The Plague Maiden

Kate Ellis

Piatkus

PIATKUS

First published in Great Britain in 2004 by Piatkus Books Ltd

9 11 13 15 17 19 20 18 16 14 12 10

A CIP catalogue record for this book
is available from the British Library.

ISBN 978-0-7499-3461-3

Typeset in Times by Action Publishing Technology Ltd, Gloucester
Printed and bound by CPI Group (UK) Ltd, Croydon, CR0 4YY

Papers used by Piatkus are from well-managed forests
and other responsible sources.

MIX
Paper from
responsible sources
FSC® C104740

Piatkus
An imprint of
Little, Brown Book Group
Carmelite House
50 Victoria Embankment
London EC4Y 0DZ

An Hachette UK Company
www.hachette.co.uk

www.piatkus.co.uk

To Ruth Smith and Pat Grigg with many thanks for their
patient reading and their honest advice

September 1991

The intruder stood quite still and listened. But he heard nothing: no voices, no distant babble of a television or radio, no creaking of boards on the floor above. It seemed that he was quite alone ... except for the lingering, blood-scented presence of death.

From time to time the noises of the country night pierced the deep silence; a screeching owl, a barking fox, the mournful lowing of a discontented cow in a nearby field. The intruder shuddered. The sounds of the countryside were frighteningly unfamiliar, not like traffic or the chatter of pub voices.

As he walked on tiptoe into the hallway he noticed that a door to his left was standing open to reveal a large shabby room, bathed in the jaundiced light of a tall standard lamp. He hesitated on the threshold before creeping in, his heart beating so strongly that he could hear the blood pounding in his ears. Stopping by the faded chintz sofa, he gazed for a few seconds at the framed photograph on the mantelpiece – a pale image of a woman cradling a tiny baby. But after a quick glance around he decided it was time to move on. He might have more luck upstairs.

The intruder climbed the stairs, and when he reached the landing a brief tour of inspection only confirmed what he already suspected ... that the house's occupant was more interested in books than in material possessions. Every shelf and surface was crammed with the things, all dull scholarly works with titles such as *Theology Understood* and *Wessler's Principles of Biochemistry*. The intruder had assumed that a big house in a place like Belsham would provide rich pickings for the casual thief. But you could never judge a book by its cover.

In the main bedroom – a room furnished with almost monastic simplicity – he spotted a shabby leather wallet lying on the bedside table and he pocketed it quickly before making his way back downstairs by torchlight. It wasn't much but he supposed it was better than nothing.

He crept back into the room where the French window stood ajar, its lock splintered where it had been forced open. But the unexpected sight of a man's corpse, lying half hidden behind the cluttered desk in the centre of the room, brought him to a sudden halt.

As soon as he saw the staring eyes and the mess of battered skull beneath the blood-matted grey hair his hand went to his mouth. The seeping blood had spread outwards and soaked into the patterned carpet, staining the dead man's snowy-white clerical collar a rusty red.

The intruder felt a wave of nausea rising in his gullet and he knew that he had to get out of that place of death before he was sick. Although his legs felt unsteady, he took a deep breath and hurried past the mortal remains of the Reverend John Shipborne, his eyes fixed ahead.

And as he stepped through the French windows, out into the still country night, he was quite unaware that he was being watched.

Chapter One

*I thought little of it when William Verlan asked me to
help one of his PhD students research the history of
Belsham in the middle of the fourteenth century. I'm
used to visitors looking around the church, asking
their questions, and I usually smile sympathetically
and hand them a guidebook.*

*But I can hardly fob Barnaby Poulson off with a
potted history of the place, can I? He wants to dig
deeper and uncover more than the bare facts.*

*He tells me that he has discovered some old manu-
scripts in the archives at Exeter and he hopes they'll
yield valuable information about Belsham's past. His
particular field of interest appears to be the Black
Death of 1348.*

*I confess that I'm beginning to regard Poulson's
frequent visits to the church and his constant questions
as a bit of a nuisance.*

*From a diary found among the Reverend John
Shipborne's personal effects*

The jar of jam was taken from its clean white carrier bag
and held at arm's length. There must be no fingerprints –
no clues – and the damage to the seal must be undetectable.
This job had to be done properly.

3

The jam was Huntings' own brand, new and unopened, and when the carpet of crumbs had been brushed aside, the virgin jar was placed on the table next to a slice of half-chewed toast and a cracked mug containing muddy dregs of coffee: the squalid remains of a hasty breakfast.

The ancient fridge in the corner of the kitchen had been salvaged from a skip but it still worked after a fashion. The fridge door was opened to reveal a trio of shrivelled vegetables, a bottle of milk and a packet of ham just past its sell-by date. Beside the ham lay a small glass dish with a glass cover, an object more suited to a laboratory than a kitchen.

Hands encased in blue rubber gloves lifted the dish off its filthy wire shelf and carried it over to the table, where a white carrier bag bearing the words 'Hunt for good prices at Huntings' was smoothed out, waiting.

It was time to get to work. Time to spread death.

'It's called Pest Field.'

'Does anyone know why?' Neil Watson looked around the field, his eyes drawn to the roofs of the new executive homes that peeped over a hedge a few hundred yards away.

Dr William Verlan scratched his balding head and looked slightly embarrassed. He was a tall man with a neat moustache and a trim, muscular build that suggested he kept himself in shape. He spoke with a soft American accent and his clothes looked as though they'd been taken straight from the retailer's shelves. But in spite of the immaculate appearance there were telltale dark shadows beneath his eyes: he looked tired. 'I've been taking a year's sabbatical and I only got back from the States on Saturday,' he said defensively. 'I didn't hear about your dig until this morning. If I'd known about it I could have done some research.'

Neil shuffled his feet impatiently. They were working to a deadline and he hadn't come to hear excuses. 'I read somewhere that there was supposed to be a leper hospital around here.'

Verlan blushed. 'I've heard that too but . . . '

'Well, a medieval leper hospital shouldn't be too hard to find,' said Neil, pulling his green wellington boot out of a cow pat with a satisfying squelch. 'If it's an important site we might even be able to halt the wheels of commerce for a little while.' He grinned as though this prospect pleased him. Dr Neil Watson, field archaeologist for the County Archaeological Unit, was only too aware of his own mildly anarchistic tendencies. 'I'll get the team up here later on to do a geophysics survey. That should tell us if there's any sort of building under here ... with any luck.'

He shielded his eyes against the sun and studied the squat church tower protruding above the hedgerow not far from the new executive homes. The old village of Belsham – a settlement that had once earned itself a mention in the Doomsday Book – was being swallowed rapidly by the spreading suburbs of Neston.

He looked at Verlan, who was standing beside him looking rather nervous. He taught medieval history at Morbay University and there was no harm in picking his brains.

'What do you know about the church?'

'It's the parish church of St Alphage. Most of it dates from 1276 and the chancel was added in 1424.'

At least Verlan seemed to know his dates. 'Worth a look?'

Verlan shrugged. Neil waited for some comment about the church, its architecture, its history or the quirky little features that, in his experience, each ancient church could boast. But Verlan remained silent, his long, pale face unreadable. With his inscrutable expression and his small, dark eyes he reminded Neil of a watchful lizard. But perhaps he was being unfair. The man had only just got back from the States – perhaps he was still feeling the effects of jet lag.

'Fancy showing me around?'

Verlan looked at his watch. 'I haven't time right now. I'm teaching in an hour. I seem to recall there are some interesting tombs in the tower but it was closed off years ago for safety reasons.'

'So it's dangerous?'

'It was locked up in the early nineties and it's not been opened since as far as I know.'

'You lived in Belsham long, then?' As Verlan was American somehow Neil had assumed he was a relative newcomer.

Verlan smiled. 'Over twenty years now. My father was stationed over here during the Second World War and he used to talk about how beautiful Devon was so when I had the chance to come over here to teach, I took it.' He suddenly frowned. 'When are you starting to dig?'

'As soon as we can. We're working to a deadline so there's no point in hanging about. Maybe you can show me the church some other time, eh?'

'Maybe.' There was little enthusiasm in his voice.

Neil Watson stared at the mellow stone tower, resolving to investigate it himself if he got the chance. But time was tight and the next branch of Huntings supermarkets would be built on this site in due course, whatever his team discovered beneath the earth.

Verlan turned and began to walk towards the gate that led out onto the main road. Neil watched him go, thinking his behaviour had been a little odd. Perhaps William Verlan didn't like hanging around old churches, which would be unusual for someone who claimed to be interested in medieval history. Or maybe there was some other reason. From the expression on Verlan's face it was clear that something was worrying him.

The West Morbay branch of Huntings stood on the sprawling outskirts of the ever-expanding resort town, in the unlovely scrubland where the town was nibbling at the country as the sea nibbles at a beach when the tide flows in; relentless and unstoppable, even by the toughest-minded official in the local planning department.

Unlike its neighbouring DIY superstore – a monolithic construction in grey corrugated iron – Huntings had at least tried to ensure that their store didn't offend the eye. Its architect had taken his inspiration from a picture of a Roman villa in his daughter's school history book and had considered the style so pleasing that every branch of Huntings had ended up with neatly pitched roofs and elegant columns that would have gained the approval of any Roman matron with an eye for contemporary architecture.

Inside the supermarket Keith Sturgeon, the branch manager, sat in his office at the back of the building. Or offstage, as he liked to think of it.

He held a small mirror in his left hand and smoothed down his wiry hair with his right, frowning at the silver hairs that were encroaching on the brown. It was nearly time to go onto the shop floor. Keith used his office as an actor uses his dressing room, somewhere to prepare for his public appearance. It was here he ensured that his appearance was immaculate, that no hair was out of place and that the flower – newly plucked each morning from the reduced bunches of flowers that, having reached their sell- by date, stood in green plastic buckets by the supermarket entrance – stood pertly to attention in his buttonhole.

He stood up and performed a final check on his appearance in the full-length mirror near the door. It was time to go down and show his face to his staff, like a general riding before his troops prior to a battle. Then he would tour the aisles and greet his public. The personal touch was important, especially in a supermarket. He looked at his watch. Ten o'clock. It never occurred to Keith that his staff were aware that he did his grand tour at the same time every morning and were fully prepared for his inspection. The thought of introducing the element of surprise and varying the time to keep them on their toes never crossed his mind.

He glanced back at the monstrous stainless-steel creation sitting proudly on his desk. The Manager of the Year award ... the highlight of his career. But that had been twenty years ago and that early promise hadn't transformed itself into the promotion he had expected ... and at one time craved. Now he had to be satisfied with his wife bringing home the lion's share of the household income. Her golden career, uninterrupted by childbearing, had flourished while his had stagnated. But there was nothing else to do but carry on.

There was a knock on the office door and Keith uttered what he considered to be an authoritative 'Come in'. The door opened and a young Asian woman entered the room. Her glossy, raven-black hair was swept back into a neat ponytail, and the only thing that stopped her from being a stunning beauty was an over-large nose. She wore a businesslike navy blue suit and held a pile of open letters in her left hand.

Keith straightened his back. 'Come in, Sunita. I was just going down on the floor. Is that the post?'

'Yes. It gets later every morning. There's nothing urgent. Shall I leave them on your desk?'

'Thank you, Sunita.'

She placed the letters on the desk, keeping back one unopened envelope. 'This one's marked strictly private so I didn't open it.' Their fingers touched as she handed the letter over and Sunita withdrew her hand quickly.

Keith examined his watch. Five to ten. Just time to see what the long envelope with the neatly hand-printed address contained. He tore it open while Sunita hovered in the doorway, curious. She watched as he read the letter inside and saw his face turn deathly pale.

He looked up at her with panic in his eyes, and as he slumped down in his chair the flower fell from his buttonhole onto the carpet.

Detective Sergeant Rachel Tracey leaned forward and her blouse gaped open, revealing a glimpse of the scanty white lace bra beneath. Detective Chief Inspector Gerry

Heffernan scratched his tousled head and stared for a few seconds before averting his eyes, feeling a little embarrassed by his fleetingly impure thoughts. He was getting too old for that sort of thing, he told himself firmly; and besides, it wasn't good for his blood pressure.

'This has just arrived in this morning's post, sir. It's addressed to a Chief Inspector Norbert. Do you know ...?'

'Someone's a bit out of date. The poor sod had my job many moons ago ... before your time.' He frowned. 'Open it and read it to me, will you.'

Heffernan, a large, untidy man with a prominent Liverpool accent, leaned back in his sagging black leather chair with his hands behind his head in an attitude commonly reserved for sunbathing.

Rachel brushed a strand of fine fair hair off her face, opened the envelope neatly and cleared her throat. 'It says "Dear Mr Norbert"' ... She hesitated.

'Go on.'

'"Dear Mr Norbert, I wish to inform you that there has been a great miscarriage of justice."'

Gerry Heffernan snorted, opened his eyes and raised them heavenwards. 'Which innocent man are we supposed to have banged up this time?'

Rachel assumed the question was rhetorical and continued to read. '"I would urge you to look again into the case of Chris Hobson. I know he is innocent but I had a very good reason for not coming forward at the time. When I saw him on the television ... "'

'Television? What was he on? *Crimewatch*?'

Rachel smiled. 'No, sir. He was on that series ... *Nick*, it's called ... a fly-on-the-wall documentary about life inside a prison. My mum watches it,' she added, slightly disapproving.

'So they're giving villains their own TV shows now, are they?' Heffernan shook his head in disbelief at the topsy-turvy nature of the modern world. 'What else does it say?'

Rachel read on. '"When I saw him on television I felt I

should write to you. I know it's a long time ago but I beg you to look into Chris's case again."' She looked up. 'That's all.'

She handed the letter to Heffernan, who took it by the corner, as if it were something contaminated, dirty. 'It's signed "J. Powell (Mrs)" ... address in Morbay – the posh end,' she added.

Heffernan placed it on the desk in front of him and stared at it for a while before speaking. 'Probably a crank,' he murmured as he pushed it to one side.

Rachel looked sceptical. 'Cranks don't usually provide their name and address.'

'I suppose we'll have to follow it up ... send a couple of uniforms round. No hurry.'

'How much do you know about the case, sir?'

Heffernan sat forward and thought for a few moments. 'It must have been about twelve years ago ... I was a DS in Morbay at the time so I wasn't involved. A vicar was murdered in the course of a burglary and Chris Hobson was arrested. Witnesses had seen him in the village around the time of the murder and the stolen goods were found in his flat. It was an open-and-shut case as far as I can remember.' He sat back and gave a long sigh. 'No use rocking the boat just because someone wants to start a "Chris Hobson is innocent" campaign. If he was that innocent why didn't this Mrs Powell come forward before? Why wait all this time? Forget it, eh.'

Rachel nodded. Perhaps the boss was right: sleeping murderers should be allowed to slumber on undisturbed ... especially if the only justification for waking them was some vague letter.

'Did this Chris Hobson have a history of violence?' she asked, just out of curiosity.

Heffernan shrugged. 'Can't remember. Probably. Even if he didn't, there's always a first time. Anything else to report?'

'Inspector Peterson and Steve have brought Lee Tepple in for those thefts from boats in the marina.'

Heffernan grinned. 'Lee Tepple? That figures. Has he been charged?'

'Yes. And apparently he's asked for thirty similar cases to be taken into consideration.'

'Our Lee was never afraid of hard work.'

Rachel smiled and left the boss to his paperwork, picking up Mrs J. Powell's letter on the way out. She had just sat down at her desk when a young man strolled into the CID office, walking between the desks with his hands thrust into his trouser pockets, a faraway look in his intelligent brown eyes. Detective Inspector Wesley Peterson stopped by the window and stared out at the view over the river, as though deep in thought.

'I believe congratulations are in order, sir.'

Wesley looked round, puzzled.

'Lee Tepple. Should do our clear-up rate no end of good.'

'I told him confession was good for the soul and he seemed to take my word for it. Anything new?'

'Nothing much. Except this.' Rachel picked the letter up off her neatly ordered desk. 'I've just shown it to the boss. It arrived this morning.'

Wesley took the letter from her and read it carefully.

'What's it all about?' he asked as he returned it to her.

'Back in the early nineties Belsham vicarage was burgled and the vicar was murdered. The thief got away with some valuables and they turned up at Chris Hobson's flat. He denied it, of course, but he was seen near the murder scene. Open-and-shut case. He got life.'

'So who's this DCI Norbert the letter's addressed to?'

'He was before my time. I presume he was in charge of the case.'

'And this Mrs J. Powell wants him to reopen it after all this time? Strange.'

'The boss thinks it's a crank.'

Wesley smiled. That was Gerry Heffernan's verdict on anyone who threatened to disturb his status quo. 'And what do you think?'

11

'Why would you want the opinion of a humble detective sergeant?'

Their eyes met. 'You know I always value your opinion. What do you think?'

Rachel considered for a moment. 'If I was in charge I'd follow it up, just to cover myself. These miscarriage-of-justice cases can get nasty for the police if we don't watch our backs. If there does turn out to be new evidence and we just ignored it ... '

Wesley nodded. Rachel was right. 'I'll have a word with the boss, then I'm taking an early lunch.'

'Going anywhere nice?'

'It's Pam's antenatal class and I promised I'd look after Michael, that's all.'

Rachel looked away. 'Good job we're not busy.'

Wesley sensed the reproach in her voice. 'I couldn't do it if we were,' he said, wondering why he felt so defensive. He had just cleared up the marina thefts. He deserved an hour off for lunch.

Rachel stared down at her hands, regretting her sharpness. But the thought of Pam, Wesley's wife, always seemed to have that effect on her. It was something she hadn't yet managed to control. And she prided herself on being a controlled person.

'I'll have a word with the boss about that letter if you like.' He held out his hand and she gave him the letter.

'Thanks.' Her lips twitched upwards into a brief smile. She was glad that the responsibility had been taken out of her hands. As Wesley walked away DC Steve Carstairs swaggered into the office, caught her eye and winked. She ignored him. As far as she was concerned Steve could piss off. Young and good looking though he was, he was a sexist, racist pain in the arse.

Wesley pushed open the half-glazed door to Gerry Heffernan's lair. The older man looked up and grinned.

12

'Wes, come in. Nice work getting Lee Tepple for those thefts. Has his place been searched yet?'

'Oh yes. His garage was like Aladdin's cave. The stuff's being brought in now.'

'Well, if you find my CD player ... It was nicked from the *Rosie May* six weeks ago. I went through the motions of reporting it but I didn't hold out much hope of getting it back.' The chief inspector looked quite indignant that any thief had had the audacity to trespass on board his precious boat.

'When the stuff's brought in you can come down and see if it's there. Rachel showed me the letter ... about that vicar's murder.'

'Did she now?' Heffernan began to rearrange the pile of neglected papers on his desk.

'I presume this Chief Inspector Norbert was in charge of the case. Do you know him?'

Gerry Heffernan frowned, trying to recall times past. 'I didn't know him well. He was DCI here before he retired about seven years ago. I presume he must have dealt with the Shipborne case.'

'Shipborne?'

'The Reverend John Shipborne. Blameless and well-liked vicar of St Alphage's, Belsham, before he ended up as a crime statistic.' He muttered something disapproving that Wesley couldn't quite make out. 'Murdered for an old silver cup. If Hobson had asked nicely the Reverend Shipborne would probably have given him the bloody thing.'

'Was Hobson regarded as dangerous at the time?'

'I can't remember him being one of our most wanted, let's just put it like that. But I wasn't involved in the case so I can't remember the details.'

'Perhaps we should have a word with ex-DCI Norbert, then.'

'That'd be difficult unless you're thinking of holding a seance. He's dead. Keeled over two weeks after he retired, poor sod.'

Wesley's mouth formed an 'o' and he stood there for a few seconds, lost for words. Then he looked Heffernan in the eye. 'I'm willing to have a look at the case file, just to make sure everything was done by the book.'

'I don't think we're giving you enough to do if you can find time for cases that were dead and buried years ago.'

'It's got me curious, that's all.'

Heffernan scratched his head. Wesley Peterson, archaeology graduate and son of two doctors from Trinidad, possessed an intellectual curiosity that Heffernan found incomprehensible. The Heffernan family motto – so Gerry always claimed – was 'Why make work for yourself?'

'Stan Jenkins used to be Norbert's sergeant around that time. He'll tell you all about it if you're really that interested.'

'I know Stan's retired now but do you think he'd mind if I had a word with him?'

'Mind? I should think he'll be delighted. Last time I saw him was in the supermarket. He was pushing the trolley,' he added significantly. 'You never met Mrs Jenkins, did you?'

'No. Why? What's she like?'

'If Stan Jenkins's missus was put in charge of the prison system crime'd be wiped out in a year and we'd all be out of a job. I don't know why you're so keen to follow this up. These nutters crawl out of the woodwork from time to time.'

Wesley knew that only too well but there was something about the letter. It was literate. Controlled. As if the sender was an educated person who'd thought about the implications of what they were saying. 'Perhaps we should pay Mrs J. Powell a visit sooner rather than later.'

Heffernan shrugged his shoulders as though he were shrugging off all responsibility. 'Go ahead if it keeps you happy, Wes. But remember it's probably not our problem.' He looked at his watch. 'Shouldn't you be off?'

There was a sudden panic in Wesley's eyes. Stan Jenkins wouldn't be the only one in the doghouse if he wasn't home in fifteen minutes.

He hurried out of Tradmouth police station and half walked, half ran up the steep narrow streets towards his home. Proving the guilt or otherwise of Chris Hobson would have to wait for a while.

Neil Watson watched as the small mechanical digger took the top layer of turf and soil off his carefully marked-out trench. The digger's arm did the job surprisingly gently, scraping up the earth delicately and depositing it on the spoil heap to the side. When Neil judged that the machine could go no deeper without disturbing what was below, he raised his hand and the driver cut the engine.

The geophysics team had already been over the field with their impressive array of bleeping machines. Neil knew that these expensive playthings for the technically minded were often useful but today they had found nothing conclusive. No outline of a building; nothing that might resemble a leper hospital, however small. But as usual the guardians of the strange instruments had hedged their bets and talked about interesting anomalies that were worth investigating. And as Huntings were footing the bill, Neil thought he might as well give them their money's worth. He strolled over to the human diggers, who were watching patiently, leaning on their spades, and told them it was time to start work.

Neil began to dig, thrusting his spade into the rich Devon earth and watching the ground closely in case anything interesting turned up in the upper layers of reddish soil. But he was so engrossed in what he was doing, so busy anticipating what he might discover, that he failed to notice a dark, hooded figure half hidden behind the thick trunk of one of the trees that edged the undulating field. The watcher observed the diggers intently for a full half-hour before slipping away silently into the churchyard near by.

Chapter Two

William Verlan tells me that there used to be a leper hospital somewhere in the village, possibly near the school. But I was more concerned about the plague pit Barnaby mentioned. Pest Field near the church appears as Pestilence Field on some old tithe maps and he suspects there could be a connection.

I saw Verlan in the village and he said Barnaby's research seems to be progressing well. I sense Verlan has no liking for me and I sometimes wonder if he knows the truth ... but of course that's not possible.

Barnaby hasn't visited for a few days. He rang last night to say that he's made some exciting discoveries. But what is exciting to Barnaby might not be exciting to the rest of us.

From a diary found among the Reverend John Shipborne's personal effects

Gerry Heffernan noticed as soon as Wesley walked in that he didn't seem his usual calm self. He had the harassed look of a father who had just been called upon to baby-sit a lively toddler for an hour or so. Who said motherhood was an easy job?

'Pam okay?'

'She's had a few twinges. The baby's not due for another

six weeks but she's seen the doctor, just to be on the safe side. Rachel's just told me there's been a call about a threat to a supermarket.' He tilted his head to one side, awaiting more details.

'That's right. The manager of Huntings supermarket on the outskirts of Morbay had an anonymous letter this morning saying there's something nasty on his shelves. He wasn't at all happy when a couple of uniformed constables turned up in answer to his 999 call under the impression they were going to arrest a shoplifter – he got on his high horse and demanded the services of CID. In the meantime he's searching his stock for anything suspicious.'

'What kind of thing? A bomb or . . . '

'The letter just said there was something on the shelves that would make Huntings sit up and take notice.'

'Is that all?'

'It said when someone died, Huntings'll be put out of business, or words to that effect.'

'That bad, eh?' Wesley supposed that for a threat to be effective, it had to be fairly dramatic.

Heffernan nodded. 'The manager's a Mr Sturgeon – no jokes about the fish counter. And he's not a happy man.'

'Did the sender make any demands?'

'No. That's what's strange.'

'Could be a disgruntled member of staff trying to put the wind up the manager.'

'Very probably. Shall we nip along to Huntings and see for ourselves?'

Wesley looked at his watch. 'It's probably nothing but I suppose we'd better show our faces.'

They drove out of the police station carpark, Wesley at the wheel as usual – Heffernan saved his navigational skills for the water. The car ferry was the most direct route and, as the tourist season was well and truly over, there was no queue of vehicles waiting to be taken over the river. They were soon on the chugging ferry, sandwiched between a post office van and a BMW, unable to smell the fresh river air for the diesel fumes wafting from the engine of the strange vessel. The river was as grey as the small navy patrol boat speeding across their bows, its crew standing neatly to attention like toy sailors. The huge naval college on the hill used the River Trad to instruct its young recruits in the arts of seamanship; arts that were a complete mystery to Wesley but familiar territory to Gerry Heffernan, who had served as first officer in the merchant navy before swallowing the anchor, as they say in seafaring circles, having been lured ashore by the charms of his late wife, Kathy.

The ferry docked to the noise of clanking chains and revving engines. Once on dry land, Wesley steered the car through the narrow streets of Queenswear and then out into the stretch of open country that divided Queenswear from the ever-expanding conurbation of Morbay. Morbay was creeping outwards stealthily and the empty fields that stood next to each new piece of development had taken on a scrubby, no-man's-land look, as if they were aware that they were next and were just waiting for their hour of execution to come.

Huntings was easy to find, a fake Roman villa that shared a massive carpark with a monolithic grey DIY warehouse. A petrol station guarded the entrance: Huntings Petrol, undercutting all the small garages in the area, many of which were now boarded up and abandoned. The small food shops, of course, had gone years ago.

'Do you and Pam shop at these places?' Heffernan asked as Wesley parked the car in the only available space, far away from the supermarket entrance.

'You don't have much choice these days.'

'I can't stand them. You nip in for a bottle of milk and you're wandering round like a lost soul for hours. Waste of ruddy time,' Heffernan concluded as they marched towards the entrance, a modern version of the old revolving door, which shuddered to a halt when a woman inadvertently touched it with her laden trolley. After a few long seconds the contraption began to move again and they shuffled on, sandwiched between huge glass doors.

18

When they were eventually disgorged they found themselves next to customer services. They flashed their warrant cards at the plump middle-aged woman behind the counter whose thinly pencilled-in eyebrows shot up in surprise as she assured them that they hadn't reported any shoplifters to the police that morning. When Wesley told her they wanted a word with Mr Sturgeon, she made a great show of telephoning through to the manager's office to announce their arrival. From her unworried manner, Wesley guessed that if something unsavoury had been hidden in the wide and well-stocked aisles of Huntings supermarket, the staff weren't aware of it yet.

Keith Sturgeon greeted the two officers with a brisk, worried handshake and led them to his office where he invited them to sit down. Without offering tea or observing any other social niceties, he handed Heffernan a sheet of paper encased in a plastic folder. He knew all about fingerprints from the television.

Heffernan cleared his throat and read aloud. '"Dear Manager, Huntings is ruining the environment and ruining lives, spreading like an infected sore over the countryside. It has to be stopped."'

'Whoever wrote that has an imaginative turn of phrase,' Wesley observed.

Heffernan carried on. '"Just to make sure you sit up and take notice, I've added a new product of my own to your shelves but you'll never find it. You won't even know what it is until someone dies. Just think of it as biological warfare against the system. Happy hunting, Huntings."' He looked up. 'That's all.'

Wesley looked at Keith Sturgeon, who was sitting behind his desk, twisting his tie around his fingers. He looked nervous. More than nervous . . . terrified. 'You've had no phone calls? No blackmail demands?'

Sturgeon shook his head.

'And you've searched all the shelves for anything out of place, any tops that have been removed or replaced?'

19

'Most stuff's security-sealed nowadays to prevent tampering and there's no obvious sign that anything's been interfered with. Sunita and I went down ourselves to check and the departmental supervisors helped too. We went through everything. I didn't want the rest of the staff alerted in case word got out and it spread panic.'

'Don't you think you should tell all your staff? Someone might have noticed something unusual. And who's Sunita?'

'My assistant manager.'

'What's she like?' Wesley asked. He had detected a slight change in Sturgeon's expression, a hint of unease, when her name had been mentioned and wondered what had caused it.

'Very good at her job. Extremely efficient.'

Wesley mentally filled in the gaps: ambitious; waiting for the boss to get egg all over his face so she could step coolly into his executive swivel chair. Perhaps if he mishandled this situation . . . But Wesley stopped himself: he'd not even met the woman yet and he was letting his imagination run away with him.

'Have you sacked anyone recently?'

Sturgeon looked embarrassed. 'Two people. One of the warehouse staff was found stealing cigarettes and dismissed.' He hesitated.

'And the other?'

'A young woman. She, er . . . didn't really fit in and . . .'

'What do you mean, didn't fit in?'

'She had the wrong attitude. I couldn't keep her on.'

'If we could have their names and addresses . . . '

Wesley saw a brief flash of panic in Sturgeon's eyes. 'Of course. I'll ask Sunita to dig them out for you. I suppose Mr Hunting will have to be informed?'

'Mr Hunting?'

'Aaron Hunting. The owner. I mean, I would rather it was kept from him but . . . '

'I think he'd want to know, don't you?'

The manager didn't answer. Wesley knew little about

Aaron Hunting apart from the fact that he lived in Tradmouth in a large white house on the banks of the River Trad and kept himself to himself. His place had its own boathouse and private moorings and he was almost a neighbour of Gerry Heffernan, who owned a cottage on the nearby quayside – a near-neighbour but a social world away. There had been pieces about Hunting in the paper, of course, but he wasn't a man who courted publicity. He was a businessman who owned a chain of successful supermarkets all over the South-west, so perhaps he didn't feel the need to wash his clean – or dirty – linen in public. Why should he?

'Of course, it's probably all a hoax,' said Gerry Heffernan cheerfully. 'Someone's idea of a joke ... maybe someone you've fired or some environmentalist who doesn't like Huntings for some reason and wants to see you running around like blue-arsed flies.'

'So what do I do?' Sturgeon spread his hands out in a gesture of despair. Wesley noticed that they were surprisingly small hands, almost like a woman's.

Heffernan and Wesley looked at each other. 'We'll have a discreet word with your sacked employees,' said Wesley. 'And I'd advise you to tell your staff to search your shelves again for anything unusual. There's nothing else we can do until the letter writer gets in touch again ... unless you want to close the store while you make sure ... '

Sturgeon shook his head. 'No. That's out of the question.'

'Then all I can advise is that you tell your staff to be vigilant and if anything unusual happens, however trivial, let us know.'

Wesley stood up and shook Sturgeon's hand in a businesslike manner. The manager buzzed through on his intercom and a young Asian woman entered the room. Wesley assumed this was the efficient Sunita, and he was soon proved right on both counts. She produced the details of the sacked employees with effortless ease and answered

21

the few questions posed to her in a calm, practical manner, replying mainly in the negative: she knew nothing. Wesley found himself believing her but wondered why. Perhaps she was just a convincing actress.

'What do you make of all that?' Wesley asked as they drove back towards the car ferry.

Heffernan wrinkled his nose. 'Probably someone's idea of a joke. It'll be the same sort of idiot who calls out fire engines to false alarms – spreading a bit of panic gives them a thrill. And if they've got some grudge against Huntings they'll get a kick out of having them in their power just by writing a few words on a piece of paper.'

Wesley didn't reply. Gerry was probably right. It was another of his cranks.

At least, he hoped it was.

In the dead centre of Pest Field the diggers worked away under Neil Watson's supervision, scraping at the earth until the heap of soil to the side grew larger as the trench grew deeper. It had rained overnight and the soil was heavy with water, so they worked with cold, reddening hands as the weak October sun tried its best to peep through the mass of thick grey clouds. The trench was now around three feet deep and if there was a medieval leper hospital down there, surely they would find it soon.

Neil climbed out of the trench and examined the contents of the finds tray. The team had been given the use of the church hall to record and clean whatever they brought to the surface, and Neil wished that he was in there now, out of the stiff east wind that was blowing dead brown leaves from the surrounding trees across the field. He did up the top button of his combat jacket and shivered. There was one remedy, of course. Hard work. He picked up a spade and climbed carefully back into the trench. Supervision was a cold business.

'Neil, are we expecting burials?'

Neil turned round. His colleague, Matt, looked worried,

frowning as he twisted his ponytail with mud-caked fingers.

'If it's a leper hospital there'll probably have been some sort of chapel with a graveyard. Why? What have you found?'

'A large bone. Looks human.'

Neil picked his way through the mud to where Matt was standing protectively over his discovery. The two men stood together and looked down at the pale brown object standing out against the darkness of the soil. It was a bone, all right. But human? He squatted down and took his trowel from his jacket pocket. Two worked quicker than one.

As they scraped away at the damp soil Neil heard excited voices drifting across from the other end of the trench. A female voice called his name and he turned round.

One of the younger diggers, a large, dark-haired young woman fresh from university, had stood up and was waving at him excitedly. From her expression Neil guessed that she had found something more interesting than another piece of medieval pottery.

'I think we've got at least one complete skeleton down here ... maybe more.'

'I'd better take a look,' Neil said calmly, smiling as he thought of the delay this could mean to the construction of Huntings' new store. A spanner – or rather a bone – in the works.

There was no word from Huntings that afternoon, which meant there had been no further threats and no demands for money. As Gerry Heffernan had said, the letter had probably been sent by some poor inadequate with a grudge, trying for his fifteen minutes of anonymous fame; hoping to see the panic he had caused reported on the local news ... or even on the national bulletins if he struck lucky and it was a slow news day. The letter had gone to Forensic to be checked out for fingerprints but, other than that, there was little else they could do until there were more developments.

As things were quiet Wesley took a stroll down to the station basement where the old case files were kept. He was looking for 1991 – the Shipborne case. If he was going to pay a call on Mrs J. Powell it would be wise to familiarise himself with the details of what had gone on all those years ago. With the help of a ginger-headed young constable who seemed to know his way around the station's records, two large and dusty box files were found and Wesley made his way back upstairs, bearing his trophies. When he reached his desk he let go of them and they fell with a loud thud.

Rachel looked up when she heard the noise and wrinkled her nose at the musty smell that was wafting towards her. 'What are you doing with those?' she asked, her curiosity getting the better of her.

'I thought I'd look up that case. The vicar who was murdered back in 1991.'

Rachel shrugged and returned her attention to a statement from a witness to a more recent crime. If Wesley wanted to waste his time on yesterday's wrongdoings it was up to him. He was the inspector and she was the sergeant, although to give him his due, he never used the fact to his advantage and always behaved towards her with polite propriety. She glanced up at him. There were times when she wished he were less of a gentleman.

Wesley, unaware that he was the focus of Rachel's thoughts, began to flick through the files, giving each sheet of paper a cursory read. As Gerry had said, it seemed to be an open-and-shut case. An intruder forced the French window of the Reverend Shipborne's study. The vicar, a widower, was found dead on the floor by his cleaner, a Mrs O'Donovan. He had died of severe head injuries inflicted by the traditional blunt instrument but the weapon was never found. Mrs O'Donovan made a statement to the effect that a silver chalice and paten – vessels used in the communion service, given to the church by some wealthy medieval benefactor and carried to the vicarage after each service for safe-keeping – were missing, along with the vicar's wallet. The stolen silver was found hidden at Chris Hobson's flat a week later after an anonymous tip-off. Hobson was a known burglar and it was assumed by everyone concerned that he had panicked after being disturbed.

Hobson couldn't explain how the silver came to be in his flat. He had admitted that he was in Belsham on the night of the murder but he claimed that when he had come out of Belsham's only pub, the Horse and Farrier, he had gone straight home to his flat in Morbay where he had spent the rest of the evening. Even Hobson's defence barrister reckoned this tale was a bit feeble and played it down in court. Witnesses had come forward to say that a man answering Hobson's description had been seen drinking alone in the Horse and Farrier. And according to these witnesses he had seemed nervous and had left the pub around the estimated time of the murder.

Hobson had offered no explanation for his presence in Belsham and no alibi for the time of Shipborne's death. Then, later on, he had tried to change his story, saying that he'd met a woman in Belsham on the evening of the murder but, as she was married, he hadn't wanted to involve her. However, when he said that the woman had conveniently left the country – whereabouts unknown – nobody took the story very seriously. The stolen silver had been found in his flat and the evidence against him was overwhelming. Wesley closed the file slowly. Gerry had been right. It did seem to be an open-and-shut case. No question about it.

The telephone on his desk rang and he picked it up. Perhaps it was a good job the Chris Hobson case looked so clear cut. Although the criminals of Tradmouth and district were suffering an attack of communal sloth this week, they were bound to start working at their usual frantic pace soon enough.

'Wes?'

Wesley recognised the voice at once. 'Neil. I hope this is a social call.' He spoke softly, not wishing his colleagues to overhear, especially Steve Carstairs, who was looking in his direction disapprovingly.

'Not exactly. We've found a couple of skeletons. I've let the coroner know and I'm just reporting it to you. Okay?'

'A couple?' Wesley's heart sank. He thought of undiscovered serial killers; overtime; not getting home till all hours and Pam turning into a vengeful harridan with a down on the police force. Would Michael forget what he looked like? And the new baby due next month ... would he ever see it? These thoughts flashed through his mind in a split second, then Neil answered, confirming his worst nightmares.

'Well, it's only a couple so far but I shouldn't be surprised if there were more down there.'

'Where?'

'Place called Belsham, just outside Neston.'

'Sure you're not digging up the graveyard?'

Neil didn't dignify Wesley's flippant question with a reply. 'It's a field on the edge of the village. Huntings supermarkets have bought the land and we were just investigating the site prior to the concrete going in. Routine stuff.'

'Are they proper burials?'

'Not exactly. They look as if they've all been chucked in.'

'Is it near the church? Could it be an old part of the graveyard that's fallen into disuse over the centuries?'

'It's not that near the church and they're certainly not in individual graves.'

'Any idea how old they are?'

'There's a bit of medieval pottery around but not much else. Do you want to come down and have a look? Bring Colin Bowman with you.'

'Is there any chance they could be modern?' Wesley closed his eyes, hoping, praying, that the answer would be no.

'I can't rule it out at the moment.'

26

Wesley's heart sank. 'Great.'

'Don't be like that, Wes. Could be worse.' Neil sounded inappropriately cheerful.

'Could it? Look, carry on excavating the bones and seal off the site. I'll come down and have a look and I'll let Colin know. Okay?'

He put the phone down and sank his head into his hands. If Neil had accidentally stumbled on the mortal remains of some serial killer's hapless victims, leisure time would soon be a distant memory.

'Anything wrong?' He looked up and saw Rachel looking at him, concerned. 'Is it . . . is it your wife? Is everything all right?'

'Neil . . . you remember Neil?'

She nodded. Wesley's scruffy, long-haired friend from his university days wasn't the sort of person who was easily forgotten.

'He's found some skeletons.'

'Isn't that what archaeologists do?'

Wesley smiled patiently. 'Yes. But they weren't expecting to find any human remains and there's nothing to date them at the moment. They could be old, of course. They could be the victims of some battle or . . .'

'Or there could be a crazed serial killer about.'

'Let's not jump to any conclusions. I'm going down there to see for myself. Fancy coming?'

He glanced to his right and saw that Steve Carstairs was listening intently to their conversation. Wesley turned away.

'I'll get my coat,' Rachel said, standing up.

Steve watched them go, a knowing smirk on his lips.

Edith Sommerby didn't like supermarkets. But you didn't have much option nowadays and Huntings was very near the bungalow she had shared with her husband, Fred, since his retirement. But walking through the vast carpark was a nerve-racking experience for someone of her age, with the

27

cars coming at her fast from every direction and everyone so impatient, blasting their horns and revving their engines when she stepped into their path. Fred didn't realise what it was like.

She had to go every other day, of course. Not like those who could pack their car boots with a week's worth of provisions. Edith's tartan shopping trolley didn't hold that much and the only freezer she possessed was the small compartment at the top of her fridge, large enough to accommodate a couple of packets of frozen vegetables but little else. The visits to Huntings were part of Edith's routine; part of her life. She even knew the checkout girls well enough now to exchange a few pleasantries about the weather when there wasn't a queue behind.

Edith began to unpack her trolley, placing her purchases carefully on the small kitchen table. Bread and milk, of course. A tub of margarine. And two nice slices of gammon for their evening meal – a bit expensive but Fred was partial to gammon – which would go nicely with a slice or two of tinned pineapple. A bottle of tomato sauce – Fred insisted on his tomato sauce. And sausages for tomorrow: his favourite. He would only allow his favourites in the house – never hers: not in the forty-five years since their wedding. It was his house and he laid down the law.

She looked at the open door and stood quite still for a few moments, listening. Then she reached into the depths of the trolley, brought out a small jar and held it, examining the label with a sly smile on her face. It was the first time she had bought jam in ages and she had popped it into her basket on impulse, feeling like a naughty child indulging in some secret mischief. She liked a bit of bread and jam; it reminded her of her childhood – of the time when she had felt safe and loved. Fred would be angry if he ever discovered her little indulgence: he would say she was wasting their pension money on stupid rubbish. But with any luck he'd never find out. It was Edith's little secret . . . and everybody needs secrets sometimes.

She put the jam carefully back in the trolley and surveyed the purchases lined up on the table before sinking down on the wooden kitchen stool. She took her purse from her coat pocket, emptied the coins on the table and counted them, her face solemn. Money didn't go far nowadays. Especially in places like Huntings.

She heard a shuffling outside. Fred was crossing the hall slowly in his carpet slippers. She thrust the purse back into her pocket and glanced at the trolley, reassuring herself that the jam was well hidden. Then she held her breath, waiting.

The door burst open to reveal a big man with snow-white hair. He stooped slightly and leaned on a gnarled stick. 'Make me a cup of tea, woman. Did you get my gammon?'

Edith nodded, glancing at the tartan trolley.

'And make sure you stir the sugar in this time.'

He raised the stick slightly and Edith slid off the stool and made for the sink.

As Wesley Peterson stood in the muddy field he wished he had worn something more substantial on his feet. He had studied archaeology at Exeter University and had taken part in many digs, wet and dry. He really should have known better, he thought as his shoes began to sink into the damp Devon earth.

Rachel stood beside him and said nothing. At least the drizzle had stopped falling from the low, grey sky, but she just wanted to be out of there. Her new black leather boots, bought on a shopping trip to Plymouth the previous week, were probably ruined, and she wondered why she had agreed to come. Perhaps it had been the prospect of spending time alone with Wesley, she thought fleetingly, before dismissing the idea from her mind.

Neil Watson was walking over, sensibly dressed in sturdy wellingtons, mud-caked jeans and combat jacket. He looked cheerful. But then Neil usually did when he was up to his armpits in mud.

'We've found three complete skeletons so far ... '

'You said two.' Things were getting worse.

'Matt's found another since I called you. And there could be more. It looks like some sort of burial pit.'

'How big is it, do you reckon?' Wesley asked.

'The geophysics results showed up all sorts of strange anomalies that look like pits or ditches. There could be loads of bodies down there.'

'Any thoughts?' If Neil said they were Civil War battle victims he and Rachel could go back to the office, have a warming cup of tea and dry their feet. A chilly breeze blew across the field, making him shiver. He zipped up his jacket and made a valiant effort to look professional.

Neil turned and looked at his colleagues, who were scraping away at the soil down in the trench, their faces set in concentration as they uncovered the bones carefully and recorded their finds. 'We've found a small amount of medieval pottery, mostly dating from the fourteenth century. Of course, there's one possibility we haven't mentioned.'

'A plague pit?' Wesley suggested tentatively.

Neil nodded, assuming a suitably solemn expression. 'Devon was hit badly by the plague in 1348 and it's possible that there was no room in the churchyard for all the dead so . . . '

'So they just dug a pit in a field and buried them? Like . . . like the animals during the foot-and-mouth outbreak?' Rachel shuddered. Coming from a farming family she had an almost superstitious aversion to the words 'foot-and-mouth'. They conjured too many horrors.

'Something like that,' said Neil. 'About a third of England's population died and this area was particularly badly hit. Tradmouth was an important port so the disease would have come in there and spread to the surrounding countryside. Do you know that half the clergy in Devon died between 1348 and 1351?'

Rachel looked puzzled.

'The parish priests would have tended the sick, giving

them the last rites and so on, so they were bound to bear the brunt of it. I've read they used to gather up the corpses in carts and . . . '

'Thanks, Neil. I think we get the picture,' said Wesley. He looked over to the trench, the focus of activity. It was time he had a look at what had been found.

As Neil led the way several of the diggers stopped and stared at Wesley, but when Matt looked up from the pelvic bone he was uncovering and greeted him cheerfully, they resumed their work.

'What's the score so far?' Neil called out.

Matt put down his trowel and squatted on his heels. 'Three so far but when we extend the trench I'm sure we'll find more. In fact you can just see a bone protruding from the side there.'

'There could be dozens of them,' Rachel said, matter-of-fact.

Wesley squatted at the edge of the trench, staring down at the emerging bones. 'How long would you say they've been down there?'

It was Matt who answered, scratching his head with a filthy finger. 'At the moment I'd guess they were old. But I'm no bone expert.'

Neil's eyes suddenly focused past Wesley's shoulder. Wesley looked round to see Dr Colin Bowman striding across the field. He wore a waxed jacket and sturdy walking boots – a wise choice in the circumstances – and carried a bag, the tools of his trade. He greeted Wesley and Neil cheerfully.

'Good to see you, Colin,' said Neil. 'How are you?'

'I'm very well, thank you, Neil. And yourself?'

'Mustn't grumble. Spot of archaeologist's knee and a permanent empty feeling around the wallet but apart from that . . . '

'Wesley said you've got some corpses for me.' He spoke with eager anticipation. Perhaps things had been quiet down at the mortuary recently.

'Three complete skeletons,' Neil announced, almost with pride. 'Now we've dug a bit farther we think there are probably more. It's possible it could be some sort of burial pit for battle victims ... or even plague victims. If you could have a quick look and see what you think ...'

The archaeologists had all stopped digging and watched as Matt helped Colin into the trench. Colin squatted down beside him, examining the bones that lay exposed. After a few minutes he looked up.

'Well, I can say life is definitely extinct,' he began with a grin. 'But I'd need to do a proper examination down at the mortuary to tell you any more. I can see no obvious traumatic injuries ... no broken heads or obvious sword wounds. But just because these three don't show anything, it doesn't rule out the possibility that they died in battle. As for plague ... well, it's possible, I suppose. Wouldn't there be records of burials?'

'Not in the fourteenth century,' Neil replied. 'Church registers weren't kept until the sixteenth.'

'But you think they're old?' Wesley asked warily, hoping that his official involvement was about to end.

Colin hesitated and scratched his head. 'I'll tell you more when I've had a chance to examine them properly.'

Wesley smiled. It was typical of the pathologist to hedge his bets. He looked at his watch. Half past five. Time to get back to the office to finish his paperwork and then get home to Pam at a reasonable time. There was nothing more he could do here until they knew the age of the skeletons for certain.

'Going, Wes?' asked Neil.

'I'll leave you to it. I can rely on you to make sure everything's done properly according to Home Office regulations, can't I?'

'Of course.'

'In that case, I'll leave it in your capable hands.' He glanced down at the skull that grinned up at him from the soil. 'And hope they turn out to be well and truly medieval.'

Wesley had taken a few steps when he heard Neil's voice loudly behind him. 'Oh look, Colin, this one's got three fillings and a metal pin in his right leg.'

Wesley swung round, his heart pounding. But when he saw Neil and Colin Bowman standing in the trench, helpless with laughter, he couldn't help joining in. The laughter was liberating; it lifted his spirits.

Rachel, he noticed, was staring at them disapprovingly.

'I'll be in touch,' Wesley called, raising a hand in farewell.

He walked to the car, Rachel following a little behind. They didn't say a word to each other on the journey back to the station.

Wesley arrived home to find Pam reading a story to Michael. The three little pigs. Pam's mother, Della, had bought him the lavishly illustrated edition, saying it was very appropriate for a policeman's son. That was Della all over: never one to miss out on a dig against authority.

Pam looked up as he walked in.

'How are you?' he asked, concerned.

'Fine. Don't fuss.' She shifted her position to make herself more comfortable. She felt bigger with this pregnancy than the last: or perhaps it was just her imagination. Little Michael grabbed at the book, longing to know more about the Big Bad Wolf's efforts to earn his bacon.

'I'll take over if you like.'

Pam smiled. 'Thanks. I'll see if the supper's ready.'

'Unless you'd like me to see to supper and ... '

'No, I'll do it. Good day?'

Wesley hesitated. Had it been a good day? It had been a frustrating one with hints of possible trouble to come. First the letter about the vicar's murder all those years ago: the letter claiming that Chris Hobson, the man put away for it, was innocent after all. But it was a rare villain who wasn't thought innocent by somebody.

Then there had been the threat to the supermarket.

33

Probably nothing. Probably some disgruntled employee or an over-enthusiastic environmentalist with a grudge. And of course there were Neil's skeletons. But then Neil had always had an irritating habit of uncovering bones at inconvenient moments.

'I saw Neil today.'

Pam looked at him, her face expressionless. 'How is he? We've not seen him since he was working on that shipwreck.'

'Is it that long?' He was surprised at the swift passage of time. Probably a sign of advancing age. 'He was up to his knees in mud in a field just outside Neston. Village called Belsham. They're building a new supermarket there and he's found some skeletons on the site.'

'Old ones?'

'I sincerely hope so. What about you? Done anything exciting?' For the sake of equal opportunities, he thought he'd better ask, although now that she was on maternity leave from her teaching job her days were usually filled with matters domestic.

'Your sister rang.' She paused, as if preparing to make some momentous announcement. 'You know Mark's family come from near Tavistock?'

'Yes,' he said, wishing she'd come to the point.

'Well, it turns out he's been applying for vacancies in the Exeter diocese and he's got a job, or a living or whatever it is they call it, near Neston ... a church called St Alphage's. He starts quite soon but Maritia's staying on in Oxford until she's finished her GP training. She wants to do locum work around here when they're married. Isn't that great?'

This was good news. Wesley had always been close to his sister, Maritia, who had studied medicine at Oxford and had worked at the John Radcliffe hospital there before training for general practice. A year ago she had met Mark, a young curate, and that spring they had become engaged. Wesley's parents had taken an instant liking to Mark. But

34

even if they hadn't been regular churchgoers, delighted at the prospect of having a clergyman in the family, the kindly and sometimes over-enthusiastic Mark would be a hard man to disapprove of.

The early misgivings Wesley's parents had experienced over their son's choice of a white partner hadn't seemed to arise in Maritia's case. At one time the Petersons had expected Wesley to settle down with his former girlfriend – a bright and beautiful black solicitor who attended their church, now married to an up-and-coming MP. Pam's unexpected appearance on the scene had been a shock for them and they had urged caution. But, as far as the Petersons were aware, Pam and Wesley's mixed race marriage had encountered few serious problems so far, which eased any anxiety they might have felt about Maritia and Mark's future.

'That's fantastic news.' Wesley put his arms around Pam and they kissed, first quickly, then more passionately. He held her as close as their growing child allowed until she broke away. 'I'll get the supper. I'm starving, I don't know about you.'

As Wesley watched her disappear into the kitchen, he suddenly thought of the bones Neil had found, and he had the uneasy feeling that he was experiencing the calm before some sort of storm.

'Pigs, pigs,' cried a small voice from the sofa, reminding Wesley that peace and relaxation were rare and precious commodities.

At eight o'clock, within the three-foot-thick walls of A-wing at Her Majesty's Prison Hammersham, Chris Hobson sat on the bottom bunk preparing for yet another quiet night in. He pulled the rough blanket over his knees as though for protection. Not that he needed much protection. He was a lifer: a murderer. And as his victim hadn't been a woman or a child, his conviction had appeared to earn him some respect in the closed, strange world of the prison. The others gave him a wide berth. Even in the damp and dangerous territory of the showers nobody had bothered him after that initial incident: the other man had lost two teeth.

Chris Hobson had developed a tough shell out of necessity. If you weren't hard, you didn't survive. He'd learned a lot in prison: some of the regulars even referred to the place as 'the university'. Some university.

He'd served twelve years of a life sentence and the fact that he still proclaimed his innocence at every opportunity seemed to irritate the authorities. They didn't like an unrepentant sinner. Especially a sinner who insisted he'd never been a sinner in the first place. But as Chris had told anyone who cared to listen time and time again, he wasn't going to own up to something he hadn't done just to satisfy a load of smug do-gooders.

There were times when he felt angry and times when he despaired. But today was different. Today he'd had Janet's letter. Today there was hope.

The metal base of the top bunk creaked dangerously as Big Jim Toolan turned over. 'I can't read this fucking word. What is it?' Chris glanced up. A page from the *Sun* came fluttering down and Chris caught it in mid-flight.

'What word's that, then, Jim?'

Toolan was an armed robber who'd done a bank job but neglected to make sure that the getaway car had enough petrol. Big Jim Toolan wasn't known for his towering intellect.

'The one under the picture of the slag ... begins with "e".'

Chris scanned the page and began to read. '"Educated Mandy has five GCSEs but her brains aren't her biggest assets." Is that it?'

'Yeah. She's all right, isn't she?'

'Wouldn't push her out of bed,' Chris replied automatically, even though he found it best not to dwell on such things in his current situation. It would be foolish for a starving man to think of fresh-baked bread or ripe, succulent strawberries. An occasional glimpse down the front of the creative writing teacher's blouse had to suffice for the time being.

'Wish I could read as well as you.'

Chris smiled but didn't answer. At least in prison he wasn't at the bottom of the pecking order, not like in the outside world. Although in the weeks before his arrest things had started to look up ... until Janet had gone off to the States.

'You got a letter today, didn't you?'

'What about it?'

'You just looked pleased with yourself, that's all.'

Chris threw off his blanket and jumped to his feet. He leaned forward until his face was level with Big Jim's. If it had been anyone else, he would have told them to piss off and mind their own business, but Big Jim was the nearest thing he had to a mate inside. And he had to tell somebody: he couldn't keep it to himself any longer.

'I'll let you into a secret.'

'What?' Jim sat open mouthed, an expression of anticipation on his large, pallid face.

'I'm getting out of here. They're going to get new evidence. Told you I was innocent, didn't I?'

Big Jim Toolan's jaw dropped. 'But what about me? What will I do?' he asked in a desperate whisper. As he turned towards the wall, the bunk shuddered dangerously.

It was 10.30 that evening when Edith Sommerby staggered from her bed and slumped down by the lavatory. The world was spinning and there seemed to be two of everything, which didn't make sense to Edith. She closed her eyes tight and felt sweat dripping down her face, even though she was shivering. She retched again, clutching her aching stomach.

'What's the matter with you, woman? You've woken me up.'

Edith waited in terror, her lips pressed together, suppressing gasps of pain. Not wishing to disturb Fred, she

37

hadn't switched the light on and she lay now in the jaundiced glow of the street light that stood outside the window. She could hear Fred's shuffling footsteps, his slippers on the fitted carpet in the hallway. He mustn't find her like this. If she had been able to summon the strength she would have locked the bathroom door. But she could only lie, as though paralysed, on the cold lino floor. Helpless. At that moment, Edith wished for death.

By the time Fred Sommerby pushed the door open and pressed the switch that flooded the small, shabby bathroom with light, Edith had lost consciousness. He walked slowly up to her and prodded her backside with his stick. 'Get up, woman. What are you up to? Get up.' His orders lacked their usual certainty. Perhaps this time she wasn't pretending.

He stood listening to her rasping breath for a full minute before making his way into the hallway to call the ambulance.

It was half past midnight and as the Horse and Farrier, Belsham's only pub, had thrown out its last customers an hour before, there was nobody about. The full moon cast a pale light on the scene but the hooded man felt safe as he flicked the switch on the side of his machine. He had taken precautions. He had thought of everything.

The archaeologists had erected temporary fencing around the site to shield it from view. But from the hooded man's point of view, their efforts were futile. They wouldn't keep him out. Rather they would help him: the fencing would hide his activities from prying eyes.

He began to walk slowly, sweeping the machine over the ground, waiting for the sound in his headphones; the sound that would tell him he had struck lucky. It wasn't long before he heard the piercing electronic whine in his ears. He paused then he made another sweep, and there it was again. He had to locate the exact spot and he sent up a silent prayer that this was it.

He took his spade and began to dig.

Chapter Three

Barnaby called today and left me a draft copy of the first section of his thesis. As I began to read, I became so absorbed that I was almost late for a meeting with the parish council.

The thing I found saddest about the events he writes about so vividly is that death appears to beget death. One would think that the unhappy folk of Belsham back in 1348 would have been heartily sick of death, sated with watching the suffering of their loved ones. And yet it seems from Barnaby's research that one of their number developed a taste for death, a love of evil. I ask myself how this could be, but as yet I have found no answer.

From a diary found among the Reverend John Shipborne's personal effects

The next morning Wesley opened the file bearing the name 'Hobson' and the musty scent of slightly damp paper wafted towards his nostrils. The station cellar probably wasn't the best place to keep old records but it was the only space they had. He was about to start reading when the telephone rang. He picked up the receiver and recited his name.

'Nighthawks.'

'What?'

'Nighthawks. They've been over the bloody site. I don't know what they've got away with.'

'Now calm down, Neil, and give me the details. Nighthawks? You mean people with metal detectors?'

'That's what I said. Bloody nighthawks. What are you going to do about it? There should be a police guard on the site and ... '

Wesley smiled at his friend's naivety. 'We haven't got the manpower. Why don't your team take it in turns to stay up there? Give the police a call if there's any trouble. Sorry, but that's the best thing I can suggest. Now tell me exactly what's happened. Has anything been stolen?' he asked before Neil could raise any objection to his suggestion.

'How should I know? I don't know what's down there yet, do I?'

Neil was right; it had been a stupid question. But then he didn't feel fully awake yet as Michael had kept them up half the night complaining about a newly erupting tooth. 'Is there much damage?'

'They've dug a few holes.'

'I presume the skeletons you found have been removed.'

'Of course. But it looks as if there are more down there.'

'Still think it could be a plague pit?'

'I'm having a look at the church today to see if there's anything there that might give us a clue. You'll be coming down to interview me about the damage to the site later.' This was a statement rather than a question.

'If I've got time.'

Neil grunted and put the phone down, but before Wesley had a chance to return to the Chris Hobson file Gerry Heffernan lumbered out of his glass-fronted office. He stopped in the middle of the floor and held up a sheet of paper.

'Mr Sturgeon from Huntings has just been on the phone again. He's had another letter this morning.'

Wesley looked up expectantly. 'And?'

Heffernan read from the paper in his hand. '"I see the jam's been sold already and when your customer dies you'll realise that I really mean business. A lot more will die and so will Huntings when people start avoiding the place like the plague. Watch and wait." That's it.' The chief inspector looked up. 'Presumably this means that whatever they've planted in the store has been sold to some poor unsuspecting sod. Sturgeon's taken all the jam off his shelves.'

'It might still be a hoax. Have there been any reports of suspicious deaths? Poisonings?'

'Not yet, Wes, but give it time.'

Wesley thought for a few moments. 'Most of Huntings' customers probably live in the Morbay area so it might be worth contacting Morbay General Hospital to see if anybody's been admitted with symptoms of any kind of poisoning. The first letter mentioned biological warfare, and at a guess I'd say that implies some kind of food poisoning or something from a poisonous plant or fungus rather than an industrial poison or something like broken glass.'

Rachel was looking at Wesley as though she was impressed by his reasoning ... which was more than Wesley himself was. It was sheer guesswork and he knew that he could be completely wrong.

Heffernan raised his eyebrows. 'Okay, get in touch with the hospital ... if you think it's worth it.'

'Even if nothing's happened yet it might be wise to alert them in case anything does.'

'You believe this nutter, then?'

'Do we really want to take the risk of ignoring him?'

Heffernan shrugged. Wesley was probably right.

'The fact that our letter writer knows that whatever it is has been sold implies that he or she is keeping a close eye on the place. Sturgeon's said he's told his staff so they're all on the lookout for anything suspicious.'

'About time too. Of course, one of his staff might be responsible.'

41

Wesley noticed that Rachel was sitting at her desk, unusually quiet. He would normally have expected some contribution, some comment or theory, but she looked preoccupied, lost in her own little world. He wondered whether there was anything wrong. Then he turned his attention to his own desk. Unlike Heffernan's it was neat and organised apart from an untidy, discoloured file lying open in its centre.

'I've started reading up on the Chris Hobson case.'

Heffernan grinned. 'I heard you'd asked for the files. Always making work for yourself. Are we going to pay a call on this Mrs Powell, then?'

Wesley sighed. 'When I've got a moment. Neil rang. He's had nighthawks. I promised I'd go over there.'

'Nighthawks? Is that infectious? Has he seen a doctor?'

'Nighthawks are people with metal detectors who dig up archaeological sites at night.'

'So what does he expect you to do about it?'

'Show my face. Make it look as if we're doing something. I told him that his team should take it in turns to watch the site at night and call the uniforms out if anything happens. I think he was hoping for a round-the-clock police guard.' Wesley grinned.

'Hasn't he seen our overtime budget?'

'I'm afraid Neil inhabits a parallel universe where the police's main priority is the protection of his site.' He stood up. 'I'll make that call to Morbay General. I know it's a long shot but if anyone's been poisoned by eating something they've bought at Huntings, at least we might get to know right away. Then I'd better go and calm Neil down, and if I've got a spare moment I might get a chance to go and see this Mrs J. Powell. And I've asked Steve to trace those two people who were sacked from Huntings. It might be worth having a word.'

Wesley looked at his watch, wondering how soon he could get out to Belsham. And what he'd find when he got there.

*

42

In the intensive care unit of Morbay General Hospital Dr Vikram Choudray looked down at the patient and shook his head. She had been rushed in by ambulance in the early hours of the morning and in Dr Choudray's professional opinion it was touch and go. She looked so fragile lying on the bed, a pile of flesh and bones in a pale blue hospital gown, tubes sprouting from her parchment skin, her thin grey hair soaked in sweat. The monitor bleeped monotonously but that was a good thing. It was when it emitted a constant whine that the staff would know that all their best efforts had been in vain.

'Doctor . . . '

Choudray turned. Sister Atkins was standing there. She was a statuesque woman with fair hair folded into an immaculate French pleat, giving her the look of some serene Roman goddess come among mortals disguised in a nurse's uniform. She towered over the doctor as she smoothed down her thin plastic apron.

'There's been a call from the police. They want to know if anybody's been admitted with any sort of poisoning, particularly food poisoning.' She looked at the grey figure on the bed. 'I think we should tell them about Mrs Sommerby.'

'We won't know if it's poisoning until we get the results back from the lab.'

'I've seen something like this before when I worked up North. I'm sure it's . . . '

'The husband told me that she didn't eat anything he didn't eat.'

'How can he be sure of that? He can't have been with her twenty-four hours a day. She might have gone shopping and had a cake or an ice cream . . . '

'So why haven't there been other cases? I say we wait until we're sure. We'd only be wasting the police's time if we were wrong.'

Dr Choudray turned his attention to the patient in the next bed while Sister Atkins checked Edith Sommerby's blood pressure. The readings weren't good. She was weakening; Sister Atkins knew the signs.

If Dr Choudray hadn't been so pedantic, she would have rung the police already. But perhaps he was right. They should wait and see.

'Much damage?'

Neil Watson stared down at the series of neat holes in the ground. 'If I knew what they'd taken I'd tell you. They're usually after coins or jewellery.'

'They probably only got away with a couple of old horseshoes and a rusty nail,' Wesley observed optimistically.

'Let's hope, eh. We're taking it in turns to keep watch from now on.' He shuddered. 'Wish the weather was better. Not brought the lovely Rachel with you today?'

'I thought I was just about capable of tackling this one on my own. Why do you ask?'

'No reason,' Neil said with a meaningful grin.

'What's the latest on the skeletons?'

'We found two more this morning. They're being lifted now. Again no sign of battle wounds.' He shrugged. 'It could be a plague pit, I suppose. There's certainly no trace of any building which seems to knock our leper hospital theory on the head.'

Wesley could see the diggers working in the trench at the other end of the field. Plastic boxes sat on the side of the pit, waiting to receive the carefully excavated, recorded and labelled bones. A young woman sat on the edge, face intent and feet dangling, sketching the bones and their relative position, while a young man near her was measuring and taking photographs.

'Let's go to the church,' Neil said suddenly. 'I've not seen it yet.'

Wesley's brain suddenly made the connection. 'Is it called St Alphage's?'

Neil looked at him, surprised. 'Yeah. How did you ...?'

'My future brother-in-law's just been appointed as vicar

44

somewhere around here. I'm sure St Alphage's is the name of his new church.'

Neil looked unimpressed. 'Small world. We've got to call at a Mrs O'Donovan's for the key.'

Wesley frowned as he tried to recall why the name seemed familiar. Then it came to him. A Mrs O'Donovan had cleaned for the late Reverend Shipborne and she had found his body. If she had the church keys, then surely it was the same woman. He didn't know why he felt an inexplicable thrill of anticipation at the prospect of encountering someone directly connected with the Shipborne case.

Neil ignored the other diggers as they made their way across the field and out of the gate. But Wesley looked over to where they were working. Bones were being lifted carefully out of the trench and placed in their waiting boxes. If Neil's theory about a plague pit was correct, there would probably be enough human remains in there to keep Colin Bowman busy for weeks.

When they reached what had once been the village street, now just a section of the main road from Morbay to Neston with houses either side, they had to stop and wait for a break in the stream of traffic. Things would get a lot worse once the new branch of Huntings was built. But then presumably someone in the lofty ivory tower of the local planning department had considered that possibility ... or perhaps not.

Mrs O'Donovan lived in a small brick council house, banished to the outer edge of the village next to an electricity sub-station. Her house had a neat look, with fresh green paintwork and a tiny, weed-free front garden. She had been the late vicar's cleaner, Wesley remembered, and presumably she still had some links with the church if she was entrusted with its key. He knocked on the door.

'Is she expecting us?' Wesley asked.

Neil nodded. 'I rang earlier. She said it was no problem.'

The door opened to reveal a plump woman in her sixties with untidy grey hair, bright blue eyes, apple cheeks and a generous mouth. In her youth she would probably have resembled a buxom milkmaid, but time had given her a maternal appearance. Everybody's idea of the perfect granny. When she smiled it was dazzling.

'You must be the archaeologist,' she said, her accent pure Devon. She stared at Wesley for a few seconds, trying hard to hide her suspicion but not quite succeeding. 'And you're not from round these parts?' It was a question rather than a statement.

'I'm a friend of Neil's. We were at university together.'

The suspicion disappeared from Mrs O'Donovan's eyes. After the initial few moments of uncertainty, Wesley seemed to have passed some sort of test. 'You'll be wanting the key to the church. Now don't go in the tower ... it isn't safe in there. And mind you lock up after you and bring the key straight back, if you please.'

'Of course.' Wesley gave her a reassuring smile. 'You cleaned for the late Reverend Shipborne, I believe?'

The suspicion reappeared on her face. 'Who told you that?'

'I'm a policeman, a detective inspector. I heard about the case. It must have been a terrible shock.'

There was no mistaking it. As soon as Wesley announced that he was a policeman her attitude had changed. And he didn't think it was anything to do with the case bringing back disturbing memories. For some reason Mrs O'Donovan was wary of the police. And he wondered why.

'Well, that went down like a lead balloon,' Neil said as they strolled up the church path.

'What did?'

'You saying you were a policeman.'

So Neil had noticed it too. It hadn't just been his imagination.

They crossed the busy road again, dashing across when there was a gap in the traffic, and made straight for the church. The building, set in its graveyard like a ship anchored in open water, was clearly ancient, but there was

46

a slight air of neglect about the place. The grass that surrounded it had been trimmed but some of the grave-stones had toppled over and the parish notice-board beside the lychgate was in need of a coat of paint. There was one tattered notice pinned to it, announcing a parish jumble sale a year in the past.

They walked up the path and Neil put the key in the church's great oak door. It turned stiffly and the door opened with a creak worthy of any horror movie. They stepped inside the church and stood for a minute or so as their eyes grew accustomed to the gloom. The place smelled of musty prayer books, and particles of dust swirled and danced in the shafts of light creeping in through the plain leaded glass windows. Only the large window above the altar at the east end contained stained glass.

Wesley scratched his head. 'What are we looking for exactly, Neil?'

'Is there any sort of guidebook?' Neil looked round the building. Most churches in his experience had some sort of bookstall selling books or leaflets telling the casual visitor something of the place's history. But there was nothing like that at St Alphage's and he thought this was a strange omission.

They strolled slowly around the church, noting that the rood screen was finely carved and still bore its medieval paint in parts. The walls had been whitewashed. In some churches this had been done to cover up medieval wall paintings in the days when that sort of thing was considered undesirable, so who knew what lay beneath the whitewash here? But at first sight, interesting features were thin on the ground. A motley selection of eighteenth-century memorials lined the walls, all commemorating members of a family called Munnery ... probably the local squires.

As they wandered into the chancel Wesley noticed a fine tomb to their right bearing two recumbent figures in Elizabethan costume. The text around the tomb announced that they were Sir John and Lady Elizabeth Munnery, which seemed to confirm that the Munnerys had been big noises in Belsham for quite some time. At his feet Wesley saw a fine medieval brass set into the floor, informing him that a Ralph de Munerie had been a power to be reckoned with back in 1466.

Neil had his notebook out and was scribbling furiously, but Wesley wasn't sure what he had found that was worth writing about. They knew that the lords of the manor were called Munnery but that was about all they knew. According to the tomb inscriptions all the Munnerys appeared to have died in their beds at a ripe old age. Nothing about them being serial killers who buried their victims in a mass grave in Pest Field. But then Wesley wasn't really expecting it to be that easy.

They strolled back down the aisle side by side, and they were about to leave by the south door when Neil stopped. 'What about the tower?'

'What about it?'

'It's sometimes the oldest part of a church. It'll be worth a look. I was told that some old vicar had it locked up a few years ago. Makes you wonder, doesn't it.'

'Mrs O'Donovan said it was unsafe.'

'I wonder who told her that.' There was a hint of cynicism in Neil's voice. 'It looks solid enough from the outside.' He tried the tower door. It was locked but one of the keys on the ring Mrs O'Donovan had given them fitted the lock. 'Let's see what the vicar was trying to hide, shall we.'

'Dry rot, I should think,' said Wesley, pouring cold water on Neil's fiery imagination.

Neil took no notice and pushed the door until it opened stiffly with a loud creaking and scraping. The space beyond was pitch dark and reeked of bat droppings, or at least Wesley assumed it was bat droppings. Neither he nor Neil had come prepared with a torch, but Neil produced a box of matches from the inside pocket of his combat jacket. He struck one and the flickering gold light lit up the small, square chamber for a few seconds, showing up a fine array of cobwebs and six dust-shrouded bell ropes. Wesley had once harboured a fleeting fancy to try his hand at bell-ringing but he certainly wouldn't have risked it here: if the bells were still up there, one pull on the rope would probably bring them crashing through the rotten ceiling on top of them. He could just make out some sort of pattern on the far wall but he assumed it was just many years' accumulation of bird droppings: it was impossible to see in that light.

Neil stepped farther into the tower and lit another match, illuminating three recumbent figures lying to one side of the bell ropes. There were two men carved in alabaster, the colour of Devon fudge, their armour as battered as their features; their noses had gone, as had their hands and toes. They wore helmets and, judging by the position of their wrists, they had been lying in an attitude of pious prayer. The woman had fared somewhat better. Her nose too was no more, but the rest of her body, the carved folds of her alabaster gown and wimple, had survived remarkably well.

Neil lit yet another match and shuffled his way over to the effigies. 'They're quite early. Fourteenth-century, I reckon from the armour and the dress. If those poor sods in the field were plague victims then this lot could have been around at the time. I wish we had some light in here. I think there's some sort of inscription on this one but ... shit ... bloody hell.' The match had burned down to his fingers and he shook it frantically until the flame was out and they were left in darkness.

Undeterred, he lit another and squatted down, reading the indistinct Latin on one side of the woman's tomb. 'I think her name's Eleanor, wife of ... hang on a minute ... wife of Urien de Munerie. Well, well. The Munnerys had this place sewn up back then and all.'

Wesley was hovering just inside the doorway. 'How long are you going to be? I've got to get back to the office.'

But Neil wasn't listening. In spite of a scorched finger he

49

was enjoying himself. 'So this one must be Urien and this one ... '

'I'll have to go.'

Another match was struck. 'Hang on. This one's Guy and it says he was the son of Urien and Eleanor de Munerie.'

Wesley took a deep breath of stale air. Neil couldn't be hurried. He would have to leave him to carry out his historical detective work alone.

'I've nearly finished. Just hang on a minute. Hey, this is interesting. The inscription continues round the other side of Urien's tomb. It says "Pray for the soul of his son Robert be he alive or dead". What do you think that means?'

Wesley shrugged. 'Went missing in the crusades? Ran away to the bright lights of London like Dick Whittington and lost touch? How should I know? Perhaps there might be something in the manor records if they exist.'

'They don't. I've asked.' Neil stood up, dusting himself off in the heavy darkness. 'It might be worth looking into, just out of interest, if nothing else. We'll come back again with some proper torches so we can see what we're dealing with.'

'Good idea,' Wesley said, relieved to be going at last.

Neil lit his last match and held it up. In the brief flare of light Wesley thought he could make out something that looked like graffiti gouged into the stone behind the effigies.

Neil had seen it too. 'Bloody vandals get everywhere,' he muttered before stepping out into the church and shutting the tower door firmly behind him.

The woman stood near the fountain at the entrance to the memorial gardens and stared across the road at the police station. She was a lady of a certain age, with the svelte look of one who had the money to take good care of herself. She wore a simple cream wool coat with a neatly tied silk scarf at the throat and her blonde hair had been expertly cut into a neat bob. Every so often she raised her left hand to push an imaginary strand of hair off her face. It was a nervous reaction ... but then Janet Powell felt nervous.

Janet had never had anything to do with the police before, apart from attending a neighbourhood watch meeting a week after her return to England. Even then she had never actually talked with the plump and amiable community constable who was obliged to be present at such functions. Her only knowledge of the police was from the television ... and from what she had been told. And it was the latter source of information which made her fearful now. She felt bad about what she had failed to do all those years ago – her sin of omission – even though that omission hadn't been her fault. But at least she could put things right now.

Posting the letter had seemed like a good idea at the time ... rectifying matters while staying out of it herself. But the moment it had disappeared into the letterbox she realised that the action had been foolish and cowardly. The police needed statements, evidence, not just unverifiable hints. If she was to make amends for her silence, she had to face them.

And as for the most awkward question of all, why she hadn't come forward at the time, she would simply tell the truth: until a month ago she knew nothing of Chris Hobson's conviction. By the time he was arrested she'd already been in the States with her husband for several weeks, all contact with Hobson severed: he hadn't even known which city she was in – she'd thought it was best that way.

For twelve not very happy years she'd been living in New York. But then the years before that hadn't been particularly happy either ... perhaps that was why she had thrown caution to the wind and taken up with Chris Hobson. Chris had been a member of what her soon-to-be-ex-husband habitually called 'the criminal classes': he had been the ultimate defiance.

51

Her mouth was dry and her heart pounded in her chest as she walked across the road. A van narrowly avoided her and the driver wound the window down and shouted something that she couldn't quite hear, but she was sure it was obscene. Oblivious to everything but her coming ordeal, Janet Powell pushed at the swing-door of Tradmouth police station and it opened smoothly to admit her.

A large policeman with a short, neat beard stood behind the reception desk. He had three stripes on his arm and looked the gentle-giant type; not the sort of man to subject her to hours of fierce interrogation. But then what happened to her in that building probably wouldn't be up to him. She thought of the tales Chris Hobson had told her about the police and suddenly lost her nerve. She was about to turn and leave when the large sergeant addressed her.

'Can I help you, madam?'

His voice was warm with a distinct Devon accent and his expression was sympathetic. She swallowed hard. It was too late to back out now.

'Er ... is Inspector Norbert ... er ... does Chief Inspector Norbert still work here?' She suddenly felt stupid. Perhaps Norbert had been transferred or retired years ago.

The large sergeant looked solemn, like one about to break bad news. 'I'm afraid Mr Norbert passed away some time ago. I'm sorry.' He lowered his eyes respectfully and observed a couple of seconds' silence. 'Can anyone else help you?'

Janet hadn't known what to expect after all these years but somehow the news of Norbert's death made her mind go blank. Perhaps she should never have sent the letter.

'Would you like to see someone from CID?' the sergeant asked. He was a pleasant, fatherly man, eager to be helpful. Not the sort of policeman Chris had described – but perhaps the next officer she encountered would be.

But she could prove Chris Hobson's innocence. She had seen him on the television, older and haggard, with a hardness, a bitterness, that he hadn't possessed when she had known him. Prison had changed him. And she felt uncomfortably responsible for that.

'Yes,' she heard herself saying.

'Can you give me some idea what it's about?' The sergeant looked at her expectantly.

The words came out quickly. 'It's about Chris Hobson ... the Shipborne case ... the vicar who was murdered in 1991. I wrote to Mr Norbert about it.'

Sergeant Bob Naseby smiled and invited her to take a seat before picking up the phone on the desk.

Five minutes later a young black man emerged from a door to Janet's right. He was slim, average height with delicate features and intelligent eyes. He didn't look like a policeman ... or at least not like the type of policeman Janet was expecting. The sergeant whispered something to him which Janet couldn't quite hear, then the young man came towards her, smiling and holding out his hand.

'I'm Detective Inspector Peterson. I believe you want to speak to someone about the Shipborne case?'

'Yes.' Janet shook hands with the inspector, although her own hand was clammy and trembling with nerves. The inspector was well spoken and seemed pleasant enough, but she reminded herself that it might all be part of a routine ... nice cop, nasty cop. Maybe she would meet up with the nasty one next.

But Inspector Peterson led her into one of the ground-floor interview rooms and ordered tea for them both. There was no sign of the nasty cop as yet.

'I presume it was you who wrote the letter we received ... Mrs Powell, is it?'

She felt her heart racing in her chest. 'Yes. Janet Powell.'

'I was about to pay you a visit, Mrs Powell. Thank you for saving me the trouble.'

She glanced up and saw that he was looking at her intently. She suspected that nothing much would get past him.

'What is it you want to tell me? I've looked up the Shipborne case and it really did seem to be cut and dried at the time.' He inclined his head, waiting for a reaction.

Janet felt herself blushing. She looked down at her trembling hands and tried to think of the right words to say. Inspector Peterson waited patiently.

'Take your time,' he said gently after a minute or so. Janet looked up at him again and he smiled encouragingly. 'Why don't you start at the beginning? What was your connection with Chris Hobson?'

At least this gave her a starting point. She took a deep breath and began. 'I met Chris a couple of months before the murder. He did some work at my house ... clearing out the gutters. I invited him in for a cup of tea. His colleague had gone off somewhere – I can't remember where exactly – and it seemed ... well, I was making a cup of tea for myself so it seemed like a friendly gesture, if you know what I mean.'

'Yes. Go on.'

Her cheeks turned a bright shade of red. 'Well, my husband was out. I'd never done anything like that before or since and ... it just happened.'

'You, er ... went to bed with him?' Wesley tried hard to keep his voice neutral. Some of his colleagues would have found Janet Powell's confession a source of gleeful amusement ... the stuff of the more salacious Sunday newspapers: the stereotypical bored housewife rutting with any male who happens to walk up her outwardly respectable garden path.

'We didn't go to bed. We did it in the utility room,' she mumbled. Then she looked Wesley in the eye. 'Look, it was completely out of character for me. I don't make a habit of that sort of thing. But Chris ... well, I'd never been attracted to anyone like that before. It was ... ' She hesitated, trying to find the right words.

'Love at first sight?' Wesley suggested, aware that he was sounding like a clichéd romantic novel.

54

Janet shook her head. 'I don't know. It was more like a magnetic animal attraction. I ... I couldn't help myself. And neither could he.'

'And your husband? Did he know about all this?'

She shook her head vigorously. 'No way. I made sure he had no idea what was going on. Chris wanted me to leave Derek but after the first couple of weeks ... well, I realised that I couldn't give up everything. It was physical, you see, and after the first flush of excitement was over I think I realised. We'd meet and go back to Chris's place in Morbay and ... '

'You compared that with what you'd have to give up?'

'That sounds awful, doesn't it? It sounds as though I'm a hard, mercenary bitch.'

Wesley shook his head. 'Not at all. It sounds as if you're a realist. Did you know about Chris's criminal record?'

'He told me. I think the affair was more serious on his part than mine ... in fact I know it was. He said he wanted to be completely honest with me. He said he'd been done for burglary and car theft ... and receiving stolen goods. But he said that if I went to live with him that would all change. The night that vicar was killed was the last time I saw him. Derek, my husband, decided to go and work in New York – it all happened very quickly. I met Chris to tell him I was going to the States. I told him it was all over.' She hesitated. 'Do you think what Chris said was true? Do you think he would have changed if I'd ... ?'

Wesley didn't answer. Who could know what might have been? But it was obvious that the question had preyed on Janet's mind. His instinct was to reassure her, to tell her that most men like Hobson, although they might mean what they say at the time, usually slip back into their old ways once the novelty of a new relationship has worn off and their old mates reassert their influence. But for all he knew, Chris Hobson might have been the exception to the rule, so it was probably best to say nothing.

'So why don't you tell me what happened on the night of

the Reverend Shipborne's murder?' It was time to get down to the nub of the matter ... her claim that Chris Hobson was innocent.

'Chris was with me all that evening.'

Wesley looked her in the eye. 'If this is true why didn't you come forward?'

She blushed again. 'I feel awful about it now, believe me. I'd heard all about the vicar's murder on the news the next day, but of course I never connected it with Chris. Then I moved to New York with Derek a week later so I didn't know Chris had been arrested for it.' She took a tissue from her coat pocket and dabbed at her eyes, although Wesley could see no tears there.

'So you and Chris Hobson had no contact once you'd moved to New York?'

'No. It was a clean break ... a new start. I didn't even tell him what part of America I was going to.'

'But you've decided to come forward now?'

'Yes.'

'After twelve years.' He tried to keep his voice neutral, to hide any hint of reproach.

'As I said, I didn't even know Chris had been arrested. I've been living in the States for twelve years ... we only got back to England a couple of months ago.'

'So how did you find out Hobson was in jail for Shipborne's murder?'

Her restless fingers began to play with the silk scarf she was wearing. 'About four weeks ago I saw him in an episode of that TV documentary ... *Nick*, I think it's called. It said he was serving life for murder and I couldn't believe it. I had to know what it was he'd done ... I assumed that whatever it was must have happened while I was in the States. Anyway, I went to the local newspaper office to look through their archives and I had the shock of my life when I found he'd been convicted of the Belsham murder. I mean, he can't have done it. We were together that night. We met in Belsham but we didn't stay there long.'

'Why have you waited four weeks to come forward?'

She looked sheepish. 'I didn't know what to do. I didn't know whether it was too late to come forward or . . . then there was the thought of Derek finding out about . . .'

'But you've decided to tell us now?'

'When I saw Chris on TV he looked so old. I couldn't just let him rot in that awful place. I had to tell the truth.'

She paused and took a packet of cigarettes from her handbag. She waved the packet vaguely in Wesley's direction but when he refused she took out a cigarette, lit it with a gold lighter and inhaled deeply.

Then she sat forward and looked Wesley in the eye. 'And besides, last week Derek, my husband, told me he's having an affair with one of the barmaids at the golf club and he wants a divorce. After all these years he wants a bloody divorce.'

Wesley saw anger in her eyes. More than anger . . . the fury of a woman scorned. Perhaps this confession of infidelity had nothing to do with sympathy for Hobson's plight. Perhaps it was a means of revenge . . . a way of humiliating her errant husband with the public revelation that she had had to seek satisfaction elsewhere in the course of their marriage. Or perhaps it was just that her reason for staying silent had gone.

'I've been wondering what to do for the best,' she said piously. 'I've been feeling so guilty.'

But not guilty enough to come forward before your husband ran off with a barmaid, thought Wesley. He didn't really know what to make of Mrs Janet Powell – was she a basically honest woman motivated by a fit of conscience or was she a manipulative bitch playing some sly game? He sat back and watched her, giving her the benefit of the doubt.

'I think it would be best if you told me exactly what happened on the evening of the Reverend Shipborne's murder, don't you?'

She paused, gathering her thoughts, before embarking on

57

her story. 'I'd decided I was going to the States with Derek and I knew I had to finish my affair with Chris. It had been nice while it lasted but I suppose I knew it was just sexual on my part. I'd realised that Chris was just a petty villain and we came from different worlds ... different ways of thinking and behaving. Does that sound snobbish?'

Wesley didn't know how to answer so he just shook his head.

'Anyway, I was starting to suspect that he was getting too serious and that was the last thing I wanted. I arranged to meet him outside the pub in Belsham ... the Horse and Farrier. I didn't know anyone in Belsham so I thought it'd be safe. I met him at seven outside the pub as arranged. He'd been in the pub and had a drink ... I could smell the beer on his breath. We talked in my car for ages ... must have been almost an hour. I told him about America and I said I couldn't see him again. Then we went for a drive.'

'Where to?'

'Just around. I think I drove through some villages – I remember we passed Berry Ducis castle – and then to Morbay. We ended up at his flat. He wanted me to go in so I did ... for old times' sake. I was there till after midnight. I left him in bed,' she added coyly.

'How did he react when you told him you were going to the States with your husband?'

'He said he loved me. He said he'd wait for me no matter how long it took. I didn't know what to do. I didn't feel like that and by then I just wanted to get him out of my life.'

'So when did you find out about the Reverend Shipborne's murder?'

'I read all about it in the paper the next day, of course. I took a particular interest because I'd been in Belsham around that time and I still recall all the details.' She closed her eyes tight, as though trying to remember. 'It said the vicar was killed between five to seven when his cleaner left and ten when she went back and found him. I remember I'd met Chris at seven on the dot and we talked in the car in the pub carpark for ages. We were probably there at the time of the murder but I certainly didn't see anything. And Chris definitely couldn't have done it because he was with me all that time.' She looked Wesley in the eye. 'How did he come to be arrested? Surely they didn't have any evidence against him.'

Wesley said nothing.

'Didn't he tell them he was with me?' she asked, puzzled.

'Not when they arrested him.'

'He probably wanted to keep my name out of it,' she said quietly.

'Later on, when he was charged, he changed his story. He said he'd been with a woman who was no longer in the country and he didn't know where to find her. But by then the evidence against him was overwhelming so I don't think this tale of a mystery woman was taken too seriously.'

In the file this last-minute alibi had been mentioned as an afterthought and Wesley couldn't even remember seeing Janet's name. His only thought was that if Hobson hadn't told the police about Janet's involvement as soon as he was questioned because of love, he had been a complete fool.

'At least I can put things right now,' she said, smiling shyly.

Wesley stood up. It's a pity for Chris Hobson that you didn't put things right twelve years ago, he thought to himself as he took a witness statement form from the drawer.

Fred Sommerby didn't cry as the nurse covered his wife's face with the sheet. Fred had never cried. Crying was for women. He looked at the small shape beneath the sheet and felt no emotion: no sadness, no elation, no regret. Nothing.

The nurse looked at him. She was plump with a kind face and she reminded him of a cow. Her eyes were full of sympathy – the smooth sympathy of the professional carer.

She was asking him whether he would like a nice cup of tea. He stared at her, wanting to wipe the smug, do-gooding smirk off her stupid face. He mumbled something that she took for a yes and she hurried away.

He stared down at Edith's body. She looked so small and insignificant. They'd taken all the tubes out, which was good. He hadn't liked the tubes. They'd made her seem strange, inhuman – not like his Edith at all.

The nurse returned with tea and ushered him into a side room with practised efficiency. The small room was carpeted and the low coffee table in the centre was covered with a selection of two-year-old editions of *Country Life* and last year's Sunday supplements. Around the pale pink walls stood six institutional easy chairs, upholstered in light blue tweed. This was the room set aside for grieving relatives.

The nurse announced that the doctor would be along in a moment to speak to him, as if this was some honour he should be looking forward to. Fred said nothing. There was nothing to say. Edith had gone. And he would mourn her in his own way. Not here in front of others.

Fred ignored the magazines and sat staring ahead for ten minutes until Dr Choudray entered the room.

'I'm very sorry about your wife,' the doctor began, his face solemn. 'We did all we could.'

Fred stared at him and said nothing. He didn't like Indian doctors . . . in his opinion there were far too many of them. He stood up. He had nothing to say and he wanted to get home, back to the bungalow.

Dr Choudray, seeing that Fred intended to leave, put a gentle hand on his sleeve. 'Please, Mr Sommerby, sit down. There are some questions I need to ask you.' He spoke in English more precise, more perfect, than Fred's own, another mark against him.

Fred ignored the hand and stayed standing. 'She's bloody dead, isn't she? There's nothing more to be said. She's gone.'

60

The doctor stood looking at him for a few seconds, flummoxed. They didn't usually behave like this. But then grief affected people in different ways. Or was it grief? Dr Choudray wouldn't have been surprised if it was relief. He put himself between Fred and the door.

'We were rather puzzled by some marks found on your wife's body. Bruises.'

'She was a clumsy cow.'

Choudray looked at him, shocked, fearful that his and Sister Atkins's worst suspicions were about to be confirmed.

'They weren't consistent with falls or accidents, Mr Sommerby. It was almost as if someone had been beating her over a long period of time. And we found evidence of untreated fractures. Now I'm a doctor and I don't know the legal position but . . . '

The doctor was quite unprepared for Fred Sommerby's strength as he shoved him aside and made for the door, waving his walking stick like a weapon before him. The doctor lost his balance and fell against one of the easy chairs, the upholstery softening his inevitable fall.

By the time Dr Choudray had stood up, unhurt apart from his dignity, Fred Sommerby had disappeared out of the swing-doors.

As the doctor walked out of the room, looking slightly shaken, Sister Atkins hurried over to him.

'Are you all right, Doctor?' she asked. She sounded worried.

'I've just had a rather unpleasant encounter with Mr Sommerby.'

'Did you ask him about . . . ?'

'Yes. But I don't think I handled it too well.'

'Well, we can mention it to the police when we tell them about the other thing.'

'What other thing?'

Sister Atkins looked smug. 'It might take a few days for the results to come back from the lab but I'm as certain as

61

I can be that Mrs Sommerby was suffering from botulism poisoning. I think I told you before that I'd seen a couple of cases of it when I was working up North. Mrs Sommerby showed identical symptoms. I really think it's time to report it to the pubic health authorities . . . and the police, in view of that request they made.'

Dr Choudray hesitated. He was a cautious man but Sister Atkins seemed so sure of herself. 'I still think we should wait until we're absolutely certain. We don't want to waste their time, do we?'

Sister Atkins said nothing and turned to go.

As she bustled off, Dr Choudray noticed that one of the contract cleaners was standing leaning on a floor polisher, watching her departure with interest. He had not seen the cleaner before – they changed so often: high turnover of staff – but he was sure that every word he had exchanged with Sister Atkins had been overheard.

But as it was only a contract cleaner Dr Choudray carried on and thought no more about it.

'Let's put it this way, Gerry, the ghost of Lady Chatterley was hovering in the air.'

Gerry Heffernan grinned. Even he, with his limited literary knowledge, had heard of the lustful Lady Chatterley.

'Chris Hobson was Janet Powell's "bit of rough". They had it off in her utility room after he'd cleaned out her gutters. I don't suppose she wanted to get her sheets dirty.'

'You're sounding very judgemental today, Wesley.'

'Well, I don't think it was true love on her part. He, on the other hand, might have had different ideas. He wanted her to leave her husband. It sounds like he was starting to get serious and that's when she decided to call it a day. If he was in love with her that explains why he didn't tell the police he was with her on the night of the murder when he was first questioned. However, later on he did say that he was with a woman – said he hadn't wanted to involve her because she was married.'

Heffernan snorted. 'A gentleman thief ... whatever next?'

'He said she was somewhere in the USA but he'd no idea where. DCI Norbert obviously didn't think it was worth following up.'

'And Hobson never named her?'

'If he did it's not in the file. I wonder how Hobson feels now after he's served twelve years in the nick while his lady friend's been living the high life in New York. She found out he was serving time a month ago and she's only come forward now because her husband's just run off with a barmaid and she's nothing left to lose.'

'If I was Hobson I'd be harbouring uncharitable thoughts about Mrs Janet Powell ... but maybe he's a nicer person than me.' Heffernan grinned angelically, sat back and put his feet up on the desk. 'But I doubt if twelve years inside will have done wonders for his better nature.' He picked up a thick file that was lying on his desk, on top of an untidy heap of similar files. 'I suppose I'd better go and have a word with the Chief Super ... tell him the bad news.'

Wesley didn't reply. He was already two steps ahead, wondering who, if Chris Hobson was really innocent, had actually killed the Reverend John Shipborne all those years ago.

He looked at his watch. He wanted to get home, away from thoughts of the fickleness of humanity and violent death.

If you want a job doing, do it yourself had been one of Neil Watson's grandmother's favourite sayings. And now he knew exactly what she'd meant.

The police were useless. They used any pretext to shirk their duties – lack of manpower being their usual excuse. He had told Wesley quite firmly that the site needed a twenty-four-hour police guard but Wesley, to his disgust, had seemed mildly amused by his high expectations. That was why Neil had pitched a small ridge tent in the corner of Pest Field and now lay curled up in his sleeping bag, fully dressed, with only a torch, a thermos flask and an alarming selection of creepy-crawlies for company.

It was just after one o'clock in the morning and the field was silent apart from the usual country noises: screaming owls, barking foxes, lowing cows and a passing local who'd had a few too many during an after-hours drinking session at the Horse and Farrier and was now convinced that he could give Pavarotti a run for his money.

Neil lay on the hard ground, alert at first, but then he closed his eyes. One of the young female diggers, a red-haired girl called Emma, popped unbidden into his drowsy thoughts and he experienced a warm tingling in his loins. He had spoken to her only about professional matters so far, but there was plenty of time for that to change, he thought to himself as he laid plans that he knew in his heart of hearts he would be unlikely to keep to.

After a while he drifted into sleep, but when the noise came he awoke, confused, thinking he was in his own bed at his Exeter flat, reaching for the clock on his bedside table. It took him a few seconds to realise that he was in a tent in the corner of a field, alone apart from an unknown quantity of buried skeletons.

As soon as his situation dawned on him, his heart began to pound. What had seemed like a good idea in the light of day now seemed the height of folly. If he encountered the nighthawks, what exactly was he supposed to do if they didn't run off as soon as they realised he was there?

The sounds were getting nearer. Faint electronic bleeps magnified in the still night air. A metal detector. There were no voices. Perhaps whoever it was had ventured there alone. Neil held on to this optimistic thought as he extricated himself from the warm embrace of his sleeping bag.

The noises stopped and Neil sat for a minute or so, listening. Perhaps it had been his imagination, or perhaps he had been dreaming. But he felt he ought to make sure.

As he unfastened the front of the tent the noise of the zip

seemed as loud as a cannon roar in the darkness. He squatted at the tent's entrance, perfectly still, listening, before crawling out into the damp and cold.

He stood up and walked, shivering, towards his trench. There was no breeze and the trees around the edge of the field stood motionless, as if in expectation.

Then a blow to his back caused him to stumble and fall down into the depths of the open trench, clawing at the damp ground. The fall knocked the breath out of him, and when he tried to open his mouth to call for help he found he couldn't move. He could taste blood in his mouth as he curled himself up defensively and the only thought in his brain was survival. All other thoughts were subsumed to this most basic of instincts, his flesh feeling as though it had been ripped apart with red-hot pokers.

As he listened to retreating footsteps padding away across the muddy ground, he lay there, fighting oblivion, his mouth filled with blood and earth. Then, with a great effort, he managed to open his eyes for a few moments.

Staring up at him were the empty eye sockets of a skull, a death's head. The thought that this was the end, that death had come to claim him, flitted through his head before he finally lost consciousness.

Chapter Four

I have read more of Barnaby's work and I find myself fascinated by the character of Hammo, who was priest of Belsham all those years ago.

He must have been an ordinary parish priest, rather like myself – a fallible, sinful man doing his best to come to terms with evil. I wonder what became of him. No doubt I'll find out if I have the time – or the courage – to read on.

Barnaby's thesis begins to disturb me for I can't help seeing myself in the place of the man at the centre of his story. I sometimes feel my conscience is eating away at my very soul.

From a diary found among the Reverend John Shipborne's personal effects

Neil had been found half conscious and disoriented at seven that morning by a postman on his early round. The postman had taken the trouble to peep over the fencing in Pest Field because he was curious about what was going on in there, and as soon as he noticed a man lying there bleeding and dazed in one of the deep trenches, obviously the victim of some beating or accident, he had rung the police and the ambulance service. All Neil could say to the uniformed officers who answered the call in their patrol car was that he hadn't seen who had attacked him. In spite of his weakened state he had objected at first to the idea of going to hospital to get checked over. However, when he found that every movement was torture and he could hardly keep his eyes open, he realised that he was in no position to refuse, so he allowed himself to be placed on a stretcher and whisked off in an ambulance to Morbay General as Tradmouth Hospital had no available beds.

At nine o'clock Neil's colleagues arrived to continue their work, only to find Wesley Peterson waiting for them, hands in pockets, with DC Trish Walton standing solemnly by his side like a professional mourner at a funeral. Wesley had hardly said a word to Trish on their way there. The thought of Neil being a victim of violent crime seemed unreal, but he told himself that every victim of every crime he had ever dealt with was somebody's friend or relation. Although this one was different somehow. This one was personal.

Trish glanced at Wesley, not knowing quite what to say, and she was relieved when she saw one of the archaeologists approaching, a lean man, a little older than Wesley, who wore his hair tied back in an untidy ponytail and was dressed in mud-caked jeans and a combat jacket similar to the one Neil habitually wore.

'Any news?'

'They've taken him to Morbay. Last I heard it was concussion and possibly a few broken bones.'

'Any idea what happened?' Matt mumbled awkwardly, glancing at Trish.

Wesley shook his head. 'According to Neil someone gave him a hefty shove into the open trench. Don't worry, we'll get them.' The quiet determination in his voice made Matt believe what he said.

'If there's anything me and Jane can do ... '

'Just carry on with the dig ... that's what Neil'd want.' He turned to Trish. 'Trish, can you make sure everyone on the site's interviewed and asked if they've seen anyone suspicious hanging around. And have a word with the occupants of any houses that overlook this site. Someone might have seen something.'

Trish nodded solemnly and rushed off, although Wesley wasn't too hopeful that her questions would bear fruit. The good people of Belsham would have been tucked up in their own or each other's beds at the time of the attack, and it was doubtful that the archaeologists would have taken much notice of anything that hadn't been buried in the ground for the past few hundred years. But it was worth a try.

'So what was Neil up to?' he asked Matt as soon as they were alone.

'Apparently he asked for a police guard on the site and was told it wasn't on.' Matt looked at Wesley with more than a hint of reproach and Wesley looked away. He felt bad enough already without having his nose rubbed in it. 'He said he'd stay on the site and keep watch. We were going to take it in turns ... do alternate nights.'

'Didn't he have his mobile? Why didn't he call ... ?'

'Maybe he didn't have time.'

'Can you tell if they got away with anything?'

'They've dug some holes but I guess Neil disturbed them before they could ... '

Wesley thought for a moment. 'Have you had experience of nighthawks before?'

Matt nodded. 'Unfortunately, yes.'

'Are they usually violent?'

Matt shrugged. 'Not the ones I've come across. I should have thought they'd be more likely to run for it if they were disturbed. It's not as if we're expecting to find anything particularly valuable on this dig. We've no reason to think it's another Sutton Hoo or Tutankhamun's tomb. Unless the bastard who attacked Neil knows something we don't.'

Wesley turned and stared at the church tower that peeped over the trees – the last place he'd gone with Neil. Matt might be right – Neil's attacker or attackers might have known something about the site that the archaeologists didn't. Perhaps there was something more down there than ancient horseshoes and old coins.

'I'm going to put a police guard on this site,' said Wesley. 'If the attacker comes back for whatever it is he was after, we'll get him.'

'Bit bloody late,' said Matt under his breath.

As Wesley walked away towards the road, Matt found himself regretting his words. He guessed that Wesley was feeling bad enough as it was.

Sister Atkins hadn't been absolutely sure about the cause of Edith Sommerby's death at first, but she'd thought about it overnight, lying awake in her single bed, turning it over in her mind, and she was now as certain as she could be without the final confirmation of the laboratory results. And, according to the memo that had been going around, the police wanted to know as soon as possible.

She glanced out of the office window. She had a good view of the ward from there so she could keep a watchful eye on her staff and patients. The man who had been admitted that morning with concussion and broken ribs was stable now, but when he had first arrived and had lost consciousness she had feared that his head injuries might be more serious than was first suspected, or that one of the broken ribs had punctured a lung. But he had been X-rayed since and nothing sinister had shown up. It seemed that he had been lucky.

Her newest patient was an archaeologist who had been keeping an eye on his dig and minding his own business when he'd been attacked. Sister Atkins didn't know what the world was coming to ... it certainly wasn't getting any better. The police probably did their best but it seemed that, like King Cnut, they were trying to hold back the rushing tide of crime and wickedness.

The thought of the police reminded Sister Atkins of Edith Sommerby and her extremely unpleasant husband. Dr Choudray may have advised caution, but she was as sure about Edith's death as she could be. She stared at the phone on her desk for a few moments before picking up the memo from hospital management saying that the police wanted to know of any poisoning cases, even cases of food poisoning. After re-reading it several times, she dialled the number printed at the end of the memo.

Wesley was holding his emotions in strict check but Gerry Heffernan could tell that the attack on Neil had upset him. Even when you deal with crime and violence day in, day out, it's different when the victim is someone you know. He told him to sit down and shouted into the outer office for someone to bring two cups of tea. There was nothing like tea for shock, in Gerry's opinion, and it usually helped in cases of frustrated anger as well.

'So how is he?' he asked.

'He's been taken to Morbay ... there weren't any beds at Tradmouth. I rang up and they said he's comfortable.'

Heffernan nodded solemnly. 'They always say that. Don't worry, Wes. He'll be back digging his holes again in no time. All we've got to do is find the bastard or bastards responsible. Have you told Pam yet?'

Wesley shook his head. 'I don't want to upset her ... not with the baby so near and ... '

Pam and Neil had gone out together at university. They were close ... or as close as anyone could get to Neil. Wesley wasn't sure how she'd take the news in her present condition.

'Any leads?'

'One of the archaeologists thought he saw someone hanging around by the trees the other day but it was all a bit vague ... no description, no time.'

'What about the damage?'

'A few holes have been dug but it was all very haphazard. The attacker exposed another skeleton near the ones they've already dug up. There was a dagger next to the bones – pretty well preserved, apparently – and a few medieval coins just lying there in the ground: whoever dug them up had made no attempt to take them. Matt said it almost seemed as if they were looking for something specific, something they knew was there. Not like usual nighthawks who are after any coins and buried treasure they can lay their hands on. Matt reckons it's very odd.'

Heffernan scratched his head. 'Sounds odd to me an' all. Any ideas?'

Wesley shook his head again. For once he hadn't a clue. Neil, his friend since their first year at university, was lying in a hospital bed, fighting for his life for all he knew, and Wesley felt useless, helpless. 'House-to-house haven't come up with anything. Nobody saw any strange cars or ... '

'So whoever did this just melted into the night, did he? Someone must know him. Would he have been bloodstained?'

'Probably not.'

'Maybe we should start by tracking down everyone with a record for this sort of thing and checking their alibis. Get Steve onto it right away.'

Wesley took a deep breath, forcing himself to be detached, professional. 'I'll see to it.'

The chief inspector's phone rang and he answered it. After a brief conversation he looked across the desk at Wesley. At least this was something to take his mind off Neil's plight. 'That was a Sister Atkins from Morbay Hospital.' He noticed a sudden look of panic flash across Wesley's face. 'Don't worry, it wasn't about Neil. This Sister Atkins has seen our memo. A woman died yesterday and she reckons it was botulism poisoning. And guess where the dead woman lived ... '

'Where?' Wesley didn't feel up to guessing games.

'Just across the carpark from Huntings supermarket. Now the sister said they can't be sure about the cause of death until after the post-mortem, and of course it might have nothing to do with Huntings, but ... '

Wesley nodded. 'I once shared a flat with a biochemistry student who told me that it's possible to culture botulism if you know what you're doing, and it's just the sort of thing guaranteed to put a supermarket out of business. Shop at Huntings and get food poisoning. It could be what our anonymous letter writer meant.'

'We need confirmation before we go any farther. I think we should go and have a word with this Sister Atkins, and we can drop in on Neil while we're there, eh,' Heffernan said gently. 'Don't worry, Wes. He's in good hands.'

Wesley didn't comment. 'Let me know when you want to go,' he said quietly, before leaving the boss's office and making for his own desk, head down. He didn't feel much like talking.

Matt and Jane looked down at the bones. After the events of that morning neither of them felt in the mood to do much about them. But the work had to go on, and soon Jane began to record their finds, even though her heart wasn't in it.

But it was the dagger which interested Matt. He could tell it was medieval, possibly fourteenth-century. The blade was badly corroded but the handle seemed better preserved, and it was just possible, beneath the rust and soil of centuries, to discern some sort of symbol or decoration carved into it. It had been lying close to the skeleton's left hip, as though he had been wearing it in a scabbard that had long since rotted in the earth. There was a ragged hole the size of a small apple in the back of the skull. The man with the dagger was the first of the skeletons they had found in the pit to bear any signs of violence.

Of course, they couldn't be sure without further investigation, but it was just possible that they might have a murder victim on their hands. At least it would take their minds off other things for a while.

Neil Watson lay helpless on the bed, filled up with

painkillers and feeling sick. Heffernan made himself comfortable on the plastic visitor's chair provided and Wesley went off in search of another and returned a few minutes later, his mission successful.

'Don't worry about the dig,' Wesley began. 'Matt's taken charge. It's all going fine.'

Neil tried to nod weakly and winced with pain.

'So have you had any more thoughts on who did this?' Heffernan said loudly, earning himself a disapproving look from a passing nurse.

Neil began to look agitated, whether from the memory or from the frustration of not being able to remember, Wesley couldn't tell. 'It happened so fast. I think I heard a noise and went out of the tent but I don't really remember. It's all hazy.'

Heffernan grinned. 'It wasn't an irate husband, was it?'

Neil tried to smile. 'Chance'd be a fine thing. Sorry, Gerry, but I've not had much luck in that direction recently. Is there much damage to the site? Did he get much?' His voice was feeble, shaky. Wesley found his friend's weakness faintly disturbing. Evidence that even healthy flesh is fragile and vulnerable.

'You say "he". You think there was just one?' Wesley asked.

'Yeah. I'm pretty sure there was only one. But he was a big bastard. Took me by surprise. You haven't told me how much he got away with.'

'According to Matt he didn't get much. He uncovered a medieval dagger and some coins but he just left them lying there on the ground ... almost as though he was looking for something else. I don't think your attacker was your average nighthawk.'

'More like a bloody heavyweight boxer.'

Wesley smiled. At least Neil had managed to retain a sense of humour.

'Do you think it could be something to do with Huntings? Do you think they could be trying to warn us off?'

73

Wesley looked across the bed at Heffernan, who was chewing at a fingernail, listening intently. He hadn't considered a connection with Huntings and he wondered why it had leapt into Neil's mind.

'What makes you think that?'

'No reason. Just prejudice against greedy supermarkets who build on archaeological sites, that's all.' Neil closed his eyes, as though the effort of conversation was becoming too much for him.

Wesley and Heffernan looked at each other. Neil's words had reminded them of the primary reason for their visit ... to have a word with Sister Atkins.

They took their leave of the invalid, promising to return.

'He seems cheerful enough,' Heffernan said as they approached the sister's office.

Wesley smiled. Now that he was satisfied his friend's life wasn't in immediate danger, he felt more relaxed. Sometimes the victims of beatings or falls weren't so lucky.

A statuesque woman wearing the dark blue dress of a ward sister emerged from the office. Wesley flashed his warrant card, as did Heffernan, who was standing behind him looking rather awestruck.

'Sister Atkins?'

'That's me. I've been expecting you.' Her voice told Wesley that she was from the North – Yorkshire probably. She opened the office door and stood aside to let them in.

Wesley sat down and looked at Sister Atkins expectantly. 'You reported a suspected poisoning?'

Sister Atkins blushed. 'I've probably jumped the gun a bit but an elderly lady was admitted a few days ago with poisoning symptoms. Her husband assured us that she hadn't eaten anything that he hadn't.' She hesitated. 'When I was working up in Leeds I saw a few cases of botulism. It was traced back to a batch of cooked ham at a butcher's shop. Five people died: it was on the news.'

'Go on.'

'Well, Mrs Sommerby's symptoms were identical. I've

been half expecting there to be more cases ... if it originated in a shop or ... '

'But there haven't been?'

'I rang round some other local hospitals and they haven't had any cases.'

'Thanks. That saves us a job,' Wesley said, giving the woman a grateful smile.

'So what's this all about?' the sister asked. 'Isn't it usually the public health people who investigate outbreaks of food poisoning?'

Wesley looked apologetic. 'I can't really tell you at the moment. Sorry.' It was probably best if their suspicions weren't made public just yet. He didn't want to start a panic. The sister raised her eyebrows but made no further comment.

The lone case fitted perfectly with the threat to Huntings ... the letter saying, 'I see the jam's been sold already and when your customer dies' – customer in the singular. And the first letter Huntings had received had referred to biological warfare, and there was nothing more biological and warlike than introducing a hint of botulism to one of Huntings' products. It was a fair assumption that the dead woman was the letter writer's first victim. Although at this stage it was still very much an assumption.

Maybe, like Sister Atkins, Wesley was jumping the gun, assuming too much. Maybe it was a coincidence; perhaps there would be other cases and the source would be found to have nothing to do with Huntings after all.

Sister Atkins shifted in her seat. 'There's something else I haven't told you. I don't know if it's relevant or ... '

Wesley and Heffernan sat forward expectantly.

'I think Edith Sommerby's husband used to beat her up. She had a mass of bruises and the doctor found a number of untreated fractures. It's my guess she'd been the victim of domestic violence for years. Her husband was an unpleasant man. Aggressive. Just the type to think it was his right to use a poor defenceless woman as a punch bag.

One of my nurses thought he was going to lash out at her on one occasion. And he pushed a doctor over ... he wasn't hurt, luckily, but it wasn't a pleasant incident. Violence towards hospital staff isn't unknown these days,' she added sadly.

'So you suspected the husband might have had something to do with Mrs Sommerby's poisoning?'

'It did cross my mind. I might be mistaken about the botulism, and if it's something else ... some poisonous substance ... But they say poison's a woman's weapon, don't they?'

'So they do. But there are exceptions to the rule.' Wesley thought for a few moments. 'However, from what you've told me about the dead woman's husband, I'd expect him to use less subtle methods to dispose of his wife. And anyway, bullies tend to like their victims alive.'

Gerry Heffernan was nodding sagely in agreement. 'If you give us his address, love, we can go and have a word.'

Sister Atkins hesitated for a moment as thoughts of patient confidentiality flitted through her head. But then Edith Sommerby's husband had never been her patient ... and the thought of him receiving a visit from the police gave her an unexpected glow of satisfaction. She walked over to a tall steel filing cabinet standing in the corner of the room and pulled out a file.

She wrote an address on a piece of paper and handed it to Heffernan. 'Don't say where you got it, will you. And I'll ring you with the post-mortem findings as soon as we get them.' She smiled conspiratorially, happy that she'd done her bit for the rights of women like Edith. She wasn't a vindictive woman by nature, quite the reverse, but Sister Atkins hoped that Fred Sommerby would get everything that was coming to him.

Wesley drove back to Tradmouth with Heffernan slumped in the passenger seat. He chose the shorter, scenic route via Queenswear and the car ferry. As they crossed the river where scores of yachts bobbed at anchor, their steel masts ringing like gentle wind chimes in the autumn breeze, Gerry Heffernan stared out of the car window, longing to be out there on the *Rosie May*.

When they reached Tradmouth, Heffernan suggested lunch. A pub, he said: somewhere to get away from the office. Wesley had to agree with him. He was in no mood to return to the station either. They settled on the Fisherman's Arms: it was the right sort of day for a good hotpot by a roaring pub fire.

'So what do you make of it?' Wesley asked as soon as they were settled, Heffernan with a pint of best bitter and Wesley with an orange juice, as he would probably be driving later.

'Make of what? Your mate getting shoved into one of his own trenches or that poor old dear getting poisoned with botulism?'

'Both.'

Heffernan took a long drink and stared at his glass. 'Well, we can't do anything about the old dear until we get the post-mortem results. I mean, that Sister Atkins could be wrong. Or it could be that the loving husband added a little something extra to her tea. And as for your mate Neil ... you sure it wasn't an irate husband who gave him a push? If nothing was taken from his dig ... '

Wesley smiled. 'As far as I know Neil's love life is going through a dormant period at the moment. I'm not aware that he's been bedding any married women ... or any other women for that matter. I don't think there's been anyone since that girl at Earlsacre last year ... remember?'

Heffernan nodded. 'The one who ... ?'

'That's the one.' Wesley hesitated, gathering his thoughts. 'I can't think of anybody who bears Neil a grudge so I doubt if it's anything personal. That leaves us with the nighthawks. They probably didn't take anything because they realised Neil was hurt and they panicked.' Wesley sat back, looking pleased with himself. 'I reckon if we make enquiries among the local metal detectorists we'll come up with a name sooner or later.'

Heffernan looked at his watch. 'I'll leave that in your capable hands, then, Wes. I'm seeing the Chief Super in an hour. He wants a word about the Hobson case. He reckons it might be best if someone has a look through the evidence before the lawyers and the miscarriage of justice industry get wind of it. They'll be circling like a load of ruddy vultures if they think Hobson's got a chance of getting his conviction overturned and a hefty wad of compensation. I still can't think why that Janet Powell didn't come forward at the time.'

'She claims she'd left the country by the time Hobson was arrested and she knew nothing about it. If she hadn't, I'd be tempted to think it was a case of aggravated snobbery. Keeping quiet would have disposed of her embarrassing bit of rough while making sure she held on to the big house, swimming pool and Mercedes.'

'What makes you think she was rich?'

'I've been checking. Her husband, Derek Powell, was one of these high-powered executives. He lived here and commuted to London until he was sent to the States to run the company's New York office. Who'd want to be Chris Hobson's bit on the side living in a squalid Morbay bed-sit off the fruits of love and petty crime when you've got all that?'

'Who indeed?' Heffernan took another long drink.

'Janet Powell claims that when she went off to live in the States she cut off all contact with Hobson and put her past behind her. Apparently she didn't know about Hobson's conviction until she saw him on that TV documentary, *Nick*. She says she had the shock of her life when she discovered he'd been done for Shipborne's murder.'

'But she still didn't come forward right away?'

'No. She waited a few weeks. She says her husband's just run off with a barmaid at his golf club so she feels she's got nothing to lose now by confessing to a bit of how's-your-father with a petty crook back in 1991.'

'Do you believe all this?'

'Her story seems to check out so far.'

The steaming hotpot arrived, and the tempting aroma made Wesley realise that he was hungry. His mind had been on other things.

An hour later they returned to the station and went their separate ways; Heffernan to the well-furnished splendour of the Chief Superintendent's retreat on the top floor and Wesley back to the more utilitarian surroundings of the CID office.

As soon as Wesley entered the office Rachel Tracey walked briskly up to him, her face serious as though she had some momentous news to impart. 'Huntings supermarket in Morbay has received another letter. It came by hand this time, left on the customer services desk.'

'What did it say?'

Rachel lifted up her notebook. She glanced at Wesley and began to read. '"So someone died yesterday in Morbay Hospital after eating something bought at Huntings. That'll look good in the papers, won't it? It's so easy to add new products to your stock ... with a little added botulism for flavour. There's one dead so far. What's the final score to be? Happy hunting, Huntings."' Rachel looked up. 'That's it. No demand for money, just threats. What are they after?'

Wesley pondered the question for a few moments. 'To create a climate of terror? The killing is probably a means to an end. For some reason they want to get at Huntings. I suppose they might be preparing the ground; letting Huntings know that they mean business and their demands might come later.' He thought for a moment. 'We'd better pay the manager a visit. I wonder if it's just the Morbay branch they've got it in for or is it Huntings in general?'

'Did someone really die of botulism at Morbay Hospital?'

'Yes. That's what's strange. The sister in charge of the

ward told us she thought it was botulism poisoning because she's seen cases before, but the post-mortem hasn't been carried out yet so it's not confirmed. There's no way anybody outside the hospital could have got to know.'

'It's not been in the papers that there was a suspected case or ... ?'

'No.' He took a deep breath, getting his thoughts in order. 'Sturgeon, the manager, provided the names and addresses of a couple of people who've been dismissed from that branch of Huntings recently and I asked Steve to check them out. See if he's done it, will you. Then we'll pay a visit to Huntings and see if Mr Sturgeon can throw any more light on all of this.'

Rachel said nothing and turned away.

'Anything wrong, Rachel?'

She swung round. 'No. Why should there be?' She hesitated, as though wondering whether to confide in him. 'I'm just fed up with living on the farm, that's all. I'm thinking of moving out. I went to see a flat in the High Street last night ... above a shop.'

'Are you going to take it?'

She shook her head. 'I've seen better pigsties.'

'You'll find somewhere eventually,' Wesley said, looking at his watch. If he finished at Huntings at a reasonable time, he might have time to visit the dig. He was sure Matt would appreciate a police presence, however fleeting.

As he was leaving he met Gerry Heffernan in the doorway. The chief inspector took him by the arm and led him into his office. Wesley assumed the worst. The Hobson case was open again.

'We're to make a thorough investigation ... go through all the evidence. It'll mean talking to Stan Jenkins to see whether there were any doubts about Hobson's guilt at the time.'

'Or any other suspects?'

'Precisely, Wes. I don't have to spell it out to you, do I? What the Chief Super said, in effect, is that we don't want any more cock-ups. He didn't put it quite like that but ...'

Wesley nodded. He got the message. But there were more pressing problems than a twelve-year-old murder case. 'I'm off to Huntings again. They've had another letter and whoever sent it knows that Edith Sommerby died in Morbay Hospital.'

'How the ... '

'That's what I want to find out.' He searched in his inside pocket for the written transcription Rachel had made of the latest letter and handed it over.

'Still no demand for money,' said Heffernan as he handed it back.

'I think he's keeping them guessing; making them so jumpy they'll agree to anything when the time comes.'

Heffernan slumped down in his chair. 'Off you go to Huntings. And don't bring me anything back ... I don't think I'd fancy it.'

The words 'nobody is indispensable' passed through Matt's head as he stood at the edge of Pest Field watching the busy diggers. Although things were going well without Neil, everyone seemed uncharacteristically quiet. No one felt like laughing and joking when the man in charge was lying in hospital with concussion and broken ribs.

Jane walked over to him, her blonde hair tied back and a smudge of mud on her nose. He raised a hand and she allowed him to wipe the smudge off before giving him a quick peck on the cheek as a reward, glancing round to check that no one was watching them.

'So what's the final verdict on those bones?'

'What bones?'

'The ones you thought belonged to a murder victim.'

'I've shown the skull to Margaret ... she's had a lot of experience digging up battle sites. She reckons it's definitely a blow with a blunt instrument.'

'Funny it was that skeleton Neil's nighthawk dug up.'

'Not really. That dagger with the body would have given

a strong signal on a metal detector so he'd have dug there.'

Matt shrugged. Jane was probably right. In all the years they had been going out together he'd found that she usually was.

'But if he didn't take a fine example of a medieval dagger – and he didn't help himself to the Edward III coins – what was he after?'

Jane shook her head. The workings of the criminal mind were beyond her.

Keith Sturgeon looked thinner than the last time Wesley had seen him. His body seemed to have shrunk in his immaculate suit and his face was gaunt and drawn as though he had been suffering sleepless nights.

When Sunita showed Wesley and Rachel into his office they found him sitting in front of a TV monitor, staring intently at the black-and-white moving pictures on the screen. Wesley cleared his throat and he swung round, startled.

'Oh, Inspector Peterson. Good of you to come. I'm just going through the CCTV footage. There's a camera focused on the customer services desk.'

He returned his attention to the screen and Wesley looked over his shoulder. Rachel hung back, watching. 'Found anything yet?'

Sturgeon shook his head. He looked near to tears. 'It could be anyone. People are passing there all the time . . . staff and customers. And the spot at the end of the desk where he left the letter is just off camera. Is it true?'

'Is what true?'

'Has someone died in Morbay Hospital?'

'There has been a death but the cause hasn't been established yet,' Wesley stated cautiously. 'Would a member of the public be able to tell which part of the desk was off camera?'

Sturgeon shrugged. Wesley noticed that he wasn't wearing his buttonhole that day. Perhaps he hadn't been in the mood. He swung his swivel chair nervously to and fro. 'I suppose Mr Hunting will have to be told.'

'What did he say about the other letters?'

Sturgeon's pale face turned a sickly shade of pink. 'I thought it was probably a hoax so I haven't actually told him yet. I didn't think it was worth bothering him with . . .'

Wesley read between the lines. He had seen the monstrous stainless-steel award sitting on the desk: it was hard to miss. Sturgeon had once been Manager of the Year and wanted to stay that way in Hunting's eyes. But keeping quiet and hoping it would all go away wasn't an option now. 'I think he should be told, don't you?'

The manager nodded, resigned to his fate. It crossed Wesley's mind that Aaron Hunting might not be the most understanding of bosses. Self-made men rarely were.

'Sunita gave us the names of two employees who've been dismissed recently but I'd also like to have the names and addresses of everyone dismissed in the past, say, five years. Can you arrange that for me?' He smiled as though he assumed the answer would be yes. The tactic usually worked. 'And if the post-mortem findings suggest that this lady did die as a result of something she might have obtained from this store, I'll have to interview all your present staff, of course.'

Sturgeon swallowed hard. 'Of course. You can be assured of our full cooperation. What exactly did she die of? Was it botulism? What are we dealing with here?'

'I'm sorry, but we can't really say until the cause of death has been confirmed, but you'll be one of the first to know, I promise you.' Wesley tried to sound reassuring but Sturgeon looked anything but reassured. He began pacing up and down the office.

'Will we have to close the store?'

'That might be wise . . . at least until all your shelves have been searched for anything suspicious.' Wesley continued, 'Of course, it makes it more difficult for us that the letter writer has made no actual demands. And it's usual in cases such as this for the writer to instruct the recipient not to call in the police, so this doesn't quite fit the normal pattern. There have been cases of supermarkets being targeted like this but the motive has always been the extortion of money. Is there something you're holding back, Mr Sturgeon?'

'No. Nothing,' Sturgeon snapped. 'I've told you everything. There's been no demand for money. Nothing like that.' He was jumpy ... but then that was hardly surprising.

As Wesley and Rachel waited for the list of past employees, Sunita offered them a cup of tea. Wesley politely declined.

Wesley walked across the supermarket carpark, avoiding shoppers with fully laden trolleys, Rachel walking silently beside him. He looked at his watch. It was four o'clock now. Just time to return to the station via Belsham and call in at the dig to see how things were progressing without Neil. He told Rachel his plans but she made no comment.

When he'd parked on the road opposite Pest Field he turned to her. She was staring ahead, uncharacteristically silent. As he was about to open the car door she suddenly spoke. 'I've had a postcard from Dave.'

Wesley looked puzzled. 'Dave? Dave from Australia? Your ex?'

She nodded. 'He's done his tour of Europe and he's coming back in a couple of weeks.'

'For how long?'

'I don't know. But he's coming to stay on the farm. As soon as my parents found out they went out in search of a suitable fatted calf to kill.' Her mouth turned upwards in a bitter smile. 'I wasn't going to mention that he'd written but my little brother went and found the postcard. He could never keep his mouth shut.'

'What's the problem? Won't you be pleased to see him?'

'My mother will be.'

Wesley thought he understood.

'I'm fed up of being treated like a child. I just need a place of my own.'

'Is it your parents who are the problem or is it Dave?'

There was no reply.

'Running away's not the answer. Maybe when he comes back you should start introducing him to some other women. What about Trish Walton, if he's got a thing about police officers?'

Rachel gave a mirthless laugh. 'It's worth a try.'

Wesley thought it best to return to work matters. 'I want to ask Neil's colleagues if they know of any local metal detectorists who might be able to give us some names.'

As they walked across the road side by side Matt spotted Wesley and waved him over.

'Look, Wes, I'm sorry about what I said earlier about the police ... '

'Forget it.'

'Have you seen Neil?'

After receiving the latest bulletin, that Neil was in pain but recovering fast and even attempting jokes, Matt climbed out of the trench and led the way to a pile of plastic boxes. Rachel followed and said nothing.

'Come and see our latest finds. I think we've got ourselves a murder victim.'

Wesley looked at him, worried. 'How do you mean?'

'The more I see of these bones, the more I'm convinced they're medieval. Everything points to it – the fourteenth-century pottery and coins found in the trench, the wear on the teeth, you know the sort of thing. Now it appears to be a mass burial, which means either a battle ... '

'Or the plague?'

'Quite right. There's only one skeleton with any signs of injury so I reckon we've found ourselves a plague pit. Fourteenth-century ... right date. The great plague of 1348.'

'What a place to build a supermarket,' Wesley said,

thinking of Huntings' latest little problem. 'So what's this about a murder victim?'

'I was just coming to that. We found one skeleton with severe injuries to the back of the skull. There was a high-status medieval dagger with the bones and a number of Edward III coins – from the time of the plague – all bunched together as if they were in a purse that's rotted away. Now I don't expect the plague victims would have been buried with their worldly goods, but if someone was murdered and tipped into the plague pit before it was filled in ... A perfect way to dispose of a body.'

'Ever thought of joining the police, Matt?'

Matt answered with a dismissive chuckle, as though the very idea were preposterous. 'The bones were disturbed by the nighthawks. The dagger and coins would have given a signal on any metal detector.'

'So why weren't the coins and dagger taken?'

'That's what I've been asking myself.'

'Where's the dagger now?' This had got Wesley intrigued.

'In the village hall. We're using it as the site headquarters. Have a look when you've got time. Lovely dagger; corroded, of course, but in remarkable condition, considering. You can even see that there was some sort of decoration on the hilt ... possibly a coat of arms. We're having it X-rayed.'

Wesley glanced over his shoulder. Rachel was still standing there patiently. Much as he would have liked to have a look at Matt's finds, he felt it would be pushing it a bit.

'What I really wanted to ask is can you give me the names of any local metal detectorists?'

Matt frowned. 'None of the local ones'd go in for violence. I'm positive of that.'

'Even so, they might know of someone who would. Is there anyone I should talk to?'

Matt thought for a moment. 'Well, there's Big Eddie. He used to be a bit of a bad lad but he saw the error of his ways when he got nicked for liberating a horde of Roman coins. After he got a hefty fine he saw the light and decided to cooperate with the archaeological establishment rather than set himself up in competition, as it were. He's helped us out a couple of times on large digs. You could have a word with him. He probably knows what's going on in the weird and wonderful world of metal detecting.'

'Where do I find him?'

'I believe he can be found in the Cat and Fiddle most evenings . . . in Neston near the castle.' He grinned. 'Don't go in there looking too smart, will you. And don't let appearances put you off. Big Eddie may look like a human Rottweiler but I've been assured that his bark's worse than his bite.'

Wesley laughed. He felt it was expected. He looked at his watch and saw that it was nearly five. As he was feeling a little uneasy about Pam's state of health he wanted to get home at a reasonable time. Big Eddie could wait for another day.

He returned to the police station with Rachel and stayed shuffling papers on his desk for a token half an hour before heading home.

Pam had been tired when Wesley got in from work and he noticed with some concern how the dark circles beneath her eyes stood out against the pale skin. He had told her of Neil's attack gently, assuring her that his life wasn't in danger, and she had received the news with a heavy sigh, almost as if she felt too tired to take it in. But the next morning she looked a little better. As he rushed round getting ready for another day making life uncomfortable for Tradmouth's criminal fraternity, she sat propped up in bed, as big and helpless as a beached whale. He salved his conscience by taking her a cup of tea and assuring her that he'd try not to be late.

As he was on the point of saying goodbye she informed him that she planned to leave Michael with a neighbour and drive over to Morbay to visit Neil in hospital, which awakened a whole new set of worries in Wesley's mind. Should she be driving? What if she had an accident or went into premature labour? He set off for Tradmouth police station telling himself not to be so foolish. Pam had always taken care of herself. But the worm of worry still gnawed away.

An hour later he found himself driving out to Morbay Hospital with Gerry Heffernan in the passenger seat. He hoped he would see Pam there and that his mind would be put at rest. But it was half past nine in the morning and it was doubtful whether she would have left the house yet. He concentrated on driving up the busy dual carriageway that led to the hospital and tried to put her out of his mind.

At the hospital Dr Choudray greeted them with weary resignation. 'Are you back again?'

Wesley had a vague feeling of guilt about adding to his workload but Gerry Heffernan had no such misgivings and insisted that they go into the doctor's office to have a quiet chat.

'We've come about Edith Sommerby,' he announced. 'Any news on the cause of death yet?'

The doctor sighed. 'I think something arrived first thing this morning from Pathology. Hang on.' He began a search of his desk and soon found the piece of paper he was looking for. 'Here we are. Botulism. The relevant public health authorities have been notified and we're on the alert for any new cases. If there's a danger to public health they'll need to track down the source.'

Wesley nodded. 'Of course.' What the public health officials had in mind was inadequate hygiene or some accidentally contaminated batch of food. Wesley knew different.

They could see no reason to keep the doctor from his duties any longer so they left, dropping in on Neil on their way out. He had been moved to another ward and he still looked weak, not his usual self. He gave a brave smile when Wesley told him that Pam might call in to see him later and lay back on his pillows, as though exhausted.

Neil's recollection of the night he was attacked was still vague. He remembered hearing a noise and going to investigate. Then being pushed by strong hands into an open trench and ending up face to face with a grinning skull. He hadn't seen his assailant and still had no idea who it could be. When Wesley mentioned Big Eddie, Neil said he was sure it hadn't been him. He wasn't the type. Wesley refrained from saying that if he had five pounds for every convicted criminal who 'wasn't the type' he'd be a very rich man.

When they left the hospital it was only a short distance to the address Sister Atkins had given them for Edith Sommerby. Get to know the victim and you get to know the murderer was what Wesley had always been taught. He had his doubts in this case but it was always worth a try.

Fred Sommerby was at home. He answered the door in cardigan and carpet slippers, towering above both policemen as he stood holding the front door as though ready to slam it in their faces.

Heffernan showed his warrant card and announced himself. Wesley did likewise and let the boss do the talking.

'We'd like a quick word, Mr Sommerby. Nothing to worry about.' Heffernan stepped forward and Fred Sommerby had no choice but to move aside. 'Thanks. Sorry to hear about your wife, by the way,' Heffernan said, barging his way into a lounge full of clashing patterns – red swirly carpet, green floral wallpaper and a large sofa covered with a faded flowery cloth: the result was slightly nauseating and the low ceiling made it seem oppressive, like a cell either decorated by a jailer with appalling taste or carefully calculated to drive its inmate to the point of insanity. Sommerby bent and switched on the gas fire. Tea wasn't offered.

Heffernan sat down without being invited. 'They reckon your wife died of botulism poisoning.'

Wesley watched the old man's face but his expression gave nothing away.

'Do they?' He didn't sound particularly interested.

'The public health people'll want to know what she's been eating and where she got it from, you do realise that, don't you? If she's bought something contaminated, they'll want to know if anyone else has bought any ... prevent an outbreak, like.' Heffernan sat forward eagerly, waiting for some response. He didn't get one.

'Can you tell us what your wife ate before she was taken ill?' Wesley asked, earning himself a hostile look.

'She ate the same as me.'

'How can you know that? She might have eaten something when she was out of the house. Where did she go that day?'

'Nowhere. She doesn't ... didn't go anywhere without me.'

'Did she go shopping?'

'She wasn't out for long ... only went across the road. She didn't have time to eat anything. I'd have known.'

Wesley had an uneasy feeling this was true, that Edith Sommerby had lived like some sort of slave, controlled by this overbearing man. But maybe she had her small rebellions. He had to find out.

'According to the sister at the hospital there were a number of unexplained injuries on your wife's body. Can you cast any light on that ... sir?' He added the 'sir' as an afterthought, an attempt to hide his contempt for the man.

'Mind your own bloody business,' was the reply.

Gerry Heffernan stood up. 'We'd like to have a quick look at your kitchen.'

Sommerby looked as though he was about to object.

'Just a quick look. If it's not us it'll be the public health people and they'll be a lot more thorough ... wouldn't surprise me if they half demolished the place taking their little samples with their test tubes and what have you. If we find what we're looking for it'll save you all that and we promise we'll leave everything as we found it, won't we, Inspector Peterson?' He grinned wickedly. Wesley thought he might be pushing things a bit far but he knew better than to utter the magic words 'search warrant'.

Sommerby said nothing and, taking silence as consent, Heffernan marched straight to the kitchen, Wesley following. Sommerby stood at the door and glowered as they both pulled on plastic gloves and went through the motions of searching the cupboards and fridge.

The letters had mentioned jam. That meant they were looking for a fairly new jar, bought at Huntings recently. After searching the cupboards they turned their attentions to the fridge. There was milk, butter, eggs and a packet of cooked ham. When Sommerby was asked whether there was anything his wife had eaten that he hadn't, he had said there was nothing. They'd eaten the same things. And the way he said it suggested that Edith had had little choice in the matter.

Wesley looked around the kitchen in despair. Back to square one. Perhaps Edith had eaten something from some café or food stall ... a small act of defiance against her tyrannical husband. Perhaps it was all a coincidence and her death had nothing to do with Huntings after all.

Heffernan had just drawn a curtain aside to reveal a small alcove. Inside the alcove stood an ironing board, a Hoover, a mop and bucket and a small tartan shopping trolley, well used with worn tyres that would have been illegal if they'd been on a motor vehicle. The trolley had had a lot of use, presumably backwards and forwards to Huntings most days. Wesley, standing beside his boss, imagined that Edith Sommerby would make the most of these little journeys: they were probably the only times when she could escape her husband's watchful eyes. Perhaps she had used the time to venture farther afield. But she wouldn't have been able to go far, as he guessed that Fred would probably have timed her outings. As he looked down on the trolley he felt a wave of sympathy for Edith, who had been as much a prisoner in her way as anyone enjoying Her Majesty's hospitality in one of the nation's jails. And Edith had committed no crime.

Heffernan was about to draw the curtain across again when Wesley stepped forward and took hold of the trolley's handle.

'What are you doing?'

'Just seeing if there's anything inside.'

Heffernan shrugged. He assumed Edith would have used the trolley for transportation rather than storage, but he said nothing as Wesley knelt down and delved into its depths.

Wesley felt around for a few seconds and pulled something out. A jar of jam ... Huntings' own brand. It had already been opened but was still almost full. Wesley wondered why Edith hadn't put it away in the cupboard. As he turned he saw that Fred Sommerby was watching him, glowering with anger.

'Can you explain why this jam is in the trolley, Mr Sommerby?' Wesley asked reasonably.

'No. I don't like jam so she never bought it. She didn't go wasting money on things that wouldn't get eaten. It's not easy on a pension. We had to watch the pennies.'

'So your wife didn't like jam? She wouldn't have eaten it?'

The question was answered with silence. Wesley put it another way. 'Neither you nor your wife ever ate jam? Neither of you liked it? You can't explain what this jar is doing here?'

Silence again. Then Sommerby growled, 'I didn't like it. Don't know about her.'

'And she wouldn't have bought anything just for herself?' Wesley was beginning to see the way Sommerby's mind worked.

'We couldn't afford to go spending money on fripperies. We had to live on a pension,' he repeated, looking at Wesley with distaste.

'So if she did buy something that she fancied, that only she liked, she might have kept it hidden from you?'

There was no answer.

'Well? Is it possible that she was so afraid of you that

she wouldn't tell you she'd bought a jar of jam?' Wesley asked, aware that he was raising his voice.

Fred Sommerby shrugged, the ghost of a smirk on his face, as though he was pleased at the thought that, like the axe-happy tyrants of history, his whims had aroused such fear in another.

Wesley packed the jar into a plastic evidence bag. He needed something, some activity to keep his hands occupied and away from Fred Sommerby. From the moment he had met the man he had seen him for what he was, a self-centred bully. But now he knew that he had gone so far as to deny his wife anything that he didn't personally approve of, even something so trivial as a jar of jam, he felt anger overwhelming him like a tide. He had to get out of there before he said or did something that he would regret.

He delved into the depths of the trolley again, just to make sure that there was nothing he'd missed. There was a scrap of paper in the bottom, a till receipt. He pulled it out and handed it to Heffernan. It listed the jam and it was dated the day the first letter was received. The two men looked at each other before Heffernan said, 'We'll have to take this jar with us, Mr Sommerby. Okay?'

Sommerby scowled. 'Have I got any choice?'

'No.'

'Do what you bloody like, then.' Sommerby concluded by muttering something about a police state and wandering out into the hall.

Heffernan followed him out, Wesley trailing behind.

'Tell me, Mr Sommerby, what did you do before you retired?' Wesley asked.

Sommerby looked round at him, surprised. 'I was a warehouseman at Huntings. Why?'

'No reason,' was the casual reply.

Wesley was only too pleased to get out of the oppressive little bungalow. He found the cells beneath Tradmouth police station more inviting. 'What did you think of Sommerby?' he asked once they were safely on the street side of the rusty wrought-iron front gate.

The chief inspector made a noise of disgust. 'The bugger's got "bully" written all the way through him like a stick of Blackpool rock. He must have led his missus a dog's life.'

'He worked at Huntings.'

'Mmm. Are you thinking what I'm thinking?'

Wesley looked at him and grinned. 'I reckon I am.'

Matt was feeling harassed. He was unused to being in charge, preferring to be cast in the role of trusty lieutenant. The contractor who had been engaged to build Huntings' latest branch had just paid him a visit, making vague and threatening hints about time limits and legal penalties. Matt had seen Neil deal with such people and send them away blinded with science and feeling bad about raping the nation's archaeological heritage. But as he had been unsure of his ground, Matt had listened politely and said little. He was all right with the archaeology but commerce and politics were a mystery to him. He only hoped that Neil's absence wouldn't be a long one.

At least the drizzle had cleared up and the sun was making fleeting appearances, hiding behind the scurrying clouds like a coy fan dancer, tantalising yet unattainable. Neil had planned to open up a new trench nearer the trees, about fifty feet away from the main excavation, to find out how far the burials extended. Work on it had just begun and Matt watched as the small mechanical digger gently removed the top layer of earth. He held up his hand to stop it when he had judged it had gone deep enough.

As the digger manoeuvred away, Jane and three archaeology students who had been waiting patiently near by descended on the embryonic trench and began to work away at the earth, scraping with their trowels. Matt was quite content to be an onlooker until Jane ordered him to lend a hand. They had been going out together for several years and Matt obeyed her instantly out of habit.

94

After half an hour's intensive scraping they had very little to show for their efforts apart from what looked like a medallion of some sort on a thin chain, buried about two feet down. Jane gave it a cursory examination, and as she scraped the soil away she recognised the image of the man carrying a child on his shoulder ... St Christopher, patron saint of travellers. It might have been silver but it was certainly modern. Someone had lost it ... and that someone hadn't lived in the Middle Ages so it wasn't of much interest to her. She threw it into the plastic box by her side with a grunt of disapproval.

They carried on until one of the students announced that he had found what appeared to be a skull. He worked away for a couple of minutes, and when he announced that the skull still had hair attached and it didn't really look like all the others they had found, his fellow diggers crowded round to see. The student looked at Matt, who told him to carry on but work slowly and carefully. It would be good practice.

But when the teeth began to emerge from the dark earth, complete with what appeared to be several dark metallic fillings, Matt thought he'd better finish the job himself.

Chapter Five

*According to Barnaby Poulson, some people used to
think the plague was caused by 'the pungent fumes of
man's lust'. I mentioned this to William Verlan when
I saw him in the village and it raised a smile. Rat fleas
are far less colourful and we all need a little colour in
our lives from time to time.*

*My conversation with Verlan brought to mind
Barnaby's thesis. I read another section last night and
found myself unable to sleep. When Verlan asked me
to help Barnaby in his research, he can't have known
how disturbing the subject matter is to me ... how it
conjures demons from my own past.*

*I don't expect the one who brought the plague to
Belsham all those years ago thought about what he was
doing any more than I ever did. Do we ever consider the
consequences of our actions when we are young?*

*From a diary found among the Reverend John
Shipborne's personal effects*

Detective Constable Steve Carstairs parked his black shiny
Ford Probe outside the small terraced house and sat for a
few moments looking at it. Standing in a road that had run
parallel to Neston's main shopping street since the late
nineteenth century, this two up, two down with its rotting

window frames and flaking door was about as close to the inner city as it was possible to get in the quaint – and self-consciously New Age – town of Neston.

Its neighbours, in contrast, bore the telltale signs of creeping gentrification with bamboo blinds hanging neatly behind sparkling windows and colourful pansies sprouting in tubs beside their glossy front doors. Number forty-three, however, the home of Edward Baring, sacked warehouse-man previously employed by Huntings supermarkets, stood defiantly among these desirable bijou residences like a stubborn weed in a well-tended flower bed.

Steve and DC Paul Johnson, a tall, lanky young man whose face still bore the signs of adolescent acne, got out of the car. Steve made sure it was locked while Paul went ahead of him and pressed a plastic bell-push that had been mended with a sticking plaster. The two men heard the bell ring within and the excited barking of what sounded ominously like a large and vicious dog. After a few moments the door flew open with such violence that Steve and Paul took a step back.

'Yeah?' The man who stood on the threshold glowering down at them was big in every sense of the word. He was at least six feet five inches tall, and although his wild mop of long hair was turning grey, his equally wild beard remained a rich shade of chestnut. His checked shirt and worn denim jeans gave him the appearance of some monstrous lumberjack. The only thing missing, much to Steve's relief, was an axe.

The dog continued to bark somewhere in the back of the house until the big man shouted over his shoulder at it to shut up. There was instant silence. The beast was clearly well trained.

'Mr Edward Baring?'

The man grunted in the affirmative and looked mildly alarmed when Steve and Paul introduced themselves and flashed their warrant cards.

The big man stood aside to let them into the narrow

hallway. It was quite a squeeze, and Paul Johnson could smell Baring's sweat. When they were shown into a shabby front parlour Paul looked around, thinking that the furniture, carpet and curtains had probably been purchased some time back in the early 1980s and hadn't been cleaned since. The two officers sat down gingerly on the edge of the brown Dralon settee. In one corner of the room stood a huge wide-screen television, as shiny and vulgar in its dull brown surroundings as a showgirl in a nunnery. Next to it stood a strange upright instrument like a skeletal vacuum cleaner: Paul recognised it as a metal detector ... a good one, state of the art.

Steve was sitting silently, his eyes fixed on Baring, who stood in front of them, shifting from foot to foot. Paul guessed that his colleague had decided to play the mean, moody cop today so it would be up to him to ask the questions. Steve, he thought fleetingly, watched far too many cop shows on the TV.

'I believe you used to work for Huntings, Mr Baring. Is that right?' He kept his voice neutral with just a hint of sympathy. Steve would have gone for the aggressive approach.

Baring lit a cigarette. His hand was shaking slightly. 'Yeah. Why?'

'And why did you leave Huntings?' Paul asked, aware that he was sounding like a clerk at the jobcentre.

Baring took a long drag on his cigarette then looked down at his large feet. His body language told Paul that he was experiencing some embarrassment. 'I was stupid ... I ran out of fags and I took a couple of packets from the warehouse. I was going to pay for them but ... '

'But what?'

'The warehouse manager caught me taking them, didn't he? Wouldn't listen to my side of the story. He reported me and I got the sack. I was just told to get out and they'd send my P45 on. Said I was lucky they hadn't brought in your lot.'

'So what did you do?'

Baring assumed an expression of injured innocence. 'What could I do? I'd taken them and nobody believed me that I was going to pay for them. I even saw Sturgeon, the store manager, but he wouldn't listen ... just said that he trusted the judgement of Tanner ... the warehouse manager.'

Paul leaned forward. 'So you think Huntings treated you unfairly?'

Baring stared at him as though he suspected it was a trick question. 'Suppose so,' he mumbled in reply.

Paul and Steve looked at each other. Paul opened his mouth but Steve spoke first. 'Have you sent Huntings any letters?'

Baring let a caterpillar of ash fall to the floor. 'Letters? How do you mean?'

'It's a simple question,' snapped Steve. 'Have you sent Huntings any letters?'

The big man looked uncomfortable. 'Why?'

'Just answer the question.'

Baring bit his lip. 'No. Why should I?'

'So you don't know anything about the threatening letters that have been sent to the manager recently?'

Baring's mouth fell open. 'No. It's got nothing to do with me. I never wrote no threatening letters. What do you mean by threatening? What was in 'em?'

There was no mistaking the fact that he looked anxious. But then, thought Paul, it was natural to be worried when someone was accusing you of something you hadn't done and you had no means of proving your innocence.

But Steve, less imaginative, took his panic as a sign of guilt. 'Mind if we have a look around?' There was a thinly veiled threat behind the question.

'You got a search warrant?' The words came out as a squeak.

'We can get one,' Steve growled as the loud barking started up again. A deep, gruff sound ... an Alsatian at the very least. Steve had been about to say that if Baring had nothing to hide he wouldn't mind them taking a quick look around, but he thought better of it. 'When was the last time you went to Huntings supermarket in Morbay?'

Baring glowered down at him and Steve did his best to glower back. 'Not been back there since I got me marching orders. I've not set foot in the place since then ... that's God's honest truth.' The barking seemed to have increased in volume.

Steve stood up but it was Paul who spoke first. 'Thank you for your time, Mr Baring. We might want to speak to you again.' He made for the door and Steve followed, annoyed that Paul was letting the man get away with it. But as he was halfway out of the front door, Paul turned to Baring, who was hovering there, anxious to see them gone.

'Have you ever worked in a hospital or a laboratory, anything of that kind?'

Baring looked at him suspiciously. 'I was a hospital porter once ... not for long. Why?'

'Know anything about botulism?'

'What?' The man's face was expressionless.

'Botulism. A particularly nasty type of food poisoning.'

'No. Why should I?' Baring said quickly before shutting the front door on the two men and hurrying into the back kitchen.

As the neatly clipped poodle greeted him, leaping up with a barrage of loud barking and a busy wet tongue, he bent down to make a fuss of the animal, burying his face in its coat. You could trust animals. They understood you ... not like people.

Matt's worried call came straight through to Wesley in the CID office. When Wesley heard his voice he expected some routine report of more medieval bodies, or perhaps some snippet of information about Neil's mishap.

He was totally unprepared for Matt's news and his heart began to beat a little faster when he was told that another

100

skeleton had been discovered on the site all right ... but this one was different: this one wasn't buried with the others and had what looked like modern dental work. It appeared, Matt said breathlessly, to be relatively recent. Matt had sealed off the trench where it was found and informed the coroner. As he recited the story to Wesley his voice shook slightly, unsteady with shock. Neil, Wesley thought, would have taken it in his stride, even enjoyed the drama of the situation. Matt was probably a more sensitive soul.

Wesley made soothing noises and said he'd be over as soon as possible. Then he called Colin Bowman, only to be told that he was in the middle of a post-mortem but that he would meet them at Belsham as soon as he could.

If Matt was right about the date of these latest bones – and Matt was an experienced archaeologist who had seen plenty of bones in his time – then it was possible that they would soon have a murder inquiry on their hands. Wesley sat back in his chair and sighed, earning himself an enquiring look from Rachel Tracey, who had just glanced up from her computer screen. She gave him a shy smile and got back to work. She had been quiet for the last couple of days ... since she had learned of Dave's impending return. But Wesley thought it was best to say nothing. He was no agony aunt.

He knew the thing to do now would be to break the news to Gerry Heffernan. He could see the chief inspector through the large glass windows of his office. Gerry had often complained that he felt like a zoo exhibit in there, his every movement so visible to his underlings. He had once threatened to put up net curtains but the threat had never been carried out, probably through sheer sloth rather than a change of heart.

As Wesley walked up to the office door he could see Heffernan inside, pretending to read a file. When he looked up and saw Wesley, his eyes lit up. Company. It was lonely in the splendid isolation of his glass cage.

Wesley shut the door behind him and sat down.

'I've just been making some phone calls,' Heffernan said unenthusiastically. 'Tomorrow we're being sent directly to jail – do not pass go, do not collect two hundred pounds.'

Wesley looked at him questioningly.

'Jail. We're paying Chris Hobson a visit. See what he's got to say for himself. I've rung Stan Jenkins but he wasn't in. He's been sent out to do the shopping, poor sod. I'll ring again later ... ask if he can come out to play.' He grinned mischievously. 'They said in church on Sunday that you should always try to help your fellow man.'

'Actually, Gerry, I've just had a call from ... '

But Heffernan wasn't listening. 'I've been reading through the Hobson files and it still looks like an open-and-shut case to me. If we can prove this Janet Powell's lying ... Perhaps there's something we don't know about her. Stan might be able to throw some light ... '

'Gerry. A body's been found. Looks suspicious.'

The chief inspector looked up, alarmed. 'Where?'

'Neil's dig.'

Heffernan's shoulders sagged with relief. 'Another one?'

Wesley took a deep breath. 'This one's got fillings.'

'Fillings?'

'Modern dental work. The coroner's been informed and Colin Bowman's going over there as soon as he can get away ... he's in the middle of a post-mortem.'

Gerry Heffernan picked up a pen from his chaotic desk and began to twirl it around in his fingers.

'We should get over there. See what they've found. If we set off now we'll probably meet up with Colin. I've told Matt to seal off the site.'

'It is a skeleton, I take it?' Heffernan asked. He sounded weary.

'Yes, but ... '

'Then it's not going to get up and go anywhere. It's not top priority ... not like the Hobson case. Or the Huntings threats.'

'If it's murder ... '

'Look, Wes, we've got some madman poisoning people because he doesn't like the supermarket they shop in and we've got a potentially embarrassing miscarriage of justice case that could make the officers of Tradmouth CID stars of the silver screen for all the wrong reasons. The Chief Super's taken to transcendental meditation ... when I walked into his office just before I found him in the lotus position. And don't stand there looking so ruddy calm. Why aren't you panicking like any normal person?'

'I'll go over to Belsham on my own, then, shall I?'

Heffernan ignored Wesley's question. 'Have the lab results on that jar of jam from Edith Sommerby's trolley come back yet?'

'I was told it might take a few days. I think it has to be incubated and ... '

'I don't want to know the details. I just want to know whether that jam was planted by the nutcase who wrote those letters.'

'I'll keep chasing them up and let you know as soon as I hear,' Wesley replied, doing his best to keep his voice at a soothing pitch.

'And don't forget our little outing tomorrow.'

Wesley didn't answer. He had seen the boss in this mood before and he knew to leave well alone until he had calmed down. He was tempted to say that perhaps following the Chief Super's example and indulging in a spot of meditation wouldn't be a bad idea ... but he thought better of it and let himself out of the office quietly.

He looked around. Paul Johnson and Steve Carstairs were out talking to Huntings' former employees and Trish Walton was finding out all she could about Fred Sommerby. He knew that Rachel Tracey was examining the details of the Hobson case and was due to have another word with Janet Powell later on. Wesley walked across to her desk and she looked up, smiling.

103

'What can I do for you?' she asked with a scintilla of suggestion in the innocent enquiry.

'We're going over to Belsham. Matt says that a body's been found.'

Rachel opened her mouth to speak.

'And before you say anything, this one's got modern dental work.'

Rachel viewed the heaped files on her desk with a sinking heart. Then she stood up and took her jacket from the back of her chair. 'We'd better get it over with, then,' she said with forced cheerfulness. Someone had to be positive about the situation.

When they reached Belsham, Matt was waiting for them by the roadside, looking out for their car and pacing up and down nervously like an expectant father. Colin Bowman hadn't arrived yet, he told them as he led them across the field. Rachel trod carefully; the rain had stopped but the field was still muddy. Wesley forged ahead with Matt to where the archaeological team had erected a makeshift shelter out of a few spades and a large sheet of tarpaulin. A number of young diggers, probably students, stood near the main trench, staring silently like curious cattle. Old bones were one thing but murder and police involvement were another.

Jane was waiting for them; tall, blonde, dishevelled and anxious. Matt touched her hand reassuringly before he rolled the tarpaulin back to reveal a partially excavated skeleton. He stood aside to let Wesley have a better view.

'I thought I'd wait until you arrived before I went any further. We opened a new trench to find out how far the burial pit extended. We found this single skeleton . . . obviously nothing to do with the others.'

Wesley crouched down. He picked up a trowel and brush lying beside the trench and began to tease away the soil caked around the jawbone. He worked carefully until the teeth were fully revealed. Whoever this had been in life, they had probably had a liking for sweet food and an aversion to toothpaste. Wesley counted nine fillings in all. A hank of long brownish hair clung to the skull, somehow giving it a more human look.

'Well, you'd better carry on and uncover the rest,' he said to Matt as he stood up and brushed himself down. The damp soil had soaked through the knees of his trousers – another dry-cleaning bill. 'I'd be grateful if just you and Jane could work on it and not . . . ' He glanced over at the students. An experienced archaeologist knows how to deal with delicate evidence and he had known Matt long enough to trust his abilities.

Rachel watched, expressionless, as they got down to work. Wesley stood beside her in silence, watching as the rest of the skeleton emerged, pale against the darkness of the soil. Scraps of cloth clung to some of the bones and what looked like the rotted remains of a leather belt lay loosely around the pelvis.

Wesley stared down at the emerging remains. Ideas and theories began to flit through his mind but his thoughts were interrupted by an inappropriately cheerful voice. Dr Colin Bowman had arrived, and not for the first time Wesley wondered how a man who spent his working life cutting up corpses could be the life and soul of any party going.

'I believe you've found something interesting for me,' the pathologist began, striding towards the trench like a terrier who'd just spotted a rabbit. 'How's Neil, by the way? Anybody know?'

Wesley conveyed the latest bulletin. Last he had heard Neil was comfortable and starting to complain about the quality of the hospital food. On the mend. But they were still no nearer finding out exactly what had happened to him, he said with a frown. Rachel watched his face and guessed that this failure was bothering him.

The doctor, having conducted a brief examination of the bones, straightened himself up. 'Well, she's not medieval, that's for sure. She appears to have undergone a certain amount of modern dental work but I'll know more when I've got her back to the mortuary.' He looked up and smiled. 'If I were you I'd get your forensic people out here right away, Wesley. I think you've got a murder victim on your hands.'

Wesley had had the same thought himself but he had been putting off making the call. Once the process was begun it would blossom into a full murder inquiry. And they had enough on their plates already.

But he took the mobile from his inside pocket and slowly punched in the number.

Steve Carstairs looked up at the house. It was hardly what he had expected. He glanced at Paul Johnson, who was standing beside him, before consulting his notebook again.

'Well, this is the address she gave. Number eight.' Paul sounded uncertain as he looked at the large number scrawled drunkenly in white gloss paint on the rotting front door.

'It's a dump,' was Steve's verdict. 'She worked for Huntings last year, didn't she? They'll have given us her old address. She's probably moved on.' His last words were drowned out by a seagull shrieking raucously overhead.

The house had certainly seen better days. It had been built when Morbay was a newly fashionable seaside resort for the Victorian middle classes, and now it was about to be swept aside to make way for some brave new redevelopment scheme ... a shopping complex, Paul had heard. The windows of the neighbouring houses were boarded up but there was still filthy glass in the rotting frames of number eight.

'We'd better knock.' Paul marched up the crumbling stone steps, rapped on the door and waited.

When there was no answer he knocked again, and after a few seconds there was a thunderous noise from above. The two policemen stepped back in time to see a small sash window at the top of the house opening stiffly. A young woman with bleached blonde hair rising Medusa-like in tiny plaits poked her head out and asked what they wanted.

'Police. We're looking for Patience Reid,' Paul shouted up. Steve stood by his side, staring at the apparition above.

'What's it about?'

'Routine. Are you Ms Reid?'

There was no answer. The head disappeared from the window and they waited.

As Paul was about to knock again, the door swung open. They had expected to see the young woman with the Medusa plaits standing there but instead they were facing a young Asian woman wearing a businesslike black suit. She was about to shut the front door behind her when Steve put out a hand to hold it open.

The young woman said a haughty 'Excuse me' and sidled past them before hurrying down the street, almost breaking into a run. Paul watched as she climbed into a newish Renault Clio and drove off, noting the car registration number in his notebook.

'She looked a bit posh for this place,' Steve commented as he stepped into a hallway that was every bit as uninviting as the house's exterior.

'Maybe she's a social worker ... or works for the landlord. I took her car number just in case.'

'Trying to arse-lick your way to sergeant, are you?'

Paul didn't reply. He knew Steve of old and his barbed comments had long ceased to bother him. He made for the stairs. A threadbare carpet of indeterminate pattern still clung to them here and there but it didn't do much to muffle their footsteps. Music seeped from one of the closed doors on the first floor ... heavy metal, hardly Steve's taste. When they reached the top of the stairs, the old servants' quarters in the attic, the blonde Medusa was waiting for them, leaning against an open door, arms folded. There was a number on the door. Presumably the place was divided into flats, although there had been no row of bells by the

107

front door. But then this place was at the rock bottom of the letting market.

'Patience Reid?' Paul spoke first, fearing Steve would say something tactless. 'Can we have a quick word? Won't take long.'

The girl appeared to think about this for a few moments, then she turned and walked into the flat without checking to see whether they were following.

She led them into a smallish room. There had been some effort to make the place cheerful: brightly coloured throws disguised a sagging sofa and lurid posters protesting against environmental pollution decorated the walls. An ornately embroidered Indian wedding arch was nailed to the wall above a double mattress in the corner, adding an exotic touch to the stained woodchip wallpaper. It was a bed-sit. They were called studio flats these days, but this one scarcely merited the euphemism.

The girl was standing by the window facing them. She took a packet of cigarettes from her pocket and lit one. 'Well?' she said, exhaling a plume of white smoke. 'And I prefer Pat to Patience, by the way ... for obvious reasons. My parents had a weird sense of humour.'

'We were given your name by Mr Sturgeon, manager of Huntings supermarket in Morbay.'

'And?'

'You used to work there, I believe.'

'You believe right.'

She gave a smirk that made Steve's hackles rise. He wanted to wipe the smile off her smug face. But Paul was there, so he had to mind his p's and q's. 'You got the sack,' he said. 'Why was that? Did they catch you with your hands in the till?'

She gave a snort, as though the idea were amusing. 'According to Sturgeon I had an "attitude problem".'

'What made him think that?' asked Paul.

'I threw a can of beans at a customer, didn't I?' She smirked again. 'Well, the stupid cow kept going on about all the prices being wrong on her till receipt. She kept on and on and she was holding up my queue so I just lost my temper.'

Patience by name but not by nature, Paul thought to himself. 'Was the customer hurt?' he asked, just out of curiosity.

'I missed,' she replied with what sounded like regret.

'Have you been back to Huntings since you left?' Paul tried to make the question sound innocent.

'No way. I'd never set foot in that place again. What's this all about anyway?'

'Huntings have received some threats and we're doing routine checks on any employees who've been dismissed recently.'

'Well, you've come to the wrong place. I've found myself a better job ... I work at the arts project on the Winterham estate. Why should I have it in for those brain-dead no-hopers at Huntings? I feel sorry for them.'

'But you wouldn't mind teaching Huntings a lesson, giving them a bit of a fright?' Paul watched her face.

'They're not worth the effort, believe me. I've moved on.' She hesitated. 'Did Sturgeon really think it could be me?' She sounded slightly worried.

'As I said, Ms Reid, it's just routine.'

'Who else are you questioning, then?'

'Is there anyone you can think of? Anyone we should have a word with?'

Again she hesitated, as though making a decision. But in the end she just shook her head.

Paul moved towards the door. He sensed that Patience – or Pat – Reid wasn't going to give them any more. It was time to go.

'How much do you pay for this place?' Steve asked her as he reached the door. Paul detected a sneer in his voice.

But she didn't appear to have taken offence. 'Nothing. It's a squat. They're supposed to be knocking these places down some time but we've been living here two years now.'

'We?'

'There's five flats. Why?'

Steve said nothing. He had a low opinion of squatters. He had a low opinion of a lot of people, come to that.

'Thank you, Ms Reid,' said Paul with scrupulous politeness as he made his exit.

Colin Bowman had made a preliminary examination of the bones as soon as they had been delivered to the mortuary and he was able to tell Wesley that they were almost certainly those of a young woman aged between twenty and twenty-five. As well as the fillings, the fact that when her left arm was eventually uncovered she was found to be wearing a wristwatch confirmed that she was no medieval peasant struck down by the plague.

Colin had been uncertain of the cause of death at first. But when he examined the neck area in detail he found that the hyoid bone was fractured, indicating that death may have been caused by strangulation. There were fractures to the pelvis and the leg bones that might have been caused after death, perhaps when the killer was disposing of the body, but he had seen similar injuries in road traffic accidents. When Colin had given this tentative verdict, Wesley had shuddered inwardly at the thought of the poor girl's departure from this life.

The forensic team were already at work, with Matt and Jane donning white overalls to help them lift the evidence from the ground. The dig had been held up, of course, but that couldn't be helped, and Huntings could hardly go ahead with their building work until the ground was cleared of all human remains, ancient and modern.

Rachel went straight back to the station but Wesley had elected to return to the hospital with Colin. After he'd been there an hour he looked at his watch and felt a pang of guilt: it was time he got back to the CID office to do his bit.

He knew there was one task that he couldn't put off for

much longer: he would have to break the news to Gerry Heffernan that it was definitely a case of murder, just when they were about to face the awkward questions the Hobson case was bound to throw up ... not forgetting the fact that some madman might be going around poisoning the stock of a large supermarket.

As he walked back through the quiet, damp streets of Tradmouth, he thought of Pam and the imminent baby ... and wondered, as he did on such occasions, why he had chosen a career in the police force. If he'd stuck with archaeology at least his interest in the bones would have been purely academic and nobody would have expected him to come up with a culprit. But as he walked on past the boat float and the memorial gardens, he realised that was exactly what he needed to do ... he needed to find out who had ended the life of the young woman buried in Pest Field and bring the culprit to justice.

The trouble was, Pam probably wouldn't see things as he did.

When he reached the office he found the chief inspector holding court. Steve and Paul had returned from their quest for disgruntled Huntings employees and as Wesley entered Paul was giving their report. No luck. Nothing suspicious about Edward Baring or Patience Reid ... at least nothing definite. Paul suggested that they examine the security videos from Huntings to see whether either of them appeared, as both had denied visiting the store. But that was the only thing they could suggest. When Heffernan gave them the go-ahead, they rushed off, apparently eager to begin a couple of hours of boring video viewing.

Janet Powell had made an official statement, reiterating her claim that Chris Hobson was with her at the time of the Reverend Shipborne's murder. And the governor of Hammersham Prison was expecting Detective Chief Inspector Heffernan and Detective Inspector Peterson to arrive around lunch-time the next day to interview Hobson. Wesley was dreading the visit ... he hated prisons; hated the smell; hated that atmosphere of repressed violence. He wished he could get out of it but it seemed that Gerry wanted him there.

He knew it was time to announce the bad news. He cleared his throat. He couldn't put it off any longer.

'I've just come back from the mortuary. A body's been found buried in a field in Belsham ... ' He noticed that some of his colleagues who knew about Neil's dig and the supposed plague pit were looking sceptical. 'A recent body with modern dental work ... a young woman. I want details of any women aged between twenty and twenty-five who've been reported missing in the area in the past, say, twenty or thirty years.' Heffernan mumbled something under his breath and slapped Wesley on the back. "I'll leave it in your capable hands then, Wes," he said before disappearing into his office.

As officers began to scurry off towards desks and filing cabinets, an idea began to form in Wesley's mind. What if the person who pushed Neil into the trench hadn't been interested in archaeological treasure? What if he – or she – had been trying to find the body he or she had buried years ago and remove incriminating evidence? If the killer knew about the dig perhaps he had decided to take action before the archaeologists found his victim, and if this was the case it meant that the killer was still around. It was a tentative, half-formed theory ... but it was worth bearing in mind.

As he returned to his desk Rachel followed him.

He sat down and she perched herself on the edge of the desk. He looked up and smiled, expecting her to say something. But she didn't.

Wesley looked at his watch. It was six o'clock already and, as he hadn't eaten since he had grabbed a cheese sandwich from the station canteen at midday, he began to feel pangs of hunger. He thought of Pam, pregnant and looking after a tired toddler, waiting for him to get back. Perhaps he'd ring her to say that he'd bring back a takeaway from the Golden Dragon. Appeasement was sometimes the only way.

He looked up at Rachel. 'Can you see if anyone's turned up anything on those missing women yet?'

She slid off the desk and strolled over to Trish Walton, who was earnestly tapping away on her computer keyboard. Wesley watched Rachel, mildly surprised that he needed to remind her there was work to be done. It was almost as if her mind wasn't on the job. Perhaps Dave's imminent return was responsible for this unusual state of affairs.

Trish Walton had left the statement she had taken from Janet Powell on his desk and he picked it up and scanned it but found nothing new. She hadn't changed her story, and he wondered whether that was a good sign or a bad. He picked up the telephone, and he was about to dial his home number when Trish bustled over to his desk. There was excitement in her large brown eyes, as though she was about to impart some momentous news.

'Eight young women have been reported missing in this area over the past thirty years,' she began breathlessly. 'One of them disappeared from Belsham about a week after the Reverend Shipborne was murdered. Her name was Helen Wilmer ... aged twenty-one. The report states that she went out one evening saying she was going to a friend's in Neston but she never made it and she was never seen again. Do you think ... ?'

Wesley smiled at her. Trish was a good officer, bright and keen. And now that she had made it quite clear to Steve Carstairs that she wasn't interested, the fear that she would fall into bad company had been removed. In fact there were rumours that she had been seen in the Fisherman's Arms with Paul Johnson on more than one occasion. There was nowhere like a police station for salacious gossip.

'It's a good place to start. Get me everything you've got on her disappearance, will you? The sequence of events, who her friends were, who was interviewed at the time – that sort of thing.'

As Trish marched off purposefully towards her desk Wesley made his phone call. Pam assured him that she was fine: her mother was there and they had just eaten, leaving his share in the microwave. She said she'd visited Neil in hospital that afternoon and was shocked to see him looking so bad. Wesley mumbled some cliché about not being able to keep Neil down for long – the first thing that came into his head – and told her he'd see her later, taking care not to give a specific time.

He stood up. Rachel was sitting at her desk, staring into space. She didn't look to be in the mood for paperwork. Wesley went over to her and bent to whisper in her ear. 'Fancy coming for a drink in Neston?'

She looked up at him, surprised, then pleased. 'Why not? Where did you have in mind?'

'The Cat and Fiddle near the castle. I've been told it doesn't do to look too smart.'

'Why there?' She was beginning to suspect this wasn't a social invitation after all.

'A bloke called Big Eddie is supposed to hang out there. He might know something about what happened to Neil.'

Rachel was careful to hide her disappointment. Maybe a tête-à-tête over a drink after work had been too much to hope for ... but she had hoped.

'Or perhaps you want to get home ... '

'I'm in no hurry, honestly. I'll get my coat.' She seemed too keen. Wesley heard faint warning bells. But it was too late now to do anything about them. He poked his head around Heffernan's office door and told him he was off. The answer was a preoccupied grunt. The boss was still wrestling with paperwork.

As Wesley walked out of the office just ahead of Rachel, he saw Steve Carstairs smirk and nudge one of the other young DCs.

Rachel said nothing as they drove out to Neston. She sat in the passenger seat staring ahead, a faint Mona Lisa smile on her lips. When they turned into the carpark nearest to the Cat and Fiddle, Wesley broke the silence.

'Any more thoughts about your little problem?'

114

'Not really. I'm still looking for a place of my own but I'm taking each day as it comes. At least we've got all these cases to keep us occupied. With any luck I'll be able to work till midnight most nights and not see Dave at all.' She hesitated. 'Do you find that? The job's useful when you don't want to go home.'

He had attended enough court cases to recognise a leading question when he heard one. And it was a question he preferred not to answer. He opened the car door. 'We'd better go and track down this Big Eddie.'

They walked into the Cat and Fiddle, a small drinking establishment with a dark, narrow frontage, squeezed between two terraced cottages on the steep road leading up to the castle. Wesley hadn't been in there before, and as soon as he stepped over the threshold he knew he wouldn't be going there again if he could possibly help it.

The clientele was almost exclusively male, with checked shirts, shaved heads and an interesting display of tattooed flesh. The place full silent as Wesley walked in, like a saloon in the old cowboy movies when a stranger rode into town. It wasn't only the colour of his skin which set Wesley apart, it was the fact that his clothes were what is usually described as 'smart casual'. The rest of the men in the bar were casual to the extreme, but by no stretch of the imagination could any of them have been described as 'smart'. Rachel too was out of place, the other two females in the place being a barmaid – in her thirties, bottle blonde and with the sort of plunging neckline that gives barmaids a bad reputation – and a thin woman who Wesley guessed was probably Neston's oldest lady of the night – fifty if she was a day with thick caked make-up, a dyed black mane of hair and a skirt that left nothing to the imagination. This apparition was perched on a high stool by the bar with a leather-clad biker's hand resting on her knee.

Wesley took a deep breath and walked to the bar. It was nearly seven o'clock and the place was already comfortably full. The crush would most likely come later, nearer closing time. It was smoky, his eyes were starting to sting and he longed to be out of there: it wasn't his sort of place at all. In fact he was surprised to find such an establishment in such a New Age place as Neston – a town more accustomed to vegetarian cafés, healing centres and cards in newsagents' windows advertising didgeridoo lessons. But then those inhabitants who preferred less peaceable pastimes had to congregate somewhere.

Fortunately the hum of conversation had resumed by the time Wesley leaned across the bar and ordered a half of bitter for himself and a lager for Rachel. When the barmaid was pouring the drinks, presenting a fine display of cleavage, he asked whether Big Eddie was in. She looked at him suspiciously but seemed to soften a little as he handed his money over and explained that he was a friend of an archaeologist Big Eddie helped out from time to time. Satisfied that his credentials explained why he didn't fit the Cat and Fiddle's usual customer profile, she pointed to a large man in a checked shirt, sitting on what looked like a church pew in the corner with a large, neatly clipped poodle sitting obediently at his feet.

Wesley was never too sure about dogs, but this one looked no problem. He walked confidently over to Big Eddie, Rachel following behind awkwardly, trying not to spill her lager.

'Big Eddie?'

The man looked up from his pint suspiciously. 'Who wants him?'

The poodle began to emit a low growl.

'My name's Wesley Peterson. I'm a friend of Neil Watson. You know Neil?'

'Aye. I've helped him out. What do you want? Shut up, Fang.'

The poodle gave his master a reproachful look and obeyed.

Up until now, Wesley had been reluctant to utter the word 'police', fearing that it might not go down too well in the Cat and Fiddle, but now was the time to come clean.

But as soon as he'd admitted that he and Rachel were representatives of the law, Big Eddie stared at him morosely. 'I've already had two of your lot round today asking questions.'

Wesley must have looked puzzled because Big Eddie began to expand on this statement. 'I used to work at Huntings and they came round asking me about threats ... I didn't know nothing about no threats ... don't know why they asked me.' He sounded indignant.

The light was dawning. 'You're Edward Baring.'

'Who else would I be?' he asked accusingly.

Wesley was unprepared for this, and as he assumed that no new information about the Huntings case would be forthcoming, he explained that he was interested only in the possible attack on Neil. Obviously Big Eddie hadn't heard about it ... either that or he was a good actor, which Wesley doubted. Wesley explained that whoever had attacked Neil had been using a metal detector but he didn't mention the body they'd just discovered. He wanted to keep things simple for now.

But Big Eddie hadn't heard anything ... and he claimed that no metal detectorist he knew would resort to physical violence. Wesley had to take his word for it and, with Big Eddie's assurances that if he heard anything he'd let them know at once ringing in their ears, he and Rachel made a hasty retreat from the Cat and Fiddle.

'Remind me to put that place in my bad pub guide,' Wesley said lightly as they reached the car.

'I reckon most of the blokes in there were known to Neston nick. I think I recognised a few myself. I was hoping you wouldn't go in flashing your warrant card.'

'Credit me with more sense.' Their eyes met. 'You want a lift back to the farm or ... '

'Drop me off back at the station. I've got some work to catch up on. I'll start going through the files on missing girls. Trish found one called Helen Wilmer who lived in

Belsham. I'll start with her and see what I can come up with. What about you?'

Wesley looked away. 'I'd better get home. I'm going up to Bristol to see Chris Hobson tomorrow . . . and Pam'll be expecting me back.'

Rachel didn't say a word for the rest of the journey.

At eight the next morning Wesley was in that limbo between sleeping and waking. He had heard the alarm clock but had put his head under the pillow, trying to ignore it.

'It's eight o'clock. Are you going into work today? Or have the criminals all decided to mend their ways and start helping old ladies across roads?' Pam sounded wide awake. But then she had been roused by Michael's demanding cries at six, so sleep was a distant memory for her.

Wesley turned over and groaned. He couldn't face humour at that time of the morning.

'They say they might discharge him later today.'

'Who?'

'Neil. As soon as they can get out of bed they send them home. I don't know how he's going to manage.'

Wesley swung himself out of bed. He couldn't think of the practicalities of Neil's plight at the moment: he had other things on his mind.

But Pam wasn't going to let the subject drop. 'He's sharing a place with Matt and Jane while the dig's on. But they'll be out working. They won't be in a position to look after him . . . I can't see him going back to his flat in Exeter. It's on the second floor and I don't think he'd be able to get himself up the stairs, never mind shopping and feeding himself. What do they think people who live alone are supposed to do?'

Wesley turned to her. 'Don't worry about Neil. He'll fall on his feet, he always does. You should be more concerned with yourself. When's your next appointment at the hospital?'

Pam ran a hand over her pregnant stomach, feeling as

ungainly as a hippopotamus with a weight problem. 'It was yesterday. I went after I'd visited Neil. I did tell you when you got in last night but I don't think you were taking it in,' she answered with a hint of reproach in her voice. 'Everything's fine. No problem.'

'Good. I've got to drive up to Hammersham ... near Bristol ... today so I might be late again.' He leaned over and kissed her on the cheek. As he glanced at the bedside clock, he realised he'd better get a move on. There was no sound from Michael's room, indicating that he'd probably gone back to sleep, so he told Pam to stay in bed and grab some rest while she still could.

He made himself a slice of toast and rushed out, making his way down the steep streets towards the centre of the town. It was drizzling and the air was damp and cold. This walk was an easy pleasure in the summer but an effort when the weather was less kind. Wesley kept it up throughout the year, however, because he knew the exercise was good for him.

Rachel was already at her desk surrounded by paperwork when he reached the office. It looked as if she'd been there some time. Wesley asked her what time she'd left work the previous night and she answered ten o'clock with a meaningful smile.

'Have we got a name for our skeleton yet?' he asked, sticking to work matters.

'I've looked through the files and this Helen Wilmer seems the most likely candidate. She was a third-year student at Morbay University and she lived at home. She told her parents she was going out to see a friend one evening but she never came back. And guess what ... '

'What?'

'Before she started at university she had been a Sunday school teacher at the Reverend Shipborne's church. And she went missing a week after he was murdered. Coincidence?'

Wesley raised his eyebrows. It was sometimes difficult

119

to believe in coincidences. 'Do we have an address for her parents?'

Rachel nodded and handed him a file. 'Help yourself. It's all in there. The boss wants to see you, by the way. He's gone to the Chief Super's office but . . . '

Before she could finish her sentence Wesley heard Gerry Heffernan's voice; he was in the corridor outside the CID office and getting nearer. He sounded as though something was annoying him.

He halted in the doorway and looked around. His eyes lighted on Wesley. 'Wes. Glad you could make it. You ready for our little jaunt?' With a jerk of the head, Heffernan summoned him into his office. Wesley followed.

'The Chief Super's had Aaron Hunting on the phone wondering what we're doing about the threats to his stores.'

'We're checking out former employees and we're still waiting for the results of the tests on that jam we found at the Sommerbys'; Steve and Paul found nothing on the security videos . . . certainly no sign of Edward Baring or Patience Reid; and Forensic have found nothing on the letters. According to Mr Sturgeon nobody working in the store has noticed anything unusual. The store was shut while they made a search but Aaron Hunting's reluctant to keep it closed just on the off-chance that something'll happen. So until our poisoner makes his . . . or her . . . next move, I don't see what else we can do.'

'Aaron Hunting's a neighbour of mine, you know, although I don't think I've ever seen him. He lives in one of the big waterfront houses beyond the tower at the end of Baynard's Quay. Huge place . . . own mooring, swimming pool, the lot. I've seen his yacht on the river . . . a vulgar gin palace called the *Hunting Moon*.' There was no envy in Heffernan's voice. The *Hunting Moon* wouldn't have been his style even if he could have afforded it. 'Tell you what, Wes, let's send Rachel and Paul round to reassure him that we're doing all we can. They can be trusted not to make dirty marks on his carpets or fart in public.' He looked at his watch. 'Isn't it about time we set off? Hobson's brief is coming in for the meeting. Apparently our Mrs Powell wrote to her former bit of rough in prison, saying she was going to tell us the whole story. He'll be well prepared.'

'Pity. I would have liked the element of surprise.'

'So would I, Wes. So would I.'

Neil Watson still bore the wounds of his particular battle bravely but he was definitely on the mend. He pushed himself up onto his pillows when he spotted Matt hovering at the entrance to the ward holding a large envelope and a bag of grapes and looking mildly confused, as though he had encountered some alien culture and wasn't quite sure of the etiquette. Neil attempted a hearty wave but paid for his effort with a stab of pain across the ribs.

Matt ambled over. He had come straight from the dig and hadn't made much attempt to clean himself up, but the staff seemed too busy to notice, the days of the fearsome ward sister with all-seeing eyes being long in the past.

As Matt sat down on the visitor's chair, they mumbled meaningless pleasantries before getting down to the subject nearest to their hearts – the dig.

'You've missed all the excitement. We opened up a new trench hoping to find out how far the burial pit extended and we found another skeleton ... just on its own.' He looked at Neil, preparing for the punch line. 'Only this one had fillings.'

Neil sat forward and winced with pain. 'What?'

'It had modern dental work and it was definitely a separate burial, not related to the others – we only dug in that spot because there was a small geophysics anomaly there ... the skeleton was bang on top of a fairly modern drain. Dr Bowman thinks she was strangled so they're treating it as suspicious.'

'So you've been seeing a lot of Wesley, then?'

'I reckon he was hoping the body was old but no such luck.'

'Has he identified it yet?'

Matt shrugged. Neil took that as a no.

'So how's the dig going?' Neil sounded worried. If modern bodies had started to turn up, maybe things were getting too much for Matt.

'We've had to stop for a while.'

'Has someone told the developers?'

'They're not pleased but there's nothing they can do about it. And they know they can't go ahead until all the plague skeletons have been removed ... if it is the plague.'

'That's something I can be getting on with while I'm out of action – I can do a bit of research into local history. If half the population of Belsham was wiped out there's bound to be some mention of it somewhere.'

Matt looked sceptical. Neil hardly looked up to trawling round the archives of Exeter just yet: even driving up there would probably be out of the question in his state.

'There's a bloke I met when we started the dig: Dr William Verlan ... he teaches history at Morbay University and he's just got back from a year's sabbatical in the States. He lives in Belsham and he seems well up on local history.'

'Think he'll be willing to do your leg work for you?' Matt smiled. After working with Neil for several years, he knew how his mind worked.

'It's term time so I expect he'll be otherwise engaged.' Neil looked at the large brown envelope Matt was clutching in his hand as though he was reluctant to let it go. 'What's in there?'

Matt handed it to Neil. 'Have a look. You remember I told you that a corroded medieval dagger was dug up when you were attacked? It looked as if it belonged to the skeleton with the head injuries ... '

'What about it?'

'We had it X-rayed and the image has come up really well. Have a look.'

Neil slid the X-ray from the envelope and held it up to the light. He could just make out the shape of the dagger

... and something on the hilt. It took his eyes a few seconds to adjust but as he stared he could just make out a shape on the thickest part of the hilt ... a barrel perhaps ... no, a half-moon. It was so clear now that he was annoyed with himself for not seeing it right away.

'Probably a coat of arms,' Matt said. 'If we can find out whose ... '

'When I get out of this place I'll get working on it,' Neil said with determination. He felt a lot stronger and his head had almost stopped throbbing. He was just longing for freedom.

'When are they letting you out?'

'Could be later today, they said. They don't tell you much.'

'And what'll you do when you get out? I mean, will you be able to look after yourself or ... ?' Matt asked the question tentatively, fearing that it would be assumed that he and Jane would be responsible for the invalid: neither of them was any good with illness.

'Don't know yet,' Neil answered with a vague smile. 'Play it by ear, eh.'

Somehow Matt suspected that he had something planned: he just hoped those plans didn't involve him.

Rachel Tracey was looking through sheets of paper. She seemed to spend a lot of time doing that recently, and she presumed that it was just the unacceptable face of modern policing.

Today's batch of papers contained details of Huntings' former employees, gleaned from the personnel files by Keith Sturgeon's efficient right-hand woman, Sunita. Rachel trawled through them with only half her mind on what she was reading.

She had begun to make a list of possibles, people who might be worth interviewing, people who hadn't really fitted in at Huntings. At the same time she had crossed out other names; students who had been there only a few weeks

123

in the holidays and had left for bigger and better things, and people who had led a blameless life at Huntings and left for better-paid jobs or for legitimate family reasons. She was aware that her mental profile of the Huntings poisoner might be too rigid, but they had only limited manpower so she had to start somewhere.

Her eyes were tired. She had hardly slept the night before. She had lain awake, tossing and turning in the single bed she had slept in since childhood, and she had avoided a conversation with her mother over breakfast by getting up late and grabbing a slice of toast on the way to her car. Sometimes she felt that she couldn't live at Little Barton Farm for much longer, being treated like a child ... but then again it was convenient and somehow comforting to go home to the farmhouse after a day tackling the district's low life. But she did worry about Dave's arrival, about the hints her parents would make about her settling down. In their eyes Dave, the good-looking, unassuming Australian brought up on a large sheep farm, was the ideal catch for a farmer's daughter. But Rachel wanted more ... longed for the forbidden. Sometimes she thought that if her mother could read her thoughts, she'd be shocked.

She scanned the paper in front of her, hardly seeing the words. She needed a coffee to wake her up, so she walked to the machine in the corridor outside and got herself a plastic cup full of a brown liquid that claimed to be coffee, although one could never be quite sure.

She took a sip, hardly noticing the taste, and as she sat down again a name at the bottom of the printed sheet on her desk caught her eye. Frederick John Sommerby.

She leaned forward, feeling suddenly awake. Frederick John Sommerby, warehouseman. Dismissed on 30 April 1993 for punching and injuring the warehouse manager. Immediate dismissal was followed by a ban from Huntings premises because of threats made to management.

It was a few words at the bottom of the page in very

small print, but it told Rachel everything she needed to know. She took another sip of coffee and sat back feeling pleased with herself. When Wesley got back she'd have something to tell him.

Chapter Six

I have heard the fourteenth century called 'the Devil's Century', and from everything I've ever heard or read about it I can see why. But then hasn't our own been even worse with two bloody world wars and atrocities across the globe? Perhaps our smugness, our self-satisfied arrogance and our blind confidence in the great god Science prevent us from seeing our own faults. I was guilty of all that once so I have no cause to feel superior.

When I read the results of Barnaby's research and learned of the tragic events that occurred in this very village all those centuries ago, I suddenly saw the truth. King Death reigns now just as he has always reigned. And I have been his servant.

I had taken little note of the tombs and graffiti in the bell-tower but yesterday I went to see them for myself. When I read the inscriptions I knelt on the floor there and wept, begging the Lord's forgiveness. Afterwards I told the churchwardens that the tower had to be kept locked for safety reasons. I cannot tell them the truth. I cannot say that facing those horrific reminders of my own sin fills me with terror.

From a diary found among the Reverend John Shipborne's personal effects

Christopher Elvis Hobson sat next to his solicitor, eyes downcast, fidgeting with a packet of cigarettes. Wesley studied him. Initially nature had dealt Hobson a generous hand: he had good bone structure and in his youth he would have been classically handsome in a Hollywood kind of way. But his hair – raven black when Janet Powell had known him – had turned a dull pepper-and-salt grey during his years spent as a guest of Her Majesty, and his lined and sallow skin displayed an unhealthy pallor. A spot of fresh air and sunshine would probably have done him the world of good. And perhaps after today those things wouldn't just be an unattainable dream.

'So she wrote to you and all?' Heffernan folded his arms and leaned back, awaiting an answer.

'Yes.' The monosyllabic reply was barely audible. Hobson took a cigarette out of the packet and lit it.

'You must have been surprised that she'd come forward after all this time.'

Hobson looked him in the eye. 'Yeah. I knew she'd gone off to the States. I'd given up hope of her ever coming forward. Have you seen her?'

'Yes.' It was Wesley who spoke. 'One thing that puzzles me is why you didn't mention this alibi at the time of your arrest. If she could have proved your innocence, why didn't you tell the police?'

'I did tell them later on ... when I was about to be charged. But that bloody Norbert ignored it ... never seemed interested in checking it out. I didn't mention it before because I didn't want to involve her – she was married ... had a lot to lose. And I knew she was living in the States but I'd no idea where or how to get hold of her. Besides, I never thought I'd go down for it. I never thought they'd have enough evidence. I knew I was innocent and ...'

'So as well as being chivalrous, you had a touching faith in British justice?'

He looked at Wesley as though the policeman had just said something in a foreign language. 'You what?'

'Nothing. Go on.'

Hobson didn't need much encouragement. He was just getting into his stride. 'I never thought I'd need Janet's alibi at first ... my brief swore they didn't have enough evidence to convict.' He leaned forward. 'I was fitted up by your lot, you know that.'

Heffernan straightened himself up. 'How do you mean, fitted up?' He had heard this story before ... in fact he'd rarely met a villain who hadn't been fitted up by somebody or other.

'That bloody Norbert, that's who I mean. I told him I never knew how that silver came to be in my flat. I'd never seen it before, I swear.'

'Is there anything else that's come back to you?'

Hobson glanced at his solicitor, who was sitting there expressionless. He looked as if he was bored with the proceedings, but Wesley sensed he was taking in every word.

'Yeah. I've had plenty of time to think about it, haven't I? There's one thing that's stuck in my mind. There was the lad in the pub. He was talking to a couple of other lads while I was in there, then later on, when I drove past in Janet's car, I saw him hanging round outside the vicarage.'

'How do you know it was the vicarage?'

'Saw it on the telly the next day ... on the news. I recognised it.'

'Can you describe this young man?'

'He was just a lad. Young ... about eighteen. Dark hair, round face. Denim jeans and jacket. That's about all really. He was standing under a street lamp outside the vicarage, looking around as if he was up to no good, so I got a good look at him. I told them all about this at the time.'

Wesley and Heffernan looked at each other. 'There's nothing in the files about any lad.'

'Well, I told that Norbert.' There was an edge of bitterness in Hobson's voice, but then, Wesley thought, if he was indeed innocent, this was hardly surprising.

'I'm surprised that this story wasn't followed up. I presume the police made some effort to trace this young man?' Wesley tilted his head to one side, awaiting a reply.

'Norbert didn't seem interested. He reckoned it was a fairy story. But it's true.'

The two policemen exchanged glances again. Norbert had probably made up his mind about Hobson's guilt and was reluctant to waste time checking out his story. The line between sloppy policing and corruption was sometimes a fine one. Wesley suddenly found himself wishing he knew more about ex-DCI Norbert.

'Now think hard, had you ever seen the young man in the pub before?'

Hobson looked at him, puzzled. 'I told the police all about it at the time. I did a job for one of them posh private schools. Now I could be wrong, but I'm sure I saw him there.'

'What was he doing there? Working or . . . '

Hobson shook his head. 'No. He was in school uniform . . . he was one of the kids. I'm good on faces and I swear it was him. I told Norbert but he didn't want to know.'

'Which school was this?' Wesley's mind was working overtime.

'It was opposite the church . . . in St Peters.' St Peters was a district of Morbay. 'Now what was it called?'

Wesley hadn't lived in the area long so he looked at Gerry Heffernan expectantly. But when Gerry looked blank and failed to come up with a name, he found himself thinking that Rachel would have known: she was a mine of local knowledge, her family having lived and farmed in the area for generations.

'We'll find it,' said Wesley confidently. If they made for St Peters and headed for the local church, they would be bound to find something as conspicuous as a school.

'So tell us what happened on the night the Reverend Shipborne died,' Heffernan said, watching Hobson's face. He used to pride himself on knowing when people were lying to him, but that certain confidence had vanished with the onset of middle age and these days he wasn't so sure.

Hobson took a deep breath, preparing to retell a story he must have gone over a thousand times. 'I'd arranged to meet Janet in Belsham at seven. Nobody knew us there. I arrived about quarter to and had a couple in the pub while I was waiting for her, then at seven I went outside to meet her ... she was just pulling up in her car when I left the pub.'

'Go on,' Wesley prompted. So far his account matched Janet Powell's perfectly.

'We talked in the car for ages, probably about half an hour or it could have been longer ... we had a lot to talk about. That's when she told me she was going to live in America and she couldn't see me any more. Then we went for a drive around some villages 'cause she didn't want to go in the pub ... she was scared someone would see us together and tell her husband.' He looked down at his fingers, yellow with nicotine. 'Then we went back to my place in Morbay.'

'How did you feel about her going to the States?' Wesley was aware that he was sounding like some sort of counsellor but he didn't know what else to say.

'Gutted.' He sighed. 'I suppose I was stupid to think she felt the same as I did. If she'd left her husband I would have gone straight ... '

'What time did she leave your flat?'

'Around midnight.'

'And you haven't seen each other since that night?' Heffernan asked, mentally adding the words 'to concoct this story between you'.

'No. I never heard from her again 'till I got the letter a week ago, honest. I didn't even have an address for her. I knew she'd gone to America but that's all I knew.'

'So there have been no phone calls, no contact whatsoever?'

Hobson shook his head.

130

'We can check.'

'Check, then. I'm telling the truth.'

The solicitor stirred in his seat. He had been so still Wesley had thought he had fallen asleep. 'I think we have grounds for an appeal, Chief Inspector. Don't you?'

'That's not for me to decide but I shouldn't be surprised.'

Chris Hobson was sitting there with a smug grin on his face, thinking of the compensation he'd get for his years of wrongful imprisonment.

But Wesley's mind was still on the Shipborne case. If Hobson hadn't killed the vicar, who had? 'Do you think you'd be able to recognise the young man in the pub again . . . from a photograph maybe?'

Hobson looked up at him and stubbed out his cigarette. 'I reckon I would. I never forget a face . . . and I've had the last twelve years to think about it, haven't I.'

As Wesley watched the prison officer usher Chris Hobson out of the room, he thought that maybe it had been worth the journey after all.

Rachel Tracey was angry, prickling with injured pride. Her status had been called into question and it rankled, irritated, annoying as a pursuing wasp. As she sat at her desk and tried to concentrate on her paperwork, she couldn't quite get the slight out of her mind.

And somehow the fact that Aaron Hunting had been scrupulously polite didn't make it any better. He had even apologised for taking up her and Paul Johnson's time when he had dismissed them. Some might have talked of organ grinders and monkeys, but he had merely stated that he wished to speak to a senior officer about his problem and left it at that. But the effect had been the same. It was the organ grinder he wanted to see rather than being fobbed off with his monkeys, and no amount of protestation that Chief Inspector Heffernan was otherwise engaged on an important case would convince Aaron Hunting to make do with anyone more lowly.

But she had managed to get a look at the house ... the entrance hall and main room anyway. She had stood – she hadn't been invited to sit – in the spacious living room and looked out on the river through the massive window that took up the entire end wall of the room. The light from the water reflected on the polished oak floor and white walls, forming ever-changing ripples of light, and she could hardly take her eyes off the scene outside; the boats skimming to and fro across the water and the hill-hung town of Queenswear on the opposite bank with its pastel houses and old stone church. It was quite a view. But then if you owned a chain of successful supermarkets you could afford such luxuries.

There had been no sign of a Mrs Hunting, but, Rachel thought, such a woman – if she existed – might be out lunching or doing good works or whatever it was wealthy men's wives did to pass the time. There was no sign of any children either – in fact the whole place seemed impersonally neat ... like a very expensive hotel suite.

Rachel was a naturally curious woman – probably a genetic condition inherited from her mother – and she found herself longing to find out more about Hunting's private life.

But she told herself firmly that she was becoming as bad as her mother and turned her attention to the heap of paper on her desk. The details from Huntings about former employees – and Fred Sommerby in particular – lay in pride of place in the centre, a trophy to be displayed when Wesley returned from his interview with Chris Hobson. She picked up the missing-persons file on Helen Wilmer. Wesley hadn't had a chance to examine it but there was nothing to stop her having a closer look ... and maybe ferreting out some valuable snippet of information that they could follow up together. Wesley always figured in her plans somehow.

She leaned on her elbows and opened the file. Helen Wilmer's photograph lay on the top. A pretty girl with

132

thick brown hair, freckles and a wide, generous mouth smiled up at her. Rachel looked at the intelligent, watchful eyes and thought that if she had met the girl she might not have trusted her. She had no reason for this assumption . . . it was a gut feeling. But if Wesley's theory was right, Helen Wilmer had been reduced to a heap of bones in the cold earth of a Devon field and that smile had been extinguished for ever.

She put the photograph to one side and began to read the sheets of paper in the file. Helen had been twenty-one, so her disappearance hadn't been treated with the urgency it would have been if she had been much younger. She had had a blazing row with her parents before she disappeared – a row about an unsuitable boyfriend – and this fact had led to her having been treated as a missing person rather than a potential murder victim.

The unsuitable boyfriend had been questioned at the time but had denied all knowledge of her whereabouts. The police had circulated her description but had had no response. She had said she was going to Neston to visit a girlfriend but had never arrived. She had never caught the ten-to-seven bus into Neston as planned. She had disappeared somewhere between her house on the outskirts of the village and the bus stop next to Pest Field on the main road into Neston. It had been a fine, clear night in November and it seemed as though the last person to have seen Helen alive was a Mrs Bettison, who knew her from St Alphage's church where she had once taught in the Sunday school. It seemed that Helen, Mrs Bettison and Helen's killer were the only people out and about in Belsham that night, and Rachel wondered whether this had anything to do with the Reverend Shipborne's brutal death. Perhaps the residents of Belsham had locked themselves in their homes, fearing that the killer would strike again. There was nothing like a murder in the neighbourhood for keeping people indoors.

According to Mrs Bettison's statement, Helen had been

heading for the bus stop and she'd smiled and said hello as though everything was normal. But according to the bus driver on duty that night, nobody answering Helen's description had boarded his bus. She had vanished into thin air ... or into Pest Field.

If the bones did turn out to belong to Helen Wilmer, then the people mentioned in the file would have to be interviewed again. She flicked through, noting names and addresses. But she knew from experience that the person who would come under the closest scrutiny was the boyfriend. His name was Dermot O'Donovan and his mother had cleaned for the Reverend Shipborne. In fact she had found his body.

Rachel's mind began to work overtime looking for some sort of connection.

Wesley felt tired when they arrived back at the station. They had become snarled up in the Bristol traffic and a fresh set of roadworks on the busy M5 had cost them a good hour. It looked as if the Shipborne case was well and truly reopened and the police were about to get egg all over their faces. Another miscarriage of justice. No wonder Gerry Heffernan seemed to be in a foul mood.

It was four o'clock ... too early to slope off home. But that was where Wesley longed to be.

As soon as they set foot in the CID office Heffernan received the news that the Chief Super wanted to see him and Wesley urgently. Rachel had stood up expectantly as if she had some important news to impart but they had no choice. They had been summoned to what Heffernan always referred to as the 'Ivory Tower' and they had to obey.

Chief Superintendent Nutter's name had been the cause of many jokes when he was a raw young officer. Perhaps that was why he had been so determined to ascend the promotion ladder, so at least the jokes would be made behind his back and he wouldn't have to hear them. Nutter was a serious-minded sort of man, good with jargon, paperwork and networking with senior ranks. Gerry Heffernan, whose talents lay in none of these directions, had always suspected that he would go far: most people did who were more at home in budget meetings than grilling villains in smoky interview rooms. But as far as Gerry was concerned, he was welcome to it.

Wesley and Gerry stood side by side at the Chief Super's door like two naughty boys summoned to the headmaster's study. Wesley knocked and a voice from within shouted, 'Come.' The use of the single word irritated Wesley momentarily: it sounded almost like the sort of order one gave to a sheepdog. But perhaps that was how Nutter considered them – sheepdogs to round up the villains and herd them into the courts while he watched from afar, leaning on his stick. The thought made Wesley smile.

But Nutter wasn't smiling as they entered the room. His long face and monastic-style bald patch gave him a serious look at the best of times. He told them to sit down and looked at them over half-moon glasses.

'I've had a complaint,' he began, leaning across his impressive desk.

'Sorry to hear that, sir. Seen the doctor?' quipped Heffernan. Sometimes, thought Wesley, he pushed his luck.

But Nutter ignored him and carried on. 'Aaron Hunting thinks you're not taking the threats to his supermarket seriously enough, especially in view of the fact that one person's died already.'

'Now we won't know for certain there's a conection until the tests come back.'

'Don't nit-pick, Gerry, I'm not in the mood. Aaron Hunting has every reason to complain. Someone makes serious threats against his business and you send round a couple of junior officers. He's an important man.'

'The officers I sent round were perfectly capable of dealing with it.'

'That's beside the point. He expected to see the officer in charge of the case. We have to be seen to be taking it seriously.'

'You mean because he's got a bob or two we let him have a DCI when every other poor sod who's attacked or robbed has to make do with whoever's available ... sir?' Heffernan looked at him innocently. Wesley sat tight in his grey upholstered office chair and said nothing.

Nutter began to shift awkwardly in his seat. Heffernan had hit a raw nerve.

'Well, it was you who wanted the Shipborne case sorting out,' Heffernan continued. 'We've just been up to interview Chris Hobson at Hammersham prison. Inspector Peterson and I might be men of many talents but being in two places at once isn't one of them, is it, Inspector?'

Again Wesley stayed silent. Presumably Heffernan knew Nutter well enough to gauge exactly how much he could get away with. But he was a relative newcomer to station politics in Tradmouth: he was taking no risks.

'Seriously, though, Gerry, I want you to go and reassure Mr Hunting that we're doing everything we can.'

'There's not much I can tell him. We've no strong leads as yet.'

'Just make the right noises – you know the sort of thing. Perhaps you could leave the talking to Inspector Peterson here. Tact was never your main strength, was it, Gerry?' The grin on Nutter's face told Wesley that the two men understood each other well.

'Is tomorrow okay?'

'It'll have to be. How did you get on with Chris Hobson?' The question was directed at Wesley.

He sat up straight, feeling like a child answering questions in class. 'His story matched Janet Powell's. And there was one lead he gave us that I don't think was followed up at the time.'

'From what you know already, do you think an appeal could go ahead?'

'I think there's every possibility, yes.'

Nutter nodded solemnly, like one who has just received bad news from his doctor. 'This could reflect very badly on Tradmouth CID,' he pronounced.

'It was a long time ago,' observed Heffernan. 'There aren't many at this station today who were involved at a senior level. Apart from you, that is.'

Nutter blushed. 'Well, yes, I did work on the case as a DI ... '

'So you'd know if Norbert took short cuts ... bent the rules ... ?'

'If he did I wasn't aware of it, Gerry ... but he played things close to his chest on that particular case I seem to remember.' He took a deep breath. 'I'm putting you in charge as you weren't involved at the time, but try not to let too many skeletons out of the closet, eh.'

'You mean I should sweep Norbert's mess under the carpet?' Heffernan sounded indignant.

'No, no, Gerry, you misunderstand,' Nutter said quickly. 'I just want you to bear in mind that if mistakes were made it was because DCI Norbert was under considerable pressure ... And of course Janet Powell's evidence wasn't available to him at the time.'

Heffernan glanced at Wesley, who had been listening to the exchange with considerable interest.

'And of course I'm glad to have Inspector Peterson involved. It might get us more credibility with the media – make us look more inclusive and in touch – if we were to have an officer from the ethnic minorities dealing with the press and giving out statements. I'm sure you'll be excellent in that role, Inspector. Raise your profile, eh.' He leaned forward and looked at Wesley hungrily, as if he were some prized trophy.

If Wesley had felt courageous he would have told Nutter to get lost, but instead he sat there expressionless, seething with resentment that it would even cross anyone's mind to use him in that way. He wanted to be working on the cases,

137

not fielding awkward questions to make some political point.

He was about to say something to that effect, considering the most tactful way of phrasing it, but Heffernan got in before him. 'I can't possibly let my inspector be sidetracked like that, sir. I need him working with me, not having his time taken up playing silly buggers with the press.'

Wesley looked at him gratefully. He couldn't have put it better himself.

'You'll have heard that another body's been found at Belsham ... a young woman buried in a field. Now I need Wesley on that one because of his special knowledge of forensic archaeology and ... ' He hesitated, racking his brains for more ammunition. 'And that sort of thing. My department's stretched at the moment, you know. There's the Shipborne case, the threats to Huntings and now this body at Belsham ... not to mention the rest. Crime's a growth industry, you know. We need all the manpower we can get. I can't let a valuable member of my team ... '

Nutter knew when he was beaten. 'Very well, Gerry. I take your point in this instance.' He looked at Wesley with some regret.

'Can we go now?' Heffernan stood up.

'Yes, of course.'

Wesley hurried out. Rachel had been about to tell him something before his summons to Nutter's office and he was anxious to find out what it was.

As Heffernan was about to follow him, Nutter spoke. 'If I can have a quick word, Gerry.'

Heffernan swung round. 'What?'

'I hope you're not trying to hamper Inspector Peterson's career.'

'Why would I do that?'

'You tell me. Some prejudices run deep but there's no room for them in the modern police service.'

Heffernan looked at him open mouthed. 'Are you saying I'm a racist?'

Nutter blushed again. Perhaps he could have made his point more tactfully. 'Well, you did seem quite averse to the idea of the inspector taking a more public role ... '

Heffernan drew himself up to his full height. 'I notice you never asked Wesley what he thought about being paraded in front of the media as the token black to show how modern and inclusive we were, did you? It never occurred to you that he might prefer to use his brains to do some honest police work instead. He's a bloody good detective, you know ... one of the best I've ever worked with.' He turned to go, but then stopped as another thought struck him. 'And isn't it racist to take someone away from the job they're good at and trot them out like some sort of performing seal just because of the colour of their skin?'

It was Nutter's turn to sit there speechless with his mouth open.

'If that's all ... sir.' Heffernan lumbered out, hoping that he'd won some kind of victory. Heffernan one, the Establishment nil. He'd had enough of politics for one day. Give him a good straightforward thief any time.

Rachel looked up as Wesley entered the CID office. She smoothed her hair unconsciously before speaking.

'Can I have a word, sir?' She glanced to her left and saw that Steve Carstairs had been distracted from the forms he was filling in and was watching her with an unpleasant smirk on his face.

Wesley walked over to her desk without looking in Steve's direction. 'What is it?'

She fumbled for her notebook. 'I've discovered two interesting things while you've been out. First of all Fred Sommerby was dismissed from his job in the warehouse at Huntings for punching the warehouse manager. It seems that it wasn't just his wife he used his fists on.'

Wesley raised his eyebrows. They were getting a clearer picture of Edith Sommerby's husband ... and it wasn't a pleasant one. 'What's the other thing?'

139

'I've found out something interesting about that girl who disappeared in Belsham ... Helen Wilmer. It seems that she had a boyfriend and her parents didn't approve ... ' She paused tantalisingly before she delivered the punch line. 'His name was Dermot O'Donovan and he's the son of the Reverend Shipborne's cleaner ... the one who last saw him alive and discovered his body.'

Wesley stayed silent for a few seconds as he turned the implications over in his mind ... if there were any implications. Coincidences did happen.

'If the body's identified as Helen's, I think it might be worth paying Mrs O'Donovan a call, don't you?'

Rachel looked up at him and smiled.

The call from the mortuary came just as Wesley was putting on his coat in the hope of sneaking out of the office and going home. Rachel was still at her desk and she looked as though she would be there for some time to come.

Colin Bowman, as always, sounded inappropriately cheerful on the other end of the phone. He said that if Wesley had a few moments to spare before heading home, perhaps he'd like to pop round for a cup of tea and a chat. Colin had the knack of making everything sound pleasant ... even an invitation to take tea among corpses. Wesley looked at his watch and said he'd be there in ten minutes.

It was almost six o'clock when he reached the mortuary. The place was quiet, most of the staff having headed off to spend an evening with the living rather than the dead. The silence made Wesley feel uneasy as he wandered down corridors floored with highly polished linoleum and breathed in the scent of the air freshener that was used to mask the stench of decay and formaldehyde. He was relieved when he reached Colin's office and found him sitting at his desk catching up with his paperwork, a picture of normality in a disconcerting place.

Colin turned in his swivel chair and smiled as though he were genuinely pleased to have Wesley's company. Not for

140

the first time Wesley found himself wondering why a naturally sociable soul like Colin Bowman had chosen to work with the unseeing dead rather than with patients who would be in a position to appreciate his affable nature.

'Earl Grey?' was the first question. Wesley nodded. As always, Colin liked to get the social rituals out of the way before he got down to business.

The sipping of tea and the exchange of polite enquiries about their respective families' well-being and the state of Neil's health took around ten minutes. When the bone-china cups were empty, Colin stood up. 'I thought you might like to have a look at our skeletons now they've been cleaned up.'

'Skeletons?' He was puzzled by the plural.

'The two from Belsham. The recent one, the young woman, and the early one ... the apparent murder victim from the plague pit ... if it is a plague pit: the archaeologists seem to think so.'

'And you don't?'

'I never said that. It's just that I haven't had much first-hand experience of medieval plague pits ... haven't had any experience, in fact. But there were no signs of violence to any of the skeletons – except this one – so I feel I'll have to take the experts' word for it. What do you think, Wesley?'

Wesley thought for a moment. 'I've never actually excavated a plague pit but I've read site reports and seen pictures of them and they do look remarkably similar to the one in Pest Field. The dead at that time would normally have been buried individually in the churchyard, so if a large number were buried hurriedly in a pit, that means that something overwhelming must have happened to cause the usual burial customs to be abandoned. Probably a battle or some catastrophic outbreak of disease.'

'Well, from examining the bones I think I can safely rule out the first option. Also the plague would explain the name Pest Field. Probably derives from pestilence ... plague.

141

That fits, I suppose. *Yersinia pestis* ... the bubonic plague, commonly known as the Black Death because of the characteristic dark blotches and bruises on the victim's flesh. It spread rapidly, you know ... carried by rat fleas.'

They had reached a pair of plastic swing-doors. Colin went ahead and pushed them open. They stepped into a white room, furnished with stainless steel. In the centre lay a trolley, a white sheet covering a hard, uneven shape, giving the appearance of a hilly model snowscape. Wesley looked at it uncertainly, wondering whose remains lay beneath: the unknown medieval man's ... or Helen Wilmer's.

Colin whipped the sheet off with a dramatic flourish and it fell to the floor in a crumpled heap. 'Our friend from the pit. I asked them to bring him here so that I could have a closer look. Nasty head wound. Even if all his companions had died of the plague that was almost certainly the cause of his death. He was found sprawled out untidily, whereas someone had made a bit of an effort to lay the other bodies out in a vaguely east–west orientation. He was also lying slightly above the others, as though they'd been buried and while the earth was still soft someone opened the grave again and tipped him in on top ... good way to dispose of your victim.'

Wesley stared down at the battered skull, the grinning teeth and the cavernous eye sockets.

'It's a young man, early to mid twenties. Five feet eight inches tall, slightly built. No obvious sign of disease. He had good teeth ... not much sign of wear which, according to the archaeologists, might indicate that he wasn't a member of the peasant classes who survived on gritty bread. That's one theory, anyway. Apparently a richly decorated dagger was found next to him, which would seem to fit with him being a member of the higher social classes.'

'So what do you think caused the head wound? A sword or ... '

'I'd say the proverbial blunt instrument ... something

142

large and heavy. He wouldn't have stood a chance. And I think he was attacked from behind.'

'And he's definitely medieval?'

'I'd say almost definitely ... and the archaeologists agree.'

'Not my problem, then.' Wesley felt relieved: he had enough on his plate. He turned his back on the grinning skull. 'What about the other skeleton?'

Colin covered up the bones and made his way through another swing-door into an adjoining room. This room was lined with steel drawers, like a giant filing cabinet. Colin pulled one of the drawers out to reveal another white sheet covering another set of bones. Only this one *was* Wesley's problem.

'I did my examination earlier this afternoon and you'll be getting my report in due course.'

'And?'

Colin drew the sheet back, gently this time. This skeleton was smaller, more delicate than the other. There was still hair attached to the skull and somehow Wesley found this disturbing, as though it made her more real.

'I think my first supposition was correct – she was strangled. Then something pretty violent happened to cause her post-mortem injuries ... perhaps she was thrown about ... or possibly run over by a car.' He thought for a moment. 'Yes. The injuries are more consistent with the car theory.'

'Would there have been a lot of blood?'

'Not if she was already dead when the injuries happened. But if they occurred before or at the time of death – if, say, he ran her over before strangling her – then he might have had blood on his clothes. In which case, you'd think someone would have noticed.'

Wesley had been staring at the bones but he looked up. 'You underestimate the loyalty of some people. Some wives and mothers wouldn't give their loved ones up to the police whatever they'd done.'

'Don't know that my wife would be that understanding,' Colin muttered.

'Nor mine.' This reminder of Pam made him look at his watch.

Colin sighed. 'Well, samples have been taken for forensic analysis and I've done a rough dental chart. All the remnants of clothing have been bagged up for the lab, including the belt she was wearing.'

'What about shoes?'

Colin frowned, as though annoyed with himself for not noticing the obvious. 'Do you know, Wesley, it doesn't seem she was wearing any.'

'Interesting. It indicates that she might have died somewhere else and her body was brought to Pest Field for burial.'

'It's possible. Any idea who she is yet?'

'Nothing definite, but a twenty-one-year-old Belsham girl disappeared in 1991. Name of Helen Wilmer.'

'Well, at least that gives you a starting point.' Colin hesitated. 'I've been wondering if your murderer knew the history of the field. It seems like a tremendous coincidence that he should choose that particular field to bury her in ... after all, Devon's hardly short of fields, is it?'

Wesley nodded. He had had the same thought himself.

Colin covered up the bones and walked over to a steel filing cabinet in the corner of the room. He opened the top drawer and took out three plastic bags containing objects that Wesley couldn't quite see. 'These were found on the body.'

He handed the bags to Wesley, who held them up for examination. One bag contained a small heart, a locket; silver, probably, although its time in the earth had turned it black as iron. Another contained a small watch with a rotting leather strap; the face was discoloured but Wesley could just make out the small Roman numerals on the dial.

Colin pointed to the third bag. 'This wasn't found on the body but just above it, buried in the same hole. It's a silver

St Christopher . . . looks like a man's to me, but I could be wrong.'

Wesley peered at it. 'It's possible the killer may have lost it when he was burying her . . . it's the best clue we've got so far. Thanks. Mind if I take these with me? They might come in handy for identification.'

'Sure, help yourself. I was going to have them sent over anyway.'

'How soon can I have your report?'

Colin smiled. 'Tomorrow okay?'

Wesley hurried from the mortuary. It was getting dark and Pam would be waiting for him, trying to entertain a tired toddler and wondering what time her husband would put in an appearance. But somehow he didn't feel like going home just yet.

Wesley called in at the station to drop off his three new items of evidence. Rachel was there alone in the CID office – avoiding going home . . . just as he was. She looked up as he entered the office, her eyes welcoming and hopeful. But Wesley just greeted her with a friendly hello and made no attempt to strike up a conversation.

He sat down at his desk without taking off his coat, as he knew he shouldn't be staying, and took the plastic bags from his pocket. When he looked at the necklace and the watch, he suddenly felt sad. These little things, these personal things that the dead girl had chosen or had been given as a present by those who loved her, brought home to him the enormity of what had happened to her. A young girl's life had been cut short. Death had triumphed over hope. And the St Christopher . . . had that belonged to Helen, or her killer? Or had someone lost it in the field, in which case it had nothing to do with the case at all?

He sat gazing at the things for a few moments before placing them carefully in his drawer. He couldn't put off the journey home any longer. He stood up and looked at Rachel, whose attention seemed to be focused on her computer screen, and when he said goodnight she looked up and gave a shy half-smile. Wesley hesitated for a second before walking out.

The evening air was cold as he headed for home up the steep, narrow streets that led away from the old part of the town by the waterfront, up towards the newer properties that had been built over green fields in recent decades. Wesley's was one of these houses; a modern detached in a cul-de-sac full of similar dwellings. He and Pam had hankered after something with more character – but these days character came at a price they couldn't afford.

As he climbed he could feel the strain on his thighs and his heart rate increasing: this was his daily exercise. But today every step was an effort and he found himself longing for a warm, comfortable car.

When he reached the house he put his key in the door but hesitated for a second before turning it, gathering his thoughts. Pam would be tired and it would be up to him to get his own meal, bathe Michael and put him to bed. Normally he didn't mind a spot of father–son bonding, but tonight he felt drained and exhausted and he imagined that Pam would be in no position to offer tea and sympathy.

But as he opened the front door he heard the sound of voices drifting across the hall from the living room. Pam had a visitor. A male visitor. Wesley took off his coat and hung it up before pushing the living-room door open.

'Wondered what time you'd be back.' Neil Watson was sitting stiffly in the armchair Wesley usually occupied. His face was still bruised and discoloured and his voice was weak, as though every breath were an effort. He looked as though he shouldn't have been allowed out of hospital.

'What are you doing here?' Wesley knew it wasn't the most original of questions but it was the only one he could think of on the spur of the moment.

'Your wife is an angel of mercy. They discharged me from hospital and she said I could stay here for a while.'

'The alternative was going back to his flat on his own. I

don't know how they expected him to cope.' Pam sounded indignant.

'So why did they discharge you?'

'They said I was well enough and they needed the bed, simple as that.' Neil looked at him pathetically. 'Hope it's okay . . . Pam said . . .'

'Yeah, yeah. 'Course it's okay.' Wesley felt he could hardly say otherwise. He wasn't the sort of man who could turn away an injured friend . . . his sister had always said he was too soft, which probably wasn't a good trait in a policeman.

'I've made up the spare bed.'

'I won't be any trouble,' said Neil weakly. Wesley didn't believe a word of it. Neil had always been trouble to someone.

Wesley looked at his wife, noting the dark rings beneath her eyes. 'Are you all right?'

'Yes. Of course I'm all right.'

'You married a wonderful woman,' Neil observed.

'I know,' Wesley replied automatically, feeling a pang of guilt as he wondered whether Rachel was still keeping her lonely vigil in the office.

June Seward pushed her trolley down the cereals aisle of Huntings supermarket at nine o'clock. The place was busy, but then it always was in the evenings when people with lives similar to June's own grabbed themselves a spare hour to do the weekly shop.

June was a mother of two pre-school children working full time as an administration assistant in Morbay Council's planning office, and each Friday evening her husband, Bob, baby-sat while she took the car to Huntings to forage for essential provisions. Bob himself couldn't be allowed to tackle the job, of course, as June knew that he'd be away from the house for three hours and would return home with a car boot full of chocolate biscuits, beer cans and crisps. If you wanted a job doing properly, sometimes you had no choice but to do it yourself.

June's shopping didn't take long because over the years

she had developed a system. When she reached an aisle she left her trolley in a central spot and scuttled to and fro between the shelves, consulting her neatly written and comprehensive list. Not many chocolate biscuits made it into her trolley. June favoured healthy eating.

When she reached the chiller cabinets she observed that there was nobody near the speciality cheeses so she parked the trolley there and made for the far end of the aisle. As she hurried back to the trolley with an armful of organic fruit yogurts she noticed something out of place among her neatly organised pile of shopping.

What looked like a folded sheet of white paper had been placed in her trolley on top of a packet of wholemeal bread rolls. June leaned over and picked it up, thinking that someone had dropped their shopping list into her trolley by mistake.

She turned it over and saw that it was an envelope addressed to the manager and marked urgent. The address had been printed neatly by hand but there was nothing out of the ordinary about the envelope's appearance. June placed it in the metal child seat next to her eggs and, when her shopping was done, she handed it to the woman on her checkout, explaining that she had found it in her trolley.

The woman on the checkout rang the bell under her till three times before she began to deal with June's shopping. June was just beginning to pack her bread carefully into a carrier bag when a middle-aged man wearing a smart suit appeared as if from nowhere. The checkout woman handed him the letter and he tore it open in panic as June watched, surprised by his melodramatic reaction. She saw the colour drain from his face before he barked the order that the fire alarm should be sounded and the store evacuated immediately.

June went home that evening without her shopping.

Chapter Seven

*There, I've said it ... got it off my chest ... confessed
- I don't really know what to call it. A public
announcement, I suppose ... and you don't get more
public than a pulpit, even in these days of dwindling
church attendances.*

*Somehow I feel better now my involvement in the
trial is out in the open and people know what I really
am. If there is to be forgiveness, there must first be
honesty ... a frank acknowledgement of one's wrongdoings.*

*I think that, on the whole, my congregation took it
very well, except for a couple of people who walked out
of the church afterwards ignoring my outstretched hand
and looking at me as though I'd disappointed them ...
as though they'd thought me one thing and I'd turned
out to be something else, something far inferior.*

*And yet perhaps they were just being honest.
Perhaps the rest of them were thinking what they were
thinking but hiding behind the mask of British good
manners. People do not expect their vicar to be a
sinner. They expect him to preach about God, not to
attempt to emulate Him.*

*From a diary found among the Reverend John
Shipborne's personal effects*

'They evacuated the store last night and it's being kept closed this morning while they do another thorough search. Sturgeon said he doesn't want to take any more chances.'

Wesley nodded solemnly.

'The shelves are being searched now.'

'So what did the note say exactly?'

Heffernan picked up the notebook on his desk and read. '"You've already seen what I can do. Make enquiries about the death of a Mrs Edith Sommerby in Morbay Hospital if you have any doubts. Today six extra items of stock were placed on your shelves. That means there could be six people dead, or even more. The items haven't been sold yet but it's only a matter of time, and the only sure way to prevent any more deaths is to close the store at once. And keep it closed. Or will you put profit above people as your sort usually do? I'll be in touch."' He looked at Wesley. 'It was the same as the other note ... letters cut out of the local newspaper.'

'How unoriginal.' Wesley flopped down in the chair by Heffernan's desk. 'I think this confirms that our friend is pursuing some kind of vendetta against Huntings.'

'Mmm. I still think past employees with a grudge are our best bet.'

Wesley thought for a moment. 'Or present employees. Whoever sent that letter knows exactly what's going on in that supermarket ... even down to whether a certain item's been sold or not. And there's quite an anti-capitalist sentiment there too ... putting profit above people.'

'I think all the staff should be interviewed, don't you?'

'I'll get onto it right away. I'd like to talk to Keith Sturgeon again. He might have some ideas. And don't forget we're supposed to be seeing Aaron Hunting this morning. I don't know what we're going to say to him ... I suppose it'll just be a matter of making reassuring noises. Let's face it, we haven't got very far.'

'Don't be such a pessimist, Wes. We smile nicely and

tell him we're doing everything we can. Leave it to me. He'll be putty in my hands, you'll see.'

Wesley looked at his boss, at his tousled hair and the slightly fraying shirt cuffs protruding from the arms of his well-worn jacket, and felt sceptical about his last statement.

It took the best part of an hour to organise a team of officers to visit Huntings and interview all the staff. Wesley told Paul Johnson to keep going through the files on employees, past and present. He was certain that the name of the poisoner would be found somewhere in Huntings' personnel records. It was just a matter of sifting through the information, of finding the proverbial needle in the haystack. Police work at its most boring.

But at least they could tell Aaron Hunting truthfully that something was being done, Wesley thought as he and Gerry Heffernan walked through the damp, narrow streets. It was difficult to see Hunting's house from the road. There was a rough stone wall low enough to allow the passer-by a breathtaking view of the river beyond, but it wasn't until they looked downwards that they spotted the roof of Hunting Moon House, an expanse of slate clinging to the river bank. There was an entryphone by the discreet gate and Heffernan, never at home with technology, allowed Wesley to press the relevant button to announce their arrival. There was a buzzing sound as the gate was unlocked electronically. Wesley pushed it and it opened.

'I only live down the road and I'd no idea all this was here.' Gerry Heffernan looked about him in wonder as they walked through a neatly manicured terraced garden. The path was gravel, as immaculate as in a miniature Zen garden, and there was a rockery on either side. Even in the autumn there was a subtle, well-planned display of colour, probably the work of a professional gardener: somehow he couldn't imagine Aaron Hunting getting his own hands dirty.

'Nice,' was Wesley's only comment. At last they had reached the front door, a grand affair in oak. Only a small section of the house itself was visible from here. The rest, like the garden, was on different levels, built into the bank of the River Trad with its own private boathouse beneath. Wesley, who kept a weather eye on the local housing market, guessed that Hunting Moon House was one of the most desirable properties in the area. Worth a million, at least ... possibly much more.

The great oak door opened to reveal a middle-aged man with steel-grey hair. He was just below average height, around five feet six, but his almost military bearing made him appear taller. After the policemen had introduced themselves, Aaron Hunting looked them up and down with intense blue eyes, as though assessing their suitability for the task. After a few seconds he addressed Wesley, ignoring his boss.

'Thank you for coming, Inspector. I'm sorry for turning your colleagues away yesterday, but I did want the matter dealt with by someone more senior.' He stood aside politely to let them into the large, airy entrance hall.

'I assure you, Mr Hunting, we're taking the threats to your supermarket very seriously indeed. I suppose you've been told about the latest letter?'

'Of course. But I want to know what the police are doing to catch this lunatic.'

'We're doing everything we can, sir. We're examining lists of your staff, past and present – trying to trace anyone who might have a grudge against the company. And we're interviewing all your employees and examining the footage from your security cameras for the relevant times.'

Hunting, satisfied that Wesley was talking sense, led them through into the main living room. The view of the river through the huge windows was breathtaking, and Wesley noticed that Gerry Heffernan's eyes had been drawn to the boats gliding up and down beyond the glass.

But after a few moments Heffernan turned to face Hunting. 'Can you think of anyone who might want to get at your company?' he asked bluntly. Appearances had been deceptive: he hadn't been distracted by the scenery after all. 'What strikes me is that our letter writer doesn't seem interested in blackmail ... he hasn't asked for money. He just wants to get at Huntings ... to close you down. Can you think of anyone who might fit the bill?'

Hunting shook his head. 'Not all successful businessmen get to the top by treading on other people, you know. I like to think I've treated my staff and customers pretty fairly.'

Heffernan was about to open his mouth to answer but Wesley got in first. 'I'm sure you have, Mr Hunting. But anybody in your position can have enemies. Envy itself can be a powerful emotion.'

Hunting sat down and signalled the policemen to do likewise. He smiled sadly. 'I suppose you're right.'

'So can you think of anyone who could be jealous of your success ... or bear a grudge against you for any reason?'

It could have been Wesley's imagination but for a split second Hunting looked uneasy before he shook his head vehemently. 'Nobody at all. Can I offer you tea?' He looked from one to the other hopefully, as though anxious to keep them there. Perhaps, Wesley thought, he knew exactly who was after him and was glad of some temporary police protection.

Hunting pressed a bell-push by the great stone fireplace: Wesley had associated such arrangements with grand houses of past centuries and he was surprised when a maid, dressed in demure black and white, appeared in answer to the call. She was a small, dainty woman, not young, not old, of oriental appearance, Filipina perhaps. Hunting gave his orders and she scurried out, as unobtrusive as a mouse.

'I wonder if your wife is aware of any animosity against your company, Mr Hunting,' said Wesley tentatively when the maid had gone. He didn't even know whether Hunting was married but it was worth a try. Maybe Mrs Hunting, if she existed, had a vindictive lover. Or maybe he was being over-imaginative again.

153

'My wife isn't well, Inspector. She rarely goes out these days.' Hunting's face was a neutral mask.

'I'm sorry to hear that.' Wesley regretted bringing the subject up.

When the tea arrived, he quickly steered the conversation back to the subject of the threats. Hunting seemed genuinely shocked at the news of Edith Sommerby's death. And he remembered the case of Fred Sommerby – he had been a violent, unpleasant man and his manager had had no choice but to sack him. It was quite possible, he thought, that a man like Sommerby might still bear a grudge against the company.

This idea had occurred to Wesley as well. What if Sommerby had used this ruse to kill two birds with one stone – to get rid of his wife and to revenge himself on Huntings? In which case there need have been no poisoned goods planted on the shelves at all – Sommerby could have poisoned the jam in his wife's bag at his leisure. But then would Sommerby have possessed the necessary skill to create the bacteria? It was something he'd have to find out.

As they talked, Hunting refused stubbornly to live up to Wesley's preconceptions. He had assumed that the founder of Huntings supermarket chain would be a hard-nosed businessman, a ruthless entrepreneur. But Wesley was struggling to see him as the spiritual heir to Dickens's wicked Victorian factory owners, who sent ragged children to an early grave and lived in luxury while their workers starved in squalor; in fact, by the time he was leaving Wesley was beginning to like the man, against his instinctive prejudices. However, he told himself that it took a certain ruthlessness to get ahead in business: the amiability could be an act, a ploy to get what he wanted ... whatever that was.

But it seemed that Gerry had struck up some rapport with Hunting, especially when the subject of sailing came up. As the two men began to discuss the merits of various types of radar and global positioning systems, Wesley asked for directions to the lavatory and excused himself. But it wasn't the demands of his bladder which were making him restless; he found himself wanting to see more of the house, perhaps to pick up some clue about the invalid Mrs Hunting. Her absence intrigued him, but he didn't know why.

He ignored the directions to the downstairs cloakroom and made for the wide staircase. It was solid polished wood, a thing of beauty, but at that moment Wesley wished it had been thickly carpeted to mask the sound of his footsteps. He walked up on tiptoe, ready with the excuse that he was lost if anybody appeared to challenge him.

He strode along a wide landing. On his right a row of large windows looked out onto the river, letting dappled light flood in, and the doors leading off the landing to his left were heavy oak in the Arts and Crafts style. As in the small portion of the house he had already seen, everything here was elegantly simple and much to Wesley's own taste.

When he was halfway down the landing he stopped suddenly, stood quite still and listened. The sound was there, soft but unmistakable. Somebody in one of the rooms was crying, sobbing their heart out.

Wesley listened for a few seconds and then turned back.

Neil Watson sat stiffly in the passenger seat of Pam's VW Golf, wearing the stoical expression of the brave invalid.

When they stopped at a set of traffic lights on the outskirts of Neston, Pam turned towards him. 'Are you okay?'

'I'll live,' he replied in a martyred voice, enjoying the attention. He hadn't been so well looked after since he'd lived at home with his mother . . . and that seemed like a long time ago.

'Are you sure you're up to this? Surely Matt can cope . . .'

'I only want to see how far they've got. I don't intend to do any digging.'

'I'm glad to hear it.' She knew Neil of old and she wouldn't have been surprised if he had hobbled from the car and grabbed a spade. 'You'll have to take it easy, you know.'

'Do you know, Pam, motherhood suits you.'

She didn't consider the remark worthy of a reply. 'Where did you say this place was?'

'Just follow the signs to Morbay and Belsham's about a mile down the main road. You can't miss it.'

Pam had never connected the words 'urban sprawl' with the small town of Neston, but as drove she noticed that small factories, stores and housing estates had sprung up like grey fungi on either side of the road. Belsham, once a separate settlement on the road to Morbay, was becoming joined to Neston by an umbilical cord of brick and concrete. It was still a village, but only just.

It was also the perfect place to build a new Huntings supermarket to serve Neston's hungry population: just out of town and with plenty of parking.

Neil had been right; you couldn't miss Belsham with its older houses and cottages, its church and its pub. Neil told Pam to park by the church and she pulled in. 'So what exactly do you think you'll be able to do here?' she asked as she helped Neil from the car.

'I want to find out what made this place tick at the time of the Black Death.'

'So you're sure it's a plague pit you're digging up?'

'Sure as I can be ... but I need proof. There must be some mention of it somewhere.'

Neil was hobbling painfully towards Pest Field. Pam locked the car quickly and followed after him, hovering behind with a frown of concern like a nurse whose convalescent patient is trying to walk for the first time after an accident. 'Take it easy,' she said with the firm tone of the experienced schoolteacher she was. Neil ignored her and pressed ahead.

The field had been screened off with temporary wooden

fencing so that the lifting of the skeletons would be shielded from public view. Neil squeezed through a gap, as determined as a guided missile. Pam followed, not quite knowing what to expect on the other side of the barrier. This was Neil's world, and it had once been Wesley's before he chose to join the police; but Pam knew little of bones and trenches and she wasn't sure that she wanted to know more. The gap was just wide enough for her to squeeze through, hampered as she was by her growing belly.

Once through, she stood by the gap and waited, watching as Neil made his painful way over the rough terrain to where a group of people were digging. The first thing that struck her was that they weren't dressed like archaeologists. They wore hooded white overalls and some had covered their faces with white masks. When they saw Neil, one of them stopped what he was doing and walked over to him. After a brief conversation, Neil turned back and rejoined Pam.

'Well?' she said as he limped towards her.

'They're not working on our trench today. The police forensic team are giving the field a good going over and Matt and Jane are helping. It's about that body that was found . . . '

'Wes mentioned it . . . said it was recent . . . a murder.'

'Yeah. I reckon whoever attacked me was the murderer after the body. Probably buried her there and got the shock of his life when he saw all these archaeologists digging near the place where he'd left her and thought it would only be a matter of time before his dirty deed was discovered. I bet he intended to remove some incriminating clue but I disturbed him.'

'Does Wes agree with this theory?'

He grinned. 'He will do if he's got any sense. I wonder if the bastard knew about all those other skeletons buried in the field. What a place to dispose of a body. Quite funny when you think about it.'

157

'The best place to hide a tree is in a forest. Perhaps he thought if it was ever found it would just be taken for another plague victim.'

'But some of the things that were buried with her were obviously modern ... her belt, her watch ... the coins in her bag. Matt said they found a chain with a St Christopher near the skeleton too ... obviously fairly modern.'

'Perhaps that's what he was intending to remove when you disturbed him. If they hadn't been with the bones then she could have been taken for just another medieval skeleton. That could be why he was using a metal detector ... her belt buckle, and so on. In which case it means the murderer knew all about the other skeletons ... about the plague pit.'

Neil shrugged but the movement made him wince with pain. 'It's possible, I suppose. But we didn't know about them when we started the dig. We were told it might be the site of a leper hospital so I don't see who could have known what was down there.'

Pam glanced at him. He looked pale. 'Well, now you've seen that Matt's got everything under control perhaps we ought to get back.'

'I heard something odd the other day. That vicar of Belsham who was murdered had the church tower locked up permanently ... even stopped the church bells being rung. He said it was dangerous but Wes and I went in and it didn't look dangerous to me.'

'Perhaps he didn't like bells ... or his bell-ringers.'

Neil wasn't listening. 'Wes and I saw some tombs in the tower from the time of the Black Death. I'd like to go there again and take a better look. And I'd like to know why the vicar closed it up.'

Pam smiled patiently. 'You think he was hiding something in there?'

'You'd think he would have been proud of having some fine medieval tombs in his church.'

'Perhaps not everyone is as fascinated by that sort of

158

thing as you are, Neil.' She turned round and started to head for the car. 'And perhaps he was telling the truth: perhaps the tower is dangerous. Are you coming back or what?' She looked at her watch. Her mother was looking after Michael so there was no rush, but her legs were beginning to ache. She wanted to sit down, preferably with a refreshing cup of tea.

But Neil had other ideas. 'There's an American bloke in the village who lectures in history at Morbay University. He's just got back from a sabbatical in Boston and I want to see if he's at home. He only lives on the other side of the church. He might know something about the tombs.'

'He'll be at work,' Pam mumbled hopefully.

She saw that Neil was wavering. Perhaps, in his present state of health, he didn't feel up to chasing this American for information after all. But Belsham offered other possibilities. 'Isn't Wes's sister's boyfriend going to be vicar here?'

'Yes. I believe he is. Why?' She looked at Neil suspiciously. He was up to something.

'Well, I thought, as there's going to be a family connection, you might fancy looking round the church.'

His hopeful expression reminded Pam of an appealing spaniel. She knew when she was beaten. At least churches had pews where you could rest your weary legs. 'Why not?' she answered with a sigh.

'I think we handled Mr Aaron Hunting quite well, don't you?' Gerry Heffernan sounded pleased with himself.

Wesley didn't answer. He turned the car onto the main road out of Tradmouth. The traffic was heavier than usual at that time of the day and he found himself wondering why.

Heffernan looked at him. 'Anything the matter?'

'Why should there be?'

'You've been quiet ever since we left Hunting's place. Something wrong?'

Wesley hesitated before answering. 'While I was looking for the loo at Hunting's place I heard a woman crying in one of the upstairs rooms. I wondered if it was the wife.'

'Well, being an invalid must get her down. Or maybe it was some homesick foreign maid. Is it bothering you?'

Wesley shrugged. 'As you say, it's probably nothing.'

'Worth looking into?'

'Not at the top of our list of priorities, I shouldn't think. What's Stan Jenkins's address?'

'Topiary Cottage, Wishburn, near Stokeworthy. According to Stan, we can't miss it.'

'That's what they always say.'

He took the Stokeworthy turning off the main road and drove on down a narrow lane, just wide enough for two smallish cars to pass. After half a mile the road narrowed to a single track with the occasional passing place. The hedgerows either side of the lane rose up like solid walls. These roads had terrified Wesley when he had first arrived in Devon and he still viewed them with some trepidation. If an idiot with a fast car and slow concentration happened to be coming the other way, you wouldn't stand a chance.

They passed through the village of Stokeworthy and Wesley shuddered as he drove past the churchyard. The sight of the great yew tree in its centre – where, a couple of years before, a woman had been found hanging, murdered – brought back unpleasant memories of death. Wesley had found her killer but it had been a tragic case and it still filled him with sadness whenever he thought of it. He averted his eyes and carried on past the thatched Ring o' Bells. Gerry Heffernan gazed out at the pub longingly from the car window but there was no time for a lunch-time pint, however swift. There was work to do.

Stan Jenkins had been right. You certainly couldn't miss Topiary Cottage, although the term 'cottage' was a little misleading. It was a modern bungalow with pale pink walls and fussy floral curtains at the gleaming picture windows, and it stood on the edge of the village of Wishburn, next

160

door to the new village hall and set back from the road behind a long expanse of garden. But what set it apart from the average rural retirement bungalow was its display of hedges cut into a variety of startling shapes. A pair of proud green cockerels guarded the gleaming white wrought-iron gate and leafy birds and squirrels formed a guard of honour either side of the garden path. Nearer the house a rather phallic green truncheon grew out of the weedless soil – or at least, Wesley assumed it was a truncheon – next to what looked like a pair of beautifully clipped handcuffs. He assumed this was Stan's little joke. And from what he had heard about Mrs Jenkins, Stan needed all the laughs he could get.

Stan opened the door to them before they had a chance to ring the bell. He had been waiting. He invited them in with almost pathetic eagerness, greeting them as a man stranded on a desert island for a year would greet his rescuers.

'Come in, come in. Good to see you. Ursula's out at the moment,' he gabbled. 'I'll just go and put the kettle on.'

'Good topiary,' was the first thing Wesley said. 'Who does it?'

'It's become rather a hobby of mine since I retired. The place is called Topiary Cottage and the previous owners had attempted a couple of deformed ducks but I think I've made it a bit of a landmark.' He grinned with pride.

'I like the truncheon and handcuffs,' said Wesley.

'Well, I thought I should make some mention of my former profession. The truncheon caused a bit of a stir, though ... until I explained what it was, of course.'

'Good to have a hobby to get you out of the house, eh, Stan.' Heffernan winked conspiratorially.

'I've got a very nice shed. Want to take a look?'

They allowed Stan to lead the way out of the kitchen door, through the back garden and into a large shed screened from the house by a tall hedge. Stan had cut crenellations into the top of the hedge and Wesley guessed

161

that this was symbolic. It was his castle, his fortress: all it lacked was a drawbridge to keep the marauding Mrs Jenkins at bay.

Stan's shed turned out to be a little home from home. A selection of gardening tools were stored neatly in a cupboard in one corner but the rest of the structure appeared to be dedicated purely to pleasure. Wesley spotted a radio and CD player; a small drinks cabinet (well stocked); a kettle and toaster; and even a battered chaise longue. As well as all this there was a pair of well-worn wicker chairs to provide rest for the weary gardener.

'Nice place you've got here,' Heffernan said appreciatively, and Wesley nodded in agreement.

'Thank you, Gerry. You're welcome any time. Drink? And don't give me any of that "not while I'm on duty" nonsense. Boddingtons okay?' He took a bright yellow beer can from the drinks cabinet and handed it to Heffernan. 'What about you, Wesley? What'll you have?'

'I'm afraid I'll have to use the "not while I'm on duty" excuse. I'm driving.' He smiled. Stan was trying so hard.

'That's a pity. I've got some tonic water somewhere. Will that do?'

'That'll be fine. Thanks.'

Stan poured himself a rather large vodka, explaining that Ursula wouldn't be able to smell it on his breath, and settled down on the chaise longue, looking at his former colleagues with eager anticipation. 'I trust this isn't just a social call?'

It was Heffernan who spoke. 'I'm afraid not, Stan. We're reopening the Shipborne case.'

Wesley watched as Stan Jenkins downed the contents of his glass in one gulp.

'May I ask why?' The words had come out in a nervous squeak.

Something was worrying Stan Jenkins and Wesley wondered what it was. He found it hard to imagine that a man like Stan would have become knowingly involved in

162

any form of police corruption. Detective Inspector Jenkins had always had the reputation of being a dead straight, if rather unimaginative, copper.

'A new witness has come forward and Chris Hobson is now the proud owner of a cast-iron alibi. His appeal's going forward and the Nutter's going berserk, as you can imagine. Now you worked on the case under Geoff Norbert ...'

'That's true ... but I was only a humble DS ... his bagman.'

'But you knew everything that was going on?' said Wesley, who had recently been promoted from DS himself. 'You would have known if any evidence was suppressed or ...'

'Geoff Norbert always played things very close to his chest but I always had the impression ... ' He hesitated.

'Go on,' Wesley prompted.

Stan turned to Heffernan. 'I don't want to be disloyal, Gerry. The man's dead. He can't defend himself.'

'From which I take it you've got something to tell me.'

Stan shook his head. 'No. I mean, the evidence was there. We had a tip-off and the stolen silver was found hidden in Hobson's flat and he'd been seen in the pub near the vicarage. There was enough to convict him.'

Wesley took a drink of his tonic water and looked Stan in the eye. 'But?'

He waited. Stan was obviously struggling to make some sort of decision.

After a while he spoke. 'Well, I suppose there were some things that I thought were a bit odd at the time ... lines of enquiry that weren't followed up, that sort of thing. But as I said, we had the evidence. We had enough to get a conviction.'

'But you thought something wasn't quite right?'

'It was nothing as definite as that. It's hard to explain.'

Heffernan leaned forward. 'Try us.'

'Well, as I said, certain things weren't followed up. For

163

instance, Hobson said he saw a lad hanging around outside the vicarage. Geoff Norbert said it would be a waste of time checking it out.'

Heffernan grinned. 'He was probably right. If I had a fiver for every time a villain claimed to have seen a mysterious figure hanging around at the scene of a crime I'd be a tax exile by now.' He took a swig from his can and wiped his mouth with the back of his hand.

'But this was different?' Wesley suggested. 'There was something about his story that rang true or you wouldn't be mentioning it.'

'The difference was that he was very specific. He said he'd seen this lad in the pub and described him in detail ... even said he'd seen him before at some school or other. Now when they're lying they're usually vague ... they can't remember what pub it was, that sort of thing. But he was quite definite.'

'And it was DCI Norbert who told you not to follow it up?'

'He reckoned we had a watertight case. He probably didn't want to waste time.'

Wesley wasn't convinced. His mind was already working overtime, considering other possibilities.

'Do you remember Hobson saying he was with a woman at the time of the murder?'

Sam snorted. 'Oh yes. He came up with that one just as we were about to charge him. Said she was somewhere in America but he had no idea where. Very convenient.'

'So Norbert ignored it?'

'As stories go it was a bit thin. Can't say I believed it myself.'

'She turned up the other day. She's the new witness I mentioned.'

Stan stared at him for a moment, lost for words.

'Were there any other suspects for the Reverend Shipborne's murder before the stolen goods turned up?'

Stan Jenkins shook his head and poured himself another

drink. 'We always worked on the theory that he disturbed a burglar. There was no evidence that it was any more complicated than that. The French windows to the study where he was found had been forced open and the cleaner said that some valuable silver had been taken, so it was just a question of waiting for someone to try and dispose of it.'

'Was the cleaner ever suspected?'

'No. She'd gone home just before seven after cooking his evening meal but she found she'd left her purse in the kitchen so she went back to the vicarage at ten to get it. That's when she found him. She was never a suspect.'

'So you think it was a simple case of a burglary gone wrong?'

'Well, I presume you've read the files.'

Wesley sensed that Stan was on the defensive. 'Or perhaps that was what someone wanted us to think.'

'You'll have to excuse Wesley, Stan. He's a graduate ... always looking for the hidden meaning.' Heffernan gave a loud belch. 'Pardon me.' He turned to Wesley. 'Go on, Wes, tell us your brilliant conspiracy theory. The Reverend Shipborne was really an enemy spy and he was eliminated by a CIA agent who later planted the knocked-off silver on a petty villain. Give us a break, Wes. Too much education can be a dangerous thing.'

When Heffernan began to laugh and Stan Jenkins joined in, Wesley took a sip of his tonic water, feeling that he was being ganged up on.

When the laughter stopped Stan leaned over to Wesley and tapped him on the knee. 'If you're absolutely determined to think there's more to Shipborne's murder than meets the eye, then there was one name you might be interested in. The Reverend Shipborne was a great friend of an old villain called Barry Castello.'

'Was he?' Heffernan sounded surprised.

'They were bosom buddies. It seems that Castello claimed to have seen the error of his ways and he bought a farm up on Dartmoor ... turned it into a sort of unofficial rehabilitation place for kids who'd just come out of young offenders' institutions. He has them working on the farm, making themselves useful for a change. Shipborne was a great supporter of the scheme.'

'So what was Castello inside for?'

Heffernan and Stan looked at each other.

'His favourite pastime was armed robbery,' said Stan. 'Banks and post offices mainly. Used to like to get his victims so scared that they'd wet themselves ... gave him a feeling of power. Not a nice man.'

'So how come Shipborne was so friendly with him?'

'Repentant sinner, wasn't he?' said Heffernan. And you know how much vicars like those. Castello was a great advert for the church.'

'You think it was all an act?'

'Who can say? I'm a churchgoing man myself and I don't doubt these things can happen ... that's between Castello and his Maker. And I must say that from the time he announced his conversion to the press he never pointed another sawn-off shotgun at anyone ever again.'

'Or if he did, we never caught him at it,' said Stan, the cynic.

'He announced his conversion to the press?' Wesley sounded surprised.

'Oh yes. It seems that Shipborne visited him in prison ... he was some sort of chaplain at the time ... and when Castello told him he'd seen the light, Shipborne made sure the media got to hear of it. It was then that they started appealing for funds to set up Damascus Farm.'

'The place for young offenders?'

'That's right. It was set up as a charity.'

'And does it actually work?' Wesley asked, interested.

'Castello says so,' said Heffernan. 'He claims his lads have a remarkably low reoffending rate.'

'Was this Castello ever in the frame for Shipborne's murder?'

'Not seriously,' said Stan. 'But I've always believed that

leopards can't really change their spots ... they might manage a cosmetic job for a few years but nobody changes that much permanently. However, having said that we checked him out and it seemed he had an alibi. He was up at the farm at the time with his merry band of bad lads as witnesses. And it wasn't really his MO.'

'Unless he and Shipborne had fallen out ... '

'Who knows? But there was no hint of it. Castello claimed to be devastated when he heard about the murder. However, Damascus Farm did very nicely out of Shipborne's will.'

Wesley said nothing more but stored the information in his mind – another possible lead to be followed up when they had the time.

To Wesley's relief Heffernan declined a second can of Boddingtons but Stan, anxious for the company, continued to make extravagant offers of food and drink which it took a great deal of will-power to decline.

As they were leaving Wesley turned to Stan. 'Did you have any doubts at the time about DCI Norbert's handling of the Shipborne case?'

He saw Stan glance at Gerry awkwardly. 'Hindsight's a wonderful thing, Wesley, as I'm sure you know. And I'm not going to say anything against Geoff Norbert ... not when he's not here to defend himself.'

As they walked down the garden path past Stan's green creations, Wesley knew that Stan had told them all they needed to know. Norbert had cut corners. The only thing he didn't know yet was whether it was through incompetence, over-enthusiasm ... or for some other reason.

Wesley and Heffernan climbed into the car and drove back to Tradmouth in silence.

As he put the key Pam had just obtained from Mrs O'Donovan in the church door, Neil felt in his pocket with his other hand. He had remembered to bring a torch this time.

'Do you want me to do that?' Pam asked when she saw him struggling with the stiff lock. The trouble with broken ribs was that the most commonplace of movements produced fierce stabs of pain when they were least expected. Neil stood to one side and let Pam take over.

When the door creaked open Pam stepped inside the church first. Neil shut the door behind them, experiencing an agonising twinge of pain as he pushed it shut.

Pam walked slowly up the aisle, conscious that her advanced pregnancy had given her a waddling gait. Feeling heavy and tired, she sank down onto one of the front pews.

'I'm going to have a look in the bell-tower. Fancy joining me?'

'Are you sure it's safe?'

'Oh yes.' He sounded confident.

Pam sighed and stood up stiffly, putting a supporting hand in the small of her aching back.

They walked back down the aisle, both hobbling slowly like a pair of invalids. Neil gave Pam the key to the tower and she unlocked the door.

'It's not very clean in there,' he warned before she opened the door.

'I can cope.' She stepped inside first and the smell of dust, decay and pigeon droppings hit her nostrils. 'I see what you mean.'

He handed her the torch. She stood in the doorway, flicked it on and shone the beam around the room. 'Perfect if you were filming a remake of *Dracula*. You bring a girl to the most romantic places, Neil Watson. Are you absolutely sure it's not dangerous?'

Neil didn't answer. Something had caught his attention. He took the torch off her and began to wander around the room, avoiding the bell ropes that dangled down like hangman's nooses. The beam of light hit the west wall. Beneath a small, high window, opaque with years of grime, was what had looked in the flickering light of a burning match like a pattern of bird droppings. But now, with a

168

proper light, Neil could see it for what it was – a wall painting ... an extremely old one. He could just make out six faint figures, flaking and faded with the centuries. There were three healthy-looking individuals dressed in rich robes on one side ... and on the other stood three gruesome, bony figures, crawling with worms and topped by grinning skulls. Skeletons representing death. Neil stood quite still and stared at the image.

'What is it?' Pam whispered. She hardly liked to raise her voice in such a place.

But Neil was absorbed in his own thoughts. 'I can't believe William Verlan didn't mention this,' he muttered.

Pam repeated her question and this time Neil looked round. 'I think it's a depiction of the Three Living and the Three Dead. It was a popular story around the time of the Black Death in the fourteenth century. Three handsome young kings meet three corpses who tell them "such as thou art, so once was I. As I am now, so thou wilt be." It means all the money and power and good looks in the world can't save you from death.'

'A sobering thought.' Pam tilted her head to one side and looked at the wall painting. It was crudely executed, hardly the work of a talented artist ... but it still had the power to disturb. 'Do you think it's got something to do with your burials? Possible plague pit ... a story from the time of the Black Death?'

'I'd put money on it if I had any,' Neil replied. 'If this is the genuine article it should be properly conserved ... it's an important find.' He swung the torch beam around the tower and brought it to rest on the wall above the tombs. Letters had been gouged into the stone, crude work, more like graffiti than stone carving. The letters were uneven, hardly legible. Neil suspected vandals until he stepped closer and began to decipher the words. He had yet to come across a vandal who wrote in Latin.

'What does it say?' Pam asked quietly.

'It's not easy to read.' He squinted at the letters and

translated the clearest section slowly. 'I think it's ... "the miserable ... dregs of the people ... survive".' He shook his head. 'The rest is just scrawled ... can't make it out.'

'If we had a big sheet of paper we could take a rubbing and you could study it at your leisure.' Pam was a primary school-teacher, always ready with a practical solution to any problem.

Neil nodded. It was a good idea and he wished he'd thought of it. But this writing on the wall wasn't going to disappear ... he had plenty of time to make sure it was properly recorded and deciphered.

'What about the tombs?'

'Wes and I had a quick look at those before. They're fourteenth-century ... family called Munnery ... or de Munerie. There are some later memorials to the Munnery family in the main church ... presumably the descendants of this lot.'

He shone his torch on the first of the three tombs, on the battered alabaster figure lying on the top as though asleep. The beam shifted to the next, a woman in a wimple with her hands pressed together in pious prayer. 'That's Eleanor, wife of Urien de Munerie.' The light came to rest on the third figure, a noseless knight in armour, his head resting on what looked like a helmet. 'And that's Urien. It says round the side that he had a son called Robert.' Neil bent down stiffly to read the inscription. 'Pray for the soul of his son Robert, be he alive or dead.'

'What does that mean?'

'Presumably he went missing.'

'So do you think this lot died of the plague?'

Neil began to read the rest of the lettering carved around the edge of Urien's tomb. Pam bent down and ran her fingers over it in the torchlight. 'Is this a date here?' She pointed to what looked like Roman numerals.

'Looks like 1357. If the plague came in 1348, it looks as if old Urien survived it. What about the others?'

'Can't see any dates. I wish they had some proper lights in here.'

'When we come back we can bring something better.'

'We're coming back?' Pam sounded surprised.

'Well, I am. And I'll need someone to hold my hand, won't I?' He smiled at her hopefully. She felt her child kick within her and turned away.

'Why don't we go into Neston and pick up some tracing paper and pencils so we can make a rubbing of the graffiti?'

Pam sighed. 'Okay ... but can we go now?'

Neil looked disappointed but began to hobble into the nave. Pam followed, turning to lock the door of the tower behind her. Its secrets could wait until another day. They walked out of the church in silence, and it wasn't until they were on their way back to the car that Neil spoke again.

'I heard the other day that a woman should marry an archaeologist because the more she turns into a ruin, the more fascinating he'll find her.'

Pam began to laugh. 'Pity Wesley gave it all up and joined the police force, then.'

'You don't like him being a policeman, do you?'

Pam stopped. 'I didn't have much say in the matter. It's what he wanted to do.'

'You're not answering the question.'

She hesitated. 'I get fed up with it sometimes. The long hours he puts in and ... '

'You don't have to be a ruin for an archaeologist to fancy you, you know.'

She stopped and stared ahead of her, avoiding Neil's eyes. 'I think it's best if we both forget you said that, don't you?' she said quietly after a few moments.

Neil's face reddened and he said nothing. They got into the car and drove to Neston in silence.

Finding Helen Wilmer's parents was an easy task. They still lived in the same small bungalow on the outskirts of Belsham. They had stayed there, hoping all the time that they would hear Helen's key in the front door ... that she would have a change of heart and return to them. After a few years of painful waiting, Stephen Wilmer had suggested that it was time to move house and make a fresh start. But his wife had been reluctant ... what would Helen do, she said, if she came home and found strangers in the house? So they had stayed, growing old and waiting for the day when their Helen, their only child, would come back to them. Hope was the only thing they had left.

Wesley took Rachel with him to see them. She was good in such situations, a calm, sympathetic presence. He had the necklace and watch in his pocket swathed in plastic evidence bags. And he had brought the St Christopher found near by as well ... just in case they recognised it. As they walked up the Wilmers' neat garden path, he hoped the finds would prove to have nothing to do with Helen. He dreaded being the bearer of bad tidings. He was a parent himself now and knew how he would feel if anything happened to Michael. He knew that destroying the Wilmers' hope would probably destroy them ... but the truth had to be known so he had no choice.

It was Mrs Wilmer who opened the door. She was a tall, thin woman with limp grey hair and bloodshot brown eyes. She backed away slightly when he showed her his identity, like a frightened animal that had spotted a huntsman.

Rachel stepped forward and said something to her softly which Wesley couldn't quite hear. Mrs Wilmer turned and led them through into an over-neat lounge. She was a house-proud woman, Wesley guessed. Housework probably gave her something to do while she endured the restless uncertainty. From her expression, he imagined that things hadn't got any better over the years. She waited for Helen's return now as she always had.

As they were making themselves comfortable on the red velvet sofa, a man entered the room. He was taller than his wife and the skin stretched over his bald skull reminded Wesley of parchment. Mr Wilmer didn't look well. Wesley felt a sudden urge to get out of the room, to leave this couple alone and not to make things any worse for them than they already were. He put his hand in his pocket and felt the hard plastic of the evidence bags that held the watch and necklace, offering up a silent prayer that they wouldn't belong to Helen, that the Wilmers would still have some hope to cling on to in their declining years.

But Rachel was already speaking, telling them gently that remains had been found. He could hear the honeyed sympathy in her voice, soothing the wounds she knew she was opening. When she mentioned the watch and necklace Wesley produced them on cue, automatically, trying to stay professional and avoiding meeting the Wilmers' eyes.

There were a few moments of silence followed by a heart-rending sob. Mrs Wilmer had flopped into her husband's arms like a rag doll and stayed there for a few moments, limp and still, helpless with grief. Then her thin body started to shake, but no sound emerged.

Mr Wilmer looked up, his eyes full of sorrow. 'Where did you find her?'

Rachel told him.

'She'd been so near us and we never knew. We walked past her most days and we never even knew.' He buried his face in his wife's thin hair and said no more.

Mrs Wilmer suddenly sat up, disentangling herself from her husband's embrace. 'I want to see her,' she said. 'When can I see her?'

Wesley and Rachel looked at each other, wondering which one should explain that their beloved daughter was now just a heap of dry bones. But there was no need. Mr Wilmer patted his wife's hand. 'She's just a skeleton, love. Are you sure you want to . . .'

The woman nodded.

'I'll see what I can do,' Rachel said quickly. 'You're quite sure the necklace and watch are Helen's?'

It was Mr Wilmer who answered. 'We bought her that watch for her twenty-first. And . . . a boyfriend gave her the necklace.'

'Dermot O'Donovan?' Wesley asked.

Wilmer looked surprised. 'Yes. How did you ... ?'

'I've been reading the file on her disappearance. Do you know where Dermot O'Donovan is now?'

The man frowned with disapproval. 'You'll have to ask his mother ... she still lives in Belsham. I hear he still visits her.'

Wesley nodded. 'I think I've met her,' he said softly, adding Mrs O'Donovan to his mental list of people to see. He produced the bag containing the St Christopher from his pocket and handed it to Stephen Wilmer. 'Have you ever seen this before?'

Wilmer examined it, turning the bag over in his hands. He shook his head. 'It's not Helen's ... looks like a man's. Did you find it ... ?'

'Near the body. It might have something to do with Helen's death. Someone might have lost it.' He mentally added the words 'her murderer perhaps', but it was really too early to leap to conclusions.

When Rachel suggested that she make a cup of tea for them all, Wesley stood up and offered to do it. Anything was better than trying to think of the right thing to say.

Wesley let Rachel take the Wilmers to the mortuary to view their daughter's remains. She was better at that sort of thing than he was. She was a natural for family liaison work ... it was a gift that some had but not others.

He returned to the station and reported to Gerry that the watch and necklace had been identified as Helen Wilmer's. And Gerry had some news of his own. The lab had come back to them at last and had confirmed that the jam found in Edith Sommerby's bag was contaminated with botulism. Her weakness for conserves had been the death of her. For some reason Wesley felt better now he knew this for certain. Until now there had always been the possibility that they were barking up the wrong tree entirely.

As the news sank in, Gerry Heffernan sat on the corner

of Wesley's desk, deep in thought. Then suddenly he gave Wesley a hearty nudge, making the pen he was holding slip from his fingers. 'I've got to see the Nutter about the Shipborne case so why don't you get over to Huntings and see if the lads over there have come up with any names yet.' A number of officers were over there going through the personnel files under Keith Sturgeon's watchful eye.

Wesley looked at his watch. Perhaps a trip to Morbay would help erase the memory of the Wilmers' grief from his mind. He glanced round the office and noticed that Paul Johnson, elbow-deep in paperwork, looked as though he needed a change of scene. He would take Paul with him. He could always be relied upon to be useful.

Wesley was surprised to find the store open when they arrived. Trusted members of Huntings' staff and a forensic team had worked flat out to examine every item of stock before the doors had been flung open to the public again and nothing untoward had been found. Wesley had the fleeting thought that he still wouldn't fancy eating anything from the store, but he kept quiet. He presumed Forensics knew what they were doing. But then examining every single item in the store would be like looking for a needle in a haystack.

He noticed that the security guards at the entrance were watching everyone intently and there were more guards posted in the aisles. Keith Sturgeon had pulled out all the stops, quite rightly. To do otherwise was to gamble with people's lives.

Sturgeon was waiting for them, pacing his office anxiously. He looked as though the strain was getting to him.

'I'm afraid the lab's confirmed that there was botulism in the jam Mrs Sommerby bought from here,' Wesley said as he sat down. 'We've spoken to Mr Hunting and he says he has no idea who's behind all this. Have you had any more thoughts on the matter?'

Sturgeon stared at him for a moment and shook his head.

'I've had a look at the latest note ... the one that was dropped into the customer's trolley. Have you ever had dealings with this ... ' He consulted his notebook. 'Mrs June Seward before. Know anything about her?'

Again Sturgeon shook his head. 'You think she could have had something to do with it?'

'It's as good a place to start as any.'

'The girl on the till said she's a regular customer who always pays by credit card. There's absolutely nothing suspicious about her. The officers who came last night questioned her and she didn't see anybody around ... just found the note on top of her shopping. It can't be anything to do with her.'

Wesley looked at Paul, who was scribbling earnestly in his notebook. 'Well, this note can hardly have dropped down from heaven, can it? I'd like to send someone to show Mrs Seward some security footage ... see if it jogs any memories. You do have security footage from last night, I take it?'

'Of course. But she said she thought it was put into her trolley when it was parked by the speciality cheeses ... '

'And there's no camera there?' It was a guess on Wesley's part but it produced an affirmative nod from the manager.

'So I think we can safely say that whoever's doing this knows the store well. He or she knows where all the security cameras are situated. That means staff ... or a very observant regular customer.' Wesley frowned. 'Which brings us back to square one. I suppose we've now got a complete list of past employees?' he said hopefully.

'Your officers have been going through the personnel records. I think they've nearly finished. I presume this means that you've eliminated those two who were sacked recently. Baring from the warehouse and that girl who threw a can of beans at one of our customers ... Patience Reid.'

'They've both been interviewed but we're still keeping an open mind at this stage,' said Wesley non-committally. He hadn't eliminated anybody yet. And he was keeping Edward Baring and Patience Reid's details filed in the back of his mind ... just in case.

'Your officers seem to be going back a long way ... in the files, I mean. Back to the eighties.'

'It's routine,' Wesley said. 'We have to be thorough. You've looked at the list yourself, I take it?'

'Yes. But I couldn't see any names there that ... '

'Nobody you'd think would be capable of something like this?'

Sturgeon shook his head vigorously. 'I suppose it could be a customer. We get complaints from time to time ... faulty goods, that sort of thing. It may be someone who thinks our prices are too high or ... '

Wesley sighed. If they were going to have to start tracing everyone who had ever shopped at Huntings it would take up a fair slice of the CID budget for the year.

'I don't really see what more we can do until this person makes another move, to be honest, Mr Sturgeon. I'll just have to ask you to make sure your staff are vigilant ... if they see anything at all suspicious, contact us right away.'

Sturgeon looked disappointed, as though he'd expected Wesley to come up with something a little more miraculous.

Wesley caught Paul's eye. They'd shown their faces and now it was time to go.

'If you could point us in the direction of the personnel office, I'll see what my officers have managed to come up with.'

Keith Sturgeon jumped up, anxious to be helpful. 'Certainly, Inspector. It's down the corridor, third door on your left. I'll show you if you like.'

'No need. We'll find it.' Wesley thanked the manager and made a swift exit before Sturgeon's help became a hindrance.

As Paul followed him down the corridor, a door opened to their right and a young woman emerged, a file tucked under her arm. Wesley recognised Sunita and said hello. She gave him a brief, nervous smile and hurried off. When she had disappeared into Sturgeon's office, Wesley felt a tap on his shoulder.

'Sir. Who's that woman you said hello to?'

'She's the assistant manager ... Sunita Choudray, she's called. Why?' He turned to look at Paul, thinking that maybe Sunita had acquired an admirer.

'It's just that I've seen her before. She was coming out of the flats where Patience Reid lives.'

Wesley stopped. Paul now had his full attention. 'Tell me more,' he said, taking out his notebook.

In Sunita Choudray's experience, the words 'women's troubles' always ensured that few, if any, questions would be asked. She had whispered the words to Keith Sturgeon confidentially and watched as his face grew redder. He was eager to end the embarrassing conversation and get rid of her. Of course she could go home if she wasn't feeling well. She should get off now before the traffic became too bad.

Sunita half walked, half ran to her car. She was sure that she had seen the young man who had been with Inspector Peterson before ... possibly outside Pat's flat. And Pat had mentioned a visit from the police. Putting two and two together, she deduced that he was a plain-clothes policeman. And if he had recognised her ... She could hardly bear to think about it.

She drove too fast, hands gripping the steering wheel, slowing down only where she knew there were speed cameras. A speeding fine would be bad. But getting found out would be far worse.

Wesley flopped down in the chair that stood beside Gerry Heffernan's desk.

Heffernan sat back. 'So what's new? Any progress at Huntings?'

'We've got a comprehensive list of employees, past and present. Although I don't know how much use it's going to be to us.' He placed a sheaf of typed pages in front of Heffernan, who began to leaf through it absent-mindedly.

'So you definitely think it's someone who works . . . or worked . . . at Huntings?'

'It seems likely. Although I don't see we can do much more until he makes another move. Forensics say that the letters on the notes were cut out of the *Morbay Herald* . . . the local paper . . . not much to go on. We've drawn a blank with the security videos. Whoever it is seems to be familiar with the system and makes sure he's never caught doing anything suspicious on camera.'

'Which points to an employee.'

'But which one? Could be anyone.' Wesley looked up. 'One interesting thing happened while we were at Huntings. It might be nothing but I think it's worth following up.'

'What was it?'

'While we were there Paul Johnson saw Sunita . . . the assistant manager. Remember?'

Heffernan nodded. 'And?'

'He recognised her. When he went to interview Patience Reid, the girl who was sacked for throwing a tin of beans at a customer, he saw Sunita coming out of the flats where Reid lives.'

'Could be a coincidence. Perhaps she was visiting a friend.'

'Patience Reid lives in a run-down squat and Sunita hardly seems the squat type.'

Heffernan thought for a moment. 'Follow it up if you want to but there's probably an innocent explanation.' He picked up the list and began to study the first page. When he flicked over to the second he gave a small grunt which Wesley took to be some sort of exclamation.

'What is it?'

Heffernan pushed the list towards him. He took it and noticed that the date on the top of the sheet was 1989. 'In the middle . . . familiar name.'

Wesley's eyes scanned the page and the name jumped out at him, causing his heart to beat faster. Helen Wilmer. A temporary appointment: July till September. A summer holiday job. Helen had been a student. It fitted.

'Well, we didn't expect to find a link between our latest murder victim and Huntings,' said Heffernan solemnly.

'It probably doesn't mean anything. Lots of students get jobs in supermarkets during their vacations.'

'Funny to see her name there, though.'

The boss was right. It was strange to see Helen's name on such an ordinary list. She was now a heap of dry bones but she had once stacked shelves and put groceries through a till. Somehow it made her more real.

There was a sharp knock and the door opened. Rachel was standing there, her face serious. Wesley twisted round in his chair.

'How are the Wilmers?'

She stepped into the room and closed the door behind her. 'How do you think? They've lived all these years with this vague hope that one day she'll turn up and now . . .'

'Come and sit down, love,' said Gerry.

Rachel forgave the 'love' for once. Emotional tiredness overrode feminist principles. She flopped down on the empty chair next to Wesley and gave him a shy smile.

'So how did it go?' Wesley asked, fighting the urge to put a comforting hand on her arm.

'They kept going on about what a lovely girl she had been. How she had been a Sunday school teacher and written poetry and . . . I was almost crying myself in the end. I must be getting soft,' she added bitterly.

'Did they say anything that might be useful?'

'They didn't like the boyfriend. They said she'd changed since she met him . . . became harder and stopped talking

180

to them. I think we should start with him. According to the Wilmers he was a bad lot.'

Heffernan scratched his head. 'The case files said he was interviewed when she disappeared. He said he was in the pub with his mates around the time she was last seen. The mates all backed him up, of course. They couldn't make anything stick.'

Wesley thought for a moment. 'Did you say she was a Sunday school teacher?'

'At one time. Why?'

'At Belsham church?'

'Yes. The Wilmers mentioned the vicar who was killed ... the Reverend Shipborne. They said he thought very highly of her.'

Heffernan was watching Wesley's face. 'You don't think there's a connection with the Shipborne case, do you?'

Wesley looked the boss in the eye. It was as though he'd read his thoughts. 'She disappeared about a week after Shipborne's murder. No connection was made at the time because it was assumed that the vicar died in a robbery that went wrong. But what if there was more to it than that?'

'And she worked for Huntings.' Heffernan sounded pleased with himself.

Rachel caught Wesley's eye and gave him another shy smile.

Sunita Choudray let herself in with the key and called Pat's name. There was no answer so she walked across the room and looked out of the window onto the street below. She could hear the steady beat of music from one of the other flats ... probably from somewhere below: Loveday's flat. She knew Loveday by sight but she avoided her. She avoided everyone in the squat ... except Pat.

Pat had told her once that Loveday came from a wealthy family ... respectable. Sunita hadn't asked why Loveday had swapped all that for the squat; she didn't want to know the details of her downward journey. Perhaps, like Sunita, she had suffocated under the weight of respectability and, unlike Sunita, she had found the courage to break away.

Thinking of Loveday's background conjured thoughts of her own home and she gave an involuntary shudder. Her parents, she knew, wouldn't rest until they saw her married respectably to a nice Indian man ... and then there was Vikram, the doctor, the model son who could do no wrong. At that moment Sunita felt all the expectations of her family crushing her but one thing was certain – Pat's existence must remain a secret: it would break her mother's and father's hearts if they knew the truth and Sunita could never face that. In her family's world, breaking your parents' hearts wasn't an option.

She heard the sound of the door handle turning. Pat was home. She took a step forward, preparing to greet her, but when the door opened it wasn't Pat who stood there. Loveday was facing her, framed in the doorway, frozen like a startled animal. She wore frayed, well-washed jeans and a sleeveless black top that revealed a skinny midriff. A jewel winked in her navel, catching the light from the window.

Sunita opened her mouth to speak. Then she noticed the scars on the woman's wrist: old scars, shiny lines like snail trails on the pale flesh.

Loveday stared at her for a few seconds before she spoke. 'Where's Pat?' she asked. Her voice was accentless with the huskiness of the habitual smoker.

'I don't know,' said Sunita.

The woman hesitated for a moment before looking Sunita in the eye. 'I saw you the other day,' she said softly, before turning on her heels and hurrying away, leaving the flat door open behind her.

Chapter Eight

A woman turned up unexpectedly last night asking to speak to me in private. She was a thin, nervous creature who reminded me of a startled deer. Her name was Amy Hunting, not one of my parishioners ... or at least not one I recognised as one of my regular congregation. I invited her into the study and asked Mrs O'Donovan to make us a cup of tea. To cut a long story short, she ended up confessing that she'd committed adultery with William Verlan, which surprised me greatly. Verlan's always seemed such a quiet man, earnest in his American way: he must have hidden depths that I never imagined. I gave her the usual stuff about repentance and forgiveness and said that the affair must stop for her husband's sake. It was an awkward meeting: the woman seemed as troubled when she left as when she'd arrived, and somehow I felt I had failed her. Mrs O'D kept interrupting us with phone messages. I must ask her not to disturb me when I have visitors – but I suspect she does it deliberately: she's a woman who likes to know what's going on in the world.

I saw Dermot O'D yesterday. I've always wondered whether I did the right thing letting him go when I caught him taking the magazine money from church. I thought he had been one of Damascus Farm's successes but now I'm really not so sure. However, I hear that he's been seeing Helen Wilmer: she seems a nice girl and perhaps she'll keep him on the straight and narrow.

I drove up to Damascus Farm this morning. It's wonderful to see those young lives being changed: funny how God works through people like Barry Castello – just goes to show how you must never judge by appearances.

Barnaby Poulson was waiting for me when I got back. I've come to dread his visits and his gushing enthusiasm for Belsham's past. He wanted to know why I'd had the tower locked up. I told him the same as I'd told the bell-ringers ... safety reasons. He's asked me to read over the final draft of his thesis for him when it's ready: I could hardly refuse.

Stephen Wilmer, in his capacity as captain of the bell-ringers, is organising some sort of petition about the tower. I only hope the whole thing will blow over soon and be forgotten.

From a diary found among the personal effects of the Reverend John Shipborne

When Wesley entered the chief inspector's office he noticed how tired the boss looked. The bags beneath Gerry Heffernan's eyes were definitely growing darker and the laughter lines seemed to be furrowed deeper in his flesh. But then Wesley was feeling the strain himself.

'So where do we go from here, Gerry?'

Heffernan looked up. 'God knows, 'cause I don't. I had a dream last night. I was trying to climb this staircase and every time I took a step upwards it slid back like an escalator going the wrong way.'

'Frustration.'

'Too right. And I've just had the Nutter on to me again. He wants the Hobson case dealt with as quickly as possible. Top priority. Or he reckons it'll look as though there's some sort of cover-up.'

'We should visit that school and try to identify the boy Hobson says he saw on the night of the murder.'

'If he's telling the truth. Sounds as if it comes from the bumper book of villain's fairy tales to me.'

'He stuck to the story. It was Norbert who ignored it.'

Heffernan shrugged his shoulders. 'Okay. Put it on our list.'

'And I want a word with Sunita Choudray, the assistant manager at Huntings. She'd know the store inside out ... and she's been seen at the home of Patience Reid, the young woman who was fired. There's probably a perfectly innocent explanation but I don't think there's any harm in checking.'

Heffernan shrugged again. 'If you think it's worth following up, do it. What about the Helen Wilmer inquiry?'

'Rachel's trying to find out more about the dead girl. Dermot O'Donovan, the boyfriend, would be the obvious place to start. I'll organise someone to have a word with Mrs O'Donovan. It shouldn't be hard to track him down.'

'So everything's under control,' Heffernan said with a weary sigh. 'Until someone decides to plant something nasty on Huntings' shelves again or the press start rattling the Nutter's cage by banging on about miscarriages of justice.' He looked at his watch. 'You get on home, Wes. How's your mate Neil, by the way?'

The mention of Neil reminded Wesley that they were still no nearer finding out what had happened on the night he was attacked. He had a suspicion that Neil's nighthawk and Helen Wilmer's killer were one and the same person. But perhaps he was reading too much into it.

'He's staying with me and Pam until he's up to fending for himself.'

'Taking in waifs and strays now, are we?'

'It was Pam's idea. She said she was going to help him out with some research.' He hesitated. 'I don't know whether it's too much for her with the baby due next month.'

'I suppose she knows best. Is Rachel still here?'

'She was when I last looked.'

'Tell her to get off home, will you. She's been staying till all hours ... making me feel guilty.'

'What about you? Shouldn't you be getting home?'

Heffernan looked up at him and gave a small, sad smile. 'Not much fun going home to an empty house. I think I'll stay here for a while.' He pointed to his paperwork. 'Try and catch up on some of this lot.'

Wesley opened the door to the main CID office. At first it seemed that everyone had gone, then he saw Rachel working away quietly. She had remained at her desk, frowning over a pile of witness statements from the Helen Wilmer file. Trying to find something, anything, that would tell them what had happened to Helen between leaving her house and failing to reach the bus stop. And trying to put off going back to Little Barton Farm until the last possible moment.

'Time you went home, Rach,' Wesley said lightly. 'Had any luck with the flat-hunting yet?'

'No. I didn't realise it would be so difficult. Anywhere half decent costs a fortune.'

'Go on, get home. We've got an early start tomorrow.'

Rachel looked up at him, her face serious. Then without a word she stood up, fetched her coat from the stand and said goodnight. Wesley watched her go, then he returned to his seat at Heffernan's desk.

The first thing that Wesley noticed when he set foot in his living room was that Neil was again occupying his favourite chair. The thought lasted only a split second before he told himself firmly that a man of his age shouldn't have a 'favourite chair' – favourite chairs went with pipes and slippers, Labradors and late middle age. He was far too young for that sort of thing. And yet the lure of home comforts was strong after a day like the one he'd just had.

He forced himself to smile. 'How are you, then?'

'Surviving. Pam's been looking after me,' Neil said in the weak voice of an invalid. It crossed Wesley's mind that he was milking the situation for all it was worth. 'Hard day at the station?'

'You could say that. Where's Pam?'

'Getting the dinner. Michael's in bed.'

'What's that?' Wesley had spotted a large sheet of what looked like greaseproof paper lying on the floor beside the coffee table. There appeared to be charcoal or pencil scrawling on it. Wesley had presumed at first glance that it was Michael's work, something to do with his creative development, but now he looked at it closer he wasn't so sure ... unless his undoubtedly brilliant offspring had managed to master Latin already.

Neil shifted in the armchair and winced with pain. 'We've been over to Belsham church. Pam did a rubbing of some medieval graffiti on the wall of the tower. Remember, we thought it was vandals? And what we thought was bird droppings turned out to be a medieval wall painting ... the Three Living and the Three Dead. Know the story?'

Wesley nodded. He'd heard the gruesome tale long ago in his student days. 'Isn't the tower supposed to be dangerous?' He felt a sudden wave of anger that Neil had placed Pam and his unborn child at risk.

'It seemed sound enough to me. I can't understand why it hasn't been cleaned out and opened up. It's not every church that can boast fourteenth-century graffiti and a complete medieval wall painting. There are bell ropes in there and light fittings ... but no bulbs: someone's taken them out.'

Wesley sank down on the sofa. 'Odd.'

'I think there's something in that tower someone doesn't want anyone to see, and what better way of keeping people away than putting it about that the place is dangerous.'

Wesley leaned forward; it was hard to stop yourself

187

thinking like a policeman when you'd been doing it all day. 'So what have we got? A wall painting, possibly connected with the plague. The plague pit you've been digging up near by. The tombs ... '

'That mention of someone going missing.' Neil picked up a notebook from the coffee table in front of him. 'I've made a note of all the inscriptions, and who's this Robert – pray for him be he alive or dead?'

'There's that skeleton you found with his head bashed in. He had a fancy dagger. Could that have been Robert? He had gone missing but all the time he was there under their noses, murdered and buried in Pest Field ... like Helen Wilmer.' He realised that his imagination was running ahead of the available facts ... but it was as good a theory as any.

'That fancy dagger you mentioned was sent away to be X-rayed and Matt tells me the X-rays have shown up a coat of arms ... three things that look like half-moons. Remember the coat of arms on the Munnery memorials in the church?'

'Three half-moons.'

'Spot on.'

'So what does the graffiti say?'

'It's a bit hard to make out but I'm going to have a go at translating it tomorrow: it'll give me something to do.'

Wesley stared down at the rubbing. It was a mess of pencil with scrawled, uneven words, some legible, most unclear. A full translation would need concentration and a clear head. The way things were going at work, he'd leave Neil to it. At least it would keep him occupied.

Then Wesley suddenly remembered something. 'You didn't see Mrs O'Donovan today, by any chance?'

'She gave us the key to the church. Why?'

'Did you notice a son hanging around?'

'A son? Well, a bloke answered the door.' Neil said the words with a sneer. 'Might have been her son, I suppose. Why?'

Wesley smiled. Perhaps Dermot O'Donovan would be easier to track down than he'd expected. 'No reason,' he said as he picked up the newspaper and scanned the headlines.

Pam called out from the kitchen. The meal was ready ... getting cold. She sounded tired and impatient. Perhaps she had needed some help, Wesley thought guiltily.

Neil stayed put. He would have his on his knee. As Wesley made for the kitchen he found he'd suddenly lost his appetite.

The atmosphere in the CID office on Monday morning could best be described as subdued, and the weather outside matched the mood, grey and drizzly with an autumnal chill in the air. Winter was on its way, inevitable as death.

Gerry Heffernan too wore a funereal expression which sat uncomfortably on his chubby face. He pushed some files aside so that he could see Wesley better.

'I've had that Keith Sturgeon on the phone in a right old panic again. They had another letter in the post this morning and some uniforms went over to fetch it first thing. This time our friend has branched out into poetry.' He produced a plastic bag containing a sheet of paper covered with the familiar cut-out lettering.

Wesley picked the letter up and examined it. '"Roses are red, violets are blue",' he read. '"If I work amongst them, I may kill you." I don't think the Poet Laureate has anything to worry about.' He read on. '"Two sold, two more coffins to make. If Huntings doesn't close more lives are at stake."'

'Hardly Wordsworth is it? What does that bit about roses mean?'

'It either means our poisoner is a florist or ... ' He thought for a moment. 'What works amongst roses and violets? Flowers ... '

'Gardeners?'

Wesley frowned, then his frown slowly blossomed into a

189

triumphant smile. 'Bees. Honey. Contaminated jars of honey. It hardly needs Sherlock Holmes to work it out, does it? Almost as if our friend wants us to find them ... but it's a bit late if two have been sold already.'

Heffernan looked impressed but not convinced. 'He's playing games with us. We'll tell them to get all the honey off the shelves. Aaron Hunting's given Sturgeon the go-ahead to close the store today. I think he's getting worried.'

'I'm not surprised.'

'But Hunting's worried that the poisoner'll turn his attention to another branch if the Morbay store closes.'

'If he keeps this up, he could ruin Huntings.'

'That might be his intention. Who knows? Let's get over there and look at their honey pots.'

'It's always possible that the poisoner sent the poem to confuse us and it's got nothing to do with honey.'

But Heffernan had stood up, knocking a pile of papers to the floor. 'You know your trouble, Wes? You think too much.'

Wesley ignored this remark. 'Surely Forensics and Huntings' staff have checked all the stock?'

Heffernan shrugged his shoulders and made for the door. They wouldn't make any progress by just sitting there.

As the two men drove over to Morbay, taking the car ferry, neither said a word. Wesley's mind was on the threats to Huntings. They would have made sense if money had been demanded, but he couldn't think what the writer of the letters was after. Unless it was just to spread fear.

Huntings' carpark was empty when they arrived. Wesley watched as drivers swept in, got out to examine the large printed notice on the supermarket doors, then got back into their cars and drove out again. Whatever was going on at Huntings, it wasn't good for business.

Keith Sturgeon answered the door almost as soon as Wesley rung the bell at the staff entrance. His flesh was grey and he looked as though he hadn't slept. He led them into the building with the news that Mr Hunting was in his office and he wanted to see them.

As they walked down beige corridors Wesley asked whether it would be possible to have a word with Sunita. But Sturgeon said that she hadn't come in that morning. She had rung in sick. Wesley and Heffernan exchanged glances but said nothing.

Aaron Hunting was sitting in Sturgeon's black leather executive chair, twisting it from side to side like a restless schoolboy. He leaned forward eagerly when they walked in. 'Well?'

Wesley cleared his throat. 'We've had a look at the latest letter, Mr Hunting. I'd like to examine some of your stock, if I may.'

Hunting waved his hand dismissively but Wesley could tell he was a worried man.

It was Keith Sturgeon who led the two men down to the supermarket. He stayed silent, his eyes darting from side to side anxiously as he moved through the aisles as though he expected an ambush. When they reached the aisle near the back of the store where jars of jam, marmalade and honey stood stacked in neat rows, Wesley stopped, put on a pair of plastic gloves and started to examine each jar of honey, watched by Gerry Heffernan who never believed in getting his hands dirty if he could help it. Sturgeon tried to assure them in a small, nervous voice that his staff had checked them already. But Wesley wasn't taking any chances.

He examined the jars once, then again. And eventually he found what he was looking for. It was a small jar of organic lavender honey produced in France – a luxury jar rather than the run-of-the-mill mass-produced stuff that graced most tables. The evidence of tampering, impossible to spot on first inspection, was detectable only on very close examination. The plastic security seal around the rim of the lid had been opened and resealed very skilfully with clear tape. A cursory inspection wouldn't have found it, especially if the searchers had the entire stock of the store to deal with. Wesley bore his finds, four jars in all, back in a carrier bag to the office with a sinking heart. The fact

191

that he had found four fitted with the letter. If there had indeed been six contaminated jars, then two were already out there somewhere ... ready to kill.

Hunting's face turned pale when Gerry Heffernan broke the news of what they'd found. He buried his face in his hands for a few seconds, no longer the confident business-man, but a victim like so many other victims.

Wesley spoke practically, professionally. Someone had to keep a cool head. 'I suggest that we put out an appeal on the local TV news. We can ask anyone who bought this type of honey recently to return it to the store immediately,' he said. 'We can just say they came from a faulty batch, a manufac-turer's recall. We don't want to spread panic, do we?'

Hunting looked at him gratefully and nodded.

'It might be too late already,' Heffernan mumbled, unhelpfully in Wesley's opinion.

'We'll just have to hope it isn't. We can get someone to contact the TV studios in Plymouth and get them to put it on the lunch-time bulletin.'

Hunting sat back and sighed. This was all they could do for now. Apart from keeping the store closed, a strategy that was losing him money by the minute.

Wesley watched Hunting as he picked up a pen and began to turn it in his fingers. Now was as good a time as any to ask the question that had been on his mind since he had stepped into the office. In his experience it was always best to ask a question when it was least expected. 'By the way, Mr Hunting, I've been meaning to ask you. Do you remember a girl called Helen Wilmer? She used to work for Huntings back in the late 1980s. She was a student ... worked at this store in the holidays.'

Hunting looked slightly confused. 'I can't be expected to remember everyone who ever worked here, Inspector. I don't suppose I ever met her. But the name's familiar.' He frowned. 'Come to think of it, I do remember something about a student who used to work for us going missing. Why do you ask?'

192

'I just wondered if you remembered her.'

'I remember her going missing.' It was Keith Sturgeon who spoke. He was hovering unobtrusively in the corner of his own office, half hidden by a large filing cabinet. 'But I don't remember much about her. We used to take on a lot of students in those days.'

Hunting shrugged and looked Wesley in the eye. If Wesley were a betting man, he'd have gambled that both men were telling the truth. Helen Wilmer meant nothing to them other than a half-remembered name connected with a disappearance many years ago. But it had been worth a try.

Heffernan looked at his watch ostentatiously. There were things to do. The TV appeal to organise, the jars of honey to send for analysis ... not to mention finding the killers of the Reverend Shipborne and Helen Wilmer. Wesley caught his eye and gave an imperceptible nod. There was nothing more to be done here. They'd send some uniforms to interview the staff again and view the security footage. And hope that something turned up.

But as Keith Sturgeon showed them out of the empty store, Wesley couldn't resist asking a final question.

'Do you trust Sunita?' he asked as the manager unlocked the staff entrance to let them out.

Sturgeon stopped what he was doing and looked alarmed. 'I don't know what you mean.'

'I think you do. Would you say she was loyal to Huntings?'

'Yes. Yes, of course.'

Somehow the manager of Huntings' Morbay branch didn't sound very convincing.

'"The dregs of the people beg for thy mercy, o Lord. I Hammo, priest, set this down in the twenty-first year of the reign of King Edward, the third of that name, and beg all Christian people, if any be left alive, to pray for the souls of those cast into the pit in the church field. King Death has reigned over us and may God forgive Robert de Munerie

193

for bringing him to this place. I die now and confess my many sins. Have mercy upon us, o Lord, your miserable people."'

Neil put his notebook down with a dramatic flourish.

Pam appeared not to be listening: she was sitting on the floor helping Michael to post brightly coloured shapes into a wooden box.

'Well?' Neil prompted, vying for her attention. 'What do you think?'

Michael posted his last shape – a triangle – and let out a triumphant chuckle.

'What do you think?' Neil repeated.

'Are you sure it's genuine?'

'Yeah. What else could it be?' He sounded as though her doubts had brought on the sulks.

'It sounds as if the missing Robert de Munerie's getting the blame. But if he brought the plague to the village then surely he'd have been the first to die of it. So why is he missing? You'd think everyone would know exactly where he was ... six feet under.'

'Graves were shallower in those days,' Neil muttered pedantically. He thought for a moment. 'That murder victim was buried with a dagger bearing the de Munerie coat of arms. And it wasn't the murder weapon ... his head was bashed in.'

As Pam began to empty the box of shapes for Michael to have another go, the baby in her belly began to kick. She touched her abdomen and smiled. 'Shut up, Neil. You're beginning to sound like Wesley.'

'Am I?' he replied before falling silent.

There was something else Wesley had wanted to do in Morbay but his mind was so full of swirling thoughts that he had temporarily forgotten what it was. He fished his notebook out of his pocket and opened it, relieved to find that he had remembered to write it down. 'Check school for former pupil ... Hobson ID.' He swung the car out of

194

Huntings' carpark and took the turning for the St Peters district of the town.

'Where are we going?' Heffernan asked.

'Remember that boy Chris Hobson claimed he saw outside Belsham vicarage on the night of Shipborne's murder? He said he'd seen him at the school opposite St Peters church?'

'Well?'

'The school is bound to have copies of old class photos. I want to show some to Hobson, see if he recognises anyone.'

Heffernan looked unimpressed. 'Waste of time, if you ask me.'

'You think he was lying?'

Heffernan didn't answer. Perhaps he didn't trust Janet Powell . . . or perhaps he had been in the police force too long to take a villain's word for anything.

St Peters was the kind of area estate agents invariably describe as 'highly desirable'. The roads of large Victorian villas were lined with trees, their leaves turning brown and ready to fall onto the wide grass verges. At the centre of the district was St Peters church, built out of sandstone in the nineteenth century to accommodate Morbay's bourgeoisie; a place fit for smug, upstanding citizens to worship in. Opposite the church stood St Peters School, a private establishment housed in what was once the grand and vulgar home of one of Morbay's most prominent businessmen . . . the owner of a large department store near the promenade which had been taken over years ago by a national chain. Modern extensions, gymnasia and laboratories protruded awkwardly from the main building, doubling its original size. Wesley swung the car into the drive and parked in a space marked 'Visitors Only'.

It was plain from the start that St Peters School bore no relation to the wilder kind of inner-city comprehensive. It was a well-ordered place full of boys in smart, striped blazers walking purposefully towards their classrooms laden down with bags full of books. It rather reminded Wesley of his own schooldays when his parents had shelled out good money to keep him and his sister well away from the tender mercies of London's state secondary system. And as, many years before that, Gerry Heffernan had passed the eleven-plus exam to a similar grammar school in Liverpool, both men felt rather at home.

And it was because of this familiarity that they approached the headmaster's study with some trepidation, but they found the man within far from intimidating. In fact Mr Julian Harley, MA (Oxon), BEd, was a round, balding man with the harassed, anxious manner of a man who knows that the school's success, academic and financial, is down to him. When he asked them to sit down, he sounded slightly nervous, as though he feared that some parent or pupil had made some serious allegation against the school which warranted a police investigation. But when Wesley announced that all they wanted to do was to look at some old school photographs, the man relaxed visibly.

Wesley knew what he was looking for. Sixth-form class photographs from the late 1980s and early 1990s. They were provided with surprising efficiency by Mr Harley's secretary, a young and curvaceous blonde who was, no doubt, the focus of a few adolescent fantasies. Wesley put the photographs carefully in a folder, promising to return them as soon as they had finished with them.

'We'd better get these pictures up to Hobson as soon as possible,' Wesley said as they turned out of the school drive onto the main road.

Heffernan knew Wesley was right. There was no sense in wasting time over anything to do with the Shipborne case. 'Are we going straight back, then?'

'Yes, but there's just one thing I want to do as we're in Morbay. Have you got that list of Huntings employees handy?'

Heffernan grunted and reached onto the back seat for a file.

'Look up Sunita's address, will you? Sunita Choudray.'

'You're going to visit her?' The chief inspector sounded surprised. 'You don't think she's got anything to do with this business at Huntings, do you? She's the assistant manager.'

'And she might have her own reasons for helping Keith Sturgeon to fall flat on his face.'

'So she might be ambitious ... but she wouldn't go as far as killing anyone, surely.'

Wesley didn't reply. When it was put like that, it did seem extremely unlikely. But there was no harm in checking Sunita out while they were in the neighbourhood.

They found the house easily enough. It was a large pebble-dashed semi in a district not far from the school, a shabby but respectable part of town. Nothing pretentious ... and certainly nothing like the desirable St Peters. It was Wesley who rang the plastic doorbell; Heffernan hung behind as if he were preparing for a quick getaway.

Wesley waited a few moments before pressing the bell a second time. He tried to peer through the frosted glass of the porch but stepped back when he saw a dark shape approaching. Somebody was at home.

When the door opened Wesley and Heffernan stood there gaping at the man framed in the doorway. Even though Dr Choudray shared the same surname as Sunita, somehow he had never connected the two.

It was Wesley who spoke first. 'Dr Choudray. I ... '

'If you've come about Edith Sommerby, I don't think there's any more I can tell you.' The doctor sounded tired, as if being bothered by the police again was the last thing he wanted. 'Look, I've been on night duty and ... '

'It's not about Mrs Sommerby, Doctor. We're looking for a Sunita Choudray and we were given this address.'

The doctor's brown eyes widened in surprise and he scratched his head. 'Sunita's my sister. What do you want her for?'

'Just a routine matter, Dr Choudray. We have reason to

197

believe that the botulism originated at the supermarket where your sister works and we're just interviewing the staff again. If we could have a quick word with her . . . ' Wesley looked at the man expectantly. This tactic usually worked.

But the doctor was distracted before he could answer. A high-pitched voice from within the house, calling in some foreign tongue, made him turn round. He called back and Wesley assumed he was speaking in some Indian language. Then came a man's voice, an old man, Wesley guessed. The doctor called out again, answering his question. Probably, Wesley thought, the unseen pair were asking who was at the door.

Choudray turned back to the visitors. 'My parents,' he explained before taking a deep breath. 'Look, Sunita's not here. She spent the night with a friend.'

'She rang into work sick.' Heffernan spoke for the first time, his eyes on Choudray's face.

The doctor looked surprised. 'Sorry, I can't help you. I was on duty last night as I said, and when I got home this morning my parents told me that she'd spent the night at a friend's house . . . and before you ask, she didn't say which friend it was. That's all I know.'

That was that. Sunita had probably lied to Sturgeon . . . skived off work. She wasn't the first to do that and she wouldn't be the last. The only thing that bothered Wesley was that Sunita didn't seem like the skiving type.

But there was nothing for it: they'd had a wasted journey.

'By the way, Doctor,' said Wesley as Heffernan turned to leave. 'I'd be grateful if you would inform us right away if you come across any more suspected cases of botulism.'

Choudray raised his eyebrows. 'You're expecting more?'

'Let's hope not,' Wesley said as he handed the doctor his card. 'But it's best to be prepared.'

'So where's Sunita?' Heffernan asked as they got into the car.

'That's what I'd like to know,' Wesley answered.

*

198

Steve Carstairs was unaccustomed to the freedom of the open road. Usually, when witnesses who lived far away needed to be interviewed, either the local force dealt with the matter or, if it was important, Inspector Peterson or Chief Inspector Heffernan got all the fun and did the job themselves.

As he drove up the M5 in his nearly new Ford Probe, his pride and joy, with Paul Johnson seated nervously by his side clinging to his seat belt, Steve felt a thrill of exhilaration as he exceeded the speed limit by twenty miles an hour. This was a break from the Cinderella existence of paperwork and dull routine enquiries ... and it was too soon to think of the time when the shiny black car would turn back into an office chair.

'Great, this,' he said to Paul, who had been silent for most of the journey.

'We're going to a prison.'

'So? Gets us out of Tradmouth ... out of the office. It's nearly lunch-time. Fancy stopping at a pub?'

Paul had no objection to pubs in principle but he knew that the boss wanted this job done and he wanted it done quickly. 'It's not far now to Hammersham and we can grab something after we've been. We told the governor we'd be there by one so we'd better not waste time.'

Steve didn't reply. He wished he was with someone who was a little more amenable to the idea of cutting a few corners ... but then Heffernan himself had selected Paul as his partner for the trip, so he wasn't altogether surprised that he was doing things by the book.

Paul Johnson had been right. HM Prison, Hammersham wasn't far, and they were there within ten minutes. As Steve walked in through the massive gates, which shut behind him with an ominous and final clang, he felt, as he always did on visiting a prison, a sudden sense of desolation, of lost hope. But he experienced no pang of guilt that from time to time he had helped to put people away in such places: he reckoned that each villain he had helped to put inside deserved all he or she got.

A tall, balding prison officer led them through corridors

of painted beige brick, locking and unlocking gates and doors as they went. There was a none-too-subtle scent of boiled cabbage and urine in the air. Steve caught Paul's eye but Paul walked on with the determined expression of a man with a job to do. He was holding the cardboard folder containing the photographs the chief inspector had borrowed from the posh school in St Peters.

As the door to the interview room was opened, Steve was seized with curiosity. He had read so much about Chris Hobson in the last few days as he went over files and reports about the Shipborne case. And now, sitting there next to his solicitor, was the man himself: medium build, dark hair turned to dull grey, sallow complexion. He didn't look like a murderer ... but then murderers rarely did. It was Paul who made the introductions and produced the pictures for Hobson to examine.

Hobson was so keen that he almost grabbed the school photographs. He pored over them, peering at each of the youthful faces that stared out of the pictures, frozen in eternal schooldays. He examined every photograph carefully but he kept returning to one in particular. After ten minutes he looked up.

'That's him.' He pointed to a face on the back row. A youth with sleek dark hair and the sullen pout of a young James Dean. A face more at home in a leather jacket than a striped school blazer.

'You're sure?' Paul Johnson sounded uncertain. He hadn't really expected Hobson to remember after all this time. This had been too easy.

'Absolutely positive. I never forget a face. That's the lad I saw in the Horse and Farrier and then outside the vicarage. I swear it on my mother's life.' He looked Paul in the eye, and for a few seconds both Paul and Steve found themselves believing every word he said.

Wesley thought he'd better be the one to visit Mrs O'Donovan, as she'd met him already. Familiarity might be

200

an advantage ... or not, as the case might be. He decided to take Rachel with him. She had been going through the files on Huntings' current employees all morning and she looked as though she'd had enough. A change of scene, a spot of fresh air, would do her good.

'Any luck with the Huntings files?' he asked as they drove out towards Belsham.

She gave a deep sigh. 'I don't really know what I'm supposed to be looking for. All the staff have been interviewed and most of them seemed as puzzled as we are.'

'What about Sunita Choudray, the assistant manager?'

Rachel frowned. 'Can't really remember. I'll look her up when we get back if you like.'

Wesley didn't know why but he felt uneasy about Sunita. She'd been seen coming out of Patience Reid's squat. She'd lied to Keith Sturgeon about being ill ... and possibly to her parents about where she'd spent the night. 'Have you checked out the security staff ... and the cleaners?'

'We've done security. Nothing suspicious there. And we're doing the cleaners at the moment, but it's not straightforward. Huntings' own cleaners have been checked out but they also employ agency staff and we're having a job getting their records.'

Wesley felt his heart begin to beat a little faster as it always did when he scented a fruitful lead. 'I think we should make it a priority to get those records.'

Rachel nodded. The 'we', she knew, meant her. She put it on her mental list of things to do, a list that was growing longer by the hour.

They had reached Belsham. Wesley drove past the church and parked the car opposite Pest Field. He hesitated as he got out, fighting the strong temptation to cross the road to see what was going on. He knew that, with the help of Matt and Jane, the police search had now been completed and the dig would be resuming. Lifting the medieval bones from the ground would be a priority as it wouldn't be long before the developers started piling the

201

pressure on. Time was money. Neil was adept at standing up to such pressure ... but Matt wasn't so sure of himself.

He walked away from the field with Rachel beside him, making for Mrs O'Donovan's house at the edge of the village. He rapped on the door and it was opened almost at once, as though the woman had been watching for him behind the net curtains.

'You'll want the church key again, I suppose,' she said wearily, as though the church's recent popularity was becoming a nuisance.

Wesley produced his warrant card. 'As a matter of fact I've not come about the church ... I need to have a word with your son, Dermot. Does he still live here with you?'

Mrs O'Donovan took a step backwards. 'Why? What do you want him for?'

'Nothing to worry about, Mrs O'Donovan. I just think he might be able to help us with a case we're working on. Do you remember Helen Wilmer?'

There was no mistake about it, the colour had left Mrs O'Donovan's rosy cheeks and her face had turned white. 'My Dermot had nothing to do with that. The police said so at the time. He had no idea where she went. He was as worried about her as anyone.'

'You've heard that her body has been discovered buried in Pest Field?'

The woman looked wary. 'It said on the local news that it was her. But it's got nothing to do with my Dermot.'

'Could you tell us where we can find him?

Mrs O'Donovan hesitated, then she stepped aside to let them in. 'He's upstairs. He's helping me move some furniture.' She went to the foot of the narrow staircase and called Dermot's name, and there was an answering shuffling from somewhere above.

Somehow Wesley had expected Dermot O'Donovan to be frozen in time, to still be the teenage rebel, the undesirable boyfriend who had been questioned when Helen Wilmer had disappeared. He was quite unprepared for the present-

202

day reality. Dermot O'Donovan was a tall, sharp-featured man wearing well-pressed jeans and a pale blue polo shirt, whose dark hair was frosted with grey around the temples. He was in his thirties, self assured and apparently prosperous. For a few moments Wesley was lost for words.

'You're lucky to find me here,' Dermot began after Wesley had introduced himself. He had a slight local accent and spoke with the quick, to-the-point manner of a man used to issuing orders. 'I came to help my mother move a wardrobe.' He gave Wesley a businesslike smile. 'I heard that Helen's body had been found. It's all come as a bit of a shock. Terrible business,' he said as he arranged his features into a mask of solemn concern.

'As you were friendly with Helen at the time, I'm afraid we'll have to ask you some questions.'

'I realise that, but it seems so long ago. A lot of water has flowed under the bridge since then.'

'Her parents didn't approve of you.' It was a bare statement but Wesley thought Dermot O'Donovan wouldn't appreciate the subtle approach.

'I was a bit of a tearaway in those days. I left school at sixteen and got myself a job as a lorry driver's mate. I got talking to Helen when we made deliveries to Huntings in Morbay ... she had a holiday job there. I'd seen her before around the village, of course, but that's when we started going out together.' There was a sudden wariness in Dermot's expression that told Wesley he was hiding something. 'Look, go through to the front room ... I'm sure my mother won't mind making a cup of tea.'

As Dermot went off in search of his mother, Wesley and Rachel made themselves comfortable in a pair of tapestry armchairs. When Dermot returned, he sat on the matching sofa and leaned forward. 'I swear I had nothing to do with Helen's death. I'm as upset about it as anyone.'

'I'm sure you are, sir,' said Rachel sympathetically. 'What can you tell me about the last time you saw Helen?'

'I gave a full statement at the time.'

'We'd like to hear it again.'

'We'd had a row over something silly ... about which film to see at the pictures. She'd not been her usual self since the reverend was killed.' He hesitated. 'I went over it again and again in my head but I couldn't think what had happened to her. I was sure she wouldn't have just gone off without telling anyone.'

'She didn't,' Wesley said gently. 'You say she changed after the vicar's murder? Why do you think that was?'

Dermot looked uncomfortable. 'Search me.'

'Might she have thought you were involved somehow?'

'I didn't have anything to do with the reverend's murder,' Dermot said vehemently. 'I'd been a bit of a bad lad over the years, but that? No way.'

'What about now?' Wesley glanced at Rachel, who was watching Dermot's face intently, searching for some telltale sign that he was lying.

'I haven't returned to my old ways, if that's what you're getting at.' He spoke defensively. Wesley had touched a nerve somewhere. 'I run my own building firm now ... got ten men working for me. And I'm married ... two kids. The model citizen. And just for the record I've never murdered anyone.' He looked Wesley in the eye, challenging him to prove otherwise.

'How did Helen seem when you last saw her?'

Dermot shrugged. Again he looked uncomfortable.

'Is there something you want to tell us?' Rachel asked gently, coaxing.

Dermot hesitated, as though coming to a decision. 'She said something about seeing someone where they weren't supposed to be. As soon as she'd said it her mum came in so she changed the subject.'

'Is that all?' said Wesley, disappointed. 'She'd seen someone where they weren't supposed to be? Did she say who or where?'

Dermot shook his head and swallowed hard. He looked like a man who was aware that he'd said too much already.

He bit his lower lip and turned his head away.

As Wesley watched him he found himself thinking that either Dermot O'Donovan was genuinely affected by Helen's death ... or he was a very good actor.

'So what did you learn from Dermot O'Donovan?' Gerry Heffernan sat back and put his feet on the table. If a man couldn't make himself comfortable in his own office, where could he relax? And he had just returned from another fraught meeting with Chief Superintendent Nutter, so he felt he needed all the relaxation he could get.

Wesley pulled a face. 'Not a lot really. Apparently Helen wasn't her usual cheerful self after Shipborne's murder – but then it had shocked the whole village. And Dermot has a vague recollection of Helen saying something about seeing someone where they shouldn't have been, but she didn't say who.'

'Is that all?'

'Afraid so.'

'What did you make of O'Donovan? Is he in the frame for her murder?'

'I wouldn't rule it out. His record says he committed a number of petty offences when he was in his teens and, according to his file, he spent some time at Barry Castello's place on Dartmoor at one point ... Damascus Farm.'

'So how did he get involved with Helen Wilmer?'

'He was a lorry driver's mate and he met her when she was working at Huntings in Morbay during her vacation and he was delivering goods there. Small world.' Wesley frowned. 'Why do we always keep coming back to Huntings?' He craned his neck to look through the window into the outer office. There was a quiet bustle of activity as officers spoke on phones and typed into computers. For a few seconds Wesley's eyes were drawn to Rachel, who had her head down studying a file, then he turned back to his boss. 'Any word from Steve and Paul about how they got on with Chris Hobson?'

Heffernan nodded smugly. 'Hobson identified the boy ... seemed absolutely certain. I sent them over to the school as soon as they got back. Hopefully we'll have a name soon.'

'Why wasn't this followed up at the time?'

Heffernan gave an exaggerated shrug. 'Don't ask me. Probably an oversight ... a cock-up.'

'Probably.' Wesley sounded unconvinced. There had been a lot of coppers in days gone by who had ignored inconvenient evidence if it contradicted their own pet theory and got in the way of a conviction.

'I asked someone to contact Keith Sturgeon again ... Sunita Choudray still hasn't turned up at work. Not that I expected her to, if she phoned in sick. Where is she if she's not at home?'

'Probably quite innocent ... she might have genuinely spent the night with a friend and been taken ill.'

'But wouldn't she have let her family know?'

'Perhaps we should go and have a word with Patience Reid again ... see if she knows who Sunita was visiting at the squat. She might be able to throw some light on the matter.'

'Good idea.'

'And while we're on the subject of Huntings, has the warning about the honey gone out on the local news?'

'Yeah. It was on the lunch-time bulletin and they're repeating it tonight. And they've decided to keep the store closed until all this is sorted out.'

'Good. I'd like someone to go through Huntings' personnel records again to see if anyone working there has the necessary knowledge to culture botulism. Perhaps one of the employees has worked in a lab or studied biochemistry or ...'

'I'll let you organise that.' Heffernan suddenly sounded weary, tired of it all.

Wesley leaned forward, elbows on the desk. 'Do you think Helen Wilmer's death was connected to Shipborne's murder?'

'If she mentioned to her boyfriend that she saw someone where they weren't supposed to be it's possible she witnessed something ... or saw someone coming out of the vicarage that night. I wonder where she was on the night of Shipborne's murder? We could contact her parents again, see if they remember.'

'Is that likely?'

'People tend to remember where they were when something dramatic happens. My parents remember what they were doing when President Kennedy was assassinated ... and I was arresting a gang of art thieves in Essex when Princess Diana died.' He grinned. 'There's no harm in asking. If she did witness something she might have been killed to stop her talking.'

'And the killer buried her near Neil's plague pit ... is that a coincidence? And what about Huntings? Everyone we come across seems to have a connection with Huntings.'

'The Reverend Shipborne didn't ... unless he did his shopping there.'

Wesley put his head in his hands. It was only four o'clock but he wanted to get home. His brain was becoming overloaded with information ... and he knew from experience that most of it would turn out to be completely irrelevant.

A knock on the door made him sit up straight. He twisted round in his seat and saw Steve Carstairs and Paul Johnson standing in the doorway, looking pleased with themselves.

'We've got a name for that lad on the photo, sir ... the one Hobson picked out.'

Heffernan stood up. 'And?'

'The headmaster identified him right away. Seems he'd been a bit of a tearaway ... caused his parents no end of grief and left just before his A-levels.'

'So what's his name?' Wesley asked, earning himself a sideways look from Steve.

'Norbert, Philip Norbert ... and the headmaster said that his dad was a policeman ... sir.'

207

Chapter Nine

Barnaby Poulson called today to thank me for helping him with his research. I smiled and made the right noises: I couldn't let him know how his discoveries had affected me. I didn't mention that I had locked up the tower and destroyed all the church guidebooks that mentioned what was in there. When he read me an extract from an original document he'd discovered I sat with a fixed smile on my face, trying not to listen because the words were too painful.

I've been lying awake wondering whether Robert de Munerie felt as I do when he saw the results of what he'd done. I wonder what became of him: did he escape or was he consumed eventually by his own brand of evil?

Barry Castello rang just after Barnaby had left. I must make an appointment with my solicitor soon – it's high time I got round to changing my will and Barry's need is far greater than my niece's.

I saw Dermot O'D with Helen this morning. His mother tells me how much he's changed for the better but I'm afraid her parents see things rather differently. Last night they asked me to have a word with Helen, but I told them that she was a grown woman and it wasn't up to me to interfere. It was clear they didn't care for my answer and Stephen Wilmer then began to berate me

From a diary found among the personal effects of the Reverend John Shipborne

It was easy to find the address of ex-DCI Norbert's widow. But once in possession of the information Heffernan hesitated to act upon it, saying that he needed time to think. To barge into the home of a late colleague's widow and virtually accuse her husband of corruption and her son of robbery and possibly even murder wasn't something to be entered into lightly. He looked at his watch, then at Wesley. It was getting late, he said. They'd think about it in the morning.

Wesley supposed that Philip Norbert, wherever he was, could wait another day. And, unlike others, Wesley had never any harm in the 'softly, softly' approach.

There was a shy knock on Gerry Heffernan's office door and both men looked round. Trish Walton was standing behind the glass partition, an excited expression on her face. Wesley signalled her to come in, hoping that she had something important to tell them . . . they needed all the help they could get.

'What is it, Trish?' Wesley asked as she stepped into the office.

'You know you were asking about any Huntings employee who'd ever worked in a lab or knew anything about biology . . .?'

'Yes. Go on.' Wesley smiled encouragingly.

'Well, I got on to their human resources department and asked them if any employees at Morbay had any relevant experience or qualifications. They've just come back to me, and it seems that Sunita Choudray went to Bristol University. She has a degree in microbiology.' Trish stood there like a dog who'd just delivered a stick to its master, pleased with herself and awaiting praise.

Heffernan smiled at her, bearing a set of uneven teeth. He turned to Wesley. 'Let's see if our Ms Choudray has returned home, eh. Why don't you give her a ring? Her home number'll be in Huntings' files. It's near teatime ... maybe we'll get a decent curry if we catch 'em at the right time.'

Wesley felt uneasy. He hoped Gerry wouldn't do anything to offend or frighten Sunita's parents ... he knew that cultural sensitivities were a minefield these days. One wrong word, however innocently meant, might have Gerry up in front of some police complaints committee accused of racial harassment. 'Didn't you mention the Chief Super wants to see you about the latest developments in the Hobson case? Tell you what, if it turns out that Sunita's returned home, I'll go round there with Trish.'

Heffernan scratched his head. 'Suppose you're right ... I'd better go and tell the Nutter about the photograph.'

A few minutes later Trish reported that Sunita had still not returned home but had telephoned her family from an unknown location to say that she was staying another night with her friend. Wesley looked at his watch. It was six o'clock already. As if he had read his mind, Gerry Heffernan told him to get home to Pam. It would probably be a long day tomorrow.

Wesley put on his coat, ready to set off home. But as he was about to leave the office he hesitated at Rachel's desk.

'How are things at home?'

'Dave telephoned to say he's coming over the week after next. My mum's asked him to stay at the farm.'

'Oh. It'll be nice to see him again,' was all Wesley could think of to say.

Rachel looked away and there was an awkward pause as Wesley desperately searched for the next thing to say. Work was a safe subject, so he began to talk about Sunita Choudray and Phil Norbert and their sparse discoveries about Helen Wilmer's life and death. Rachel listened and made the appropriate noises, but Wesley suspected that her mind was elsewhere.

He saw Steve looking up from his paperwork, the ghost of a knowing grin on his lips. Wesley knew he had to be careful not to provide the office gossip-mongers with ammunition, and he told himself firmly that he should get home while he had the chance. Pam needed him. And she had Neil to deal with as well as Michael.

He walked home through the evening drizzle, pulling his coat collar up against the chill. The trees on his route had turned a rich russet red and had begun to shed their leaves. Soon they would be little more than skeletons against the grey sky, devoid of life until they were reawakened by the warmth of spring. Wesley had never liked autumn. It reminded him too much of approaching death. As he walked he thought of the skeletons in Pest Field that had lain beneath the earth for centuries, winter and summer. What sickness, what agonies, had caused them all to wither and perish?

By the time he reached his front door he was feeling quite depressed.

Wesley watched the television breakfast news the next morning as he munched a slice of wholemeal toast. The warning about the organic French lavender honey was repeated. Surely everyone must know to avoid the stuff by now, he thought hopefully.

As soon as he arrived at work he received a call from Dr Choudray. Two emergencies had been admitted to Morbay Hospital in the early hours of the morning and were now in Intensive Care. He couldn't be absolutely certain yet but they seemed to be displaying all the symptoms of botulism poisoning. The patients, a woman and a ten-year-old girl, were on the critical list.

Wesley fell silent on the other end of the line. He had somehow managed to convince himself that Edith Sommerby's death was an isolated incident . . . perhaps even

211

engineered by her vicious, violent husband. He had hardly dared to believe that the poisoner would carry out his threats. Even when he'd found that the jars of honey at Huntings had been tampered with, he had still hoped it was part of some elaborate hoax. But now it seemed that whoever was responsible was willing to kill members of the public at random. That meant they were highly dangerous . . . or sick.

He sat for a few moments, lost for words. Then Choudray's voice asking if he was still there brought him to his senses. He took the patients' details before asking the question that shock had almost driven from his mind. 'Has Sunita returned home yet?'

'No. She rang my parents to say that she was staying another night with her friend. Why?' The doctor sounded annoyed.

'And you've no idea who this friend is? The address?'

'Sorry. I've no idea . . . and neither have my parents.' The way he said it made Wesley suspect that the Choudrays weren't too pleased about their daughter having a life they knew nothing about.

'If you could let me know when she returns . . . We'd just like a word with her. Routine.' There was no way he was going to hint that Sunita was suspected of any wrongdoing . . . but now they had discovered that she had the necessary knowledge – as well as the opportunity – to contaminate goods at Huntings, she had to be a suspect. Why a capable, intelligent young woman like Sunita Choudray would do such a thing he didn't know. But he did know that appearances often deceived. Sunita was in the frame . . . and they had to find her as soon as possible.

'Thank you very much for letting us know so quickly, Doctor,' Wesley said politely before he put the phone down.

Gerry Heffernan lumbered out of his lair like a bear emerging from its cave after its winter hibernation. He stood in the middle of the main office and stretched before turning his gaze on Wesley.

212

Wesley looked up. 'I've just had Dr Choudray on the phone. There are two more suspected cases of botulism poisoning at Morbay Hospital. It'll be a while before it's confirmed, of course.'

Heffernan raised his eyes to heaven. 'That's all we need. Any sign of Sunita Choudray yet?'

'Still at her friend's, according to the doctor. I've got the address of the patients ... it's a woman and a ten-year-old girl, both called Pickering, so they're probably mother and daughter. We should go and have a word with the rest of the family.'

'And warn them not to touch the honey.'

'Of course, it might have nothing to do with Huntings.'

'And a squadron of pigs have been booked to do an air display at the Royal Regatta next year. Tell you what, we'll get round to see the family and I'll tell Rachel and Paul to pay Mrs Norbert a visit.'

Wesley picked up his notebook from his desk, wishing that Rachel was going with him to see the Pickerings ... she had a gift for dealing with people in distress. Gerry Heffernan's heart was in the right place, but that was about all you could say for him.

The Pickering family lived in a large detached house near St Peters church. It was a substantial property, built in the 1920s to ape the social pretensions of its Victorian neighbours. There was a gleaming white people carrier parked on the drive. Wesley rang the doorbell and waited.

It was a while before the front door opened to reveal a slim woman with well-cut blonde hair. The lines around her eyes and mouth suggested that she had probably reached her half-century, but she had a youthful manner which belied her age. Her blue eyes widened in alarm when they introduced themselves, and she stood aside to let them in. She introduced herself as Mrs Pickering's elder sister, Georgie Bettis. Mr Pickering – Joe – was at the hospital and she had volunteered to step into the breach to look after

213

the Pickerings' younger child, a boy, who had been unaffected by the mysterious bout of illness, which the doctors suspected was some sort of food poisoning.

Once again Wesley found himself wishing that Rachel were there. But he had to make do with Heffernan, who was standing staring at the victim's sister like a love-struck schoolboy. Wesley suggested that they sit down. Someone had to.

Georgie Bettis didn't offer tea; her mind was on other things. She looked at Wesley with puzzled expectancy, and he made the snap judgement that she was an intelligent woman who would appreciate it if he came straight to the point.

'This might seem a strange question, Ms Bettis, but do you know if your sister bought any honey from Huntings supermarket recently?' He leaned forward, expecting Georgie Bettis to say that she had no idea.

But it seemed that Georgie was more observant than he'd dared to hope. 'There's a new jar in the cupboard. I was looking for something to give to Jonathon, my nephew, but I know he hates honey.'

'So Jonathon wouldn't have eaten it?'

She shook her head. 'And neither would Joe, my brother-in-law . . . he can't stand it either. I always say it's men who are the fussy ones.' She attempted a smile.

Wesley was about to say that their fussiness might have saved their lives, but he thought better of it. 'If I could have a look at this honey . . . '

'Why the honey? Surely it could be anything. And what are two senior detectives doing looking for jars of honey? Surely if it's food poisoning it's a public health matter.'

'I'm afraid there might be more to it than that, Ms Bettis . . . '

'Georgie, please.'

'Georgie . . . er, we think that someone may have contaminated products at Huntings supermarket deliberately. A warning went out on television yesterday.'

Georgie Bettis's hand had gone up to her mouth. 'That's

awful. Poor Aaron. Do you know who's doing it ... or why?'

Wesley shook his head.

'That's what we're trying to find out, love,' said Heffernan. 'Have you heard how your sister and the kiddie are doing?'

'Joe rang half an hour ago. He said it's still touch and go.' Her eyes began to fill with tears and she took a tissue from her pocket.

Wesley sat forward. 'You said "poor Aaron". Did you mean Aaron Hunting?'

'Yes. I was his PA before I left to have my eldest.' She gave a weak smile. 'I liked him. He was a good boss.'

'We think that whoever's behind this might be trying to shut his business down. Might anyone have a grudge against him?'

Georgie shook her head. 'I suppose there are always those who resent successful people, just because they are successful. But Aaron was always fair to his staff, treated them well. Even when he had difficulties in his private life he was always courteous and considerate to me. Is this the first time anybody's been poisoned?'

'There was a lady in Morbay last week. That's why we put out warnings this time,' said Wesley, fearing that the police were about to be blamed for keeping the whole thing quiet.

'And what happened to her?'

Wesley swallowed hard and was about to answer when Heffernan got in first. 'She died, love.'

'But she was elderly ... very weak,' Wesley added quickly. 'I'm sure your sister and niece will pull through. If we could look for this jar of honey ... '

'Of course, help yourselves.'

Wesley approached the kitchen apprehensively, fearing that the honey wouldn't have been bought at Huntings and they would have to rethink everything. But he had no need to worry. As he opened the first cupboard in the newly fitted Shaker-style kitchen, there was the small jar sitting at the front ... organic lavender honey, produce of France. The same brand. They had found one of the missing two jars.

But one was still out there, waiting to strike like a hidden time bomb.

'Where are we going?' Gerry Heffernan scratched his belly where his shirt buttons had strained apart, and looked confused.

'I just thought that as we're in Morbay we might go and have another word with Ms Patience Reid. I want to see if she knows anything about Sunita.'

'If she worked at Huntings she's bound to know her.'

'Yes ... and that's why she might be able to tell us why Sunita was visiting the squat. If she saw her there she'll probably have recognised her and asked a few questions of her fellow squatters ... like what was the deputy manager of Huntings doing in a place like that?'

Heffernan didn't look convinced. 'I suppose it's worth a try.'

Outside the car window the leafy avenues of St Peters had long since given way to littered pavements and Victorian houses divided into flats. The polished brass bell-pushes of prosperous suburbia had been replaced by arrays of grubby plastic doorbells with the faded names of each flat's occupants displayed in cracked Perspex compartments underneath.

Patience Reid's abode didn't even boast these luxuries. The squat was stuck firmly at the foot of Morbay's housing ladder ... not even on the first rung.

When they got there Wesley hammered hard on the front door from the simple need to make himself heard. As he drew his hand away a flake of faded paint fluttered to the ground. Apart from the noise of passing traffic and the distant throb of a pneumatic drill in a neighbouring street, the only other sign of life was the mournful cry of a fat seagull wheeling overhead, calling to a colleague perched on a nearby chimney pot. Wesley waited, then knocked again. This time his persistence paid off and he heard the sound of footsteps within the house. A few seconds later the front door creaked open and a thin woman stood before them. She had mousey hair arranged in two lank pigtails and she stared at Wesley for a moment before speaking. 'What do you want?' She was well spoken, too well spoken for a place like that. When Wesley looked at her face closely he was surprised to see that she wasn't in the first flush of youth. She was thirty if she was a day ... or perhaps she'd just led the kind of life which made her look that way.

'Is Patience Reid at home?'

The woman looked at him suspiciously. 'Who wants to know?'

Wesley hesitated before producing his warrant card, wondering whether it might be more politic to spin some yarn about him being an old friend of the family and Gerry being her long-lost uncle. But in the end he decided on the honest approach. 'Police,' he said. 'Nothing to worry about. Just routine.'

It was obvious that his explanation was greeted with scepticism but, after a few moment's consideration, the woman stepped aside. 'It's not her day at the project today so she should be in.'

Wesley gave her what he considered to be his most charming smile. 'Thank you, Ms, er ... '

The woman didn't fall for it. She wasn't giving her name to the police. She watched from the foot of the uncarpeted stairs as Wesley and Heffernan clattered up to the top floor.

Wesley knocked on Patience Reid's door, a loud, businesslike knock. There was no answer but he could hear a shuffling beyond the door so he knocked again.

After a while the door opened half an inch and a voice asked, 'Who is it?'

When Wesley announced himself the door closed again

and he could hear the frantic whisper of voices on the other side.

'Come on, Wes, we've waited long enough. Tell her to get on with it and let us in.'

But Wesley took no notice. Patience would open up in her own time and he wasn't prepared to antagonise her without good reason.

After another minute his wait-and-see approach paid off. The door opened to reveal Patience Reid, dressed in faded denim. Her hair, still arranged in peroxide Medusa plaits, looked more unkempt than when he had last set eyes on her and the dark rings beneath her eyes stood out against the pallor of her face. She didn't look well. She blew her nose on a crumpled tissue as she stood aside to let them in.

Wesley stepped into the room, Heffernan following behind him. 'We'd like to ask you a few more questions, Ms Reid. Just routine . . . nothing to worry about. Are you acquainted with a Sunita Choudray at all? She's deputy manager at Huntings' Morbay branch.'

He noticed a flash of alarm in the young woman's eyes when Sunita's name was mentioned. 'Why?' she whispered. 'What do you want to know for?'

At that moment the door to what Wesley assumed was a bedroom opened. Patience swung round and Gerry Heffernan stood open mouthed as Sunita Choudray herself stood framed in the doorway.

'Are you looking for me?' Her voice was calm. She walked across to Patience and put a protective hand on her shoulder.

'You two know each other, then?' was all Heffernan could think of to say.

The two women exchanged glances.

Wesley stepped forward. 'We've been trying to get in touch with Ms Choudray and her family said she wasn't well and was staying with a friend.'

Sunita took a deep breath and squeezed Pat's shoulder. 'There are some things I'd prefer my parents not to know,

Inspector. And my relationship with Pat is one of them.'

'So are you two . . . ?' Heffernan blurted out.

Wesley interrupted him. 'I don't know whether you're aware that more poisoned goods have been planted at Huntings, Ms Choudray. We think they've been contaminated with botulism, which indicates that the person responsible has some knowledge of how to grow bacteria.' He hesitated and glanced at Heffernan, who was staring at the two women. 'I believe you studied microbiology at university, Ms Choudray.'

Sunita took her hand from Pat's shoulder and began to play with her hair. She looked uneasy. 'I think I see what you're getting at. And yes, I would be quite capable of culturing botulism. All I'd need is some gelatine or milk, a Petri dish and an oven. But why should I try and ruin the company I work for? I'm doing well at Huntings . . . I even hope to get my own branch in a year or so. Whoever you're looking for is sick . . . they're quite prepared to let people die for their own twisted reasons. I don't see how you can think this has anything to do with me.'

Wesley was lost for words. She had a point. 'So you and Ms Reid . . . '

Sunita stuck her chin out defiantly. 'Are lovers. We met at Huntings and . . . '

'Why did you ring in sick?'

'It was Pat who was sick. She's recovering from a stomach bug.' She took hold of the other woman's hand. 'I've been looking after her.' She hesitated, then addressed Wesley as though she assumed he'd be the more sympathetic of the two. 'There's just one thing I want you to promise me.'

'What's that?'

'That my parents and my brother won't find out about Pat and me. They're from a different culture and they see things in a different way. They wouldn't understand.'

Wesley nodded. He understood only too well. 'You have my word that they won't find out from us.'

Sunita gave a nervous smile. 'Thank you. You said more things have been planted at Huntings ... Has anybody ...'

'A mother and daughter have been taken to hospital. They're in Intensive Care.'

Sunita's hand went to her mouth and Pat put a protective arm around her shoulder.

'Is there anyone you can think of at Huntings who might be doing this? Whoever it is obviously knows how to create the bacteria and they have inside knowledge of the store. Please think hard.'

But Sunita shook her head. 'Nobody. I'm sorry.'

'What about Loveday?' It was Pat who spoke.

Sunita looked at her questioningly. 'What about her? She doesn't work for Huntings.'

'She does early morning cleaning there ... she told me. She works for an agency. She does a shift in the hospital as well.'

'Who's Loveday?' Heffernan asked, impatient.

'She lives here ... in the ground-floor flat. Wasn't it her who let you in?'

Wesley frowned, trying to remember the young woman who had opened the door. 'And does she have any grudge against Huntings?'

Pat shrugged her narrow shoulders. 'She's a bit strange, so who knows? But she was at Morbay University at one time. She told me she studied biochemistry but she dropped out 'cause of personal problems.'

Heffernan was already making for the door when Pat called out to him. 'I wouldn't just go barging in there if I were you. I'd be careful ... she's had a lot of problems. A few years back she tried to kill herself.'

Heffernan stopped in his tracks and turned to Wesley. 'I'll leave this one to you, then, Inspector.'

Wesley went out of the room first, wondering why he always got landed with the awkward ones.

*

Rachel Tracey pressed the doorbell. Mrs Norbert, widow

of the late DCI Norbert, lived in a cream-painted detached house above Tradmouth overlooking the river and the town. Above Town, the area was called, and the name was very apt. Above Town afforded the spectacular view of Tradmouth that was peddled to tourists on picture postcards each summer. From her living-room window Mrs Norbert could gaze down like some Greek goddess on Mount Olympus, and survey the panorama of the town's rooftops tumbling down to the River Trad's grey waters, where tiny boats scurried about like pond insects.

When there was no answer, Rachel pressed the bell again.

'Maybe she isn't in,' Paul Johnson suggested hopefully. There were easier ways of spending a morning than suggesting to the respectable widow of a senior police officer that her son might be some sort of crook. Even paperwork was preferable.

But Paul's hopes of a swift return to the station were in vain. The door opened a fraction and the red-haired woman inside poked her head round it and looked them up and down with guarded hostility, as though she suspected they were double-glazing salesmen or Jehovah's witnesses.

The two officers introduced themselves and held their warrant cards up for inspection. Neither recognised Mrs Norbert. They were both too young to have known her husband, and even if they'd been older, would have been too lowly in rank to encounter a DCI's wife at any social function.

As Rachel followed Mrs Norbert into the living room, she concluded that she must have been a lot younger than her husband. She didn't look a day over fifty, even though her hair colour probably owed more to the skills of her hairdresser than to the wonders of nature. Paul found himself thinking that she must have been a stunner in her youth.

She invited them to sit down and asked them whether they'd like tea. She didn't smile ... but neither did she show any hint of annoyance that they were there. Her face remained a mask of neutrality.

'We're very sorry to bother you, Mrs Norbert,' Rachel began, assuming a sympathetic expression. 'You have a son called Philip, I believe.'

'Yes.' Her response was wary, guarded; hardly the reaction, Rachel thought, of a proud parent.

'And he attended St Peters School in Morbay?'

'That's right.'

'The thing is, we'd like a word with him. Nothing to worry about ... just something he may have witnessed a few years ago.' She hated herself for lying but it was the first thing that came into her head. Paul cleared his throat and she glanced at him. The expression on his face said 'be careful'.

'I wonder if you could give us his current address, Mrs Norbert,' Paul said with a smile.

Mrs Norbert hesitated for a split second, then she seemed to realise that she had no option. 'Of course. I'll write it down for you.' She went across to a polished oak bureau, opened a drawer and took out a sheet of expensive writing paper. She wrote something down, folded the paper and handed it to Paul.

It was then Rachel noticed that her hand was shaking.

Loveday had tried to kill herself. This fact was at the forefront of Wesley's mind as he knocked on her door. The girl was emotionally fragile, and if he said or did the wrong thing he might trigger some reaction that would lead to disaster and an internal inquiry. As he waited there in the cold bare hallway he shuffled his feet on the filthy lino, avoiding Gerry Heffernan's eyes.

The woman who had let them into the house opened the door and immediately Wesley's eyes were drawn to her wrists, to the thin lines of scar tissue, pale and shiny on the flesh. What Pat had told them about a suicide attempt was true. When he asked whether he could come into the flat she shook her head, and she was about to close the door when Heffernan stepped forward.

'We only want a chat, love . . . and a cup of tea'd be nice.'

Loveday seemed too stunned to make any protest as he barged past her. Sometimes Wesley didn't know how Heffernan got away with it. But he usually did.

Wesley followed and shut the door behind him, looking around. The room was large and its high ceiling boasted an elaborate ceiling rose, its delicate plasterwork obscured and clogged by layers of paint and festooned with cobwebs. The once garish carpet was faded and threadbare, and what furniture there was was a hotchpotch of other people's tattered rejects. It was a bed-sitter, with an unmade bed near the window opposite a shabby green vinyl sofa. A thin curtain of stylised purple flowers, the height of chic in the 1970s, hung across one corner of the room, probably screening off some kind of kitchen or bathroom area. It was no palace but at least it was fairly tidy.

The woman had slumped down on the bed, chewing her nails and watching Heffernan out of the corner of her eye. Wesley squatted down at her level a few feet away.

'Loveday, isn't it?'

She stared at him for a few seconds then nodded.

'Loveday what?'

She hesitated before whispering, 'Wilkins.'

'Pat upstairs told me you went to Morbay University.'

No answer.

'She says you clean at Huntings in the early mornings. Is that right?'

Loveday began to chew her nails again, more fervently this time.

When Wesley heard a noise he glanced round. Gerry Heffernan had just drawn aside the flowered curtain to reveal a cheap chipboard sink unit, a mismatched cupboard and an ancient fridge. A small, grease-stained Baby Belling oven, its dirty white enamel chipped to reveal the black metal beneath, stood on top of the cupboard.

223

Loveday sprang up suddenly, with a cry of distress, like a wounded animal. She flew at Wesley and he was unprepared for her strength as she sent him toppling to the floor, clawing at his face like a cat. He tried to push her off, to grab her hands, but she was too quick for him. She was screaming something that sounded like 'you bastard' and scratching at his face when suddenly her shouts turned into a piercing scream as Heffernan yanked her off by the pigtails.

As soon as she twisted round to turn her attentions to the chief inspector Wesley managed to scramble to his feet and retrieve the handcuffs from his back pocket. When he grabbed Loveday from behind and snapped them on her narrow wrists, Heffernan was able to break free, breathless and winded.

'You could make a fortune in the ring, love. Ever thought of challenging Mike Tyson?'

Loveday, now at bay, stared at Heffernan as though she were about to spit in his face, but Wesley pushed her gently back down onto the bed before she had a chance. They'd be prepared from now on.

Heffernan drew the curtain back farther and stepped inside the excuse for a kitchen. 'Now what is it you don't want us to see, love? I think I can guess but I hope I'm wrong.'

He opened the fridge and bent to look inside. After donning a pair of plastic gloves, he took something out and put it on the worktop. Then he opened the cupboard. 'There're six jars of Huntings own-brand marmalade here. On special offer, was it? And by the way, what's this I found in your fridge?'

He carried a small, flat glass dish covered with a glass plate over to Wesley very carefully and thrust it under his nose. 'If I remember rightly from my school chemistry lessons it's a Petri dish. And I think our lab might be interested in what's in it.'

The two men looked at Loveday, who was slumped on the sofa with a sullen, defiant expression on her face, her lips moving as though in quiet prayer. Heffernan whispered something to Wesley, who began to search the room, opening drawers and rooting through the large wardrobe standing near the door. After a few minutes he found what he was looking for: several copies of the local paper with letters cut out, paper, glue and envelopes. They had found the source of the botulism and the source of the anonymous letters to Huntings.

Wesley held up the plastic bag containing the newspapers for the girl to see. 'A woman has died and another two people are in Intensive Care ... one of them's a kid. They've never harmed you. Why did you do it?' He knew that his question probably wouldn't be answered ... even with the help of prison psychiatrists they often failed to get to the bottom of why people did wicked things. But there was no harm in asking.

Loveday pressed her lips together and said nothing.

'As far as I can see you've never worked for Huntings, apart from this contract cleaning, so what have you got against them?'

Even when she was taken to the police station and the forensic team were searching her flat, Loveday still said nothing.

As soon as Loveday had been seen by a doctor she was put in a cell and the custody sergeant was given instructions to keep a close eye on her. The last thing they wanted was any slip-up, any accusations of neglect or heavy-handedness. They would allow her to rest and question her later, something Wesley wasn't looking forward to.

When he and Heffernan returned to the CID office they found Rachel and Paul Johnson waiting for them, looking rather pleased with themselves. They'd got Philip Norbert's address from his mother and wondered whether the DCI wanted them to go to Exeter and follow it up. Wesley was surprised when Heffernan said that he wanted to see Norbert himself, and he noted the momentary flash of disappointment on Rachel's face. She had been looking forward to a few hours out of the office.

Wesley followed the boss to his lair. 'So we're going to see this Philip Norbert?'

'I thought it might be best ... after all, his dad was one of us.'

'Rachel and Paul could have handled it.'

'I'm sure they could but I'd like to see him for myself ... see his reaction when we ask him about the Reverend Shipborne.'

'You think he might be our man?'

'Hobson's appeal's likely to go ahead, and if he didn't kill him, someone did. And if Hobson's story about seeing Norbert outside the vicarage is true ... '

'It might explain why DCI Norbert chose to ignore that line of enquiry. If he knew that his son was involved and he was trying to protect him ... '

'My thoughts exactly.'

'If the whole inquiry was tainted by corruption it's not going to look good for us if it all comes out at Hobson's appeal.'

'We weren't involved, Wes. You were still in your school blazer playing with your Lego and I was a lowly sergeant at Morbay. Nothing to do with us.'

'But what about Stan Jenkins?'

'Not his fault either, Wes. He was only obeying orders.'

'Now where have I heard that one before?'

There was a tentative knock on the office door before Steve Carstairs burst in, as though he was about to impart some exciting news. 'Sir, I've just had a report from Forensic. That St Christopher they found near Helen Wilmer's body ... it's silver and it has an American maker's mark on it ... and they found faint lettering scratched on the back: they think it says "to Billy love from Louise".'

Heffernan scratched his head. 'Do a check on the where-abouts of any Billys living in Belsham at the time of

Helen's disappearance.' Steve stared at him. 'Go on, what are you waiting for? Christmas?'

As Steve scurried back to his desk Wesley looked at his watch and made for the door. If they were going to drive up to Exeter they'd better not waste any more time. 'Should we ring Norbert to tell him we're coming?'

'No way. I want the advantage of surprise.' Heffernan grinned wickedly and followed Wesley out of the office.

An hour later they arrived at the address Mrs Norbert had given ... a new waterside apartment, all brick, round windows and wrought-iron balconies. Wesley brought the car to a halt in a space marked 'Visitors' and surveyed the scene. Things had moved on since he was a student in the city. The quaysides had moved upmarket and now boasted twee bridges, loft living and the obligatory crop of restaurants and trendy wine bars. The cars parked there were shiny and new and a high proportion wore the distinctive BMW badge on their radiator grilles. Phil Norbert had done well for himself.

Norbert's apartment had a telephone entry system which might have robbed them of the element of surprise if Heffernan hadn't thought quickly. He cleared his throat, announced that he had a delivery for Norbert and asked whether he should bring it up. Wesley stood back a little, dissociating himself from the deception.

As soon as the door opened automatically the chief inspector barged his way into the building and began to climb the stairs. Wesley followed, overtaking him on the landing to be first at Norbert's door in case tact and diplomacy were needed. He knocked and the door was opened almost at once.

'Yes?' Philip Norbert stood there, looking confused. He sniffed loudly. 'Where is it, then?'

Wesley held up his warrant card and introduced himself. 'May we come in, sir?' He looked at the man framed in the doorway. He had longish dark hair and an expensive-looking black leather jacket not dissimilar to the one Steve

Carstairs habitually wore. He had a wide mouth and a long nose which he kept touching from time to time, perhaps an unconscious nervous reaction. Wesley thought he could see fear in the man's eyes ... but it might have been his imagination.

Norbert looked as though he was thinking on his feet. 'I'm expecting something ... a delivery ... it's not convenient.'

'We've come all the way from Tradmouth to see you, Mr Norbert. We won't get in the way if your delivery comes.' Heffernan gave him an innocent smile as he stepped over the threshold. 'Cup of tea'd be nice. I'm spitting feathers.'

'I haven't got any tea.' Norbert began to follow Heffernan into the flat. 'Look, what do you want?'

Wesley watched him. Twitchy was the best word he could think of to describe the way he was behaving. Twitchy and frightened. And when they reached the main room he found out why. Lying on a sleek beech coffee table in the centre of the room was a small mirror. On the mirror was a line of white powder and beside it was a crisp twenty-pound note.

'Expensive habit,' Wesley said, strolling around the room. They had Norbert at a disadvantage now, and somehow this made him feel more comfortable about the corners they had cut. He stopped by the huge window and looked out on the scene below ... water and bars. Like cocaine, chic didn't come cheap. 'What do you do for a living, Mr Norbert? It must pay well, whatever it is. Or do you earn a bit extra by dealing in that stuff you're shoving up your nose?'

There was no answer.

Heffernan sat down heavily on a black leather sofa. 'I think you'd have been a big disappointment to your dad if he'd lived. See much of your mum, do you?'

Norbert sniffed. 'Not much.'

'Remember that time you broke into the vicarage in Belsham and pinched some silver? Your dad covered up for you, didn't he, and someone else got put away for murder. You might be interested to hear that the man your dad put away was innocent ... his case is going to appeal. That means we're looking at the Shipborne case all over again, sunshine. Did your dad plant the silver in Chris Hobson's flat to frame him? Is that what happened? Is that why Hobson's served twelve years for a crime he didn't commit?'

'I don't know what you're talking about.'

'We have a witness who's quite prepared to swear you were at Belsham vicarage that night.'

'Whoever it is, they're lying.'

'Get your coat,' said Wesley quietly. 'You're coming with us to Tradmouth.'

Norbert kicked at the sheepskin rug on the floor. 'And what if I don't want to?'

Wesley took a deep breath. 'Philip Norbert, I'm arresting you for being in possession of a class A drug. You do not have to say anything. But it may harm your defence if you do not ...'

Norbert swung round. 'Okay. Okay. I get the message.'

On the way to Tradmouth, Philip Norbert didn't say another word.

'We'll let him cool his heels, contemplate his wrongdoings,' Heffernan said when they'd handed Norbert over to the custody sergeant. They didn't make any mention of who his father had been. It was probably best that nobody knew. They didn't inform his mother either: the man was almost thirty, well beyond the need for parental protection. And besides, it would hurt Mrs Norbert to discover that her son was no saint ... although she probably knew already.

Surprisingly, Norbert had no police record, even for dealing or possession of drugs. He had been either clever or lucky. And of course, in the early part of his criminal career, he may have had some help in high places. As Wesley prepared to settle down to some paperwork while he awaited developments, a restless Gerry Heffernan ambled over to his desk.

'How's Loveday Wilkins? Is she ready to be interviewed yet?'

'The doctor says she's a very disturbed woman. He'll tell us when he thinks it's okay to talk to her.'

Heffernan rolled his eyes to heaven. 'Great. And Philip Norbert? Think he could have killed the vicar?'

'I reckon his dad thought so and that's why he suppressed so much evidence.'

'Maybe Philip confessed to his dad.'

'And Norbert put away an innocent man to keep his son out of trouble?'

Heffernan sighed. 'We've both got kids, Wes. We both know how far you'd go to protect them.'

'But that?'

Heffernan shrugged his shoulders and turned to go back to his office. Then he stopped as though he'd remembered something. 'Do you know, every time I read through the file on Shipborne's murder, I keep coming across Barry Castello's name. Before we talk to Philip Norbert, I'd like a word with Barry ... I want to see if Philip had any connection with Shipborne.'

'Surely Philip wasn't one of Castello's bad lads ... he went to St Peters.'

'But who knows where he went after he left. He dropped out before his A-levels, remember. Come on. Let's take the road to Damascus.'

Wesley looked at his paperwork, then at Heffernan. Damascus Farm won.

'Should we be doing this, Neil?' Pam Peterson tried the church door and found that this time it wasn't locked.

'I want to take photographs of the tower room ... show them to some experts.'

'How are you feeling?'

Neil began to fiddle with the digital camera he'd taken

230

from his pocket. 'Much better since Matt told me that Huntings have had to give us longer to complete the excavation because of the skeletons.' He grinned. 'Nice to puncture the tyres on the wheels of commerce from time to time.'

Neil was walking better now and complained about the pain in his ribs only when Pam suggested that he do some household chore. He had even spent the morning at the dig, supervising and giving his opinion on the finds. And there seemed to be plenty more skeletons to dig up. The archaeologists were unearthing two or three a day and placing the bones in boxes ready to be taken away for examination.

Pam had driven out to Belsham to pick Neil up but he had been in no hurry to leave and, as Michael was safe at home with her mother, neither was Pam. So when Neil suggested another visit to the church to take some photographs, she agreed. Although a visit to the pub over the road would have been preferable.

She pushed open the church door and when she stepped inside she was surprised to see a flickering light in the gloom. As her eyes adjusted she could see that a candle was burning in front of a side altar at the end of the far aisle. To her surprise she saw a man kneeling in the pew nearest to the candle, his head bent in prayer. Instinctively she stopped and Neil almost cannoned into her.

She put her finger to her lips. 'There's someone there,' she whispered. 'I think they're praying.'

Neil, unimpressed by displays of reverence, began to walk down the aisle. Pam tried to call him back in a loud whisper but Neil took no notice, so she followed him, taking hold of his arm.

When they were level with the man in the pew, Neil stopped and stared. Pam pulled at his arm. 'Come on, Neil, let's take a look at the tower.'

She had no wish to disturb the man's prayers, especially not when she saw that he was crying.

As they opened the tower-room door, surprised to find it

unlocked, William Verlan looked up at the flickering candle flame, its small light misty through a veil of tears.

It had been raining that morning but now the sun was out, shining on the rolling landscape of Dartmoor, and the rain-drops caught on the trees, ground and hedgerows sparkled like diamonds on a bed of russet, green and gold. The trees stood out, half naked, against the scurrying clouds. Soon all their leaves would be gone and they would be mere skel-etons against the vast, empty sky.

'Some scenery,' Wesley said softly.

'Bleak in winter,' was Heffernan's verdict. 'Are we on the right road?'

'Don't you trust my navigation?'

Heffernan didn't answer. He was looking out of the window, taking in the view.

Ten minutes later they pulled up outside a low, rambling farmhouse. The grey stone building blended perfectly with the landscape and looked as if it had always been there, like a pile of ancient rocks left behind by some prehistoric glacier. The name Damascus Farm was written in neat white letters above the stone porch, topped by the outline of a fish. The area in front of the house reminded Wesley of Rachel's home, Little Barton Farm: the Dutch barns packed with hay bales; the cobbled farmyard; the tractors kept under cover against the harshness of the Dartmoor winter. This was a working farm. And yet there was some-thing different about it, something Wesley couldn't put his finger on.

As they got out of the car a stocky youth with a shaved head and tattooed neck wearing green overalls and match-ing wellington boots emerged from behind the barn carrying a couple of galvanised steel buckets. The youth glanced at the newcomers but chose to ignore them and hurried off.

The two policemen walked up to the front porch and rang the doorbell. After a few moments the door was opened by a smiling man who greeted them warmly and invited them to step inside. Gerry Heffernan recognised Barry Castello from his old mug shots, even though time had ploughed furrows in his flesh and grizzled his long, wiry hair. But he hadn't been prepared for the smile ... or the openness in Castello's brown eyes. If this man still hid secrets, he hid them well.

'Welcome to Damascus Farm,' Castello said as he led them into the front parlour, a shabby room with an eclectic variety of furniture that looked like donated cast-offs. A log fire burning in the old stone hearth gave the room a homely feel.

Wesley sank down in a sagging flowered sofa while Heffernan chose a shapeless armchair, upholstered in threadbare orange sackcloth. Castello stood with his back to the fire.

'Now how can I help you, gentlemen?' he began. His voice was deep with the telltale trace of a London accent. He smiled encouragingly, as though he would welcome any questions they cared to ask ... however awkward.

Wesley spoke first. 'We understand you were a friend of the Reverend John Shipborne.'

Castello's smile disappeared and was replaced by an expression of sincere sadness. 'That's right. John was a remarkable man ... a terrible loss. If it hadn't been for him, I'd be inside now wasting my life. It was John who gave me the idea to start this place ... to give hope to youngsters who found themselves in the situation I'd been in.'

'And does it work?' Wesley asked, genuinely interested.

'Oh yes. Some of our lads reoffend, of course. Can't win 'em all,' he said with a self-deprecating smile. 'But we have a remarkably high success rate. We get them to think, you see. We make them believe in themselves and their abilities and show them there's a better way. We also tell them it might not be easy once they get out into the big wide world again with all its temptations ... but they know

233

we're always here for them if they start to backslide. Sometimes we're the first people who've actually cared what they do. Their parents don't ... and to social services and their probation officers, however well intentioned, they're just a reference number ... one in a long line. But we take an interest in them as individuals.'

Heffernan grunted. Somehow it sounded too pat ... but perhaps he had been involved with criminals for so long that he had become cynical. Wesley listened and said nothing.

'So tell us about the Reverend Shipborne,' Heffernan said. 'What kind of man was he ... apart from being a saint, that is?'

If Castello had noticed any sarcasm in Heffernan's voice, he chose to ignore it. 'John would have been the last to claim he was any sort of saint. He was only too aware of his own failures.'

'And what were they?' Wesley said quickly.

Castello turned to him and smiled again. The smiles were starting to get on Heffernan's nerves. 'I really don't know. If he had any failings, I wasn't aware of them. To me he was a sincere and humble man ... a man who'd put God before his own career.'

'Isn't that what vicars are meant to do?'

'I'm talking about the career he had before he joined the Church.'

Wesley sat forward on the floral sofa. 'Which was?'

Another smile from Castello. 'I think he was some sort of scientist ... but he never talked about it. He told me once that it was something he'd rather forget, which was strange, I suppose. I think he was quite high up ... well paid ... because I remember him saying he'd taken a huge pay cut to go into the Church. I'm sorry, but that's all I can tell you.'

'I've read the files so I know you had an alibi for the time of his death ... but did any of the boys in your care know him?'

234

'They saw him when he visited, chatted to him, that sort of thing. But I don't think any of them knew him particularly well. Why?'

'I believe Dermot O'Donovan was here at one time.'

'Yes. He was one of our success stories. I believe he runs his own building firm now.' A smug smile played around his lips: he almost looked like a proud parent, boasting of an offspring's academic achievements.

'Have you ever come across a boy called Philip Norbert?' As far as they knew Norbert had no police record, but it was still worth asking the question.

The smug smile disappeared and Castello shook his head. 'The name doesn't ring any bells. I can look it up in our files if you like.'

Wesley said that he'd be grateful and Castello strolled out of the room. There was no urgency in his movements. Damascus Farm was his territory and things moved at the pace Barry Castello dictated.

'Well? Any ideas?' Heffernan said in a low voice when he had gone.

Wesley gathered his thoughts before speaking. 'He makes Shipborne sound like some sort of saint.' He smiled sadly. 'But I suppose the concept of goodness is a difficult one for us policemen to grasp. We're used to dealing with humanity at the other end of the spectrum.'

'So?'

'I can't help wondering if everything is as it appears to be here. Were Shipborne and Castello using this place as a cover for something . . . for abusing the boys? Did Shipborne have some nasty skeletons in his closet? Did someone take their revenge?'

'If that was the case, surely Castello would have been targeted as well.'

'Perhaps Shipborne was using Castello to supply the boys and Castello knew nothing about it.' He shook his head. 'Or perhaps I'm letting my imagination run away with me . . . seeing the bad in everyone.'

235

'The job gets you like that sometimes.' Heffernan sighed. 'But it might be worth talking to some of these lads of Castello's alone ... find out if he's really as squeaky clean as he makes out. We can see how Castello reacts when we make the request.'

But when Castello returned with the news that the name Philip Norbert didn't appear on his files, he said that he would be glad to let them talk to the boys alone. He withdrew tactfully and they ended up seeing seven boys in all – all of them shifty and inadequate rather than plain wicked – who all said that they were happy enough at Damascus Farm, although Wesley suspected that a couple just regarded the place as a cushy alternative to the young offenders' institution and would probably return to their old ways in due course. He'd be looking out for them.

At the end of the interviews, Wesley found himself feeling very uneasy about the swiftness with which he'd been ready to suspect Castello of sexual impropriety with the boys in his care. He said as much to his companion. 'Have I just got a dirty mind, Gerry?'

'Nah. It's because there's so much about it in the news these days ... children's homes, naughty Catholic priests. When a couple of blokes start taking young lads to an isolated farmhouse, even if it's all quite innocent, it's only natural that you start to suspect the worst.'

'So you don't think ... ?'

'My gut reaction from talking to the lads tells me that it's all above board. Well, Castello is anyway. Although there's always a chance that Shipborne ... '

'We'll bear it in mind, then,' said Wesley. 'Maybe we should have another word with that Dermot O'Donovan and see what he's got to say about this place.'

'Maybe we're just starting to read too much into all this. Even if Hobson didn't kill Shipborne, it doesn't mean that the motive wasn't robbery.'

But their conversation was interrupted by Castello, who, knowing the interviews were over, entered the room bearing two mugs of steaming tea ... a temptation Heffernan could hardly resist. Castello settled down in an armchair next to the fire and put his feet up on a stool. It was hard to believe a former armed robber could look so relaxed in the company of two policemen.

'You can't really think that anyone here had anything to do with John's death, surely? I have heard that Hobson's case might be going to appeal, by the way.'

'And what do you think about that?'

'Pleased. I never thought Chris Hobson was capable of killing anyone, let alone John.'

'You knew Hobson?'

'Not personally. But I know the type well. Petty criminal, shies away from any serious violence. He would have run if John had caught him ... his instinct would have been flight rather then fight, and I know John wouldn't have done anything to provoke him. Hobson would never have killed, especially in a frenzied attack like that. Although God only knows what all this time in prison will have done to him,' he added as an afterthought.

'And you always got on well with the Reverend Shipborne?' Wesley asked. 'Never had any disagreements?'

'No. Never.'

'Did he seem worried about anything before his death? Had anything out of the ordinary happened?' Wesley was clutching at straws, but while he had Shipborne's old friend with him it was worth asking any questions that came into his head.

Castello frowned. 'Now you come to mention it, he wasn't his usual self in the weeks leading up to his death. He was helping a student from Morbay University with some research into local history, and I got the impression that he was uneasy about it for some reason ... although I can't think why. And he seemed a bit upset about a row he'd had with the captain of his bell-ringers – a man called Stephen Wilmer.'

'Helen Wilmer's father? The girl who went missing a

week after Shipborne died?

'That's right. John had locked up the church tower because it was found to be unsafe but Wilmer said it was unnecessary and started making a fuss ... even organised a petition. But that could hardly have had anything to do with his death.'

'Probably not,' said Wesley, looking at Heffernan.

They both sensed that they would get no more out of Castello ... if there was anything to get. They'd given Damascus Farm a cursory examination and had found nothing amiss. Whether this was because there was nothing to find or because they were looking in the wrong places, Wesley didn't know. But he was keeping an open mind.

'Was that a waste of time?' he asked as he drove south across the moor in the direction of Tradmouth.

'Who knows, Wes. Maybe Shipborne was done in by an irate bell-ringer ... it's worth following up. And I'd like to know more about Shipborne's background. What happened to his personal effects?'

'I'm sure we can find out. Maybe we should pay Stan Jenkins another visit.'

'What about Helen Wilmer ... is she connected with all this?'

Wesley didn't answer. He had no idea what had gone on in Belsham all those years ago. And he felt he was no nearer finding out the truth than when he had first heard Chris Hobson's name.

Looking at the Reverend John Shipborne's last will and testament, copied at the time of the investigation by some zealous young detective constable, Wesley found that he had made a variety of bequests. Most of his personal effects had gone to his niece, Anne Talbot, a doctor who lived up in Dundee. His books had been left to Morbay University. Mrs O'Donovan, his cleaner, had inherited a thousand pounds and various charities had benefited from his posthumous generosity. Shipborne, in spite of his modest lifestyle, had left over half a million pounds and the bulk of his estate had gone to Damascus Farm.

Wesley still found it hard to forget that Castello had started life as an armed robber. And the old clichéd saying about a leopard not being able to change its spots sprang unbidden into his mind.

Trish Walton had been asked to track down any evidence that had been stored in connection with the case, and it wasn't long before she struck lucky. There were two boxes of evidence stored in the cellars beneath the station. She looked down at her cream-coloured trousers and sighed, fearing that it would be up to her to retrieve the boxes and knowing that the station cellar wasn't the cleanest of places. She had smiled at Steve Carstairs nicely in the hope he'd be a gentleman and volunteer, but he made an excuse and left the office. So much for chivalry.

Half an hour later Trish, helped by a couple of uniformed constables from downstairs, deposited the two large dusty cardboard boxes beside Wesley's desk.

Wesley looked at them with a sinking heart. He had no idea what he would find. Perhaps he was hoping that there might be something, anything, that would tell him about the people in Shipborne's life; his friends and enemies. Anybody who would be likely to want him dead.

As he opened the lid the contents of the first box made him recoil with distaste: he could see that many of the items were stained a rusty brown . . . splashed with the victim's blood. The clothes Shipborne had been wearing when he died lay there, neatly packaged in plastic, together with the contents of his pockets. There were other items from the murder scene too; things from the desk in the study where Shipborne had died; things splattered with blood that, understandably, Shipborne's niece hadn't cared to claim.

He was staring into the box when he heard a voice behind him. 'Do you want me to give you a hand with that?'

He looked round and saw Rachel hovering there, looking at him enquiringly.

'Thanks, that'd be a help. I don't really know what we're looking for but I hoped there might be an address book or a diary, that sort of thing.'

Rachel knelt on the office floor and began to empty one of the boxes, examining each item carefully. She burrowed among the small items that had fallen to the bottom of the box and after a while stood up and placed something on Wesley's desk. It was a small book . . . a hardback notebook of the type available in any stationer's shop. Its cover was black but Wesley could see rusty patches which looked suspiciously like dried blood.

He grabbed it eagerly and took it out of its protective bag. Rachel craned her neck to see over his shoulder.

'Looks like some sort of diary.' Wesley flicked through the pages, satisfied that he had found something that could be significant. Shipborne had indeed kept a diary of sorts, not of the ready-printed kind detailing appointments; this one seemed to be more jotted thoughts. Although there was dried blood on the cover, it hadn't seeped through to the pages. The book was full, and he noticed that the last entry was dated a couple of weeks before Shipborne's death. Wesley found himself wondering whether he had started another volume in that time . . . if so, perhaps it would be in the other box.

Just as he turned to the opening page, he heard a commotion at the other end of the office. Steve Carstairs had just come in with the news that someone had come to the front desk saying that they wanted to confess to Helen Wilmer's murder.

Chapter Ten

I visited my solicitor in Morbay this morning and I feel so much better now that the will has been changed and I know that, were anything to happen to me, the money would go where it is most needed. I saw Stephen Wilmer near the church when I got back to Belsham but he ignored me.

On my return I had a rather strange visit from Amy Hunting, the woman who turned up a couple of weeks ago and confessed that she was having an affair with William Verlan. I'd sensed at the time that her confession had been an excuse, that there was really another purpose to her visit, and today she asked me if what I had said in church the other week was true – had I really been involved in the trial. When I answered her she walked out without another word.

I didn't know what to make of her visit but somehow she made me feel uneasy. It was all very odd. I wish I knew what she'd really wanted.

From a diary found among the personal effects of the Reverend John Shipborne

Dr William Verlan's face was ash pale as he sat in the interview room, toying with an empty plastic beaker that had recently contained tea.

'I believe you have something to tell us,' Wesley said, glancing at the whirring tape machine. 'You can have a solicitor present if you wish.'

Verlan shook his head. 'It's been on my conscience for all these years. I just want to get it off my chest.'

'Why don't you start at the beginning.' Gerry Heffernan sat back, ready to listen. Criminals weren't usually this obliging with their confessions, so he would make the most of it while the going was good.

'I killed Helen Wilmer.'

'What happened?' Wesley prompted.

'I was driving along and my mind wasn't on my driving,' he began, speaking slowly and clearly as if he was telling a well-rehearsed story. 'I'd just got back from a trip to the States so I guess I was jet-lagged, and I'd had a bit to drink on the plane. It was dark and wet and I'd been driving on the other side of the road for the past week or so: I should have been paying attention but ... Well, I felt a bump, as though I'd driven over something. I stopped the car and she was just lying there in the road. I took her pulse and ... ' He looked down at his hands. 'She was dead. I'd killed her.'

'So why didn't you call the emergency services?'

Verlan looked Wesley in the eye. 'I panicked. Hell, I'd just killed someone. Wouldn't you panic? There was nobody about and it was a bright moonlit night. I saw a small digger in a field near by ... in Pest Field. Someone had been digging a drainage ditch and the hole was still open and there was a spade there beside it. I suspected there might be plague burials in that particular field from research one of my PhD students had been doing, and I thought if I buried her in the ditch there was a chance that she might be taken for one of the plague victims if she was ever found. I wasn't thinking straight.'

'So you went ahead and buried her?'

'I carried her over and put her in the hole and covered her over with a layer of soil. But I've lived with it ever

242

since, Inspector. Believe me, there's not a day goes by when I don't regret what I did.'

Heffernan leaned forward. 'I bet you got a shock when Huntings announced they were going to build a supermarket on the site.'

'I've been in the States for a year teaching in Boston, so I didn't know about it. When I got back and found they were about to start the dig I guess I panicked 'cause I knew it was only a matter of time before they found her. I knew I'd been stupid to think that she'd be taken for one of the plague victims ... she'd had modern clothes ... buttons and a necklace and things.' He hesitated. 'And after I'd buried her I found I'd lost the St Christopher medal I always wore around my neck ... it was a present from my sister, Louise. She gave it to me when I came over to England ... she'd scratched our names on the back so I thought it'd be traced back to me. When I realised I'd lost it at the time I couldn't face going back to dig up her grave again to look for it.'

'So when you learned about the dig you panicked?'

'Sure I did. I bought a metal detector. I thought that if I could find my St Christopher ... '

Wesley watched Verlan's face. 'But you were disturbed ... and you attacked Dr Watson, the archaeologist in charge of the dig.'

'I was just trying to get away. I panicked and pushed him and he fell back into the trench. I didn't mean to hurt him. It was an accident.'

'You seem to be rather accident prone, Dr Verlan.'

Verlan hung his head and said nothing.

'And incidentally, you might be interested to know that the pathologist who examined Helen Wilmer's remains reckons she was murdered.'

Verlan looked up, his eyes wide with shock. 'No ... it was an accident, I swear. I ran her over. It wasn't murder. No way.'

'He thinks she was strangled. Perhaps you'd like your solicitor present after all.'

William Verlan nodded meekly and mumbled another denial.

'Well, he's sticking to his story.' Heffernan put his feet up on his desk. After questioning Verlan for over an hour he felt he deserved a rest.

'I believe him, Gerry. His statement fits in with Colin's findings ... the post-mortem injuries. If Verlan ran her body over after she'd been killed ... '

'You're forgetting the small fact that she was strangled.'

'So someone strangled her and left her body in the road. Verlan admits his mind wasn't on his driving. He might not have seen her lying there. Then he automatically assumed that he'd killed her. But what if she was dead already?'

'So there was a strangler at large in Belsham?'

'Or a boyfriend. I don't think we should discount Dermot O'Donovan. But ... '

'But what?'

'Everywhere we look we turn up more links between all these cases we're working on. The Reverend Shipborne, who'd had a row with the father of Helen Wilmer, who used to teach in Shipborne's Sunday school and also worked for Huntings, the firm that Loveday Wilkins has some sort of grudge against.'

'It's a small world.' Heffernan leaned back and scratched his head. 'Has that Loveday made a statement yet?'

'She's not saying a word. I'm getting someone to check out her background. If she does have mental health problems her family should be contacted and perhaps they'll be able to throw some light on why she's been doing all this. Because it certainly doesn't look as if money was the motive.'

'Any word on the mother and daughter in hospital?'

'Trish rang up a few minutes ago. In hospital-speak they're "comfortable" – although I'm not quite sure what that means. Keep your fingers crossed anyway. And there's good news about the missing jar of honey: it was handed in

244

unopened at Morbay nick a couple of hours ago and it's gone off to the lab.'

'That's one weight off our minds.'

Wesley shifted in his seat and looked at his watch. It was getting late and he was neglecting Pam again. Perhaps when all this was sorted out – when the web was unravelled – he'd be able to make it up to her. Or perhaps by then there would be more cases to keep him at the office. He stood up, trying not to think about it. 'I think it's time we found out what Philip Norbert has to say for himself. Coming? Or should I take Paul?'

'I'll sit in if you want some moral support,' Heffernan said, as though he were making a generous offer. 'Then I think we should pay Aaron Hunting another visit ... see what he has to say about Loveday Wilkins's efforts to ruin him and ask him if he recognises her name. Perhaps we'll get free groceries for a year for clearing this lot up.'

Wesley laughed. 'In your dreams, Gerry,' he said, making for the door.

A few minutes later they walked into the interview room where Philip Norbert was waiting for them, having just been brought up from the cells. Norbert was seated at the table, watched by a uniformed constable in the corner. When the two detectives entered he greeted them with a scowl as they sat down opposite him.

'Want a solicitor?' asked Heffernan as he prepared to switch on the tape machine.

'Piss off,' was the reply. Heffernan took that as a 'no'.

'Christopher Hobson saw you hanging around outside Belsham vicarage on the night of the murder. He was quite positive ... said he says he never forgets a face. What have you got to say about that?' Heffernan smiled benignly and waited.

Norbert shifted a little in his seat and Wesley thought he detected a new uncertainty in his eyes, as though he was weighing up his options before making a decision.

After a few seconds he spoke. 'Okay. I was in Belsham

on the night the vicar died. I was drinking with this bloke.'

'Name?'

'Can't remember.'

'Now why doesn't that surprise me?' said Heffernan quietly. 'Go on.' From the guilty look on Norbert's face there was something he was holding back. 'Did you go near the vicarage?'

'Don't know.' He shifted in his seat. He was lying.

'Your dad thought you'd killed the vicar, didn't he? Why was that?' Wesley thought the question was worth a try.

Norbert's eyes widened and Wesley knew he'd touched a nerve.

'He covered up for you ... sent an innocent man to jail to protect you. How did he know you'd killed the vicar, Phil?' He leaned forward. He could smell the garlic on Norbert's breath and he could see tiny beads of sweat on his forehead. 'Well?'

Philip Norbert began to speak quietly, almost inaudibly, his head bowed. 'I'd had a few drinks and when I left the pub I passed this big house. The lights were on and I could see the French window was open ... which was funny because it wasn't a warm night. I went up to the window, just out of curiosity, and there didn't seem to be anyone about so I went in.'

'Go on,' Wesley prompted gently.

'I had a bit of a look round and ... well, there was nothing much worth nicking so I went upstairs. I found this wallet by the bed so I just grabbed it and got out.' The colour drained from his face and he studied his hands.

Wesley could tell there was more to come. 'What happened next?'

'I saw him when I was on my way out. He was just lying by the desk. If I'd seen him I'd never have gone in ... never.'

'How do we know you didn't kill him?' snarled Heffernan. 'Your dad obviously thought you had.'

'I didn't.'

246

'How did your father know you'd been there?' Wesley was curious.

'The murder was on the TV news and I knew I had to get rid of the wallet. But my dad found it first. He'd never trusted me ... used to go through my coat pockets. I was stupid to leave it in there but I wasn't thinking straight. Anyway, the vicar's bloody cheque card was in the wallet and Dad found it and went mad ... started shouting and hitting me and ... Anyway, I got out ... left home and that bloody school. I stayed with some mates ... lay low, thinking the law would come looking for me. I thought they'd try and pin the murder on me.'

'So what happened?' Wesley asked.

'Nothing. That's the point. My dad knew I'd got the dead man's wallet but nothing happened. I read in the paper that he was in charge of the case and ... '

'And you were waiting to be named as chief suspect?'

'Something like that. But as I said, nothing happened. I couldn't understand it. Then they said this bloke had been arrested and later on when he was convicted they showed his picture on the telly. I'd seen him before but I couldn't remember where.'

'And you never thought of coming forward?' Wesley knew the question was naive as soon as he'd said it.

Norbert grunted. 'Do me a favour. I didn't fancy doing life.'

'But you said you didn't kill the Reverend Shipborne.'

'Yeah ... but how could I prove it? I had his wallet, didn't I? Who was going to believe that he was already dead when I went into that house? But I swear he was. He was lying there ... all blood on his head and his eyes open staring at me ... I've never moved so fast in my life.'

'You admit you took the wallet. Did you notice a silver cup and plate while you were searching the place?' Wesley asked, watching Norbert carefully. But Norbert shook his head.

'What about your dad?'

Norbert bowed his head. 'Never saw him again. When he died I got in touch with Mum ... gave her my address but ... '

Heffernan leaned forward. 'You owed him a lot. He put his career on the line for you.'

'His bloody career ... that's all I ever heard.'

Wesley watched him carefully. 'You didn't get on with your father?'

Norbert shrugged. 'I never saw much of him ... and I had to live up to being a copper's son ... getting teased at school. And sometimes it was like me and Mum didn't matter ... that his job was more important.'

Wesley looked away and caught Heffernan's eye.

'I didn't kill that vicar. My dad might have thought I did but I didn't.'

Heffernan stood up. 'We'll send someone along to take a statement.' He walked out of the room and Wesley followed.

'What's up?' Wesley asked when they were out in the corridor.

'I don't know what to do, Wes. Do I go ahead and ruin a man's reputation or ... ?'

Wesley put his hand on the chief inspector's arm. 'I don't think you'll have much choice ... not once Hobson's case goes to appeal. Makes you think, though, doesn't it?'

'What does?'

'If you're too busy catching villains to be there for your kids and that's how they turn out.'

'I wouldn't worry about it, Wes. Not every copper's kid turns out a criminal, you know. Mine haven't ... as far as I know. And just because your mum and dad are doctors doesn't mean you go round smoking like a chimney, eating junk food and ignoring medical advice, does it?'

Wesley forced himself to smile, but he looked at his watch, wondering how soon he could get home.

'But it makes you wonder, doesn't it? Which of us

wouldn't do what Norbert did if we found ourselves in the same situation, eh? Do you reckon he did it?'

'He had Shipborne's wallet and his story about finding the body on the way out seems a bit thin to me. If Janet Powell's version of events is true – and we've no real reason to doubt that it's not because, as far as we know, she has no reason to lie – he's the best suspect we've got.'

'He said he didn't see any silver and I believed him.'

'He might not have noticed it if he'd just been looking for ready cash.'

'So who planted the silver in Hobson's flat?'

'I think we can both guess, can't we? Norbert would have done anything to protect his son.'

Wesley glanced at his watch again but Heffernan seemed in no hurry to go home ... with Sam and Rosie being back at university up North, he had nobody to go home for. He scratched his backside. 'Tell you what, Wes, we've just got time to pay Aaron Hunting a visit and let him know we've found his poisoner. I'll be interested to see if he recognises Loveday's name.'

They spoke little on the journey to Hunting's house: at least they had cleared up the supermarket poisonings now, although Wesley still wanted to know what was really behind it ... what had driven Loveday Wilkins to gamble with strangers' lives. He held on to a vague hope that Aaron Hunting might be able to throw some light on the matter ... but he wasn't going to hold his breath.

The door of Hunting Moon House was opened almost as soon as they'd pressed the doorbell. Hunting had been waiting for them, his face a picture of relief.

'Come in, come in. Chief Superintendent Nutter called me to say that you'd made an arrest. Come through to the drawing room. I'll arrange for some tea. Is that all right?'

Wesley and Heffernan followed their host down the hallway. It was nice to be welcome for a change.

'So who have you arrested?' Hunting asked as they sat down.

Wesley's eyes were drawn to the scene outside . . . to the grey waters of the river underneath a leaden sky. A navy patrol boat glided silently past, separated from them by a sheet of glass. Heffernan stayed silent, so he cleared his throat and looked at his host. 'A young woman. We picked her up in a flat in Morbay . . . a squat.' He didn't mention Pat or Sunita's connection. As far as he was concerned it was irrelevant.

'What's her name?'

'Loveday Wilkins. I'm afraid we haven't been able to question her yet. It appears she has mental health problems and the doctor says we've got to go easy for now.'

Wesley noticed that Aaron Hunting's face had gone quite pale. He opened his mouth to speak and then closed it again.

'I'm afraid we've no idea why she did it yet.'

'But you're sure it's her? You're sure you've got the right person?' Hunting sounded anxious. Heffernan, sitting on the sofa beside Wesley, gave him a nudge.

'Have you ever heard the name Loveday Wilkins before? Is there any chance she could have a grudge against you for some reason?'

Hunting gave an almost imperceptible shake of the head and said nothing.

'She didn't actually work for Huntings but she did work for a contract cleaning agency who provided temporary cleaners at your Morbay store in the early mornings. That's how she knew so much about the layout of the store and managed to plant the goods without being detected. Does the name ring any bells? She's in her late twenties or early thirties, about five foot five, with thin brown hair which she usually wears in plaits. She has scars on her wrists.' He looked at Hunting enquiringly but the man shook his head again.

'I can't help you. I'm sorry.' There was something in Hunting's tone which told Wesley that this was his last word on the matter. Something in his eyes, however, suggested that he knew more than he was letting on.

250

'I wonder if we could have a word with your wife, Mr Hunting? She might recognise this girl's name. Is she at home?' Wesley said the words casually, watching Hunting's face.

'I'm afraid my wife's not been well for some time and she's not up to receiving visitors. Perhaps in a few days.' He stood up. 'I'll go and see where that tea is.'

Hunting disappeared through the door, leaving the two policemen gazing at the scene outside.

Amy Hunting sat in her bedroom at Hunting Moon House and stared at the wall. She spent a lot of time doing that. It seemed to be the only thing left to her. That and the cold, clear comfort of a vodka bottle and whatever pill Dr Allen cared to prescribe that month. There had been so many types of pill that she had lost track.

She ran her left hand over her mouth and felt the coarse skin beneath her fingers, remembering William Verlan ... recalling the time when she had still had her looks and had taken refuge in such temporary physical relationships to dull the pain. But now every time she looked in the mirror she saw an old woman staring back: with lank greying hair and no make-up on her thin, sallow face. She was fifty but she felt twenty years older.

Of all the men she'd taken to bed in those wild, desperate years, she remembered William Verlan particularly. He was American, a university lecturer she met at some long-forgotten party; a quiet man with clean-cut hair and a taste for corduroy jackets and neatly pressed jeans: so different from Aaron. He had spoken of history – medieval was his period – and she had listened as he'd talked of other times, other worlds. She hadn't heard much of what he'd said but she'd found his soft New England accent hypnotic as she had stood, head slightly inclined in an attitude of rapt attention, clutching her glass of Chardonnay tightly, as though afraid it would be snatched from her. Aaron had told her not to drink while she was taking the anti-depressants.

She had ended up in bed with William that night in the larger of the two bedrooms in his neat, sparsely furnished cottage near the centre of Belsham. The sheets had been clean, changed that day: she remembered that detail but little else. She supposed that sex had dulled the agony for a while ... but not for long. She buried her face in her hands. If the nightmare began again it would mean another spell in the clinic ... more drugs to blot it all out. Sometimes she longed for the sterile safety of the clinic ... and sometimes she dreaded it.

The door opened and she looked up, her heart pounding. Aaron was standing there looking at her in the cold, pitying way he always looked at her nowadays.

'Have they gone?' she whispered.

'Not yet. I've offered them tea.'

'I heard them talking. They said something about ... '

'Don't worry. The doctor won't let her talk to them yet.'

'Is she ...?'

'I don't know. They won't say much.'

'You should tell them.'

Aaron Hunting shook his head.

'You should tell them, Aaron ... tell them who Loveday is. Why don't you tell them?'

Aaron Hunting walked over to the chair and put his arm around his wife's shoulders. 'Now we don't want them bothering you ... asking you questions, do we?' He leaned across and put his face close to hers but she turned her head, avoiding the warmth of his breath. 'This is our business, Amy. It's nothing to do with the police or anybody else. Is it?'

As he started to stroke her hair, Amy Hunting flinched. Then she began to sob.

Wesley got home just as Pam was putting Michael to bed. He offered to take over, to give Michael his bath, but Pam said he'd be more use clearing up after Neil, who was sprawled across the sofa in the living room surrounded by books and papers. There's an old saying that fish and guests stink after three days, and Wesley could tell by the tone of Pam's voice that Neil had begun to over-stay his welcome. And besides, Pam said, Michael was running a temperature and the last thing he wanted was the unfamiliar excitement of Daddy in the bathroom. Her words hit Wesley like a hammer. Had he become such an unfamiliar figure to his own son? Still smarting, he made his way downstairs.

The scene in the living room reminded Wesley of his student days. Neil was sprawled with his feet up on the sofa. All around him books and papers were scattered. Dirty cups and plates stood on the floor and coffee table: Neil hadn't bothered to use mats and a couple of ominous rings were forming on the wood. Neil looked up as he entered the room and greeted him with a lazy 'Hi'.

'Just like old times,' Wesley said pointedly. 'Haven't you thought of clearing this lot up?'

Neil smirked. 'Don't be so suburban, Wes. Relax.'

'It's okay for you but me and Pam have got to clean up after you.'

'You sound like my mum. Have a beer. And before you ask, I'm feeling a lot better. Definitely on the mend. I went to the hospital today and they said I could drive again if I was feeling up to it.'

'So where did all this lot come from?' Wesley surveyed the mess of books and photocopies with a sinking heart.

'Libraries, archives. I hear they've got something about Belsham at the time of the Black Death at Morbay University, so I'm planning to go over there and have a look.'

Wesley turned away, trying to hide his irritation. He and Neil had shared a flat together at university. It was only then that it struck him how much he had changed since those days while Neil had stayed the same. He walked out of the room and into the kitchen, where he found his dinner in the microwave ... a pointed reminder from Pam of his late return.

He was about to turn the machine on when Pam came in.

She ignored him and started to search the cupboard where they kept the medicines.

'What's the matter?'

She turned to him and he saw that she looked worried. 'He's getting worse. His temperature's shot right up.'

Wesley stood there puzzled for a second, and then he realised she was talking about Michael, not Neil. She resumed her search of the cupboard.

'Shouldn't you wait and see how he is in a couple of hours?'

She swung round, looking at her husband as though he'd just suggested they abandon their child in an alligator pit. Then she put out her hand to grab the phone.

But before she could touch it, it began to ring. Wesley picked it up. It was the station. Pam stormed out, muttering something about finding her mobile, while Wesley tried to listen to what the officer at the other end was saying.

A body had been found in the river at Tradmouth and Gerry Heffernan wanted him there right away. He put the phone down and went to look for Pam to tell her he was going out again. But when he found her in Michael's brightly painted bedroom she was in no fit state to take in what he was saying. Michael was lying in her arms, emitting a grizzling whine, his body floppy, his eyes closed. She looked up when he came in.

'I've rung the doctor. He said he'll come as soon as he can.'

'Good.' Wesley hesitated on the threshold. 'I have to go.'

Pam said nothing. She was rocking Michael to and fro, crooning, her anxious eyes focused on his face. She didn't reproach Wesley ... but then she didn't need to: he was reproaching himself.

He left the house without saying goodbye to Neil and drove the short distance to the waterfront.

*

A yachtsman had seen her jumping in. She hadn't taken a

running leap, just let herself drop forward, as though surrendering herself to the embrace of the grey water. Wesley had heard a local legend to the effect that the Trad claimed a life each year, but there had been two drownings already that year so it looked as though the river's appetite was increasing.

The yachtsman had made an attempt to rescue the woman but he hadn't been able to reach her in time, and he'd called the police and ambulance as soon as he realised his rescue efforts had been in vain. But then perhaps she hadn't wanted to be saved.

Wesley and Heffernan stood side by side on the quayside as the officers on the police launch pulled her body from the river. It was dark and Wesley gazed across the river to the lights of Queenswear, wondering why he was there. It was a case of suicide . . . cut and dried.

Two officers on the police launch were placing the woman's body gently on the floor of the bobbing boat. Wesley glanced at his companion and was surprised to see that he was clutching a woman's handbag to his chest. In the darkness he hadn't noticed this odd addition to the chief inspector's wardrobe.

'That her handbag?'

Heffernan looked round. 'Yeah. She'd left it on the quayside. I'm surprised nobody had nicked it.'

So was Wesley but his thoughts were running ahead. 'So why are we here for a jumper? Surely Uniform could have dealt with it.'

Heffernan sighed. 'I'm sure they could in the normal run of things, Wes. But the name on the credit cards in this handbag is Mrs Amy Hunting. It's Aaron Hunting's wife.'

'So why did she jump in the river?'

'That's what I'd like to know.'

Chapter Eleven

In the course of my research into the effects of the Black Death on the Tradmouth, Neston and Morbay area, I came across an account of events in 1348 that brought to mind the old European legend of the plague maiden: a beautiful young witch who brings plague to a community; a feared figure, armed only with a red scarf and a broom to sweep away the living. To trace Belsham's own plague maiden the main source document I have used is a sermon of Abbot Thorsleigh of Morre Abbey (Exeter Cathedral archives) written more than twenty years after the events he describes. Thorsleigh's story seems rather like a fictional account on first reading – a cautionary tale perhaps. However, as the name of the main protagonist is Robert de Munerie and there are de Muneries buried in Belsham parish church, I began my researches with the aid of Belsham's vicar, the Reverend John Shipborne, who was good enough to allow me access to his church.

I think it best to begin with the basic narrative gleaned from Thorsleigh's writings. Thorsleigh begins with an account of the activities of Robert de Munerie, the younger son of the lord of the manor of Belsham, who, it was alleged, dabbled in the black arts; alchemy, necromancy and conjuring spirits. He travelled to Tradmouth on his father's business at the time plague broke out in the town. However, Robert never succumbed to the illness – probably because of some natural immunity – and he began to believe that he was protected by supernatural powers. While in Tradmouth he began to write up scientific observations about the effects of the plague: the proportions of men, women and children who became ill; their symptoms; how long it took them to die, etc. He appeared to use a methodical approach, common among scientists of today but quite innovative in the fourteenth century.

However, events were soon to take a more sinister turn, and I shall deal with the consequences of Robert's misguided experiment in due course.

Extract from Barnaby Poulson's PhD thesis

Wesley left it to the DCI to inform Aaron Hunting of his wife's death. Heffernan put on a suitably solemn expression and decided to take Rachel with him to break the news. It wasn't a task he looked forward to but someone had to do it.

When Wesley mentioned that Michael wasn't well, Heffernan told him to get back home. It was 9.30 and there was nothing more he could do for Amy Hunting until the morning.

Wesley was surprised, even shocked, at how reluctant he felt to leave the place where Amy had died. He stood for a while on the quayside, staring at the dead woman as she was photographed and examined. He had never seen Amy Hunting alive but there seemed to be something familiar about her face, although he couldn't think what it was. She hadn't been in the water long enough for her body to be marred in any way, and in death she looked small and delicate; her pale, almost translucent flesh seemed unlined, but perhaps that was just an illusion. She was arranged neatly on a stretcher with her long-fingered hands crossed over her chest, as though laid out for her burial. A dull gold wedding ring hung loosely on the third finger of her left hand – suggesting that she had lost weight since her wedding to Aaron Hunting – but she wore no other adornments and the plain black dress, clinging to the wet contours of her body, served as a tasteful shroud. There was a slight smile on her lips, as though she were in a deep, peaceful sleep. Amy Hunting had embraced death willingly and it had claimed her gently, like a lover.

Wesley watched the forensic team go about their work for a few minutes before creeping away. He had brought the car because he wanted to get to the scene quickly, but now he wished he had left it at home because he felt he needed a walk to clear his head.

When he arrived back home he parked in the driveway, noticing that Pam's car had gone and all the lights in the house were blazing. As soon as he put his key in the lock Neil opened the door. He looked uncharacteristically anxious and the colour had drained from his face. A sudden feeling of dread clutched at Wesley's stomach. Something was wrong.

'They've gone to the hospital,' Neil began. 'The doctor came and said to get him there right away.'

Wesley felt his heart thumping. 'What's wrong?'

Neil just shook his head. He wasn't well up on childhood ailments. Wesley got straight back into the car and drove to Tradmouth Hospital. His mind wasn't on his driving and he almost collided with a lorry coming out of a side road. He knew he was speeding but somehow the prospect of a fine seemed unimportant at that moment.

At the hospital he found Pam sitting by Michael's cot, her hand through the bars, holding onto his tiny hand, her eyes watching his face intently. Michael lay quite still, sprouting wires and drips. A monitor next to the cot emitted soft electronic bleeps. Pam didn't look up when he came in, as though she were afraid that if she took her eyes off her son for a moment she would break the flow of the invisible stream of will-power that was keeping him alive.

Wesley drew up a chair and sat beside her. 'What have they said?' he whispered.

'They've done tests to see if it's meningitis,' she whispered back. 'His temperature's rocketed.' She squeezed the little hand and the toddler stirred a little.

'He's in good hands,' he muttered, aware that he was uttering a cliché. But sometimes clichés are the only things that seem appropriate.

He put his arm around her, closed his eyes and began to pray.

'There's been a call from Wesley, sir. His little boy's in hospital. Suspected meningitis. He's been at the hospital all night so he won't be in till later.'

Gerry Heffernan looked up at Rachel anxiously. 'What did he say? How's the kid? What do the doctors say?'

Rachel, who had been told only the bare facts of the situation, shook her head helplessly. As she turned to go Heffernan picked up the phone and punched out Wesley's home number.

The phone was answered immediately. Wesley had just returned home to have a shower and grab something to eat. Heffernan was lucky to catch him in. He said that they were still waiting for the results of the tests and Pam was refusing to leave Michael's bedside for a rest, even though, in her condition, she could do with one.

Heffernan's instinctive response was to tell Wesley not to bother coming into work. They could do without him for a day and he'd call round later to brief him on the latest developments.

But as soon as he put the phone down he looked out at the busy office beyond the glass partition, at the harassed faces of the officers as they trawled through files and paperwork, and regretted his generosity. He needed Wesley's logical way of looking at things. But then he told himself that a day or so wouldn't make much difference ... unless Nutter started piling on the pressure again about the Hobson case.

A few moments later Rachel returned, poking her head around the door nervously. 'We told Mr Hunting last night that you'd call on him this morning to take a statement. Do you want to leave it till later or . . .'

Heffernan pushed his pile of paperwork to one side and stood up. 'No, love. The Chief Super's made it very clear that Mr Hunting can't be kept waiting.'

Half an hour later Rachel was ringing Aaron Hunting's doorbell, the chief inspector standing beside her, shuffling his feet like a nervous schoolboy.

It was the solemn-faced maid who answered the door and stood aside to let them in. She led them to the living room overlooking the river, gliding in front of them like a black-clad ghost. The sky was dark today and the deep grey of the river matched their mood. The house was silent, a house in mourning for its unseen mistress.

Hunting didn't keep them waiting for long. Heffernan had last seen him at eleven the night before when they had met at the hospital for the formal identification of Amy's body, but he seemed to have aged ten years overnight and black smudges beneath his eyes suggested that he hadn't slept.

Rachel had been sitting beside Heffernan on the large leather sofa but she scrambled to her feet when Hunting appeared. 'We're sorry to bother you, Mr Hunting,' she said gently. 'But we did say we'd be calling this morning to take a statement . . .'

Hunting sank down in an armchair. 'That's quite all right. I know you have a job to do.' His voice was quiet, the sort of softness that precedes tears. But the eyes were dry and he stared straight ahead.

Heffernan glanced at Rachel. 'We need to know your wife's movements, sir. And her state of mind. Did she give you any hint that she might take her own life?'

Hunting put his head in his hands for a few moments. Then he looked up suddenly. 'You might as well know that my wife hasn't been well for a long time. She's suffered

260

from depression off and on for years.'

Heffernan made sympathetic noises but felt an overwhelming relief. This one was going to be straightforward. A simple case of suicide ... if suicide was ever simple.

'We didn't find a note. I wondered if she'd left one here.'

Hunting stood up and left the room. Half a minute later he returned with a sheet of expensive notepaper and gave it to the chief inspector. Heffernan scanned it quickly and frowned, puzzled, before handing it to Rachel.

Hunting continued. 'When you came round yesterday to tell me that you'd found the person responsible for the threats to my business ... ' He hesitated. 'My wife overheard our conversation. She heard you mention Loveday's name. As you see from that note, she couldn't bear the idea of Loveday causing trouble again. That's why she felt she couldn't go on any more.'

'I don't understand,' Heffernan prompted, hoping he was about to get an explanation.

Hunting squirmed in his seat. 'There's something I didn't tell you yesterday.' There was a long silence. 'The fact is, Chief Inspector, Loveday Wilkins is my daughter. Wilkins was Amy's maiden name ... Loveday stopped calling herself Hunting when she left home.'

Heffernan glanced at Rachel, who was sitting beside him, listening intently. Somehow he hadn't been expecting this. 'Why did she leave home?' he asked. It was the first thing that came into his head.

'The usual sort of thing ... teenage traumas. She had always been very volatile ... unbalanced. Disturbed, I suppose you could call it.'

'Took after her mother?' Heffernan knew the question was impertinent but he asked it anyway.

'Possibly.' The word was whispered. Hunting began to stare out of the window, and the light from the dappled water reflected on the ceiling moved across his face so that his expression seemed to change by the second. Heffernan wished he could read his thoughts.

261

'So why did she threaten your supermarket?'

'I can't say. She was a very disturbed adolescent ... she gave us no end of trouble and rejected any help we offered. After a while you have to back off with children like that and wait for them to come to you ... or so we were told by the experts. She went to five boarding schools and got expelled from all of them. Then there were spells at various clinics. We hoped she might grow out of it. She was ... is an intelligent girl, and we hoped going to university would do her some good, but she dropped out after her first year and took a succession of dead-end jobs.'

'How do you think she'll react to the news of your wife's death?'

Hunting frowned. 'I've really no idea.'

'Would you like to see your daughter, Mr Hunting? She's at the police station. Perhaps you'd like to break the news about your wife ... '

He shook his head. 'I don't think I could tell her. In fact, after what she's done, I don't think I even want to see her.'

Heffernan could think of nothing to say. Apart from the usual teenage tantrums, raising his own children had been relatively plain sailing, even when their mother had died unexpectedly. Disturbed children were uncharted territory, something he came across only when he picked up the pieces if they turned to crime, as they often did.

But Rachel came to the rescue. 'I think we understand, sir. Perhaps in a few days ... '

Hunting glanced at her gratefully, his eyes glistening with unshed tears. Coming face to face with Loveday was the last thing he wanted right now.

'Can you think why your wife chose to drown herself?' Rachel asked gently.

Hunting shook his head. 'I've no idea. Perhaps it was something to do with me spending so much of my spare time on the river ... perhaps she wanted to make a point. I don't know.'

Heffernan gave Rachel an almost imperceptible nod.

262

'Do you mind if we have a quick look at your wife's room, Mr Hunting?' she said.

A momentary flash of alarm passed across Hunting's face. 'Of course. Corazón will show you. He stood up and pressed a bell-push by the fireplace which brought the maid scurrying in. As Heffernan and Rachel followed her out, the chief inspector noticed that the expression on Hunting's face was like an inscrutable mask. There was no grief and no relief there . . . nothing.

Corazón opened the door of Amy Hunting's room for them then left, something that Heffernan was grateful for. He didn't feel comfortable searching someone's room when he was being watched. He shut the door and surveyed the scene. It was a feminine room, full of frills and flowers. A flimsy dressing gown hung behind the door. There was no sign of masculine occupation.

'Separate rooms, sir?'

'Maybe he snores. Anyway, it's a big house and there're just the two of them . . . three if you count Corazón . . . so why put up with snoring and cold feet on your back, eh? And if you fancy a bit of how's-your-father there's nothing to stop you creeping down the landing at midnight, eh? Probably more fun that way.' He noticed Rachel press her lips together disapprovingly. 'They say a lot of rich people have separate bedrooms. One thing about this job, Rach, you get to learn how the other half lives.'

Rachel began to search. She tried a door, probably connecting to the adjoining room, but it was locked: perhaps Aaron Hunting slept next door . . . and wasn't welcome at night. She began with the obvious places like the bedside drawer, then the wardrobe. Heffernan sat on the bed and stared out of the window. This room too over-looked the river.

He watched the boats skimming over the water, all the time aware of the noises in the background as Rachel conducted her search. He told himself that it was more appropriate for a woman to delve into Amy Hunting's

263

private things ... or perhaps that was just an excuse for idleness. After ten minutes Rachel came over to him. She was carrying a box, a shoebox.

'I found this. It's full of photographs. There's a little girl on them ... could be Loveday. And there's a little boy in some of them. Mr Hunting didn't mention a son, did he?'

Heffernan took the photographs out of the box and examined them. Loveday – if it was Loveday – must have been aged around seven. Her parents featured in some of them, smiling for the camera, and so did a little boy, a toddler aged around two or three ... it was difficult to tell. He bore a resemblance to Loveday, who was holding him on her knee in some of the pictures. As Heffernan looked through the pictures he realised that, although there were many taken when Loveday was young, there was none taken when she was older. It was as if time had stopped during that one happy, golden summer.

'So who's this other kid?' said Heffernan, not really expecting an answer.

'Cousin? Friend's son? We could ask Mr Hunting.'

As if on cue, Hunting opened the door. He'd knocked politely first, which surprised Heffernan. He hung on the threshold anxiously, as though waiting for permission to enter.

'We were just coming to find you, Mr Hunting,' said Heffernan. 'We've found some pictures.' He held out the photographs. 'Can you tell us who this little lad is?' As he pointed to the child, he noticed that the colour had drained from Hunting's face.

'That's my son, Chief Inspector. That's Adam.'

Dr Colin Bowman was writing up his notes on Amy Hunting's post-mortem when Gerry Heffernan poked his head round his office door. Colin invited him in, as always, for tea and biscuits, but this time Gerry declined the offer.

'I've got to go and find Wesley. Did you know his little boy's in here ... suspected meningitis?'

Colin's normally cheerful face clouded. 'Sorry to hear that, Gerry. How's the little chap doing? Do you know?'

'Not yet.'

'I'm sure they're doing their best for him. Give Wesley my best wishes, won't you ... and his wife.'

'Sure,' Heffernan said quickly. He wanted to change the subject. The thought of Michael's illness, the thought that the life of one so young was so vulnerable to the powers of nature, depressed him. 'Are the results of Amy Hunting's post-mortem ready? You said you were doing it first thing ...'

Colin produced a file, and waved it about. 'I'm waiting for the toxicology report, of course, but all my findings are consistent with her death being caused by drowning. Want to know how I reached my conclusions?'

'Thanks, Colin, but I'd rather not hear the gory details. So there's no chance it was suspicious?'

'All I can say is that I didn't find any evidence to indicate that it was anything other than a case of suicide. And I believe you have a witness who saw her jump in. Sorry, Gerry.'

'Don't be sorry. I've got enough work on as it is. By the way, I've been talking to the man who claims to have killed Helen Wilmer.'

This got Colin's attention. 'Oh yes?'

'He says he ran her over. Claims it was an accident and denies that he strangled her. Is there any chance at all that you could have made a mistake about the strangulation?'

'I'm afraid not. There's a definite fracture of the hyoid bone.' Bowman pointed at his throat. 'Just above the Adam's apple. Classic sign of manual strangulation. But as I said before, the injuries to the lower part of her body are consistent with her having been run over so your man might still be telling the truth. If someone else strangled her and left her lying in the road, then he might have come along in his car and run over her body by accident.' Colin smiled. 'Or perhaps your man strangled her himself then drove his car over her to make sure he'd done a thorough job. That's for you to find out, I'm afraid.'

Heffernan sighed, wondering why life had to be so complicated. 'I'd better see if I can find Wesley ... let him know what's been happening.'

He lumbered through the swing-doors leading from the mortuary and on reaching the main hospital spotted a sign pointing the way to the children's ward. He marched on down the polished corridors until he saw a pair of glass doors painted with bright cartoon characters, which told him he was in the right place.

He found Wesley easily enough. He was sitting by Michael's bedside, holding the patient's small hand in his. Michael was lying as though asleep while a nurse checked the electronic instruments that bleeped and winked on the other side of the bed. Wesley looked up and greeted Heffernan with what looked like a smile of relief. He was glad to see a face from the outside world.

'Is it okay to come in?' Heffernan whispered, creeping in on tiptoe.

'Yeah. There's no change. We're just waiting for the results of the tests. Pam's gone home for a shower and a rest. She took some persuading but I said I wouldn't leave his side.'

'He's in good hands, Wes.' Heffernan repeated the mantra. 'He'll be fine. He's a fighter is your lad.' He felt tears prick his eyes as he looked down at the tiny figure in the cot and slumped down on a seat near the door. When the nurse had left the room he stood up again and walked over to Wesley.

'Sorry to talk about work, Wes, but there have been some developments since ... '

Wesley looked up at him. 'Don't be sorry, Gerry. I'm only too glad to have something to take my mind off all this. I've brought the Reverend Shipborne's diary with me – it's in my pocket. I've been meaning to finish it but I've not had a chance yet. So what's new?'

266

'I've just found out that Loveday Wilkins is Aaron Hunting's daughter.'

Wesley's mouth fell open.

'Or rather his estranged daughter. She was a nightmare teenager, according to her father ... had lots of mental problems over the years, apparently.'

'That's hardly an excuse for killing innocent people.' Wesley sounded weary.

'No, but it could be an explanation. That mother and daughter who ate the poisoned honey are out of danger, by the way. I had a call before I came out.'

'Thank God for that.'

'And the post-mortem seems to confirm what we already know ... that Amy Hunting drowned herself. I've just seen Colin ... he sends his best wishes.'

'Does Loveday know about Amy's death yet?'

'Not yet. I suppose someone'll have to tell her. How do you think she'll take it?'

Wesley didn't answer, and there was a period of silence as both men watched the sleeping toddler intently. After a few minutes Heffernan whispered that he'd better get back. He crept from the room feeling utterly useless, frustrated by his helplessness, his inability to do anything constructive.

When he had gone Wesley delved in his pocket for the plastic bag containing the Reverend Shipborne's diary. He opened it and began to read, one eye on the page and the other on Michael's monitors. He needed something to take his mind off things ... anything to remind him that there was a world outside those four walls.

Neil had opened the door to Pam when she returned. He'd asked her how Michael was but she hadn't said much. She was too preoccupied for a social chat. She had taken a shower, something to help keep her awake, she said. Neil reckoned that what she needed was a square meal and a good sleep, but he kept his thoughts to himself as he hardly felt qualified to offer advice on such matters. After show-ering and changing her clothes, Pam had gone straight back to the hospital, leaving Neil alone, wondering what to do next.

His yellow Mini was parked on the road outside but he hadn't driven it since his fall. He stared at it out of the living-room window and wondered whether he dared risk the journey to Morbay. Although his ribs still hurt they were certainly healing fast, so he decided the time had come for action. He left the house, climbed into the driving seat tentatively and, like a learner on his driving test, set off slowly and carefully, trying to avoid any sudden move-ments.

He had discovered that a student at Morbay University's history department had written a PhD thesis back in the early 1990s on the history of Belsham at the time of the Black Death, and as he was out of action as far as digging was concerned he thought it might be worth taking a look. He was surprised that William Verlan hadn't mentioned the thesis when they found the plague pit . . . but then Verlan seemed to be a man with secrets.

He had telephoned the university earlier and arranged to look at the thesis. Now all he had to do was get there. The journey seemed to last for ever as he drove stiffly and sedately, feeling like one of those old men who wore hats and drove at five miles per hour below the speed limit that people always complained about being stuck behind. But he had no choice. Each change of gear, each depression of the clutch pedal, sent a twinge of pain through his body. After half an hour he drew up in the university carpark, relieved that the journey was over.

Morbay University was expanding. Featureless new buildings had sprouted up beside the original red-brick college, founded in the 1920s to train the nation's teachers, and more were under construction. The beneficiaries of this rapid growth, the students, slogged, bleary eyed, between the buildings, chattering as they recovered from the previous night's excesses in the bar. It brought back memories, but Neil told himself firmly that he was far too young to start reminiscing about the good old days ... about the time when he and Wesley had had nothing to worry about but getting essays in on time and their social life. He thought of Wesley and Pam sitting by Michael's bedside, willing their son to live, and longed for those days of playful innocence again.

Signs directed him to the history department, where he was met by a female postgraduate student. She was plump and dark with the face of a porcelain doll – small nose, small mouth and wide brown eyes. If Neil's mind hadn't been on the ache in his ribs, he would have noticed her charms, but as it was he had enough to contend with. She led him to the departmental library where the red-bound volume awaited him on a pale wooden table. Neil thanked her and waited. He didn't relish the thought of someone standing over him as he read the text and made his notes. After a few seconds the porcelain doll seemed to take the hint and left him to it.

Neil began to read. And soon he forgot all about his pain.

Heffernan had made sure that Loveday had a cup of tea, hot and sweet, before he sat down opposite her in the interview room. Since his childhood tea had been the universal panacea for shock, bad news and any other troubles that life threw at you. But Loveday ignored the steaming cup on the table and contented herself with chewing the end of one of her pigtails.

He decided on the direct approach. It was best to get these things over with quickly. He gave a discreet nod to Rachel, who was sitting beside him.

'I'm afraid I've got some bad news for you, Loveday,' Rachel said gently.

Heffernan watched the young woman's eyes but they betrayed nothing, no apprehension about what the bad news could be.

269

'There's no easy way to say this.' Rachel hesitated. 'I'm afraid your mother's dead. She died last night.'

The two officers braced themselves for tears and hysteria ... but none came. Loveday just carried on chewing the hair as though Rachel had made some routine observation about the weather.

'I haven't got a mother,' she said after a few moments. 'She died years ago.'

Heffernan glanced at Rachel, who looked as confused as he felt. 'We've been to see Aaron Hunting. He says he's your dad. We found photographs of you. Are you saying Mr and Mrs Hunting aren't your parents?'

Loveday didn't answer.

'Are you Aaron Hunting's daughter or not?'

Another silence.

'You must have some personal grudge against Mr Hunting or his company to have done what you did. Is it because he's your father? Did he disown you?' He hesitated. 'Did he abuse you? If you don't want to speak to me or DS Tracey here, there are ... '

'No, he didn't disown me or abuse me. Can I go now?' Loveday stared ahead, her lips sealed. If she had a secret she was keeping it for now.

Heffernan nodded to the young policewoman by the door, who took Loveday's thin arm and prepared to escort her back to the cells. When she had gone, the chief inspector sat for a while, deep in thought, with Rachel watching him expectantly, waiting for some comment. His head was aching and he wished Wesley were there to give his opinion, to bounce ideas off. For all he knew he was about to get things completely wrong. He told Rachel to go home. They'd had enough for one day.

Wesley lay on the bed fully clothed and put his hand out to touch Pam's pillow. He'd come home for a couple of hours, knowing that if he didn't have some sleep he'd be no use to anybody. But, in spite of his urgings, Pam had

270

stayed at the hospital. He'd felt bad about leaving her, but perhaps when he returned to the hospital he'd be able to persuade her to take a break. He closed his eyes and felt himself drifting towards oblivion, then the cold fingers of anxiety clutched at his chest and kept sleep at bay, so he sat up again. How could he sleep when Michael might be struggling for life?

He was just putting on his shoes in preparation for returning to the hospital when the phone by the bed rang. He stared at it for a few moments, reluctant to answer it, dreading what he might hear. Then he picked up the receiver and muttered a nervous hello, his heart thumping in his chest.

'Wes?' It was Pam's voice. But from that one word he couldn't tell whether she was distressed or elated.

'What is it? What's happened?'

'It's good news. The tests are negative. And his temperature's coming down. The doctors say it's just a nasty virus.' She was gasping, starting to cry with relief.

'I'll come right down. Then you can come home for a rest. You need one.'

When Wesley looked at himself in the dressing-table mirror, he saw that tears were pouring down his cheeks.

He heard the front door opening and a voice shouting. Neil. He'd almost forgotten about Neil.

'You upstairs, Wes?'

Wesley grabbed a tissue and wiped his face as Neil burst in.

'How's Mike?'

'Pam's just rung. He's going to be okay.'

'Great. Hey, you're not going to believe this, I've found the most amazing contemporary account of the plague in Belsham in 1348. It says . . . '

'Look, Neil, tell me about it another time, eh? I've got to get to the hospital.'

Neil followed him downstairs and watched him disappear out of the front door.

*

271

It was late when Wesley reached the police station the next day. But late was better than never. He had stayed by Michael's bedside while Pam went home for a well-earned rest, but when she returned a couple of hours later he excused himself, saying there were things he had to do, although he was careful not to be too specific. However, Pam hadn't been listening anyway: she'd been too busy talking to Michael, reading him stories and chattering about this and that. He had opened his eyes and smiled.

On reaching the CID office Wesley was greeted by enquiries about his son's health. Even Steve Carstairs managed to look vaguely sympathetic. After running the gauntlet of well-meaning questions, he reached Gerry Heffernan's office and found the chief inspector at his desk, the telephone to his ear. Wesley sat down and waited.

The telephone conversation was one sided and Wesley guessed that the person on the other end was giving Gerry grief. After a minute or so of not being able to get a word in edgeways Heffernan said, 'Yes, sir. I'll see to that,' put the receiver down with a bang and blew a loud raspberry.

'Chief Superintendent Nutter?' Wesley made an informed guess.

'He wants us to charge Philip Norbert with the Shipborne murder. Says it'll make us look efficient if we charge someone as soon as Hobson's released. I told him it might be best to make sure that we've got the right man this time, but he didn't seem convinced by my brilliant argument.'

'Oh dear.'

'Oh dear indeed. I've heard the good news about your Michael ... ' He grinned widely. 'Now if we can just clear up these cases, we'll be able to start celebrating.'

Wesley looked sceptical and said nothing.

'Had any thoughts? Or has your mind been elsewhere?'

'Oh I've had thoughts. In fact, while I was at the hospital I had a chance to look at Shipborne's diary.'

'And?'

'Well, I can see why it was dismissed as unimportant at the time, but in view of recent developments I think it's worth looking at. It's full of interesting snippets. Would you believe William Verlan and Amy Hunting were having an affair?'

Heffernan's mouth fell open.

'She even told the Reverend Shipborne about it . . . went to the vicarage to make some sort of confession. Helen Wilmer and Dermot O'Donovan get a mention as well. And Helen Wilmer's father.'

Heffernan pushed his paperwork to one side and leaned forward. 'Go on.'

'There's a lot about a Barnaby Poulson, a student of Verlan's who was writing a thesis about the plague. Reading between the lines, Shipborne was worried about what this Poulson was digging up. Barry Castello features quite a lot too . . . sounds as if Shipborne had a very high opinion of him.'

'Interesting. What does he say about O'Donovan and Helen Wilmer?'

Wesley took a deep breath. 'Well, Dermot O'Donovan was a bad lad but we knew that already. And Shipborne had some kind of row with Helen Wilmer's father about the church tower being locked up.'

'So Shipborne knew Amy Hunting?'

'Yes. She went to see him and told him about her affair with William Verlan. It says she asked Shipborne about some trial in the 1970s . . . he said he'd mentioned it in a sermon. I'd like to know more about Shipborne's background. If it was assumed that he was murdered in the course of a robbery, I don't suppose anybody bothered to find out much about his past.'

'You don't think Philip Norbert's responsible, then?'

Wesley shook his head. 'I think there's more to the Shipborne case than meets the eye. The diary's full and the last entry is a couple of weeks before the murder. I'm wondering if he started another – if it wasn't bloodstained like the earlier one it might have been sent to the niece in Scotland with his other effects.'

'Why don't you give the niece a ring?'

Wesley added this to his mental list of things to do, which was becoming longer by the hour. 'So what have I been missing? What's the latest on Loveday Wilkins and William Verlan?'

'Loveday's been charged but she's waiting to be examined by a psychiatrist. Her father hasn't been to see her, which isn't that surprising in the circumstances. As for Verlan, he's stuck to this story about running Helen Wilmer over by accident, even when I told him that Colin Bowman found evidence that she was strangled. If I didn't know better, I'd say he was telling the truth.'

'Perhaps he is.'

'Then why bury her ... why try and dig her up again to destroy the evidence and attack your mate Neil?'

'And he knew Shipborne. Could Helen have seen him leaving Shipborne's house on the night of the murder? Did he kill her to keep her quiet?'

Heffernan looked impressed. 'It's possible. But we've got to prove it.'

'But why would he kill Shipborne in the first place?'

'If Shipborne knew about his affair with Amy Hunting, he might have known about other secrets from his past ... things he wanted hidden. I'd like to know if this trial has something to do with it. Could it be a case involving Verlan ... or Barry Castello?'

'I'll get someone to check it out. Although we don't even know where it was held. Was it at Exeter ... or the Old Bailey?'

'Wherever it was, there'll be a record of it somewhere. Finding it'll keep someone out of mischief for a while.' Heffernan grinned again.

The telephone rang. Heffernan answered it, and after a brief conversation he sighed and shouted to Trish, 'William Verlan's brief is here. You'd better show our next lucky contestant down to interview room two.'

'What, sir?'

'Sorry, Trish. Tell the custody sergeant I want to have a word with William Verlan. I take it he's still enjoying our hospitality . . . he hasn't escaped or anything?'

Trish looked at him, not knowing what response was expected. Erring on the side of caution, she said nothing as she left the room.

Fifteen minutes later William Verlan was sitting where Loveday had sat, his solicitor, a young man who looked as though he was straight out of the sixth form, by his side. Unlike Loveday, Verlan looked frightened. He was being held for the assault on Dr Neil Watson, but as he had decided to confess to killing Helen Wilmer, it was only a matter of time before he was formally charged with murder and the whole rumbling process of the law began. But somehow, in spite of this, he felt better for having confessed, for having got the secret sins of all those years ago off his chest.

'You had time to think about your story, Dr Verlan?' Heffernan said when the tape was running.

'Yes. I don't want to change my statement. I ran the girl over. I panicked and buried her body. It was a dumb thing to do, I know that now.'

Heffernan paused to read some papers on the desk in front of him. 'You see, Dr Verlan, the pathologist is absolutely sure Helen Wilmer was strangled. And if you really thought you'd run her over accidentally, why did you go to so much trouble to hide her body?'

'I told you. I panicked. I was tired . . . jet-lagged. I'd had too much to drink on the plane so I was probably over the limit and . . . I just panicked. And I didn't go to that much trouble. There was an open ditch dug in the field and a spade there beside it: all I had to do was tip her in and cover her up with soil. I guess it seemed like a good idea at the time.'

'And you tried to dig up the site of her grave. Why was

275

that? Why go to so much trouble? Surely, even if they did identify her, they wouldn't connect her with you?'

Verlan shook his head. 'I told you ... I'd lost my St Christopher. It was a present from my sister in the States and I thought it might have been traced to me. And just before ... just before it happened a student of mine was researching the history of Belsham at the time of the Black Death and he suspected that plague victims had been buried in Pest Field. I reckoned that someone might have put two and two together and realised that I could have known there was a plague pit there and buried her with the other skeletons. I guessed I'd be the number-one suspect. I wasn't thinking straight. I panicked.'

'How well did you know the Reverend Shipborne?'

Verlan looked surprised at the change of subject. 'I went to church sometimes but I wouldn't say I knew him well. I asked him if the student I mentioned could do some research in Belsham church. He was keen to cooperate at first but ... '

'But what?'

'Barnaby said that when he told Shipborne what he'd discovered, Shipborne's attitude changed and he said he couldn't help any more. Barnaby wanted to bring in experts to examine some medieval graffiti in the tower but Shipborne locked the place up. He said it was unsafe and nobody was allowed in there, but that was the first I'd heard of it.'

'I'd like to talk to this Barnaby. Do you have an address where he can be contacted?'

Verlan closed his eyes for a moment and lowered his head. 'Barnaby Poulson died in a car accident shortly after he was awarded his doctorate. It was a tragic business. He was such a promising historian.'

'I'm sorry to hear that,' said Heffernan. 'I'm afraid I have some more bad news for you, Mr Verlan. Amy Hunting killed herself last night. Jumped in the river.' He watched Verlan, waiting for a reaction.

The shock on Verlan's face seemed genuine. It would have been difficult to fake that momentary flash of astonishment followed by the look of utter desolation.

'We also think her daughter, Loveday, was threatening Mr Hunting's business. Did you know her daughter?'

Verlan shook his head. 'Amy mentioned once that she had a daughter but she said she hardly ever saw her.'

'Did that upset her?'

'She didn't seem too upset about it.'

'Did she ever mention a son ... Adam?'

Verlan looked wary. 'I don't remember.'

'What was your relationship with Amy Hunting?' It was the first time Wesley had spoken and Verlan looked at him curiously.

His face reddened. 'Carnal initially.'

'And then?'

'For a short time I thought I was in love with her ... or perhaps I just felt sorry for her ... I don't know.'

'Who finished it?'

Verlan looked embarrassed. 'I guess it was kind of mutual. I found out that she'd been to see the Reverend Shipborne to confess that we were having an affair ... goodness knows why. I made excuses not to see her after that. I liked to consider myself part of the village community and I went to that church sometimes so I found it embarrassing that Shipborne knew. I told Amy it put me in an awkward position, and she said that if I felt like that we'd better stop seeing each other. That suited me because by that time she was starting to act a bit weird. I mean, why tell the vicar ... ?'

'Did you ever discuss a court case with Mrs Hunting ... something the Reverend Shipborne had mentioned during a service?'

Again Verlan looked puzzled. 'A court case? Not that I can remember. Why?'

'How well did you know Helen Wilmer?'

Again Verlan looked surprised by the change of subject.

'Not well. I knew she was a student who lived in the village and she taught in the Sunday school at one time. Doesn't that prove that I killed her by accident? I had no reason to want her dead . . . none at all. I hardly knew the girl.'

'Did you find her attractive?'

The young solicitor roused himself from his daydreams and asked whether the question was relevant.

'Well, if the motive for strangling Helen wasn't personal, it might have been sexual.'

Verlan leaned forward. 'How many times do I have to tell you? I didn't strangle her. I ran her over by accident.'

'So you won't change your statement?'

It would have been too much for Heffernan to hope that the answer would be 'yes'.

Wesley and Heffernan walked back upstairs in silence. Wesley followed the chief inspector into his office out of habit and sat himself down by the desk.

'Verlan's sticking to his story.'

'Yeah. Our lecherous lecturer isn't being much help, is he? I reckon he was having a bit of how's-your-father with the lovely Helen of Belsham and it got out of hand.'

'He said he didn't know anything about any court case.'

'He might be being economical with the truth.' Heffernan sighed. 'One funny thing, Wes: when me and Rach were looking through Amy Hunting's things we came across photos of Loveday when she was a kid with a little boy a bit younger than her. Hunting said it was his son, Adam. Now Verlan knew about Loveday but nothing about any son. Funny.'

'So where is this son?'

Heffernan frowned, annoyed with himself. 'I never asked. I assumed he'd grown up and left home years ago, I didn't think it was important.'

'It might not be. But I suppose we'll have to pay Hunting another visit and find out. I wonder why Loveday hates her father so much. What went wrong?' Wesley gave Heffernan a meaningful look. 'Sexual abuse?'

'That's the first thing that springs to mind these days but she says not.'

Heffernan's telephone rang. He swore under his breath, pushed a heap of files out of the way, and picked up the receiver. After a brief conversation he looked at Wesley. 'That was the custody suite. Loveday wants to see us. She says it's important. She says she's decided to tell us everything.'

Chapter Twelve

The first sermon of Richard Thorsleigh, Abbot of Morre Abbey (Exeter Cathedral archives), states that:

'There was one in the village of Belsham near this Abbey's lands, called Robert de Munerie, an arrogant young man of good family who, not mindful of God or his fellow man, dabbled in witchcraft, and it is said by some that he conjured Satan himself. This Robert befriended a common harlot of Tradmouth when the pestilence did rage in that town, some say carried in by ships from afar. The woman was stricken but, through Satan's power so he claimed, Robert himself did not fall sick.'

There are no surviving manorial records to confirm the existence of this young woman. In fact the only contemporary references to Robert de Munerie, other than in Abbot Thorsleigh's sermons, are to be found in the tower of Belsham parish church. There is a cryptic request to pray for Robert's soul, be he alive or dead, on his father, Urien's, tomb, and a remarkable piece of graffiti survives in the tower of Belsham parish church which says, 'The dregs of the people beg for thy mercy, o Lord. I Hammo, priest, set this down in the twenty-first year of the reign of King Edward, the third of that name, and beg all Christian people, if there be any left alive, to pray for the souls of those cast into the pit in the church field. King Death has reigned over us and *may God forgive Robert de Munerie for bringing him to this place. I die now and confess my many sins. Have mercy upon us, o Lord, your miserable people.'*

This heartrending memorial to the ordeal of the villagers of Belsham can be seen on the north wall of the tower of St Alphage's church, Belsham, to this day.

Extract from Barnaby Poulson's PhD thesis

Loveday Wilkins sat on the grey plastic chair in the interview room. She shifted nervously and the chair scraped on the lino floor. Wesley had already set the tape running and now he waited to hear what she had to say. He didn't try to rush her: he knew that would have been useless. Heffernan sat beside him, watching Loveday's face. But her expression gave nothing away.

'Have you been there?' she said.

Wesley looked at her calmly. 'Where?'

'To the house. To my dad's house.'

'Yes.'

'Did you see it? Did you see the room?'

Wesley glanced at Gerry Heffernan. 'What room's this?'

Loveday sat back. There was the ghost of a smirk on her face.

'Why don't you tell us about it?' said Wesley gently.

Loveday looked him in the eye. 'Have you got kids?'

Wesley hesitated before answering. He didn't want this to get personal. 'I've got a son. Why?'

'What would you do if he died?'

Her words hit Wesley like an electric shock and Gerry Heffernan glanced at him, sensing his discomfort. 'Come on, love, what are you getting at?' he growled.

Loveday pressed her lips tightly together and sat back, her eyes focused on the empty plastic cup in front of her.

'What happened to your brother?' Wesley asked softly.

'He was ill. He died.'

'What was wrong with him?'

281

Loveday shrugged her shoulders. 'Something to do with his heart . . . he had an operation.' She leaned forward, her mouth forming the semblance of a snarl. 'They never forgave me, you know. Never forgave me for living when he'd died. She didn't want me after Adam was born. I was just in the way.'

Wesley said nothing. He waited for her to continue.

'They hardly spoke to me again after he died. I had a series of nannies and I made their lives hell.' She smiled. 'I set fire to his precious boat once and they sent me away to boarding schools but none of them could cope with me. I wish everyone had just told the truth and said they hated me.' She began to sob uncontrollably. Wesley turned to the policewoman by the door and signalled that the interview was over.

'I think that's enough for now, love. We'll carry on when you're feeling up to it,' Heffernan said after muttering the required words into the tape recorder and switching the machine off.

As she was being led out of the room, Loveday turned to them. 'Go to the house and look at the room. You'll understand when you've seen it.'

As soon as she had gone, Heffernan stood up. 'I suppose we'd better pay a call on Aaron Hunting and have a look at this room, if it exists. Get someone to go through Amy Hunting's personal effects, will you. Tell them we want any keys she had with her. You never know.'

Wesley stayed silent as he followed the chief inspector out into the corridor. An hour later, when Rachel had managed to track down the keys found in Amy Hunting's handbag, they headed for Hunting Moon House. If they found Aaron Hunting at home, they had the excuse of visiting to bring him up to date on his daughter's situation. If not, they would play things by ear. But they knew that by some means they had to see the room Loveday had mentioned. She had been quite emphatic: once they had seen the room they would understand her actions. And both Wesley and Heffernan hated loose ends.

Corazón, the maid, answered the door. She stood on the threshold and told them in heavily accented English that Mr

Hunting wasn't at home. This was the first time Wesley had been able to study her closely. It was hard to guess her age but she wasn't in the first flush of youth. She was slightly built but the baggy black dress she wore did a good job of hiding any curves she possessed, giving her body a boyish appearance, and a black Alice band held back a glossy curtain of shoulder-length jet-black hair. Her dark brown eyes, lowered modestly, gave nothing away.

Wesley, as usual, was worrying about small details like search warrants, but Heffernan had no such hang-ups. He stepped nimbly past Corazón and marched into the hallway. Wesley had no choice but to follow.

'We've just been speaking to Mr Hunting's daughter and she asked us to have a look around. That okay, love?' He didn't wait for an answer but began to march down the hallway, opening doors.

Corazón followed them anxiously. 'You should ask Mr Hunting. I should not let you . . . '

'It's okay, love. Mr Hunting wouldn't mind.' Gerry Heffernan was at his smoothest . . . not a common sight. Wesley followed and said nothing.

There was no sign of any remarkable room downstairs, although it occurred to Wesley that the room, if it existed, might have been transformed into something quite mundane like a bedroom since Loveday had lived in the house. They continued their search upstairs with Corazón at their heels, determined not to let them out of her sight, and each door they opened led to bedrooms or bathrooms, all large and well appointed. As they opened the last door, they were starting to conclude that either the mysterious room was now unrecognisable or Loveday had been lying.

But Wesley turned to Corazón; one last shot was worth a try. 'Do you know of any other rooms in the house . . . perhaps one that's kept locked?'

Corazón stared at him and said nothing. But she was useless at pretending. Her expression gave away the fact that he'd hit the jackpot.

'Where is it?'

Corazón hesitated. Then she began to walk towards Amy Hunting's bedroom. They followed her in. In one corner was a white panelled door that they had taken for a connecting door on their first inspection of the room. Corazón walked over to the door and tried the handle, as though to demonstrate that it was locked.

'Have you got the key?'

'No. It has always been locked ever since I come here. Mrs Hunting, she tell me to keep away.'

'So Mrs Hunting had the key?' Heffernan fished in his pocket, brought out Amy Hunting's keys and jangled them about triumphantly, pleased that they'd had the foresight to bring them.

He went over to the door and tried various keys in the lock. The last one he tried fitted. He turned it slowly and pushed open the door.

He stood aside and allowed Wesley to enter first. Wesley took a step into the room and stopped so suddenly that Heffernan almost cannoned into him. The gaily patterned curtains, lined with blackout material, were drawn, allowing no light to seep in from the outside world. Wesley flicked the light switch inside the door and the electric bulb above him blazed.

It was a child's room ... a little boy's room, spacious and thickly carpeted with not a thing out of place. The bed was covered with a bright quilt, decorated with capering clowns. The shelves that lined the walls were crammed with colourful toys: building bricks, cars, soft toys and brightly coloured books. The drawers and wardrobes contained an array of small clothes and a bright plastic toy car, big enough for a child to sit in, stood by the side of the bed. It reminded Wesley of an Egyptian tomb where the deceased's possessions were piled up around him for use in the journey to the afterlife. This was Adam Hunting's shrine and, as in all the best shrines, the most personal relics were placed on the altar.

Wesley walked up to the pine dressing table, which was covered with a snowy damask cloth and flanked by a pair of candlesticks with half-burned candles and rivulets of dripped wax that had spilled down and dripped onto the dark blue carpet. Two square silver boxes, decorated with art nouveau foliage, lay in the centre of the table, and Wesley picked one up and opened it. Inside he found what looked like nail clippings, and when he examined the other he found that it contained a lock of dark brown hair. Adam's hair.

'Poor woman,' was Wesley's only comment.

'I think we've seen enough, Wes. Let's get out of here.'

Wesley felt the same. They left the room, switching off the light and locking the door behind them.

The room had made them forget about Corazón, who was waiting anxiously in the bedroom. She was shifting from foot to foot. Wesley smiled at her reassuringly. 'Did you know what was in the room, Corazón?'

She shook her head vigorously. 'Mrs Hunting, she would go in there for hours and lock the door behind her. She said I must never go in.'

'Weren't you curious?'

Corazón shook her head. If she had been curious about the locked room she certainly wasn't going to admit it to a pair of police officers.

'Where is Mr Hunting? Do you know?'

'He is going to the office in Plymouth then to Morbay.'

'Thanks, love. We'll catch up with him later.' Heffernan tapped the side of his nose and put his face close to hers. 'And I'd be grateful if you didn't mention our visit. No need to upset Mr Hunting, is there? We'll talk to him about it next time we see him. All right?'

Corazón looked at him like a frightened rabbit and nodded.

Wesley didn't speak until they reached the gate. 'Do you think we're anywhere nearer understanding why Loveday did what she did?'

Heffernan shrugged. 'Rejected by her parents for being

the one who survived when the favourite didn't. I reckon I can understand ... sort of.'

'We still don't know what killed little Adam.'

'That's a question for Aaron Hunting ... when we track him down.'

On his return to the office Wesley sat down at his desk and began to play with his pen, deep in thought. He glanced at Rachel and saw that she was watching him. She gave him a shy smile and returned her attention to her computer screen. He was about to ask her how her hunt for a flat of her own was progressing but decided against it.

Nobody had actually been charged with the murders of the Reverend Shipborne and Helen Wilmer yet, although the two chief suspects were still in custody and undergoing questioning. And as for Loveday Wilkins, her case had an air of tragedy ... a disturbed young woman lashing out at her neglectful family rather than a cunning blackmailer poisoning Huntings' goods for their own gain. Edith Sommerby and the mother and daughter who had been so ill had been unwitting victims, caught up in something that they knew nothing about. Loveday had been charged and remanded for psychiatric reports.

He looked up and saw Steve Carstairs walking into the office, strolling as if he had all the time in the world.

'Have you managed to find out anything about the Reverend Shipborne's background yet?' Wesley asked him.

Steve blushed. 'I'm still working on it.'

'You could try asking Barry Castello at Damascus Farm. He might know something.'

Steve hesitated.

'Take Paul with you when you go and see him.'

Steve nodded reluctantly and ambled over to the filing cabinets at the end of the office. Wesley had always suspected that somewhere deep inside Steve Carstairs there was a good police officer waiting to get out ... it was just that he was taking rather a long time to emerge.

Gerry Heffernan was standing in his doorway, like a squire surveying his acres with proprietorial pride. He caught Wesley's eye and beckoned him into his office.

'How's your Michael?' he began as he slumped down into his executive leather chair, now rather worn at the edges and moulded to the shape of his backside.

'Pam rang me from the hospital a few minutes ago and said he was sitting up and demanding ice cream. They're letting him home later today.'

Heffernan leaned back with an ominous creak and put his hands behind his head, smiling beatifically as though all was right with his world. Disasters averted, criminals locked up. But Wesley had an uneasy feeling that this was just the calm before some kind of storm.

'I've asked Steve and Paul to check out the Reverend Shipborne's background. And then there's the question of who strangled Helen Wilmer if William Verlan didn't.'

Heffernan grunted, annoyed that Wesley had destroyed his temporary idyll. 'Well, at least we've cleared up the supermarket poisonings.'

'We still have to get a statement from Aaron Hunting.' Wesley thought for a moment. 'And I want to know how his son died.'

'Probably quite irrelevant, Wes. But we'll have to speak to him. We don't want him moaning to the Chief Constable that we've been neglecting him, do we?' Heffernan paused. 'How about having another word with that Dermot O'Donovan about Helen Wilmer? If a girl gets herself strangled, it's as well to start looking at the boyfriend.'

'He had an alibi for the time she disappeared ... I've checked.'

'Alibis can be broken.' The telephone on the desk began to ring and after a brief conversation Heffernan looked at Wesley. 'That was the Nutter. I've been summoned to tea and biscuits in his office. He wants to talk about the implications of Chris Hobson's appeal and damage limitation, whatever that is. He also said he wants Shipborne's murder cleared up as soon as possible so we don't look as if we couldn't organise a piss-up in a brewery . . . my words not his, but that's the gist of it.'

Wesley smiled, certain that Chief Superintendent Nutter's original words had owed more to corporate-speak than to Heffernan's colourful vernacular.

He left Heffernan to prepare for his 'damage limitation' meeting and returned to the main office, which was buzzing with industry. Steve Carstairs was on the telephone, frowning with concentration as he wrote on his notepad.

Wesley sat down, wondering where to begin, when he was relieved of his dilemma by his telephone. He picked up the receiver and was surprised to hear Neil's voice on the other end of the line.

'Meet me at Belsham church in half an hour. I've got something you might be interested in.'

'I'm busy at the moment. Can't it wait?'

But the line had gone dead.

The door of Belsham church was slightly ajar. Wesley pushed it and stepped inside the building, standing still for a moment as his eyes adjusted to the gloom.

The place seemed to be empty, but his nose detected a pleasant smell of lavender polish, and there were fresh flowers, white lilies mainly, on the altar and beside the pulpit. He began to wander towards the east end and noticed that someone had been polishing the memorial brasses set into the chancel floor.

He walked slowly up to the altar, then turned round. If Neil wasn't there he might as well go: he was hardly short of things to see to back in the office. But then he noticed that the door to the tower was ajar and he could just make out a pale, flickering glow around its edge. He walked back down the aisle, the route trodden by so many Belsham brides over the centuries, and came to a halt at the tower-room door.

When he pushed the door it swung open. Flickering

candles bathed the tower room in soft golden light, bringing the faded painting on the wall into dappled animation
and making the recumbent alabaster figures on the Munnery
tombs look as if they were sleeping in firelight. The bell
ropes cast shadows like blackened nooses on the stone
walls, giving the place the look of some Gothic torture
chamber. Neil was sitting at the end of the room on a large
wooden chair in the style of a medieval throne, lit by a
forest of candles on the floor. A smile was playing on his
lips. He was enjoying the effect he was creating.

Wesley stepped over the threshold. The air was warm
from the candle flames, and the smell of hot wax mingled
with the mustiness of centuries. 'What's all this about?' He
didn't have time for playing games.

'I found the candles in a box. I thought it'd create the
right atmosphere.'

'For what?' Wesley glanced at his watch.

'For the story of Robert de Munerie, follower of Satan
and all-round bad guy. Take a pew.'

Wesley looked around. Behind him was an old bench, grey
with the dust and bird droppings of years. He sat down
gingerly on the edge. 'I haven't got time for this, you know.'

'It won't take long. Sitting comfortably? Then I'll
begin.' Neil paused dramatically as Wesley watched the
words of the deeply carved graffiti above the tombs dance
in the flames. 'The dregs of the people beg for mercy, o
Lord.' He shuddered at the words as Neil began his story.

'There was a young guy in Belsham called Robert de
Munerie ... playboy younger son of the local lord of the
manor and not short of a groat or two.'

Wesley smiled. Neil's style of storytelling had rather
spoiled the effect of the surroundings.

'Anyway,' Neil continued. 'This Robert fancies himself
as a bit of a magician. He reckons he's in league with the
Devil and has special powers. And if he was bad before he
went to Tradmouth on his dad's business, when he found
that everyone there was dropping dead of the plague while

he was immune he became even worse. He thought he was invincible ... had Satan's special protection. In reality he probably had some natural immunity, but he began to imagine that he was capable of anything. Anyway, he picks up this tart in Tradmouth who was showing symptoms of the plague and brings her back here to Belsham to infect his family so that he'd inherit the lands.'

Wesley took a deep breath. The air was thinning as the candle flames devoured the oxygen in the atmosphere. He was reluctant to admit it but Neil's story had aroused his interest.

Neil carried on. 'But things didn't go to plan. His mum died of the plague but his dad only got it mildly and recovered, as did his elder brother. The immunity was probably genetic but I don't really know much about these things. Anyway, Robert didn't hit the jackpot and inherit but the plague spread through Belsham like wildfire and almost three-quarters of the population were wiped out. There were too many bodies for the churchyard to take so they had to bury most of the victims in the church field near by ... which became known as Pestilence Field, or Pest Field.'

'So what happened to Robert?'

'Nobody knew. He just disappeared one night. There were all sorts of rumours, of course, the favourite being that the Devil had dragged him down to hell. He'd just vanished off the face of the earth. Then I found out about Barnaby Poulson's PhD thesis and I went to Morbay to have a look at it.' He paused for dramatic effect. 'Remember that skeleton we found buried on top of the others with his head bashed in? The one that was found with the dagger bearing the de Munerie coat of arms?'

'Yes.'

'That's Robert. That's what happened to him. How's that for poetic justice, eh? He ends up with the poor sods he infected with the Black Death. So come on, Detective Inspector ... who did it? Who killed Robert de Munerie?'

'This is all very interesting, Neil, but it sounds to me as if Robert de Munerie deserved everything that was coming to him. And I haven't time to give my professional opinion on a murder that happened nearly six hundred years ago. I've got a mountain of cases on my desk at the moment and the culprits are all alive, kicking and likely to do it again if they're not caught and put away.' He stood up and brushed himself off. 'And make sure you put out all these candles before you go. We don't want the place to catch fire.' He started to make for the door

'I haven't finished – don't you want to know who it was?'

'Tell me tonight. I take it you're still staying at ours.'

'If I'm welcome,' was the pointed answer.

Wesley walked out, saying nothing. After the week he'd had, he really didn't have time to indulge Neil's whims. As he walked out to the car, he rang Pam on his mobile to check that everything was all right at home. She sounded quite cheerful and informed him proudly that Michael was doing well. There had been a miraculous change in him and he was almost his old self. Like animals, young children never malinger: it's only when they're older that they learn to play for sympathy.

He had just opened his car door when he spotted a figure hurrying up the church path. He slammed the door shut again and began to follow, breaking into a run. Now was as good a time as any.

'Mrs O'Donovan. Can I have a quick word?'

But the woman quickened her pace as she made for the church door.

Wesley shouted his question again but she had changed direction suddenly and disappeared rapidly round the side of the church. He followed at a trot but when he reached the back of the church she wasn't there. All he could see was a forest of old gravestones peeping out from the over-grown grass. It was as if she'd disappeared into thin air . . . a vanishing trick.

Talking to Dermot O'Donovan had suddenly leapt to the top of his list of things to do.

Chapter Thirteen

My last diary is full so I must begin this new one.
Somehow writing down my thoughts helps. Barnaby
called today to give me a copy of his finished thesis.
He was so pathetically grateful for my help and he
seems quite unaware of what he has done to me. His
discoveries have been like a scalpel delving into a
wound that I once thought was healed. How I see
myself in that man Robert de Munerie, bringing plague
and death to the innocent.

Barnaby thinks the dead are buried in Pest Field.
Perhaps there should be some memorial there ...
something to say that this is the result when man's
arrogance tempts him to emulate the Almighty.

From the diary sent to DI Wesley Peterson by Dr
Anne Talbot

'Perhaps she was just in a hurry ... or wasn't in the mood
to talk to you. Perhaps you're reading too much into it.'

Wesley shook his head. 'No. She was definitely frightened of something. She took one look at me and ran ... or
at least that's how it seemed.' He smiled. 'I suppose I could
have been imagining it. But I still think it's a priority to
have a word with Dermot O'Donovan. He might know
more about Helen Wilmer's death than he says ... and

maybe even about Shipborne's. I still reckon the two are linked.'

'So you don't believe Verlan's confession?'

'In a word, Gerry, no.'

'He could be playing it clever ... trying to pull the wool over our eyes. He was Amy Hunting's lover and she went along to see Shipborne to confess that they'd been playing hide-the-sausage with each other.' Heffernan wrinkled his nose. 'Do people still go to the vicar to confess to adultery? It seems odd ... especially if she wasn't a churchgoer.'

'In his diary Shipborne said that he confessed something in a sermon. Wonder what it was.'

'Can't have been anything that bad or it would have made the tabloids. It was probably something like forgetting to pay his bus fare.'

'We can always see if Verlan knows. He's still in the cells.'

Heffernan pulled a face. 'I've got enough on my plate with the Hobson appeal. Would you believe that the Nutter wants to drag me along to a press conference? You were first choice, of course, as you know ... but I made your excuses.' He grinned wickedly. 'See how I look after you.'

Before Wesley could answer, there was a knock on the door. Through the glass they could see Steve Carstairs with a piece of paper in his hand. Heffernan shouted a booming 'Come in' and the door was opened.

Steve stood on the threshold, as if he wasn't sure if he was doing the right thing. Then he spoke, addressing Heffernan.

'The only trial I've found that the Reverend Shipborne took part in was Dermot O'Donovan's, sir. He was done for breaking and entering and Shipborne spoke up for him ... said he'd benefit from community service and spending some time at Damascus Farm. Dermot was eighteen at the time and it looks like the vicar's contribution stopped him going inside.'

'I reckon this Dermot character could be in this up to his neck,' was Heffernan's verdict.

Steve shuffled his feet awkwardly and looked downwards.

'Have you got anything on Shipborne's background? What he did before he became a vicar?'

Steve looked up. 'Yeah. I tracked down the niece who was mentioned in his will ... a Dr Anne Talbot. It was easy 'cause she hadn't changed her address.'

'And?'

'She said he was some sort of top scientist. They were all surprised when he announced he was going to chuck it all in and become a vicar. He had a great job, she said ... really well paid.'

'Maybe he thought there was more to life than money,' said Wesley quietly. 'Was he ever married?'

'Dr Talbot, the niece, said he was a widower. His wife had died quite young, she said. Cancer. There was one kid but it had died as a baby.'

'Did she say what kind of scientist he was? Who he worked for?'

'He worked for the government ... the Ministry of Defence, she said.'

Wesley's heart sank. If this whole thing was something to do with state secrets and highly confidential MoD work, it was way out of his league. James Bond territory. Former top government scientists being murdered and the event arranged to look like a robbery was just the sort of thing the secret services got up to ... or so he'd heard. He'd had very little to do with Special Branch in the course of his police career and even less to do with MI5 and MI6 – and that suited him fine.

'Look, Steve, can you call Dr Talbot again and ask her if there was any sort of diary amongst her uncle's personal effects. There was a full one kept here ... probably because it was bloodstained ... but it's possible he might have started writing another. If she has it, ask her to send it to me by registered post, will you?'

Steve looked mildly annoyed by this addition to his workload but he hurried out.

Heffernan sighed and began to doodle on something that looked like a budget report. 'Right, Wes, what have we got?'

'Philip Norbert had Shipborne's wallet and he admits that he was in the vicarage that night.'

'Pretty damning.'

'Perhaps . . . but I'm not leaping to conclusions just yet. There are other possibilities. What if Shipborne's death was connected with what he did for the Ministry of Defence . . . or what he knew? But I'm probably letting my imagination run away with me.'

'And we need to talk to Dermot O'Donovan, Helen Wilmer's boyfriend. As we now know, Shipborne spoke up for him in court on one occasion . . . got him sent to Damascus Farm.'

Wesley stood up. 'Last time we asked Castello about his own relationship with Shipborne. This time I'd like to ask him about Dermot O'Donovan and Shipborne. Did Dermot have some unfinished business with him? Maybe something that made Dermot lose his temper and kill him.'

'Or alternatively Shipborne's death may have been just what it seemed at the time – murder in the course of a robbery. If Philip Norbert's brief advises him to say it was an accident, he could get away with manslaughter.'

Wesley nodded. He knew this only too well. Getting away with murder was a common phenomenon: there were times, as he lay awake in the small hours of the morning, when he wondered why he went to all the trouble of catching criminals at all.

'So you're off to Damascus Farm again?' Heffernan looked at his watch. 'It'll have to be tomorrow. I've got to go and see the Nutter first thing in the morning so why don't you take Rachel? She looks as if she could do with a trip out. She's been quiet recently. Know what's wrong with her?'

Wesley shook his head and left the office.

*

If an artist had been painting the Dartmoor landscape the next morning, he or she would have made good use of the colour grey: mid-grey for the vast sky; green-grey for the sodden earth; a dark brownish grey for the trees and bushes; and a cold, darker shade for the scattered rocks, walls and farm buildings. A fine drizzle fell from the sky and drifted like mist in the biting breeze. Today there was no sunshine to make the raindrops sparkle like jewels on the wild land. Untamed and lovely as this place was in summer, Wesley found himself wondering how people survived up here in the winter.

He caught a whiff of Rachel's perfume as they drove. It was musky, sensual, quite unlike the light floral scent Pam wore when she had the time to be bothered. He looked out of the window and concentrated on the scenery.

Barry Castello must have heard their car engine because he was waiting at the farmhouse door to greet them, the smile fixed on his face. He shook hands courteously when Wesley introduced Rachel and led them inside. On their way in, they passed three youths who greeted Castello with a friendly nod. They didn't seem to be in awe of him; this was no prison regime.

'I didn't think I'd see you again so soon, Inspector,' Castello said as they sat down. 'How can I help you?'

'Last time I talked to you, you said you thought the Reverend Shipborne had been a scientist. Did you know he used to work for the Ministry of Defence?'

Castello shook his head. 'He never went into detail about what he did. I presume he thought that what he did before he gave his life to God wasn't particularly important.'

Wesley sat for a few moments, considering his next question. He had hoped that Castello would know more. He glanced up at the huge stone mantelpiece. There was a photograph there, a group of people in evening dress – men in tuxedos and women in shining cocktail frocks. He hadn't noticed it before but now he stared at the faces, focusing on each fixed smile. A younger Barry Castello was in the

296

middle, a champagne glass raised to the camera in an eternal toast. Aaron Hunting, looking sleek and prosperous, stood at his right hand. And he'd seen the woman standing to Castello's left before ... but that time she'd been dead.

'Isn't that Amy Hunting?'

Castello suddenly looked solemn. 'I heard about her death on the local news ... dreadful.'

'Did you know her well?'

'She came to a couple of fund-raising dinners many years ago. Her husband had given us some generous donations.'

'You still haven't said how well you knew her.'

'No, I haven't, have I.' Castello looked Wesley in the eye. The subject was closed ... for the time being.

Wesley studied the photograph again and spotted another familiar face just behind the main party. A much younger Keith Sturgeon, wearing uniform tuxedo, held his glass uncomfortably, as though he wished he were elsewhere. 'Who's that?' Wesley asked.

Castello made a show of peering at the image. 'I don't know. Someone from Huntings, I think. Why? Does it matter?'

Wesley tried another approach. 'Look, Mr Castello, you knew John Shipborne better than most people, is that true?'

'I suppose so.'

'Is it possible he might have been killed because of something in his past?'

Castello sat back and put the tips of his fingers together to form an arch. He stared at them for a while, as though making some sort of decision. After a while he spoke. 'To be perfectly honest, Inspector, the idea of John having had enemies seems ridiculous. If you'd known him you would have realised what a gentle, generous man he was.'

'According to his diary he fell out with his bell-ringers when he had the church tower locked up.'

Castello shrugged. 'He told me the tower was unsafe. It was probably a misunderstanding. John would never have willingly fallen out with anyone.'

'Perhaps he hadn't always been like that,' said Rachel. 'People can change. You did.'

He gave her a beaming smile. 'You're quite right, Detective Sergeant. People do change, and of course John did say . . . ' He stopped himself suddenly.

'Said what, Mr Castello?'

A silence.

'Please. It might be important. Nothing you say can harm him now, and it might help us catch whoever killed him.'

Castello leaned forward. 'Okay. John told me once that he'd done something he was deeply ashamed of: he said it had caused a great deal of harm. He never told me what it was but it certainly seemed to be on his conscience.'

'Could this have been when he was working for the Ministry of Defence?'

'Possibly. Although he never said it was connected with his work. I'm sorry I can't tell you more. But I suspect that this thing, whatever it was, was what attracted him to the church . . . seeking forgiveness, I suppose. I of all people can understand that.'

'Did he ever mention a trial?'

'Whose trial?'

'I don't know.'

Castello thought for a moment. 'I remember he did speak up for one of our boys when he went to court.'

'Dermot O'Donovan?'

Castello looked up at Wesley, surprised. 'Yes, that's right. He was one of John's parishioners. His mother used to clean at the vicarage. Dermot was a sly boy, if I remember rightly – bit of a charmer. I always had the feeling that he was just going through the motions, saying what he thought I wanted to hear. To be frank, I didn't expect him to be one of my success stories.'

Wesley and Rachel looked at each other.

'Do you think he'd be capable of murder?' Wesley asked, expecting the answer to be no.

298

'Who knows? As I said, he was a sly boy, the type who would always make sure he had an alibi. I expected him to reoffend but John used to say we had to show him trust. I know he used to wander in and out of the vicarage ... "borrowed" his mother's keys. But as far as I know he never got into trouble again so John might have been right ... or at least he never got caught.'

Wesley was surprised at Castello's cynicism about those in his charge, worthy of any police officer. The man's realistic take on human nature raised him a few notches in his estimation.

Castello's face clouded. 'You don't think he could have killed John, do you? Because if he did I'd never forgive myself for not keeping a closer eye on the situation.'

'Was there any antagonism between O'Donovan and Mr Shipborne?'

'I didn't see anything like that myself but ... I don't know. It's possible, I suppose.' He looked from Wesley to Rachel. 'Do you think I've screwed up? Do you think it could be my fault?'

'Don't worry about it, Mr Castello,' said Rachel, knowing that her reassurances would be useless if Dermot O'Donovan turned out to be John Shipborne's killer.

They grabbed a quick sandwich at a roadside pub but there wasn't time to linger over lunch. They had to talk to Dermot O'Donovan. It was beginning to rain heavily as they drove back over the moor towards the Plymouth road, and the landscape looked grim through grey mist and windscreen wipers. Just outside Buckfastleigh Wesley fumbled in his pocket for his mobile phone and rang Gerry Heffernan to tell him their plans while Rachel drove on, her eyes on the slippery, glistening road. The chief inspector sounded weary on the other end of the line and said he wished he were coming with them. It seemed that he had been on the receiving end of a load of crap from Nutter about public relations and the reputation of the force, and from the tone of his voice he sounded well and truly fed up.

Gerry Heffernan wasn't one of nature's PR men. And Wesley shared his view that Chris Hobson could best be served if they discovered the truth and cleared his name once and for all. No lingering doubts. No TV documentaries in a year or so's time claiming that Hobson did it after all. By the time they reached Dermot O'Donovan's front door, Wesley was feeling quite indignant on his boss's behalf.

Rachel hadn't said much. When Wesley, making conversation, had ventured to ask her how her flat-hunting was progressing, she made a non-committal reply: she had viewed a few more flats around Tradmouth, without her parents' knowledge, but she still hadn't found anything suitable. For the rest of the journey they stuck to work matters.

Dermot O'Donovan lived on a new estate on the outskirts of Plymouth; all brick driveways, mock Tudor gables and en suite bathrooms. When Wesley had met him he had said he owned his own building firm. If his house was anything to judge by, the business must be ticking along nicely.

Wesley was surprised to find O'Donovan's front door wide open and a couple of men standing on the doorstep. They wore grey suits and looked like a pair of shifty chartered accountants. As Wesley emerged from the passenger door and slammed it loudly behind him, the men turned, frowning. He had the feeling he wasn't welcome.

He advanced on them, holding out his warrant card like a shield. 'DI Wesley Peterson, Tradmouth CID. I'm here to have a word with a Mr Dermot O'Donovan. Is he at home?' He thought it best to ignore the hostile looks that were being beamed his way. The men stood side by side in the doorway facing him. One was tall and thin, the other shorter and fatter with a moustache. Wesley was reminded of Laurel and Hardy ... but this pair didn't look funny.

The tall, thin man scowled and held out a warrant card of his own. 'Be my guest, mate. Inspector Nick Forbes, Fraud Squad, and this is DS Masters. We're here to have a word with Mr O'Donovan about his business interests ...

and we've been searching the premises.'

As if on cue Rachel emerged from the driver's seat, smiling. 'Nick. Nice to see you again. How are you?'

Forbes blushed and smoothed down his hair. 'I'm fine, Rachel. Long time no see, eh? What's all this about, then?'

Wesley, annoyed at being pointedly ignored, answered. 'We're conducting a murder investigation. We need to speak to Mr O'Donovan.'

As Wesley watched Forbes undressing Rachel with his eyes, he felt an unexpected stab of anger.

'Well, we won't be here for much longer.' Forbes took his eyes off Rachel and addressed Wesley. 'O'Donovan's inside ... help yourself.'

They stood aside to let Wesley and Rachel into the house. Dermot O'Donovan had just emerged from the kitchen, chewing at the nails of his right hand.

He looked at Wesley defiantly. 'What the hell do you want? I've got two of your lot here already.'

'Sorry to bother you, Mr O'Donovan, but we'd like to ask you a few more questions about the murder of the Reverend John Shipborne ... and Helen Wilmer.'

Wesley wasn't mistaken; for a split second Dermot O'Donovan looked frightened. 'I've told you all I know already. Look, my wife'll be back soon. I'd appreciate it if you could get all this over and done with before ... ' He spotted Forbes making for the stairs. 'What are you doing? You've been up there already.'

'We won't be much longer ... sir,' said Forbes, as though he planned to take his time if it suited him. He looked at his colleague. 'I take it we've seen all your business accounts?'

'I've told you already ... most of them are in my office.'

'Some of our colleagues are searching your office premises at the moment, sir. We're just here to make sure you're not keeping any little secrets from us.' DS Masters grinned unpleasantly and touched his moustache as he gave Rachel a knowing wink.

'Why don't we go through to your living room to have a

chat,' Wesley suggested, anxious to put some distance between himself and the pair of clowns from the Fraud Squad. O'Donovan nodded, resigned to his fate, and led the way.

'What's all that about?' Wesley asked as he sank into O'Donovan's expensive leather armchair.

'It looks as if my accountant's been cooking my books. Nothing to do with me.'

Wesley found himself almost believing this heartfelt protestation of innocence. He was beginning to think that O'Donovan should have chosen acting as a career rather than building.

'They're not going to find anything, you know. I've got nothing to hide.'

'We've been to see Barry Castello.'

O'Donovan's expression gave nothing away. 'Have you?'

'Told us you were a bad lad.'

'Surely you knew that already. I've made no secret of it.'

'Where were you when the Reverend Shipborne was murdered?'

'I was in the pub with some mates but I left early and went straight home . . . got back about the same time as my mum. I was there the rest of the evening . . . my mother'll tell you.'

'Were you asked about your whereabouts at the time?'

Dermot thought for a moment. 'No. I don't think so.'

'We've come across someone else who says he was in the Horse and Farrier that evening . . . Philip Norbert. Know him?'

Dermot frowned. 'There was a lad called Phil . . . dark hair . . . went to some posh school . . . bit of a tearaway.'

'Was he there that night?'

'Can't remember after all this time. Might have been.'

'And where were you when Helen Wilmer disappeared?'

'Home with my mum. I told the police.'

'Did you love Helen?' Rachel asked quietly.

He shrugged. 'I was very young . . . and what is love anyway?'

Rachel didn't reply.

'Look, Mr O'Donovan,' said Wesley, 'I want you to tell us everything you know about Helen Wilmer. Who were her friends? What was her relationship with the Reverend Shipborne? What kind of girl was she? Did she mention that she was worried about anything? Afraid of anybody?'

Dermot thought for a few moments. 'Well, there was a bloke at the supermarket ... at Huntings: she worked there in the holidays. He was a big bloke ... worked in the warehouse. She used to say she wished he'd stop following her about and staring at her.'

Wesley sat forward. This was a new piece of information. Edith Sommerby's unpleasant husband had once worked in Huntings' warehouse. And someone else whose name escaped him for the moment.

'That wouldn't be a man called Edward Baring?' Luckily Rachel had a better memory for names.

Dermot shook his head. 'I don't remember the name but I saw him once. Curly hair and built like a brick shithouse.'

This sounded like Big Eddie all right. 'So what did he do?' Wesley asked.

'Just used to watch her ... gave her the creeps.'

'Nothing more?'

'Not that she told me.'

Wesley and Rachel looked at each other. It might be worth paying Big Eddie another visit.

'Can you think of anything else?' asked Rachel.

Dermot was silent for a few seconds, as though making a decision. When he eventually spoke the words came out in a rush. 'It was Helen's idea. I had nothing to do with it. I just read the letter through for her.'

'What letter?'

'She wrote it and asked me to read it through. I said it was a stupid idea but she thought it'd be fun ... like an adventure. I said it could be dangerous but she said it could get us some cash ... it could get us out of Belsham and off to London.'

'What did the letter say?'

303

'I can't remember exactly. Something like "I saw you coming out of the vicarage", and she asked for a thousand pounds to keep quiet. I didn't want anything to do with it.'

Wesley leaned forward, his heart beating. 'So who was the letter addressed to? Who was she trying to blackmail?'

But Dermot shook his head. 'I've no idea. She said it was best if I didn't know. I thought she was playing a game. I never thought she'd go through with it . . . '

Wesley looked him in the eye. 'We keep hearing that Helen was a nice girl before she got involved with you. She was a student teacher . . . she used to teach in the Sunday school. Now how does a girl like that become a scheming little blackmailer? You tell me that.'

Dermot shrugged, the ghost of a smile on his face. 'She didn't need much encouraging, believe me. It was like she'd been in a cage for years and when she saw the outside world she went wild.'

'And you were the outside world?'

'Perhaps I was at first. But she was more than up for it . . . gagging to lose her virginity and try out dope. She used to like taking risks . . . she scared me sometimes. I might have taught her a thing or two about life but she was a bloody good pupil and when she disappeared I thought she'd just moved on to bigger things . . . maybe gone to London without me to try her luck.'

'Do you know if the letter was ever sent?'

'I'd told her it was a stupid idea so she never mentioned it again. I thought she'd taken my advice and torn it up.'

'And you never tried to find out what had happened to her?'

'I did at first but then later I moved on . . . as you see.'

There was a commotion outside in the hallway. Wesley looked round as a woman entered. She was bottle blonde with a thin, pinched face, and a pair of small children, a boy with a crew cut and a girl with a fair ponytail, both dressed in fancy private school blazers, stood either side of her like bodyguards.

'What the hell's going on? They say they're police . . . what's been happening?'

Dermot O'Donovan stood up, walked over to his wife and put a protective arm around her as the children looked on, half curious, half excited at having policemen in the house. 'It's just a misunderstanding, love. My accountant's been on the fiddle . . . nothing for you to worry about.'

Wesley almost found himself believing every word that Dermot said.

'So is Dermot O'Donovan in the frame or not?' Gerry Heffernan put his feet up on the desk.

Wesley was temporarily distracted by the sight of his boss's shoes, worn down at the heel, in urgent need of a visit to the menders.

'Is he our man, Wes? What do you think?'

'I think he probably knows more than he's saying and he seems to have a formidable talent in the lie-telling department. But I've no idea if he killed Shipborne or Helen Wilmer. He did say that Helen was wild . . . up for anything, as though she'd just been released from a cage.'

'That's not the impression her parents gave us.'

'Well, it wouldn't be, would it? But can we believe that she was blackmailing Shipborne's killer and O'Donovan was the one who was holding her back? What do you think?'

'She wouldn't be the first demure little miss who's forgotten what she learned at Sunday school and strayed onto the path of wickedness, Wes. O'Donovan could be telling the truth. In which case Shipborne's killer is probably Helen's killer and all.'

'Dermot said that Edward Baring, Big Eddie the metal detectorist, had a bit of a crush on Helen when she worked at Huntings . . . used to stare at her and follow her about. There's no hint that he did any more than that, but it might be worth having another word with him.'

Heffernan nodded. 'We'll put him on our list. What did you learn from Barry Castello?'

'He said that Shipborne had done something in his past that he was deeply ashamed of, but he didn't know what it was.'

'Murdered someone? Raped someone?'

'Shipborne seemed to have been the type of man who would have been deeply ashamed if his library books were overdue. But it's worth looking into.'

There was a knock on the office door. Through the glass they could see Trish Walton standing outside with a piece of paper in her hand. Heffernan beckoned her in.

'You know you asked for a copy of Adam Hunting's death certificate, sir ... well, I've got one. There was an inquest as well and the verdict was natural causes. He'd been ill for some time and he'd just had a major operation.'

Wesley took the paper from her and stared down at it. Unlike his parents and his sister, he had no detailed medical knowledge, and he could only guess what the scrawled words in the 'cause of death' section meant. He looked at Adam's date of birth. He had been five when he died ... a little boy born into a wealthy family with his life ahead of him. But at least now they knew that young Adam's death wasn't suspicious. It had probably been a waste of time going to the trouble of getting the death certificate – another dead end.

Gerry Heffernan interrupted his thoughts. 'So what did the kid die of?'

'I'm not sure yet. I think we should have another word with Aaron Hunting.'

'Well, don't mention his kid's death. The poor bugger's been through enough. I mean, his crazy daughter's tried to ruin his business and his wife's just topped herself ... '

But half an hour later they were parking outside Huntings supermarket in Morbay, Wesley still stinging slightly from Heffernan's accusations of insensitivity. They had phoned the company's head office in Exeter and been told that Hunting was at the Morbay branch, now reopened after the recent crisis. As they made their way up to Keith Sturgeon's office, Wesley noticed that the atmosphere

306

among the staff seemed lighter now that the threat of poisoning had been removed.

It was Sunita Choudray who showed them into the manager's office. Wesley asked her whether everything was okay and she nodded shyly. Presumably her parents weren't aware of her secret yet. She asked what had happened to Loveday and Wesley told her. She had been charged and remanded for psychiatric reports. Sunita appeared to have little sympathy, which was hardly surprising: Loveday had killed one old lady, made two other people very ill and put all their jobs under threat.

Aaron Hunting was sitting in the manager's chair while Keith Sturgeon sat opposite in the visitor's seat, his shirt-sleeves rolled up as though he was preparing for a hard afternoon's work, his eyes fixed on the file in front of him. When Heffernan said they wanted to see Mr Hunting alone, Sturgeon looked relieved and hurried from the room to attend to some unspecified task.

It was Heffernan who spoke first. 'I didn't expect you to be back at work so soon after ... '

'It's better than sitting at home brooding on what might have been, Chief Inspector. I've always found work helps at times like this.'

'Quite right, sir. I understand that you've had your share of tragedy. I don't know whether your housekeeper told you that we'd visited your house.'

'She said something about Loveday telling you to look round.' He gave a weary smile. 'I presume you didn't have a search warrant ... but I'll let it pass this time.'

'We saw your late son's room.' Wesley waited for a reaction but Hunting merely lowered his eyes.

'Yes. Corazón told me you'd been in there. Perhaps you'll understand now that Amy was ill ... obsessed with Adam. And Loveday's instability didn't help the situation. She was a difficult child.' He hesitated. 'Difficult to love. I suppose I'm partly to blame for what happened.'

'You can't blame yourself, sir,' Wesley said quickly. 'What

exactly did your son die of, if you don't mind me asking?'

'A lung infection, Inspector ... complications after an operation. Amy never got over it. At first she sank into terrible depressions when she wouldn't even get out of bed, then she went wild ... drank a lot ... had affairs. She had Adam's room sealed off as a shrine and she spent hours in there alone. I don't suppose I helped very much ... I just buried myself in work as I always have. Perhaps I should have paid Amy more attention but ... it's not something I'm very good at. I thought of divorce, of course ... but then I kept telling myself that it wasn't her fault.'

'No,' Wesley heard himself saying. Aaron Hunting may have loved Amy in his own way ... he just hadn't known how to handle her grief. Wesley felt that there was something profoundly sad, even ironic, about a man with all that material wealth having to endure such a wretched private life. Perhaps it would teach him that the rich don't always have things their own way.

'Can I see Loveday?' Hunting asked suddenly.

'Of course. I'll arrange it for you.'

Heffernan cleared his throat. It was time to go.

'If there's anything else you want, Mr Hunting ... '

'Thank you, Inspector. You've been very understanding.'

'I don't half feel sorry for that poor bugger, Wes,' Heffernan said as they reached the carpark.

Wesley smiled and said nothing.

It was late when they returned to the office. There had been a queue for the car ferry back from the Morbay side of the river: it was the time when most people were returning home from work ... people who didn't have murderers to apprehend.

Rachel was at her desk, looking as though she was in no hurry to get home. She stood up when Wesley and Heffernan entered the office but Trish beat her to it. She hurried up to the newcomers as if she'd been on the edge of her seat, waiting for them to arrive.

308

'I've got the full details of Adam Hunting's inquest here, sir. Apparently he'd been born with a heart defect and he'd just had an operation to correct it. A few days after he came out of hospital he picked up an E. coli infection which affected his lungs. The poor little lad was too weak to fight it and he died. It was natural causes all right.'

'Thanks, Trish,' said Wesley, dismissing the possibility that the unfortunate child's death could have anything to do with later events. It was a tragedy for his family ... but not one that could be blamed on anybody else.

As Trish hurried away, Rachel saw her opportunity. She slipped into Heffernan's office before the two men had a chance to sit down.

'I've been looking at the Shipborne case again, sir,' she said to Heffernan, her eyes bright with the excitement of the chase. 'Dermot O'Donovan said he was at home with his mother on the night Shipborne was murdered ... '

Wesley nodded. 'That's what he said. He went to the pub early and got back just as his mother arrived home from the vicarage: that would be around ten past seven. Then he stayed home for the rest of the evening.'

'Well, he wasn't asked to make a statement at the time but his mother, Shipborne's housekeeper, told the police she went round to a friend's on the other side of the village at seven thirty ... called into the vicarage on the way back and found Shipborne dead around ten. Dermot was alone. He hasn't got an alibi.'

Wesley looked sceptical. 'It was a long time ago. Perhaps he's forgotten.'

'Didn't you say that you never forget where you were when something dramatic happens, Wes? The President Kennedy syndrome? If his mum's employer had been murdered, surely he'd remember exactly what happened that evening.'

Wesley sighed. Heffernan was probably right. It would all make sense. And what if the story about the blackmail letter was a lie to put them on the wrong track? If Philip Norbert had been telling the truth about finding the body, then Dermot O'Donovan might have committed the murder earlier that evening. Wesley looked at his watch. It was getting late.

'We'll pick him up tomorrow, Wes,' Heffernan announced, beaming benevolently. 'Give him another night in the bosom of his loving family. Time's marching on and I've got choir practice tonight, so why don't we call it a day?'

Wesley reached for his coat. Then he stopped suddenly and swung round. 'You've just reminded me. We've not checked out the sermon yet ... Shipborne's confession. Verlan said he went to Belsham church sometimes. He might have been there.'

But Heffernan already had his coat on and was heading for the door. 'You ask him, Wes. I'm off home.'

Ten minutes later the custody sergeant was unlocking the door of Verlan's cell down in the bowels of the station. When the heavy door swung open Verlan was revealed, sitting on the blue plastic mattress, hugging his knees, hunched up in the fetal position, his back against the starkly painted brick wall. He looked up hopefully, as though he was glad to have some company ... any company.

'Dr Verlan, do you mind if I ask you a question ... just informally ... nothing to do with the offences you're charged with?'

Verlan straightened his body and looked at Wesley eagerly. 'Sure, go ahead.'

'According to the Reverend Shipborne's diary he confessed to something in a sermon but he doesn't say what that something was. I know you sometimes went to St Alphage's so I wondered if you were there ... if you remembered what it was he said. I know it's a long time ago but ... '

But Verlan was now sitting bolt upright. 'Sure I was there. How could I forget a thing like that?'

'So what did he confess to? What had he done?' Wesley leaned forward, awaiting the answer.

Chapter Fourteen

The priest of Belsham, a certain Hammo, had, against the rulings of the Church, taken a woman to his bed. She was a young widow by the name of Hawise and she did bear him two children and he made no secret of his dealings with them. Now when Robert de Munerie brought the whore who carried the pestilence to the village, the woman Hawise and her children fell sick and died. Hammo lived on but he was distraught for it seemed he bore this woman and her children much love. Hammo knew what manner of man this Robert was and what he had done as he had boasted of the matter before him. Some said that the priest, Hammo, was sick with grief at his loss and did slay the said Robert and did bury him with those dead of the pestilence he brought. But all we can know for certain is that Robert de Munerie was never seen again and there are those who said that Satan came for him and dragged him to hell and others that he went over the sea to France.

After tending the sick of his flock and carving words upon the wall of his church that bore witness to his despair, this sorry priest, showing symptoms of the pestilence, sinned by taking his own life, God rest his soul.

This tale was told me by a brother of this house who

*was a child at the time of the great mortality and who,
by God's will, survived, and it teaches us that it is ill
to fight wickedness with wickedness and we must trust
to the vengeance of the Almighty.*

*Extract from the second sermon of Richard
Thorsleigh, Abbot of Morre Abbey in the county of
Devon, quoted in Barnaby Poulson's thesis*

'I presumed you knew already,' said Verlan. 'John
Shipborne stood up there and said that he'd killed at least
four people … and that he was responsible for numerous
babies having been born dead or severely disabled.'

Wesley looked at him, puzzled.

'He'd been the chief scientist in charge of germ warfare
experiments at a secret government research establishment.
He'd come up with the bright idea of spraying certain areas
of South Devon with live bacteria to find out how they
would spread and survive … and to test their effect on
animals and humans.'

Wesley was annoyed with himself for not thinking of this
before. Germ warfare trials … the trial mentioned in
Shipborne's diary had had nothing to do with the criminal
justice system.

Verlan continued. 'He'd told the powers that be that the
bacteria were quite harmless, of course … that they were
ones found normally in the environment. Only he used
large quantities, and when public health reports started to
come in some time later, the authorities started to suspect
that they weren't quite as harmless as he had claimed.'

Wesley sat down on the blue plastic mattress beside
Verlan. 'Go on.'

'Anyway, a couple of years later, when the various
reports were collated, it was found that farmers in the area
had reported cattle dying of a virulent strain of E.coli at
around the time of the trials. And there were the clusters of
serious birth defects … and several deaths, mainly elderly

312

people or the young with weakened immune systems. It was all hushed up, of course.'

'Until Shipborne made his confession from the pulpit.'

'Yes. He confessed that it had been his pet project. He'd been playing God with people's lives and he wanted to take full responsibility ... although I expect he was just one of a team. That's what had made him join the Church, he said – when he found out what he'd been a party to he felt he had to change his life and try to make amends. That's what I told Amy ... Shipborne wasn't a bad man ... he'd just made a mistake – got carried away, like we all do at times.'

'You told Amy Hunting?'

'Yes. I didn't tell you the truth, I'm afraid. She had told me about her little boy, Adam, and I began to wonder if Shipborne's experiments might have caused his last illness ... the timing was right. She said she wanted to see Shipborne face to face so she came up with the idea of going to the vicarage to talk to him. I was worried about what she'd do ... but at that stage she seemed to be very calm, almost as though she was starting to accept it.'

'Do you know if she told her husband what she'd discovered?'

'I don't know. They led separate lives. In fact she once told me that Aaron Hunting wasn't Adam's father.'

This was news to Wesley.

'She told me she'd been having an affair with Adam's father and she'd got pregnant.'

'Did Hunting know about this?'

'I've no idea. Possibly not. I had the impression that she kept that particular affair very discreet.'

'Did the real father know Adam was his?'

'Yes. She said that he hadn't any other children of his own and he'd been devastated by Adam's death.'

Wesley thought, not for the first time, that Aaron Hunting seemed to have got a raw deal out of his marriage. 'And did Amy say who Adam's father was?'

'Not to me.'

'Why didn't you tell us all this earlier?'

Verlan said nothing.

'Do you think Amy Hunting could have killed the Reverend Shipborne?'

William Verlan looked him in the eye for the first time during their interview. 'Yes, I think she might have done. I should never have told her about his involvement in the trials. She was obsessed by Adam's death, and as soon as I heard about the murder on the radio news I prayed that Amy wasn't responsible ... that she hadn't let things go that far. To tell you the truth I was relieved when they said it was a robbery and they arrested someone for it. But now they're saying that man's innocent and ... Perhaps that's why she killed herself: with all the publicity about that man's appeal she might have been afraid that the truth would come out.'

Wesley left Verlan in his cell and wandered back up to the CID office.

Paul and Trish had been sent to Neston to ask Edward Baring about his dealings with Helen Wilmer. An hour later they reported back that he denied ever having had more to do with Helen than the occasional exchange of light banter and complained about police harassment. He had seemed horrified at the suggestion that he might know something about her death and had protested his innocence so loudly that he had set his dog barking and his neighbours banging on the walls.

Paul came away from the small terraced house convinced that Baring had been telling the truth. Trish, however, thought he had protested too much. Wesley steered the middle course and concluded that he was worth keeping an eye on ... just in case.

Rachel was still at her desk when Wesley set off for home. He said nothing to her about Verlan's revelations: he needed time to think, to go over the implications in his mind.

It was raining when he left the police station and there was a chill in the air. He pulled his coat closely around him and shivered. It was dark and the shining pavements reflected the headlights of the homeward-bound traffic and the lights from shop windows. It was that sad time of year; too late for summer and too early for Christmas. He pulled his collar up and set off down the high street, dodging the crawling cars on the way to Baynard's Quay, hoping Gerry wouldn't have set off for choir practice just yet.

He hurried past cafés and restaurants, half empty now the tourist season was over, and ignored the tempting aroma drifting out from the fish-and-chip shop. Soon the narrow street opened out onto a cobbled quayside with a pub at one end and a small defensive castle at the other. The water lapped to his left and boats bobbed energetically at anchor. It was high tide and slivers of reflected light flashed on the choppy water.

Heffernan lived in a small whitewashed cottage tucked away at the end of a row of grander houses, the former dwellings of customs officials and retired sea captains. Wesley hurried to his front door and knocked. When Heffernan answered Wesley noticed that he had exchanged his shirt and tie for a roll-neck sweater in a dubious shade of beige: Gerry had never been a contender for the 'world's best dressed' list.

'I would have thought you'd have been home seeing how your little lad is,' he said as he stood aside to let his colleague in.

Wesley experienced a sudden pang of guilt. 'I'm not staying long. I just thought I'd tell you I've been having a word with William Verlan.'

Heffernan slumped down on the sofa, picked up a half-empty plate of fish and chips from the coffee table and put it on his knee. He was in the middle of his meal. 'And?' he said, waving a chip in Wesley's direction.

Wesley shook his head, resisting the temptation. 'He told me that Shipborne's job at the MoD was conducting germ warfare trials. Apparently a cloud of bacteria was sprayed over this area of South Devon around the time Adam Hunting died. Later on it was found that it had caused problems ... birth defects, death in people with weakened immune systems, cattle deaths. It was all covered up, of course.'

'Now why doesn't that surprise me?' said Heffernan with his mouth full.

'Shipborne felt bad about the effects of the experiment he'd masterminded and that's why he quit and joined the Church. Anyway, one Sunday he decided to make a full confession in a sermon and Verlan was in church when he made it. He put two and two together and realised that Adam Hunting could have been one of Shipborne's victims so he went and told Amy Hunting. She went to see Shipborne on some cock-and-bull pretext and Verlan reckons she might have killed him. You saw that room. You saw how the boy's death had affected her. She was mad with grief ... obsessed ... so when someone came along and more or less confessed that they were responsible for her son's death ... '

'Well, we can hardly arrest her now, can we?'

'And there's another thing ... Verlan says Aaron Hunting wasn't Adam's real father.'

Heffernan nearly choked on a chip. 'What makes him think that?'

'Amy told him.'

'So who was the father?'

Wesley answered with a shrug. 'Just thought I'd keep you posted.'

'I presume Hunting knows the lad wasn't his.'

'Verlan didn't know. He said Amy was neglected by her husband and she embarked on a discreet affair with someone ... unlike the affairs she had after Adam's death, which apparently weren't very discreet.'

'Think it's relevant?'

'Perhaps.'

Heffernan waved the plate in front of Wesley and this time he succumbed and helped himself to a chip. It was cold but he ate it anyway.

'I'd better be off.'

'And I'd better get organised or I'll be late for choir practice again.' He looked at his watch. 'Give my love to Pam, eh?'

Wesley left him alone with his washing up and set off up the damp, cold streets, climbing towards home. When he turned round he had a spectacular view of the lights of Tradmouth below him but there was no time to linger, and besides it was too cold to stand and stare. He quickened his pace and soon reached home.

Neil was the first to greet him when he stepped through the front door.

'You ready to hear the rest of that story now?'

It took Wesley a few seconds to remember what he was talking about. 'Tell me over supper, eh? Where's Pam?' He could hear no sound from within the house.

'She's upstairs catching up on her sleep. I told her to have a rest.'

'And Michael?' He felt a sudden pang of guilt that he hadn't rushed straight up to see how his son was doing.

'He's fine. Don't worry.'

'I'd better just . . . ' He began to make for the stairs.

'He's asleep. Pam'd go mad if you went and woke him up.'

Wesley hovered in the hallway. Neil was probably right. He shouldn't be trying to make up for his long absences by waking up a sleeping child. But he felt a wave of resentment that Neil of all people should be more in tune with his own son's requirements than he was.

'Your supper's in the microwave, by the way,' Neil informed him, sounding smug.

'So what's new?' Wesley muttered under his breath, making for the kitchen. He found the room in a terrible state with unwashed dishes piled by the sink and smears of

317

butter and jam around the handles of the cupboards. In Wesley's experience Neil always left signs of his habitation for all to see, like a wild animal leaving the debris of its kill in a cave.

When he was seated in front of a plate of reheated pasta Bolognaise Neil came in and sat down opposite him. 'Now how far had I got?'

Wesley looked up at him, his loaded fork in midair on the way to his mouth. 'As far as I can recall you were asking me to reopen a six-hundred-year-old murder case.'

Neil's face reddened. 'I wouldn't put it quite like that. I'd only asked you to guess who killed Robert de Munerie.'

'Neil, I do enough of that sort of thing at work. Why don't you just tell me?'

Neil looked disappointed. 'Okay, then. I'd told you Robert de Munerie brought the Black Death to Belsham, didn't I?'

Wesley nodded, his mouth full of pasta.

'Well, it turned out that the priest, Hammo, had a girl-friend, and she had a couple of kids. Hammo didn't die of the Black Death but the girlfriend and kids did. Anyway, Robert went round boasting about how he brought the plague to the village and how his special powers made him immune. Then he mysteriously disappeared and there were various theories about what had happened to him. Some people thought he'd gone abroad and some even said that the Devil had dragged him to hell, but now I've got proof that Hammo wiped the smirk off his face by killing him and dumping him in the plague pit with all his victims: natural justice, I suppose you could call it.'

'So what became of Hammo?' Wesley said as he chased an elusive piece of pasta around the plate with his fork.

'He felt so bad about what he'd done that he killed himself. Don't know why ... it sounded as if that Robert deserved all he got.'

'So how did the story come out?'

'A kid who survived the Black Death in Belsham became a monk in Morre Abbey and told the abbot, who wrote it down as a cautionary tale ... Barnaby Poulson found the original document in Exeter Cathedral archives. I'm glad he went to the trouble ... it's nice to know the story behind what you're digging up.' He hesitated. 'I went over to Pest Field and did a bit of digging after you'd gone.'

'Does that mean you're better?' Wesley tried not to sound too hopeful.

'Yeah. I'd be thinking of moving on if you and Pam didn't need me here to help out. But I don't mind staying for a while.'

Wesley almost choked on his last piece of pasta. 'Thanks, Neil, but I think we can manage. And you'll be wanting to get back to Belsham to be nearer the dig, won't you. We'll be fine. Don't worry about us.'

Neil, oblivious to the irony in Wesley's voice, gave his old friend a satisfied grin and put his feet up on one of the other chairs. 'By the way, Pam said could you clear up in here. She says it's getting on her nerves.'

Wesley looked him in the eye. 'Tell you what, Neil, why don't you do it?'

Neil gaped at him, puzzled, as Wesley left the kitchen, making for the stairs ... for Pam and Michael.

Wesley spent half the night lying awake, going over the case in his head, turning over all the possibilities and coming up with no clear conclusion. It hadn't helped that Pam too had been awake, disturbed by the discomforts of late pregnancy. By the time the morning came they were both exhausted.

At the station the next day Rachel greeted him with the news that the boss wanted a word with him. Wesley hurried to the chief inspector's office, eager to seek Gerry's opinion on the theories and ideas that had been spinning around in his head during the early hours. However, he was disappointed to find the boss slumped at his desk, his head buried in a newspaper, uttering angry exclamations under his breath.

'What's the matter?' Wesley asked as he stepped over the threshold.

'Have you see this, Wes? "Police incompetence led to wrongful arrest." It's all over the front page.'

'I take it Chris Hobson's appeal has started.'

'It certainly has. And the full glare of publicity is on the corrupt officers of Tradmouth CID.'

'Those particular corrupt officers are long gone,' Wesley pointed out.

'That's not what it sounds like here. You know how newspapers twist things. It makes us sound like a load of useless crooks. I sometimes wonder why we bother.'

Wesley slumped down in a chair and yawned. 'I shouldn't worry about it.'

'It might help if we came up with the right man. Any thoughts? Think we should charge Phil Norbert?'

'I'd like a word with Aaron Hunting first. Even if Verlan was right and he wasn't really Adam's father, he probably thought he was. He might have wanted revenge for his son's death.'

'You'll have to be tactful, Wes.'

Wesley smiled. 'Tact isn't something you normally worry about.'

'I do when the person we're talking to is likely to take cocktails with the Chief Constable. You want to go now and get it over with? No time like the present.'

Half an hour later they found themselves at the front door of Hunting Moon House. Wesley always felt a little awkward when they called, as though he should have been using the tradesman's entrance as policemen did in old films.

When Corazón answered the door, she told them that Mr Hunting was down in the boathouse. He was about to go sailing. Gerry Heffernan's eyes lit up and he set off round the side of the house following Corazón's directions, Wesley following behind, almost running to keep up. They reached a set of concrete steps that appeared to lead down

320

to the water but a sharp right turn brought them out on a small balcony, protected on the river side with wrought-iron railings, painted black and free of any trace of rust. There was a wooden door ahead: Heffernan tried the handle and it opened. They had found the boathouse.

It was considerably bigger than Wesley had imagined; a cavernous space beneath the house where a large yacht bobbed at anchor. There was probably room there to moor a smaller boat as well, and it reminded Wesley of a scaled-down version of a villain's underground headquarters in a James Bond film. In the dim glow of the overhead fluorescent lights Wesley could see a figure moving about on the deck. Aaron Hunting looked preoccupied and unselfconscious as he made preparations for his voyage, and Wesley knew that he hadn't seen them. They had the element of surprise.

'Mr Hunting,' Wesley called. The man on the deck almost jumped.

'What is it?' Hunting sounded annoyed.

'We'd like a word, sir ... if it's convenient.'

'Is it about Loveday?'

'Not exactly.'

Hunting hesitated before inviting them aboard. Heffernan went first, eager to get his feet off dry land. Wesley trailed behind.

Hunting's expression was inscrutable as he showed them into a well-appointed cabin, fitted out for comfort as well as practicality. Red leather seating lined the spacious area, and it had the look of a floating gentleman's club ... the expensive kind. The fittings were dark oak and there was a prominent drinks cupboard on the starboard side. It was a masculine space, and Wesley guessed that Amy Hunting had never ventured aboard. This was Aaron Hunting's refuge from the world ... and all its problems.

'Nice vessel,' Heffernan commented. 'I've got a thirty-foot sloop moored just upstream. Did her up when my wife ... when I lost my wife.' He gave Hunting a nervous

321

smile. 'Took my mind off things. Great comforter, the sea.'

Hunting looked at Heffernan and smiled, as if the chief inspector's bereavement had created a bond of sympathy between them. 'Yes. You're absolutely right. Please, gentlemen, sit down. I'm sorry I was a bit brusque ... I just wasn't expecting to be disturbed. Drink? I don't usually indulge so early but I've just been making the arrangements for my wife's funeral on Monday and I feel I'm in need of a little Dutch courage.' He waved a bottle of single malt in Heffernan's direction.

'I'd better not. Sun's not over the yardarm yet. Look, Mr Hunting, I don't quite know how to say this. It's a bit embarrassing.'

'What is it?'

Heffernan glanced at Wesley as though he expected him to take over. Just when things had been appearing to go so well the boss had chickened out. Wesley cleared his throat. 'The thing is, Mr Hunting, we've been talking to William Verlan ... a friend of your late wife's ... '

'One of her lovers, you mean.' A hint of bitterness had crept into Hunting's voice.

Wesley looked down, avoiding the man's eyes. 'Mr Verlan told me that your son Adam ... that you weren't his biological father.'

A few moments of complete silence followed and Wesley waited for some sort of explosion. But none came.

'Verlan's wrong. Of course Adam was my son.' There was something in the way he said it that didn't quite convince Wesley. 'Why are you bringing this up now? Can't you just let my wife rest in peace?'

Wesley hesitated, almost wishing he hadn't started this line of questioning. But he had to get at the truth somehow. 'We think the Reverend Shipborne might have been killed because he was involved in some germ warfare trials back in the late 1970s. A huge quantity of active bacteria was sprayed in this area ... around the time Adam died.

322

Apparently the bacteria they used were supposed to be harmless but later they found that vulnerable people had been affected . . . pregnant women, old people, babies, people like your son with weakened immune systems. Amy got to know about all this . . . and she had a strong motive for revenge.'

Hunting shook his head. 'That's impossible,' he muttered without conviction.

'She was distraught at Adam's death. Don't you think she might have been quite capable of attacking a man she thought had killed him?'

Hunting sighed. 'I suppose . . . I don't know.'

'Did she tell you about Shipborne's experiments?'

'No. She never mentioned anything like that.'

Wesley watched the man's face, uncertain whether to believe him. 'Where was she the night the vicar died?'

'I've no idea. It was a long time ago and I had no reason to take much notice of the case, did I?'

'If it turns out to be true that Adam wasn't your son, have you any idea who his father could have been?'

He had expected Hunting to be offended, but instead he answered matter-of-factly, as though it hardly mattered any more. 'I spent most of my time building up the business in those days so Amy and I saw very little of each other. I probably neglected her but as far as I know Adam was mine. She never told me otherwise.'

For the first time Wesley noticed that Hunting's eyes were glassy with tears, his only sign of emotion.

'What about Loveday?'

Hunting wiped his eyes with the back of his hand and sniffed. 'I was hardly there while she was growing up because I was concentrating all my energies on my business, and with Amy's problems after Adam's death I'm afraid she was rather neglected too. And I confess that I didn't find her an easy child to love. She'd inherited her mother's instability but I just didn't realise how much she hated me.' He gave a bitter smile. 'I've made rather a mess of things on the family front, haven't I?'

Wesley glanced at Heffernan and said nothing.

'Could William Verlan have been Adam's father?' Heffernan asked with a bluntness that almost made Wesley wince.

Hunting shook his head. 'As far as I know Amy didn't meet Verlan until a few years after Adam died.' He walked over to the drinks cupboard. 'I don't know about you, gentlemen, but I think I need a drink.'

Heffernan gave Wesley a nudge. They both knew they weren't going to learn the identity of Adam's real father from Hunting ... and with Amy dead, they wondered whether they ever would.

But Wesley was game for one more try. 'What was your wife's relationship with Barry Castello? I saw a photograph of some black-tie function at his place and she was in it.'

Hunting turned round to face them, a freshly poured drink in his hand. 'I've always considered it good for Huntings to be seen supporting local charities: Amy and I went to some of Damascus Farm's fund-raising events along with some of my staff. Honestly, Inspector, I've no idea what her relationship with Barry Castello was ... and after all this time and with everything that's happened, it doesn't really seem that important any more, does it?'

The look on Hunting's face told them that he'd said all he had to say on the matter. As they left, Gerry Heffernan glanced longingly back at the yacht.

'Lucky bloke,' he said quietly.

Wesley turned to him. 'Do you really think so?'

Heffernan didn't reply.

Loveday Wilkins was being held in a secure psychiatric ward for assessment, and as Monday morning dawned Wesley decided that he'd rather go there with Rachel than Heffernan. Rachel usually knew the right things to say ... which was more than he did in such situations. Mental illness made him uncomfortable ... but then it had that effect on many people.

324

Wesley found Loveday in a room on her own. The white walls were dirty and chipped and there was nothing in there but a basin, a hospital bed, a grey metal locker and two chairs formed out of stained black plastic. A small window, set high in the wall, let in a dribble of grey light. If the fluorescent light overhead hadn't been on, it would have been too dark to see the figure sitting on the bed, clutching her knees to her chest.

The nurse unlocked the door for them and Loveday looked up as they entered the room then looked away again, as if their arrival was of no interest to her.

Wesley sat on one of the chairs and tried to move it closer to the bed. But it didn't budge. It was fixed to the floor for safety.

He said Loveday's name softly and she looked up.

'Do you mind talking to us, Loveday? You haven't met Rachel before, have you?' He used Rachel's Christian name rather than her rank, thinking it might be less intimidating ... and he wanted Loveday's full cooperation.

'We've been talking to your father.' He waited a few seconds but there was no reaction so he carried on. 'He feels bad about everything that's happened.'

'So he should.' Loveday began to rock gently to and fro.

'Why did you just target the Morbay branch of Huntings? Why not other local branches?'

Loveday shrugged. But there was a new wariness in her eyes.

'Did you have a grudge against that branch in particular or against your father's stores in general?'

No answer.

'We've heard that Adam was only your half-brother, that your father wasn't his father. Do you know who his father was, Loveday?'

'If you know, please tell us,' said Rachel gently.

Loveday stared ahead, tears brimming in her eyes. 'They used to whisper in corners: they thought I didn't know what was going on. She could have screwed every man in Devon and he would have been too busy with his bloody shops to notice. I didn't matter . . . it was all bloody Adam, Adam, Adam. Adam needs this, Adam needs that . . . be careful with Adam.'

Rachel put out her hand to touch Loveday's shoulder; a gesture of sisterly solidarity, or so it seemed to Wesley.

'Do you know who Adam's father was?' Rachel whispered gently.

Loveday gave a secretive smile. 'Oh yes, I worked it out. I made it my business to work it out and I wanted the bitch to know that I knew. I asked Auntie Jan 'cause I knew she told her all her nasty little secrets. She wouldn't tell me at first but when I said his name I guessed from the look on her face.'

'Who's Auntie Jan?'

'Her sister.'

'Where can we find her?'

'New York. You'll just have to take my word for it.'

'So who was Adam's father?'

Loveday didn't answer.

Rachel glanced at Wesley. 'Your father thinks Adam was his.'

Loveday started to speak again, as though she hadn't heard. 'I saw them . . . I caught them doing it . . . in her bed. I saw them. I was too young to know what they were doing . . . but I know now.' She gave a knowing chuckle and began to rock to and fro. 'If he hadn't got my mother pregnant . . . if Adam had never been born . . . everything would have been all right. He was always ill . . . '

'That was hardly his fault,' said Wesley under his breath. But he knew that it hadn't been logic and reason which had driven Loveday's actions. It had been blind emotion . . . kicking out. What didn't make any sense to him made all the sense in the world to Loveday's troubled mind.

When Loveday burst into an uncontrollable bout of sobbing the nurse told them it was time to go. Wesley touched Loveday's shoulder gently and told her he'd be back when she was feeling better.

*

'Rachel and I have been having a word with Loveday Wilkins. I think she knows who Adam Hunting's natural father was but she's not saying,' said Wesley as he climbed the stairs to Chief Superintendent Nutter's office. Heffernan was lagging behind, making heavy weather of the stairs.

'Could we believe her even if she named him?' Heffernan sounded sceptical. 'She is in a mental institution.'

'Just because she's ill it doesn't mean she's not telling the truth. I believed her.' As soon as he'd said the words, Wesley began to doubt his own judgement. What if it was just some strange obsession of Loveday's? That the ailing brother who received all the love and attention, her share as well as his own, had really been a cuckoo in the nest? But Amy's confession to William Verlan that Adam hadn't been her husband's child seemed to confirm Loveday's assumption. Although it was always possible that this had been a fanciful piece of mischief and Aaron Hunting was Adam's real father after all. The very thought of all the possibilities made Wesley feel tired. It had been a hard week.

Chief Superintendent Nutter's office had all the modern conveniences, including a television and video recorder in the corner. They found Nutter leaning back in his soft leather executive chair with his eyes fixed on the flickering screen.

'Come in, Gerry, come in. Come in, Inspector Peterson. They said that it was going to be on later . . . after the main headlines.' He didn't take his eyes off the television as he spoke.

They sat down on the well-upholstered visitors' chairs and watched in silence as the lunch-time news unfolded. The threat of war in some distant hot land; storms up in Scotland; an oil tanker in peril off the French coast; a prediction that the house price boom was almost over. Nothing immediately relevant to the officers of Tradmouth CID.

327

'Here it is,' Nutter announced, leaning forward.

A man was emerging from the familiar Gothic façade of the Royal Courts of Justice, punching the air in triumph. Chris Hobson, dressed in his best suit and tie, was handed a bottle of champagne by one of his supporters. He opened it, sending the cork flying towards the crowd of press photographers, and took a long swig. After twelve years of prison tea it must have tasted good.

Wesley glanced at Nutter, who was staring at the screen with an expression of despair. And things could only get worse.

A reporter had thrust a microphone in Hobson's face and asked him how he felt.

'Over the moon,' was the reply.

But Hobson's solicitor edged his way in before his client could say too much. 'We're delighted that justice has been done at last. My client has lost twelve years of his life due to police incompetence and corruption and we hope that the compensation he receives will be commensurate with his suffering.' The man sounded as though he was reading a carefully prepared statement but he was finding it hard to keep the smug smirk of triumph off his lips.

When the newsreader moved on to a report about a royal tour Heffernan turned to Nutter. 'That's all we need. Hobson one, police nil.'

'Well, he was innocent, Gerry. And Norbert did rig the evidence. But he's well out of it and we're left to clear up his mess.'

Wesley, who would hardly have described being dead as 'well out of it', sat tight and said nothing. But Nutter looked him in the eye. 'I hear Norbert's son's our most likely suspect. Are you ready to charge him yet?'

'I'd like to make a few more enquiries first, sir,' Wesley answered, thinking of Helen Wilmer's alleged attempts at amateur blackmail. If Dermot O'Donovan had been telling the truth, was it really likely that she expected to get a four-figure sum out of a schoolboy?

Heffernan stood up, poised for a quick getaway like a runner on the starting blocks. 'I've got a feeling we're going to get to the bottom of this case pretty soon, sir,' he said optimistically.

Nutter stared up at him. 'I do hope so, Gerry. What we need is a quick conviction ... to restore our credibility.'

'We'll see what we can do,' muttered Heffernan as he left the office with Wesley following close behind.

'So who killed Shipborne and why?' Wesley asked once the Chief Superintendent was well out of earshot.

'Put your answers on a postcard and send them to Chief Superintendent Nutter, Tradmouth nick. I don't know who killed him, Wes, and frankly, if we carry on like this, hitting a brick wall every time we get a new lead, I'm beginning to think we'll never find out.'

It wasn't like Heffernan to be so despondent. Maybe he was thinking of the days to come ... of the pressure from above and the press intrusion as they tried to come up with a result.

'Amy Hunting's funeral's this afternoon. Feel like going?'

'Not really,' said Wesley honestly.

'Neither do I, but I've a feeling we should go along and pay our respects. It'd be convenient if she turns out to be the murderer, wouldn't it?'

'Not for Aaron Hunting.'

'Think it'd affect his profits, do you? I can't really see anyone boycotting his special offers just because his crazy wife bumped some old vicar over the head a few years ago. It'd be a five-minute wonder.'

They'd reached Heffernan's office and both men flopped down. After being on their best behaviour with CS Nutter they needed to relax, loosen their ties, put their feet up and think.

It was Heffernan who spoke first. 'So what have we got?'

Wesley helped himself to a blank sheet of paper from

329

Heffernan's chaotic desk and began to write. 'One: Philip Norbert – admits to wandering into the vicarage on the off-chance and helping himself to Shipborne's wallet and says he saw the body. His account fits with Hobson seeing him at the scene but he has to be our number-one suspect, I suppose. Although if Dermot O'Donovan was telling the truth and Helen Wilmer was really blackmailing the killer, how did she expect to get a thousand quid out of a school-boy?'

'Unless she didn't know he was a schoolboy. Perhaps she'd met him and he spun her some yarn about being heir to a fortune ... he wouldn't be the first teenage lad to let his imagination run away with him. What about suspect number two?'

'Has to be Amy Hunting. She'd just found out that Shipborne had been in charge of an experiment that prob-ably led to the death of her son. She'd been to see him at the vicarage under some cock-and-bull pretext so she knew the lie of the land. She could have staged the robbery.'

'So how did Hobson come to have the silver?'

'Maybe DCI Norbert took it and planted it. Although in the reports I've read, the housekeeper, Mrs O'Donovan, reported that it was missing straight after the murder, and Norbert didn't know about his son's involvement when he was first called to the scene, so he'd hardly have taken it to plant on someone else on the off-chance. And there was definitely an anonymous phone call to say the silver could be found in Hobson's flat ... I've checked that out.'

'Would Helen Wilmer have known Amy Hunting?'

'It's possible she'd seen her or she recognised her from a photograph.'

'Who's next?'

'There's always Aaron Hunting. Helen had worked at Huntings so she'd be bound to recognise him. And he claims that as far as he knew Adam was his son so his motive would be the same as Amy's.'

'Any more?'

330

'Verlan's a possibility, although I can't think why. Then there's Helen Wilmer's father, the captain of the bell-ringers ... he'd just had a row with Shipborne and Shipborne's diary said he had a temper.'

'I can't see him strangling his own daughter.'

'It's been known. And under Dermot O'Donovan's influence she'd changed from a nice Sunday school teacher into a nasty little blackmailer.'

'Barry Castello? He certainly knew Amy so it's possible he was Adam's father. Or he might have had some row with Shipborne. He – or rather Damascus Farm – was the major beneficiary of Shipborne's will.'

'I wouldn't rule him out. Then there's Dermot himself. He was a thief, a nasty bit of work, and his alibi's dodgy. Shipborne may have caught him with his fingers in the poor box and Dermot hit out in panic and covered his tracks to make it look like a robbery. He may have seen Hobson in the pub, found out where he lived and planted the silver. He may have told us that tale about a blackmail note to throw us off the scent. He may have strangled Helen to stop her blabbing, then Verlan came along, ran over the body and panicked like he said.' He sighed. 'I suppose we could come up with more names if we put our minds to it, but I think that's enough to be going on with.'

'Do you think it's relevant that Adam might not be Hunting's son?'

Wesley didn't answer. He began to study the notes he'd written.

'My money's still on Philip Norbert, you know,' Heffernan said with a sigh.

Wesley looked up from his notes. The boss was probably right. He glanced at his watch. They just had time to grab something for lunch before the funeral.

They left the office and drove into the centre of Tradmouth, coming to a halt outside the pasty shop under the gaze of a predatory traffic warden. Wesley waved his warrant card at the uniformed figure before disappearing into the shop and returning with a carrier bag containing two large traditional pasties.

With any luck that would keep them going until the funeral baked meats appeared ... if they were on the guest list, which was doubtful. But some instinct told Wesley that it might be wise to be there when Amy Hunting was laid to rest.

As soon as Wesley arrived at the cemetery he had the feeling that Amy Hunting's funeral was going to be one of those restrained, polite English affairs that kept the lid firmly on emotion and referred to the hope of heaven in the same dismissive way as people touched wood for luck ... a vague superstition, hardly understood. Her remains were to be dispatched below ground in Tradmouth cemetery with the maximum of efficiency and the minimum of fuss with little religious input. But perhaps Amy had wanted it that way.

The party was gathering around the open grave when they arrived. Aaron Hunting, the chief mourner, wore an immaculate black suit, Armani probably, and black silk tie, showing up the funeral directors in their chain-store versions. His face betrayed no emotion as he fixed his eyes on the sturdy oak coffin.

Wesley was surprised to see Barry Castello there, hanging back behind a group of women, hardly any of them in black. He looked more distressed than Hunting, and a casual onlooker might have taken him for the widower. He also noticed Keith Sturgeon standing staring ahead as though stunned. He was with a group of men wearing identical suits ... an overt show of respect from Huntings' loyal staff.

But as Wesley and Heffernan watched from a tactful distance, another familiar face caught their eye. As his mind hadn't connected her with Amy Hunting it took Wesley a split second to put a name to the face. But there she was, standing next to Aaron Hunting, her face half veiled under a large and expensive-looking hat. Wesley gave Heffernan a nudge.

'What's she doing here?' Heffernan responded in a stage whisper.

Wesley didn't answer, and the two men stepped back, hoping that she wouldn't see them. The element of surprise might come in useful later on.

It wasn't until the coffin was safely underground and the mourners were walking away from the graveside that they made their move. Their quarry was walking beside Aaron Hunting, her arm linked in his. Wesley walked fast to catch up with them and Heffernan followed a little more slowly.

'Mrs Powell. I didn't expect to see you here.'

The look of horror on Janet Powell's face was fleeting. But Wesley saw it clearly. She opened her mouth to speak but no sound emerged.

'Are you a friend of the family?'

Janet looked at Hunting, who was standing there, his arm still linked with hers. His face was impassive. He was giving nothing away.

'Er ... Amy was my sister.'

Now that Wesley looked at her closely, he could see a resemblance between her and Amy Hunting. This was the Auntie Jan Loveday had spoken of ... the recipient of Amy's secrets. She was fair where Amy had been dark, plump where Amy had been thin ... but there was something about their facial features which gave away the fact that they were sisters.

'I saw your friend, Chris Hobson on the tele. I would have thought you'd have been there celebrating with him,' Heffernan tried to sound innocent.

She looked at him coldly, 'I came straight back after I'd given evidence. Amy was my sister, you know. Now, if you'll excuse me, we must get back to the house.'

Aaron Hunting put a protective arm around his sister-in-law's shoulder. 'Yes, gentlemen, if you'll excuse us. It's a very upsetting day, as I'm sure you'll understand.'

333

'We'd like a word with you, Mrs Powell. It shouldn't take long. Our car's outside.' Heffernan spoke confidently, as though he didn't expect a refusal.

Janet Powell hesitated, looking at her brother-in-law for support. But Hunting told her gently that she'd better go, his eyes meeting hers.

With a last pleading glance towards Hunting, she walked silently with them to the car.

After making sure that Janet Powell was comfortable in a spare office with tea in a proper china cup and a plate of chocolate biscuits, Gerry Heffernan led Wesley into his office.

'I don't know why we couldn't have talked to her in one of the interview rooms, Gerry.'

'Softly, softly. We're lulling her into a false sense of security. Nice cop, nasty cop, minus the nasty cop. And besides, she's got friends in high places.'

Wesley smiled. 'Then we'd better not keep the lady waiting. You seem more cheerful.'

'We're on to something, Wes. I can feel it in me water. Janet Powell just happens to be Amy Hunting's sister and the Reverend Shipborne was responsible for the experiment that killed Amy's son. Coincidence or what?'

Wesley had a similar feeling but he said nothing as they walked down the corridor and knocked on the door, hoping she'd left them some chocolate biscuits.

Janet Powell looked up when they walked in. 'I don't know why I've been brought here,' she said in a tone that suggested she was used to giving orders rather than taking them. 'It's ridiculous. I've told the truth about where Chris Hobson was on the night that vicar died and he's been acquitted. End of story.'

Wesley sat down, his face serious. 'Not quite the end, I'm afraid, Mrs Powell. You see, we've been doing some digging and we've found a link between the Reverend Shipborne and your sister . . . a tenuous link admittedly, but a link.'

334

Janet Powell glanced at Gerry Heffernan, who was sitting beside Wesley watching the proceedings with interest but saying nothing. 'I don't know what you mean.'

'Your sister visited Mr Shipborne to confess she was having an affair.'

'What?' Her eyes widened in disbelief.

'But we think she had another reason for wanting to see him. You see, Mr Shipborne had worked as a scientist for the Ministry of Defence and he felt so guilty about some of the things he'd done in the course of his work that he made a public confession in his church. He'd been involved in a germ warfare experiment. Bacteria were sprayed over a wide area and later some vulnerable people developed health problems. Your sister was under the impression that the Reverend Shipborne was responsible for the death of her son, Adam.'

Janet Powell stared down at the scattering of biscuit crumbs on the desk.

'You knew about all this, didn't you?'

'No.' She spoke almost in a whisper.

'The truth, please, Mrs Powell.' Wesley hesitated. 'I don't think this sort of thing comes easy to you, does it? I think you were used. Did you kill the Reverend Shipborne?'

She looked up, horrified. 'No, no. I could never do anything like that. And Chris didn't kill him either. I told the truth: he was with me. I heard about the murder on the news the next day but Chris had been with me all evening . . . we had nothing to do with it.'

'Did Amy know about you and Chris?'

'Yes. I'd been stupid enough to tell her all about him in glorious detail. I should have kept it quiet but there you are.'

'Did you keep in touch while you were in the States?'

'Yes. Of course.'

Wesley looked her in the eye. 'So she must have let you know he'd been arrested. You were lying when you said you didn't know about it till a month ago.'

335

'No, that's not true. I had no idea. Amy never told me he'd been arrested. She never mentioned it.' Janet sounded puzzled at this omission.

'Doesn't that strike you as strange?'

'Yes, I suppose it does.'

Gerry Heffernan leaned forward. 'Do you think your sister could have killed the vicar? Unless you cooked the idea up between you and paid Hobson to do your dirty work. We only have your word that he's really innocent, don't we?'

'That's ridiculous,' Janet snapped.

Heffernan caught Wesley's eye. 'I think we should carry this on in the interview room, don't you? Would you like a solicitor, love?'

Janet Powell nodded.

Rachel walked up to Wesley's desk. She was breathless, as though she'd been running. 'I've heard you're questioning Janet Powell.'

'We're just waiting for her solicitor to arrive then we can interview her properly. If she's in this up to her neck I suppose it casts doubts on Chris Hobson's innocence.'

Rachel tilted her head to one side. 'I wonder if she thinks we can't touch Hobson now – double jeopardy: you can't be tried for the same crime twice.'

'If she's been in the States she might not know the law's going to be changed.' Gerry reckons he was paid for the murder and the proceeds are waiting for him in some offshore bank account. I believe he's in the tender care of a national newspaper at the moment, telling his tragic and heart-warming story for an obscene sum of money. But if Gerry's right, Hobson might be waving goodbye to his compensation for wrongful imprisonment.

Rachel grinned. 'So you think he did it after all?'

'It's possible. He was besotted with Janet at the time ... but a few years behind bars is a great healer.'

Rachel's expression suddenly turned serious. 'I suppose

this could mean DCI Norbert's in the clear if he got the right man after all. And what about Philip Norbert?'

'The charge for possession of cocaine should stick and he admits going into the vicarage and pinching the wallet.'

'If we get this case cleared up we can all go out for a drink,' Rachel said, looking at Wesley hopefully. She opened her desk drawer and produced a small parcel. 'By the way, this came for you ... registered post. Got an admirer in Scotland?'

Wesley took the packet from her but before he could say anything Steve Carstairs ambled up to them, a knowing smirk on his face. 'Trish said to tell you Janet Powell's brief's arrived. They're waiting in interview room two.'

Wesley wandered down to join Gerry Heffernan in the interview room. This was it – with any luck the Shipborne case would soon be concluded. And then all they had to do was to find out who killed Helen Wilmer. His money was still on Dermot O'Donovan ... but then he hadn't predicted Janet Powell's involvement. Perhaps he was losing his touch.

Janet Powell's solicitor wore an expensive suit. But then Janet Powell was an expensive lady. Wesley wondered how it was that the Wilkins sisters had both ended up married to rich men. Luck, perhaps ... or a talent for being in the right place at the right time? But whatever it was, it didn't seem to have brought either of them much happiness.

As Heffernan set the tape running and said the required words, Janet looked nervous. But then so would Wesley if he were facing a charge of conspiracy to murder.

They went through the events of the night of Shipborne's death and Janet was adamant: Chris Hobson had been with her all evening. She'd told the truth.

She stuck to her story. She'd met Chris Hobson outside the Horse and Farrier; they'd sat in the car talking for at least half an hour, probably longer, then they'd driven to Morbay. She remembered that he'd spotted a boy behaving

337

furtively outside a large house and mentioned in passing that he'd seen him at some posh school in Morbay and he was surprised to see him hanging around in Belsham. Wesley supposed this confirmed Philip Norbert's story ... and somehow Janet Powell's account was starting to sound more convincing, even if Gerry was still behaving as though Chris Hobson's guilt was a foregone conclusion.

Wesley asked Janet whether anyone had known her plans for that evening and Janet hesitated before admitting that she'd told Amy, who had even suggested the Horse and Farrier as a place to meet. Her answer caused Wesley to spend the next five minutes deep in thought, hardly hearing the questions Gerry was firing at the woman on the other side of the table ... or her protestations of innocence.

When Wesley had gathered his thoughts, he spoke. 'Did Amy tell you Shipborne had killed Adam?'

'I told her she was talking rubbish.'

'We've been hearing that your sister had an affair and Adam wasn't Aaron Hunting's son. Is this true?'

Janet Powell's face was expressionless. 'It might be.'

'Did she tell you who Adam's real father was?'

No answer.

'Could Amy have killed Shipborne?'

She had a whispered discussion with her solicitor before answering, 'No comment.'

'She's not going to say, is she?'

Wesley was sitting on the other side of Heffernan's cluttered desk. He picked up a pencil stub and began to twist it in his fingers. 'Her sister's dead ... we can't ask her. Someone knew about Janet's fancy man's history and thought the blame could be put on him. The only person who could have known was Amy. Or Adam Hunting's real father, whoever he is, if Amy told him everything.'

'Or maybe it was Janet herself. Adam was her nephew and she hasn't any children of her own. She might have wanted to avenge his death ... especially if she had Hobson eating out of her hand. Hobson might have done it after all. Or maybe Janet and Hobson did it together.'

Wesley ignored this. He didn't know why, but he believed Janet Powell's story. 'If it wasn't Amy herself then what about Aaron Hunting? He claims he didn't know that Adam wasn't his son. And Helen Wilmer would have known him by sight and knew he was worth blackmailing.'

Wesley sighed and fumbled in the inside pocket of his jacket. He took out a small package neatly wrapped in brown paper. He also pulled out a small battered book encased in a plastic evidence bag, flecked with what looked like dried blood.

'What's that?'

'Shipborne's diaries. I just wanted to read what he said about Amy Hunting again.' He began to open the packet Rachel had given him, the packet from Scotland. He found a small book inside, identical to its blood-spattered predecessor. 'This is the diary he'd just started to use when the first was full. His niece in Scotland's just posted it to me.' He opened it and saw that the first few pages were filled with John Shipborne's neat, tiny handwriting. Wesley's heart began to beat faster: these were the dead man's thoughts in the days leading up to his murder. Perhaps they would provide the final solution to the puzzle of his death . . . or perhaps not.

'If you find anything interesting, let me know.' Heffernan stood up. 'I'm getting myself a cup of tea. Want one?'

Wesley nodded. And by the time Gerry Heffernan returned from the vending machine in the corridor with two plastic cups full of some scalding liquid that resembled tea only in its general appearance, Wesley had returned to his own desk and begun to run over everything in his mind: Loveday's attempt at sabotage; someone, perhaps Amy Hunting, framing Chris Hobson; Helen Wilmer's death. There was something he was missing.

He read through the papers on his desk for half an hour

before the idea came to him. There was one person who might be able to throw some light into the chaotic darkness. It was time he returned to Morbay.

Checking up to see how Loveday Wilkins's two latest victims were recovering gave Wesley's mission some semblance of legitimacy: it had been his case, after all. But although he was glad to see Ellie Pickering and her daughter, Chloe, home from hospital and well on the road to recovery, his real interest lay in another direction.

He found Ellie lying on the sofa, a blanket over her legs like a Victorian invalid. She bore a slight resemblance to her sister, Georgie Bettis, but she was younger and her face was more gaunt ... probably as a result of her recent misfortunes. Her husband, Joe, an amiable, balding man, made a great show of fussing over the invalid and Ellie was beginning to display flashes of irritation which Wesley took as a sign that she was on the mend.

After fifteen minutes of polite enquiries and bringing the Pickerings up to date with the police's progress, Wesley thought the time was right to come to the point of his visit.

'I believe your sister, Georgie, worked for Aaron Hunting?'

Ellie pursed her lips. 'She was his PA. It was a wonderful job and I was surprised she gave it all up when her eldest was born but she said she'd had enough.'

'Of Hunting?'

'Oh no, I think she got on well with him. It was Hunting's wife who used to make a bit of a nuisance of herself, and I think Georgie got a bit fed up with it. Wasn't she found dead recently?'

'Yes.' Wesley didn't feel like elaborating.

Ellie continued. 'There were things going on in the office that Georgie didn't like so she wasn't sorry to leave.'

'What sort of things?'

Ellie hesitated, as though she feared she'd said too much. 'You'll have to ask Georgie.'

An hour later Wesley was sipping rather good coffee in Georgie Bettis's converted barn on the outskirts of Tradmouth and immersing himself in office scandal.

And as he drove back to the station he felt the overwhelming feeling of satisfaction he usually felt when he was about to identify a murderer.

Neil Watson had arranged to meet Aaron Hunting and his entourage that afternoon. He wasn't looking forward to it. He never felt at home with commerce. He'd met Hunting on several occasions and found him more likeable than the usual run of businessmen. It was his hangers-on he couldn't stand; the po-faced yes-men who swarmed around him in their uniform suits and ties. And there was one who got right up his nose; the one called Sturgeon, a self-important prat who always wore a flower in his buttonhole. He'd heard rumours that Sturgeon was supposed to be taking over as manager of the new store when it was eventually built. Which would be a long time off if Neil had his way.

Neil was still holding himself stiffly: although he felt much better and was even able to turn without experiencing an excruciating stab of pain, he wasn't ready to relinquish his invalid status just yet. He was settled at Wesley and Pam's . . . it was somehow comforting to live in a proper grown-up house rather than a glorified student flat. And it was a long time since he had spent so much time with Pam. He was beginning to regret this omission, although he would never have said as much to Wesley. When his old friend was around – which was seldom, thanks to his job – Neil was careful not to betray his feelings. But he wondered how much, if anything, Pam had sensed.

He looked on as the others worked, still bringing skeletons out of the ground. The forensic anthropologist who was examining the bones, a large woman with cropped hair called Dr Rhodes, had concluded that the remains were those of a typical cross-section of a medieval village: old

341

and young; male and female; rich and poor. The Black Death had been no respecter of persons. None of the bodies showed any signs of injury: only the young male corpse with the richly decorated dagger had died by the violence of man . . . and if that corpse was really Robert de Munerie, Neil reckoned that he'd had it coming to him.

As he watched the bones emerge from the earth, he recalled the words on the wall of the church tower. The miserable dregs of the people survive. It must have been tough for the survivors, although from far-off history lessons he recalled that the resulting shortage of labour gave the working men who were left new power and respect. The old saying about clouds having silver linings sprang to his mind.

But the appearance of a group of people at the entrance to the site meant that his musings on the economic consequences of the Black Death were cut short. He recognised Aaron Hunting at once, standing slightly apart from the others. Neil had heard that Hunting had just buried his wife so the solemn expression on his face as he picked his way across the treacherous terrain of the dig was hardly surprising. Sturgeon, he noticed, was following closely behind him, the inevitable carnation stuck in his buttonhole: Neil found the sight of its fresh, frilly petals profoundly irritating, although he didn't know why.

Neil assumed a martyred expression as Hunting drew nearer, signalling that, although he was injured and in pain, such was his sense of duty that he struggled on regardless of the personal cost. He smiled weakly as Hunting offered his hand.

'Dr Watson, how are you feeling?'

'A little better,' Neil replied bravely.

'Good. When will the excavation be finished? I do realise that with human remains having been found, things might take a little longer than we anticipated.'

'People wouldn't want to be buying their bread and milk on top of a plague pit, would they?'

Hunting looked at Neil, surprised. There had been a hint of defiant sarcasm in his voice, suggesting that he was no longer the suffering invalid. 'Indeed they wouldn't. In fact I've been having doubts about the wisdom of siting the new store here. There's been quite a bit of local publicity about the excavation, and if the public come to subconsciously connect Huntings with the plague . . .'

'People have short memories.' It was Keith Sturgeon who interrupted. His tone was soothing and sycophantic. 'I'm sure all this will have been forgotten by the time the store opens.'

Hunting said nothing but allowed Neil to lead him across the site to the newest trench, pointing out fresh items of interest on the way.

'I'll take you over to the church hall in a minute and show you the finds. Thirty-three complete skeletons and more still coming up.'

But before Aaron Hunting could reply Neil spotted a pair of figures approaching. Even from a distance he recognised Wesley and Gerry Heffernan. Hunting, seeing that Neil was gazing over his shoulder, turned round. Sturgeon mumbled something in his ear and hurried off in the direction of the road. Neil watched him go with a fleeting feeling of contempt.

Hunting turned to face the newcomers.

'Mr Hunting,' Wesley said when they were in earshot. 'Can we have a word?'

Hunting gave a wary half-smile. 'Certainly.'

'We'd just like an informal chat with Mr Sturgeon if you can spare him for a few minutes.'

'Help yourself.' He looked round. 'He said he was going back to the car for something he'd forgotten . . . he parked it up by the church.'

Hunting's expression gave nothing away. Wesley thanked him and began to follow Keith Sturgeon, quickening his pace as he neared the church. Heffernan told him to slow down but Wesley took no notice.

343

There was no sign of Sturgeon anywhere near the row of cars parked by the church gate but Wesley noticed that the church door was standing open. He began to walk up the path and Heffernan followed.

The ground was sodden from the recent rain and their shoes were soon covered with mud. When Wesley reached the shelter of the church porch he wiped his feet on the ancient coconut mat that lay on the floor and Heffernan did likewise.

'Do you think he's inside?' Heffernan sounded unsure.

Wesley didn't answer. He led the way inside and saw that someone was sitting, motionless, in one of the front pews.

'Perhaps he's in need of divine guidance,' Heffernan whispered. But Wesley ignored him and walked down the aisle.

When he reached the front of the church he sat himself down next to Keith Sturgeon, just beneath the richly carved pulpit. Heffernan hovered in the aisle a few yards away. As it was a grey, sunless day, the interior of the church was almost dark; only a cluster of candles flickering before a small altar in the side aisle relieved the gloom: prayers for the living or the dead.

'We'd like a word, Mr Sturgeon.'

The man didn't answer but stared ahead at the stained-glass window above the altar, an image of Christ blessing a group of small children.

'We know about your relationship with Mrs Amy Hunting.' Sometimes Wesley hated intruding into people's hidden secrets, dragging the skeletons out of cupboards. But it had to be done if he wanted to learn the truth.

'Amy's dead,' he said, almost in a whisper. 'What does it matter now?'

'I'm sorry,' said Wesley quietly. 'You see, I've heard that you and Amy had an affair in the 1970s. Is that true?'

Sturgeon said nothing.

'I've been talking to Georgie Bettis. Didn't they always

344

used to say that if you want to know about a man you should ask his secretary? Georgie didn't want to discuss Mr Hunting's private life at first, but when I explained that it was a case of murder ... '

Sturgeon looked up anxiously. 'What did she say?'

'She told me that she'd called at Mr Hunting's house to pick up some important papers for a meeting and caught you and Amy Hunting together. She said your affair went on for some time. She also said you were married. You must have married very young.'

Sturgeon nodded.

'Children?'

Sturgeon shook his head violently. Wesley had touched a raw nerve. 'My wife never wanted children.'

'But you did?'

No answer.

'Did Amy Hunting get pregnant as a result of your affair?'

'Yes.' The reply was whispered, almost reverently.

'So you had a child at last ... a son. Adam, wasn't it?'

He nodded, a fond smile playing on his lips. 'Adam,' he whispered. 'He looked like me, you know. I knew he was mine as soon as I saw him.'

'Did you see him often?'

'Amy and I used to meet on my afternoon off. She knew how much I wanted to see him. She and her husband led separate lives and my wife was busy with her career ... she's a hospital manager, you know,' he said, half proud, half resentful.

'Did you and Amy ever consider leaving your partners and living together?'

'Oh yes. We considered it when Adam was born, but there was the problem of Loveday. Then there was Adam's health – he had a heart condition ... needed operations. At least if she stayed with Aaron Hunting we knew Adam could have the best medical treatment money could buy. I often wished we could all have been together ... me, Amy and Adam. It might have been goodbye to my career at Huntings but ... '

'Did Aaron Hunting know about you and Amy?'

'We were very discreet and I don't think he ever found out. Or perhaps he did and he just didn't care. Georgie Bettis caught us together once but that was our only mistake, and I was sure Georgie wouldn't have said anything. Or perhaps she did ... perhaps that was the reason why Aaron never promoted me. I don't suppose I could blame him if it was.'

'You never thought of leaving Huntings?'

He shook his head. 'Perhaps I was too set in my ways or perhaps it was out of some misguided loyalty to Amy ... I don't know. I should have moved on but I never did.'

'Did Loveday know about your affair?'

Sturgeon's face reddened. 'She walked in once when we were ... in bed. But she was only young ... about seven. She can't have known what was going on. Later on Amy had to bring her sometimes when we met up so I could see Adam. I suppose we thought she was too young to take anything in, but didn't Robert Burns say something about there being a child among us taking notes? She must have thought about it later and asked herself why one of her father's managers had been with her mother like that. She must have done her sums about Adam's birth. She must have added it all up and got the right answer.'

'So she blamed you for her problems?'

'She was a disturbed child before Adam's death and she was even worse afterwards. Amy said she'd resented Adam from the moment he was born; more than normal sibling jealousy ... real hatred. If she'd guessed I was his father then I suppose it's likely I became a focus of her resentment. Reason didn't come into it.' He hesitated. 'Adam looked so like me, you know ... the image of me when I was little.' He smiled; there was pride and love behind his bitterness.

'Adam died.'

'Yes.' There were tears in Keith Sturgeon's brown eyes, brimming onto his cheeks. 'That was the worst day of my life. My son ... my only son. The only child I'm ever likely to have. My wife had herself sterilised, you know ... she never intended to have children. I used to dream of the time when Adam was older ... when I could tell him the truth ... when I could tell him that I was his father and we could do things together ... father and son.' He buried his head in his hands.

'I'm sorry,' was the only thing Wesley could think of to say.

Heffernan had been listening intently. Now he spoke. 'You remember a girl who worked for you in the holidays called Helen Wilmer?'

Sturgeon looked up in surprise. He'd almost forgotten the chief inspector was there. 'I told you before,' he said quickly. 'I remember she went missing but I don't remember anything else about her. Hundreds of people work for me. I can't know them all.' He looked nervous and started to play with the wedding ring on his finger, twisting it round.

Wesley looked up at the pulpit, glowering down on them like some carved dark oak totem. 'Amy told you about the Reverend Shipborne being in charge of the germ warfare trials. I don't suppose it had ever occurred to you that someone's deliberate actions might have caused Adam's death. As far as you knew it had been a random misfortune. You and Amy must have been devastated when you found out about Shipborne's experiments.' He paused, his eyes on Sturgeon's face. 'How did you feel when you discovered Shipborne's experiments could have caused your son's death?'

Sturgeon stood up. He was breathing quickly. The pain in his eyes made Wesley recoil for a second. He fixed his gaze on the window above the altar.

'I can see why you wanted Shipborne dead but I can't understand why you killed Helen Wilmer.'

Sturgeon said nothing. He stood with his eyes fixed on

347

the window; on the stained-glass images of the children.

'Helen Wilmer was blackmailing you, wasn't she? She'd worked at Huntings and when she saw you outside the vicarage near the time of Shipborne's death she recognised you and thought she'd try a bit of blackmail. Only she didn't realise what she was getting into. You arranged to meet her, didn't you? You met her and strangled her.'

Sturgeon closed his eyes as if praying and stood quite still.

'She could have destroyed you so you killed her.' Wesley watched Sturgeon's face and was surprised that he felt some sympathy for the man. Avenging the death of his only son was something he could understand . . . but Helen Wilmer's murder was different. It had been wicked to end a young girl's life like that.

'You killed her, didn't you, Keith? Can you imagine what her parents have gone through all these years? You lost Adam so you must understand how they felt at losing their only child.'

There was no denial. Wesley knew his guess had been right. Helen Wilmer had paid for her amateur excursion into the world of blackmail with her life. Keith Sturgeon's obsession with Adam, his love for his only child, had triumphed over all other considerations.

Sturgeon sat back down and slumped forward, his head in his hands.

'You loved Adam. I can understand that. My own son was in hospital with suspected meningitis recently so, believe me, I know what it's like. I know what it's like to feel helpless when your child's life is in danger. Adam was everything to you . . . and that man destroyed him.'

Sturgeon nodded vigorously, as if he was glad someone understood.

'When did your affair with Amy end?'

'After Adam died. I don't think either of us had the heart to carry on. Amy suffered so much, you know. Then years later she found out by chance that that vicar . . . that bloody hypocrite ... had caused Adam's death because of some experiment: he'd used sick children like laboratory animals. Others died as well, you know ... he admitted it ... and babies were born sick and disabled. He said he was sorry but sorry wasn't enough.'

Tears were running down Sturgeon's cheeks but Wesley knew he had to carry on. He wanted the truth.

'Wouldn't it have been better to try and get a public inquiry into what happened rather than take the law into your own hands?' he asked gently. Something about this man's grief tore at him. He could imagine himself in his place ... and he wondered what he would have done.

Sturgeon smiled bitterly. 'They hold public inquiries about the siting of Huntings supermarkets. Ninety-nine times out of a hundred they just say what the party with the most power want them to. If business holds so much sway, what chance would you have against an organisation like the MoD? And I wanted the man responsible to pay. He deserved to die for what he'd done.'

'What was Amy's involvement in his death?'

'She told me about her sister's boyfriend ... she said he was a crook and if we wanted to do anything about Shipborne we could make sure he got the blame. She knew Janet, her sister, was meeting him that night in Belsham – Amy had suggested the meeting place – and she knew that a week later Janet would be in the States and wouldn't even find out about his arrest so wouldn't be able to give him an alibi. She suggested that I take something valuable when I'd ... and we'd plant it in the boyfriend's flat and ring the police anonymously. That's what we did.'

'And it worked until Janet came back. You were taking a risk.'

Sturgeon took a deep breath. 'It was worth it, believe me.'

'And Amy's suicide?'

'When Hobson's case went to appeal she must have realised the truth would come out eventually. She couldn't face it.'

Wesley hesitated and glanced at Gerry Heffernan, who was watching in silence.

'Shipborne suffered too, you know, Keith. He had a conscience. He heard a story about a man who'd done something similar, put people's lives at risk here in Belsham hundreds of years ago. The story haunted Shipborne so much that he had the church tower locked up so he wouldn't have to be reminded of it. He wasn't the heartless man you think he was. He was tormented by the thought of what he'd done. He'd made a dreadful mistake and he blamed himself for it. You didn't have to punish him ... he punished himself.'

Heffernan scratched his head. He felt out of his depth. 'I think we'd better carry on back at the station. You can ring your solicitor when we get there.'

As the chief inspector prepared to recite the familiar words of the caution, there was a great roar as Keith Sturgeon bounded across the cold stones of the church aisle towards the back of the building, like some desperate animal evading capture. The sudden movement took the two policemen by surprise and they stood for a second, stunned, before they began to follow. Wesley thought their quarry would make for the main door but instead he carried on in a straight line towards the tower. He leaned his weight against the ancient door and it gave way with a crash. Once he was inside the door was slammed in their faces.

'What does he think he's doing?' Heffernan asked, breathless.

Wesley, assuming the question was rhetorical, didn't answer but concentrated his energies on pushing the door open. There was something behind it: Sturgeon had erected some sort of makeshift barricade and Wesley cursed himself for not foreseeing the situation.

'What do we do now, Wes? Wait till he decides to come out?'

'I don't think he plans to come out.'

'What?' Heffernan looked at him.

'I think we've got to get to him before he does anything stupid.'

Heffernan joined Wesley in pushing and with each shove they felt the obstacle blocking the doorway giving way a little. After a while their persistence paid off and the door opened just wide enough for them to squeeze through into the darkness. Only a tiny sliver of grey light filtered through a high, cobwebbed window, and it took their eyes some seconds to adjust. Wesley could just make out the shapes of the Munnery tombs and the bell ropes, curled like snakes at the end to form nooses. But there was no sign of Keith Sturgeon.

'He must have gone up. Where's the bloody door?' Heffernan groped his way around the perimeter of the room, muttering oaths under his breath as he banged into tombs and discarded pews. 'It's here. It's not locked.'

There was a terrible creak as he pushed the small arched door open. 'Do we go up or what?'

Wesley dodged past him. They had been responsible for allowing him to escape so it was up to them to make sure he was brought in safely. He began to climb the narrow winding stone steps very carefully. They were steep and worn and the overwhelming smell of damp pervaded the chill, stale air. He felt his way upwards in pitch darkness, the stone walls clammy beneath his searching fingers. When he stopped and listened he couldn't hear a sound, not even Heffernan behind him. The boss had done the sensible thing and had stayed in the tower room, calling for back-up on his mobile. But Wesley knew that there might not be time to wait for reinforcements.

He felt his way up the narrow spiral staircase, his hands clinging to the cold, damp roughness of the stones. This was what it would be like to be blind: to have no idea what lay ahead. He felt his palms sweating with fear.

As he climbed he suddenly saw a shaft of dull grey light; the autumn daylight was creeping in through the louvres of the bell chamber. As he drew level with the small, arched entrance he could make out the shapes of the bells, hanging between their great wooden wheels like sleeping giants. As he stared at them, the things seemed almost to be breathing, as if they were just waiting to be wakened by the twitch of a rope below.

He paused for a few moments, listening, but he could hear only the faint fluttering of pigeons' wings in the still air, so he continued up the steps, more slowly this time. At the top he found a wooden door, covered in dull green paint, dry and flaking like diseased flesh, but when he tried the handle he found that it was locked. Sturgeon had vanished into thin air . . . or he was hiding somewhere.

He felt his way slowly back down the steps until he reached the bell chamber. He stopped at the entrance and listened, but he could hear nothing but the gentle cooing of the resident pigeons.

He was about to make his way down again when he heard a sudden frantic flutter of wings. He turned and stared into the bell chamber, and as his eyes became used to the light he thought he could just make out an alien shape among the sleeping bells . . . the shape of a man, squatting, half hidden by the solid mass of the tenor bell; the largest bell with the deepest voice . . . the bell that tolls for death.

'It's no use running away, Keith. If you come down now we can sort this out.'

Sturgeon straightened himself up. 'What's the point? It's all over. There's nothing left.' His voice echoed against the hard metal of the bells.

'There's your wife.' It was all Wesley could think of on the spur of the moment.

'If my funeral coincided with a budget meeting, I doubt she'd bother coming.'

Wesley could think of nothing more to say, other than inappropriate clichés. That night in bed, with hindsight and after hours of thought, he knew he'd be able to come up with some brilliant, life-saving speech . . . but now he was lost for words. And the helpless inadequacy he felt was almost painful. 'Just come down,' he pleaded. 'We can talk about this.'

He took a step forward into the bell chamber. He could hear the wind howling against the outside of the tower as the pigeons beat their wings in alarm. He began to tread gingerly between the bells while Sturgeon watched him, impassive.

He was a few feet away from Sturgeon, walking stiffly, testing the safety of the floor with each step. But the man had begun to back away from him.

'We'd better go down now,' he said softly.

It happened so quickly. The struggle, the flailing arms grabbing at the air as the floor splintered and gave way. The noise, echoing like thunder around the tower as it set the silent bells swinging, tolling for a death for the first time in years.

When Gerry Heffernan, waiting below, heard the cry, like some primeval creature screaming out its last breath, he ran towards the stairs, his heart thumping, mouthing Wesley's name.

Chapter Fifteen

I read in the local paper that our Member of Parliament is to ask questions in the House of Commons about the events of that summer and the effect the trials had on the population of this area. I'm not sure whether this is as a result of my public confession, whether word has got about and people have begun to put two and two together.

I did not mention my own suffering in my sermon and I have spoken of it to nobody since; to have mentioned my own loss would have made it seem as if I was asking for pity ... which I wasn't as I blame only myself. When my little Mary was born, half formed and barely alive, I did not realise at first that it was a judgement on me. I had thought it an isolated incident, a tragic misfortune of the type that happens randomly every now and then ... until I heard that there were other, similar births locally, all eight or so months after the trials I had instigated had taken place. Claire, my dearest wife, never got over the loss of the daughter who left us before we could even know her. She suffered with depression until she eventually succumbed to cancer, God rest her sweet soul.

Perhaps I should have told my congregation how I suffered, how I paid the price for playing with

354

people's lives, for playing God.

From the diary sent to DI Wesley Peterson by Dr Anne Talbot

Loveday turned her gaze towards the window when the nurse entered the room. The nurse, a woman in her thirties who was a regular at her local weight-watchers' class, assumed the capable, no-nonsense expression she always wore when dealing with her patients. But she always allowed Loveday the occasional smile. She liked Loveday: she wasn't as much trouble as some of them.

'I've brought you what you wanted, Loveday. But I'll have to stay here while you write it. You know you're not allowed to have pens unless someone's with you.'

Loveday kept on staring at the window and made no comment on the restriction. Such petty infringements of her liberty were the stuff of her life now. Pens were sharp and she wasn't allowed them in case she harmed someone . . . or harmed herself as she had done so many times in the past.

The nurse handed her the notepad and cheap Biro and sat down on the blue bedspread, leaning back against the wall and crossing her powerful legs as though she expected to be there for some time. 'Get on with it, then. I haven't got all day.'

Loveday stared at the blank white paper for a while before looking up at her companion.

'That nice black policeman who came to see me . . . the detective inspector. What was his name?'

The nurse shrugged her large shoulders. 'I haven't a clue, love,' she replied wearily.

Neil stood with his head bowed as the soil poured into the hole. He bent down and took a handful of earth and threw it in. It felt like the right thing to do somehow, but he didn't know why. He looked round at the others. Their faces were solemn. It was over.

355

'So what happens now?'

Neil swung round. Wesley was standing at his shoulder, watching as the trench was filled.

'I've heard that they might build new houses on the site.'

'No supermarket?'

Neil shrugged. 'Sturgeon's death seems to have put a spanner in the works. We'll have to wait and see. I never thought it was right to build an in-store bakery and delicatessen counter bang on top of a plague pit anyway. You got your case all cleared up, then?'

'Yes. Sturgeon killed the vicar because he blamed him for his son's death.'

'Why?'

'When Shipborne had been a top government scientist he'd authorised the spraying of this part of Devon with bacteria. He thought they were harmless but it turned out later that they caused the deaths of vulnerable people, including Amy Hunting's son, who was recovering from a heart operation. They also caused clusters of birth defects ... which was ironic because Shipborne's own baby was born eight months after the trials and died soon after ... probably as a result of what Shipborne had authorised.'

'He paid for his mistake, then?'

They stood in silence for a few minutes. Then Neil spoke. 'What about that other skeleton we dug up ... the girl?'

'Sturgeon strangled her because she was blackmailing him and left her body on the road. William Verlan ran over her, thought he'd killed her and panicked. He dumped her body in a newly dug drainage ditch and covered it over. He's been charged with concealing the death but I can't see him going to jail somehow.'

'You're sure it was Sturgeon who killed her?'

'He admitted it before he ... ' Wesley had a sudden urge to change the subject. In the dim light he had caught a glimpse of Sturgeon's face as he fell through the floor,

356

grasping at the air: the torment, the despair. He saw it in his dreams, just as he saw visions of Sturgeon's bleeding corpse lying in the tower room sprawled across Urien de Munerie's tomb, the face turned towards the terrible writing on the wall. He shut his eyes, trying to block it out. 'What's happened to the skeletons?' he asked briskly.

'They're being studied and stored at the County Museum. Then there's talk of them being reburied in the churchyard. The Munnery dagger's being put on display.'

Wesley stared at the earth. 'It's a pity we could never find out which skeletons were Hawise and her children. It would have been nice to give them a name.'

'You know your trouble, Wes? You're too bloody sentimental.'

Wesley looked at his watch. 'I'd better get back. I only dropped by to see how the dig was going.'

'How's Pam?'

Wesley was tempted to say that she was much better since Neil's departure but he erred on the side of tact and just said, 'Fine.'

His mobile phone began to ring in his pocket, emitting a tinny version of a Bach fugue. When the conversation was finished, he turned to Neil, his eyes shining with excitement. Excitement and something else – anxiety perhaps.

'Pam's gone into labour. I've got to get back. I've got to organise someone to look after Michael and take her to hospital.'

'Give her my love,' said Neil, his face serious.

Wesley turned to go. The dig was over, and so was the Shipborne case. Life had to go on.

Four hours later Neil received a phone call telling him that Wesley and Pamela Peterson were now the proud parents of a beautiful baby girl.

*

Dear nice black policeman (sorry I can't remember your name but I've met so many different people since I came here)

Dr Harvey keeps telling me that I've got to be honest. I've got to face the truth about my feelings and the things I've done in the past. There's something I told him today, a thing I've never told anyone before, and I'd like to tell you about it because I think you'd understand. Sometimes I think I must have dreamed it. But I know I didn't.

You're wondering what it is, this secret I've been keeping to myself for all these years, rotting and festering in my head. Dr Harvey says it's bad to suppress things. They always used to say confession was good for the soul, didn't they? So this is my confession.

I was nine when Adam was ill. I heard the doctor tell my mum he had a lung infection. His breathing was all funny and Mum said I wasn't to go near his room. But in the middle of the night when everyone was asleep I went in and I stood there by his bed watching him sleep. He'd stopped making the wheezing noise and they'd said he seemed a bit better. She always fussed over him. It was all 'How are you feeling, Adam? Be careful, Adam. Don't catch cold, Adam.' And he'd just smile that smug little smile of his and play nicely while I created havoc. She treated him like some precious ornament. And I hated her ... and I hated Dad ... and I hated the man who used to come to the house when Dad was out and make such a fuss of Adam and touch Mum when they thought I wasn't watching and did things with her in her bed. I worked it all out eventually when I was grown up and knew about sex: I pieced together the jigsaw, all the half-forgotten memories, until I realised that he was Adam's father. Then I made sure he paid for what he'd done to me.

Anyway, where was I? I said I went in when Adam

was asleep, didn't I? Well, I stood there watching him for a while and I started thinking that if he wasn't there they might take some notice of me. At that moment I hated him so much, really hated him. There were two pillows on his bed and one was pushed to the side. I picked it up and put it over his face. I did it gently because I didn't want to wake him up. Then I started to press down. He moved and I pressed harder. His body jerked about but he couldn't make a noise. I don't know how long I held the pillow over his face but it seemed a long time, and when I took it away he wasn't moving any more.

They said he died of natural causes ... because of the infection. Mum was never the same afterwards and it never worked out how I'd wanted. Mum still ignored me and got obsessed with Adam and Dad spent all his time at work, just like before. If my life had been a nightmare before I did what I did, it got even worse afterwards.

Dr Harvey was right. I feel better now I've told you. I'll send this to your police station. Dr Harvey says I won't be arrested but I'd like to see you again ... to talk to you.

Yours truly

Loveday Wilkins

Loveday held the letter out to the nurse, who looked up from the magazine she was reading.

'You finished, then?'

Loveday nodded. 'You'll make sure it's posted, won't you. I think he's from Tradmouth police station. He's an inspector. Can you find out his name?'

'No problem, love.'

The nurse took the paper from her outstretched hand and left the room. It was the end of her shift.

When she reached the cloakroom she crumpled Loveday's letter into a tight ball and threw it at the overflowing litter bin.

Historical Note

In June 1348 sailors from plague-ridden Gascony in France disembarked at the port of Melcombe in Dorset, only thirty miles away from the Devon border. As well as their cargo they brought with them the plague bacillus, *Yersinia pestis*, spread by rat fleas, and within eighteen months almost half the population of Britain would be dead.

The dead at that time were normally interred carefully with their feet facing east so that they could stand and face Jerusalem on the Day of Judgement. But when the plague struck there were so many corpses and so few people left to bury them that they were often thrown unceremoniously in huge communal pits. Families were split, the healthy moving away from the sick to avoid infection. In some cases parents were forced to abandon children for whom nothing could be done in order to save those who remained well. In records of the time, such as manorial rolls and lists of clergy, one can see the names of men and women struck through as they died, a poignant reminder of what the population faced as they watched their family, friends and neighbours succumb and waited with dread to see whether they would be next.

Seaports such as Dartmouth in Devon fared particularly badly as ships brought the infection in from elsewhere. Priests tending the sick and giving the last rites to the dying were especially vulnerable, and the diocese of Exeter was one of the worst hit in England, losing half its clergy.

Understandably the survivors at the time came to regard death as a constant companion and the art of the time – in illustrated books and on the walls of churches – reflects this. The story of the Three Living and the Three Dead, referred to in this book, was particularly popular, as were paintings of a grisly 'dance of death'. Two-layer (or transi) tombs depicting a dead nobleman or bishop in rich robes above and a rotting corpse beneath became fashionable. All were equal in death and 'King Death' mocked the pretensions of social superiority.

I hope the people of Ashwell in Hertfordshire will forgive me for using a variation of the graffiti on the wall of their parish church tower in this story. It was possibly carved by their despairing priest as he watched his parishioners dying. 'Miserable, wild, distracted, the dregs of the people alone survive to bear witness.' It serves as a harrowing reminder of the horrors endured by the population in the fourteenth century.

Things could never be the same in England again after the devastation of the Black Death. However, the resultant shortage of labour led to the end of serfdom and an improvement in the economic prospects of the survivors as labour became a 'sellers' market'. Every cloud has a silver lining of some kind.

To come forward in time, I was surprised to discover in the course of my research that in the 1960s and 1970s Devon had indeed been sprayed with massive quantities of E. coli 162 and *Bacillus globigii* as part of secret germ warfare tests. The government claimed that the trials posed no risk to public health; however, it was later found that the old, the young and those with lowered immunity were at risk of lung infections. Farmers lost cattle to an E. coli infection around the time of the trials and in a village at the centre of the test area many miscarriages and severe birth defects were reported.

On 12 November 1997 the Member of Parliament for

Teignbridge praised the *Western Morning News* for bringing the matter to the public's attention and reminded the House of Commons that many people in the area still suffered a growing number of unexplained illnesses and medical conditions.

When I first had the idea for *The Plague Maiden*, I feared that the notion of inflicting germ warfare trials on Devon might be considered a little far fetched. But then sometimes the truth is harder to believe than fiction.